REMAINS

THE NEW WORLD SERIES | BOOK FIVE

Stephen Llewelyn

FOSSIL ROCK PUBLISHING

For Sally
Thank you for your unwavering commitment to the cause.

The author also wishes to acknowledge:

Mum, Dad and Bill for continued support. Thanks to Sally-Marie and Fossil Rock, and Melanie at The Chapter House for all the reads, re-reads, marketing, publishing, IT help and on, and on, and on... To my long-suffering friends for encouraging my mad ideas.

Special thanks to the experts who took time out of their frantic schedules to answer my emails and questions about our favourite subject.

...And last but by no means least, to everyone who reads this book and enjoyed its predecessors, a sincere thank you.

The crew of the USS *New World* will return soon in
THE NEW WORLD SERIES | BOOK SIX | CURSED.

No dinosaurs were harmed during the making of this book.

To everyone forced to make a new beginning by the recent problems, keep your foot down and don't stop for anything – I'll see you on the other side!

Your Free eBook is Waiting...

Six people alone in the Cretaceous South American jungle. Ordered to complete a threat assessment, Corporal Heinz Engel is at a loss where to begin. Between hiding and running from the indigenous wildlife, his team must somehow complete their survey and return what they have learned to their masters.

Foolish mistakes have bloody consequences, bringing out the best in some and the worst in others, but by the end of their mission, Engel seeks only justice.

ENGEL is set during the early chapters of REVENGE, book 2 of the New World Series, and leads up to the events prior to the attack on the *Last Word.*

Get a free copy of ENGEL here:

www.stephenllewelyn.com/free-book

Chapter 1 | At The Day's End

The climb was painful but worth it. The steep-sided ridge offered commanding views across the delta and out over the Tethys Ocean towards a long, mountainous peninsula that jutted out across the westward horizon.

He liked to come here in the evening. Recent injuries plagued him, but the 360-degree vantage made this a safe place. His injuries would heal. He would recover. He always did.

The sun dipped towards the distant mountains, the becalmed ocean reflecting a perfectly bronzed bar beneath. A pleasing, almost soporific haze airbrushed all the details to insignificance. Every shade of copper and gold augmented the balmy evening's warmth, the air completely still but for the occasional twitter of a bird, late to its nest.

He lay down on his belly, grunting as his chin lowered to the dusty ground between his forelimbs. As the sun sank, so drooped his weary lids. He fought it, like a curious hound for a few moments, until the calm claimed him.

One year later
Today had not begun well, and the less said about the rest of it, the better. After leaving his ridge, a place he had commanded every single night for more than thirty years, he had taken his favoured early morning swim.

His brethren always did likewise. After the crocodilian way, they were less 'social' than willing to occupy the same location as their own; theirs, a state of near perpetual armistice. On a good day, they would tolerate one another, more in the manner of an aquatic Diogenes Club. Cooperation was rare... on a good day.

This, for him at least, was not one of those. His had been a life of combat. The endless and incessant injuries, which dogged all his kind, had taken longer to leave their mark on him than most. However, each injury was becoming more serious, regardless of degrees. Healing took longer. Pain slowed him more than it used too. He was getting old.

Many of his contemporaries at the river shore were his own offspring, but this mattered about as much to them as it had to him, when he was young – or now, for that matter. He was weakening, and although still a deadly force, was beginning the gradual decline into fair game.

There were plenty of fish to go around and catches made in times of bounty carried an understanding long preceding language or agreement. Whoever catches it, gets to eat it – at least without hindrance from their own kind.

When a hunter gets old, the cyclical slip towards prey can happen with alarming rapidity, yet often with a subtlety that catches the erstwhile hunter off guard. His catches should have been his own, but the up-and-coming buck, who had always seen him as a danger, now saw him merely as an obstacle. Although still a serious threat to life, the threat to his prowess could no longer be tolerated and the time had come to remove it.

The twenty-year-old Spinosaurus aegyptiacus was a good sixteen years his junior and, though slightly smaller, was in his prime. Full of life, power, and fight. He should have backed away, found a new place to fish; his wounds ached, but this was *his* home. The aggressor perhaps even his own son. It mattered not. He had made his stand and he had lost.

That was the morning. Now well into the heat of afternoon, he stalked along a beach where the fluvial landscape met the Tethys Ocean. His eventual – perhaps inevitable – amphibious retreat had led him here. The deep bite to his thigh made swimming painful, and so, content to go with the flow, he had wound up at the sea. Swimming usually relaxed his stiff muscles, kickstarting his hitherto prodigious healing capabilities, but not today. He was no stranger to serious injury. His lands were filled with natural dangers, not to mention other predators, some more dangerous even than he, but this felt different.

Animals have always known when their end is near. The first impulse is always to fight, to become even more dangerous. Eventually, anger subsides into acceptance, but he was not there yet.

He was limping badly when a scent pulled him up short. He raised his snout. *Sniff, sniff.* How well he knew the whiff of death. Adrenaline surged through his system. The earlier altercation had cost him breakfast. His gut growled, and so did he.

Quickening his stride as pain allowed, he headed east along the shoreline. A little way ahead a sandbar pointed out to sea. The bar was tall enough to block his view forward, while loose sand made the short climb hard work. As he crested the top, the breeze blasted his face with an oven's heat. Squinting against the baked sand flung into his eyes, his nostrils dilated, sucking in the unmistakable aroma of sun-bleached carrion.

Halfway up the beach was a corpse; a deep-dwelling leviathan deserted by the tide, and far bigger than anything that had ever lived in his river. He struggled down the opposite side of the bank, injury forcing him into a fully quadrupedal gait. The rotting body was missing a large section of its tail, amongst other things, such as fins, eyes, and vast tracts of gut.

A star attraction for miles around, the body was already surrounded by scavengers, all avid and threatening, posturing for a share. The local foragers ate, but the stench was already an eleven. Drool dripped from his mouth in expectation of 'spine dining'.

Eighteen metres long and eleven tons, his approach did not go unnoticed. Sensing the inevitability of being moved along, the revellers became ever more frantic, gulping down as much flesh, gut and dead blood as they could. The flighted menagerie, ever cocky, were last to leave. He snapped, catching three of them on the wing as a flock exploded into the air from the steadily ripening cadaver. He swallowed them, their meagre bodies barely distracting him from the banquet. Tearing a new rip through the decomposing musculature was light exercise for the robust snout of Spinosaurus. He glutted kilo after kilo of raw meat and soft innards. The repugnant reek was like amphetamine to a piscivore. He may have been old, but when it came to scavenging, size was all. The corpse was his now. Eyes widened from bloody rapture caught movement among the dunes to the south.

Sated for now, threat adrenaline warred with the somnolence of a heavy meal as he took several steps away from the bloated remains to scent clearly – ever more reliable than sight – and it was a scent he recognised.

Although lacking the foresight required to have a sinking feeling, as previously established, animals do sense their end. Following a slap-up meal, even acceptance became easier to swallow.

A huge shape crested the nearest dune. Moving quickly on powerful hind legs, the creature approached with the indolence of an alpha, further increased by the smell of recent injury from his competition.

The old Spinosaurus knew this animal. Had always known him. They moved in similar circles, always keeping a respectful distance – until this day.

The vast Carcharodontosaurus saharicus came on to stand less than twenty metres away, bobbing his head and swishing his tail expectantly.

Of an age, and a size, the giants circled one another, but like all creatures in this life, some are born with more luck than others. Spinosaurus felt his end was close, but instinctually knew that surrender would guarantee it. Attempting to disguise his limp, he bellowed challenge. This would have voided the bladder of any common adversary, sending them scurrying away. Unfortunately, this adversary was emphatically uncommon. Few grew to his size, perhaps one in a generation, and yes, he was lucky, but he was also an absolute brute.

Spinosaurus knew that, out of the water at least, he was well overmatched. His severe injury at the teeth of one of his own that morning clinched the deal. He began to circle away from the prize rotting in the baking afternoon sun, heading away from the gently lapping waves and towards the dunes.

This move towards placation only encouraged the Carcharodontosaurus to rush in. The lunge was a feint, but the injured Spinosaurus automatically moved to avoid it and stumbled on his damaged leg. Slow to get up, his enemy was upon him, all savagery and spittle. He snapped ineffectually in return but failed to get any kind of purchase on the scales of his antagonist.

The carcharodontosaur fairly danced around him, going straight for the injured leg, now running with fresh blood over that already coagulated. The bite struck with such shocking force that pain took a moment to follow. When it ballooned, Spinosaurus bellowed in furious agony. A reflexive jerk allowed a retaliatory snap at his attacker's neck. Stealing the opportunity, he sank his jagged fangs deep to draw a torrent of blood, but the neck of this Carcharodontosaurus was hugely thick. Though the wound found and left its mark, it barely registered in the mind of a killer so completely hopped up on adrenaline and rage.

Carcharodontosaurus roared in anticipation of victory, then stepped back unexpectedly. Any beast of such size and dominance needed to be lucky, but they also needed to learn from experience. Vast size could only be attained through long life, and long life through learning to minimise risk. His quarry was down and bleeding from wounds affecting his ability to stand, fight or run. There was no need to do more, so he backed away, taking an easy snack from the monstrous fish corpse washed up on the sands. He would come back to stamp his supremacy once his prey was too far gone to present a threat.

Spinosaurus knew how this game was played; he had not survived alongside this creature without learning the same lessons. He tried to regain his feet but roared in agony when his hind leg failed to support his enormous weight and collapsed again. He looked up at the sun, now firmly in the west. His mind bore an imprint, an urge... home.

With a goliath effort of will, he regained his feet, heavily favouring his now irreparably injured leg.

Carcharodontosaurus looked up from snacking. Now the undisputed king of the beach, he watched with detached interest as his longest standing competitor crawled away three-legged, dragging a ruined limb behind. He had neither the intelligence nor imagination to realise that his own relatively tiny forelimbs would not even afford him that dignity, when his time came. There but for the grace of God, he snapped at a few cheeky avians and resumed his meal.

Just this morning he had watched the sun rise from the safe eyrie atop *his* ridge. Now he felt the agony of bloody, and if he was lucky, lonely death upon him. His instincts told him to climb up to his lofty home. Only then could all be set right. The miles dragged as his leg dragged, his task Sisyphean, then he saw it – his ridge, some thirty metres above him. Failing from shock and blood loss, his gait compensated for a useless hind leg. An easy stroll the day before, now consumed his remaining energy completely.

No other creatures had bothered him since leaving the beach, but he knew they were there, circling, waiting. As he began to climb, his leg collapsed again. His cry was harsh and raw, lacking power or threat now.

The sun was setting behind him, the light softening all around as his sight began to fade with it. Scrambling exhaustedly with his good hind leg, he clawed at the earth with his forelimbs to propel himself further up the slope with the last of his strength. The top was close now. Though he could not see it, he knew every piece of this land. Knew he was close. His remaining leg failed, leaving him clawing ineffectually with his less powerful forelimbs. After a few desperate minutes scratching at the ground, his legs splayed, dropping him onto his chest. With his last strength, he craned his neck around to watch the sun set behind the peninsula.

At the top he would be safe, until the new day. It had always been so. He tried, *really* tried, with every ounce of strength and courage remaining to him, but with legs no longer at his command, he was paralysed. His head crashed down to the ground with finality as he whimpered and sighed.

A small pack of hungry Rugops looked dispassionately on from atop the now masterless ridge, as the old king took his final breath just a few metres below them.

...Many such kings have lived and died, their fates, to vanish into the pages of the Earth, but not this king. A chance discovery of some nameless bones in modern Egypt, by German palaeontologist Ernst Stromer, began a cycle of events that forever guaranteed Spinosaurus' place alongside the now-fluid history of man...

AD2112, USA

Lieutenant Colonel Davis Jonson, adjutant to the Chief of Staff, steeled himself before the closed door. The plaque in front of his nose read 'General Brassheim' followed by five gold stars. He sighed and knocked.

"Come."

The response was muffled by the door but there was no way he could pretend not to have heard, so he turned the handle and stepped through nervously. "Sir, General Green is here as ordered, sir."

"Good. Bring her in, Davis."

"Immediately, sir." Relieved, Jonson turned to go.

"And you stay too, would you? I may need a note takin'."

Jonson swallowed. "Of course, sir."

A few moments later, Jonson opened Brassheim's door once more. He stood aside respectfully, allowing General Green to enter before him.

Brassheim looked up from whatever he had been reading. "Ah, Lisa, have a seat. Thanks for coming. Coffee? Or perhaps something a little stronger?"

"Thank you, sir." Green took the proffered chair before the Chief of Staff's gargantuan desk, at the same time taking a deep breath. Jonson brought her and Brassheim a generous measure of scotch. Clearly, *he* sensed where this was heading. So, pleasantries over, she waited for the unpleasantries to nova. "How did your meeting with the President go?"

She probably should have followed Brassheim's lead, but she hated waiting for an attack – better to get stuck into it and get the hell out of there.

The Chief of Staff smiled with little humour. "Let's just say I'm finding it a little uncomfortable to sit down right now. Lisa, how in the Sam Hill did this happen?"

"Sir, I have Special Agents Harrison and Smith from Homeland Security flying in to see me this evening. Apparently, Smith had intel relating to the launch of those black ships from Argentina—"

"And...?" Brassheim interrupted as he leaned forward, scrutinising her.

Green took another breath. "He passed it along to his boss, but the information was deemed untrustworthy, so between them, they decided not to act on it."

Brassheim's expression soured even further. "His boss being...?"

"Harrison, yes, sir. I invited them both to the meeting, to expedite the firing process."

"And Harrison's boss?" he pushed.

"Denies all knowledge of this intel, sir. She threw them over, to face me."

A flicker of amusement crossed Brassheim's face. "So, I guess they do things a little differently than we do, huh?"

Green dared return his smile with a fleeting one of her own.

"I suppose it's no longer good," Brassheim continued, "but what *was* the intel?"

"A communiqué from someone called Elizabeth Hemmings, sir. She seems to have completely disappeared from the radar now. We can only guess at what's happened to her, after giving up that sort of information about such a powerful organisation."

"What did she te— *try* to tell us?"

"She offered up times and dates for the launch of some very advanced ships and weaponry."

"We noticed those," Brassheim remarked, drily. "Anything else?"

"Yes, sir. And it gets worse."

Brassheim sat back, confounded. "Davis, fix us another drink, will ya? And have one yourself. Looks like this could take a while."

"Yes, sir. Thank you, sir," Jonson replied as he buttled off.

Fortified with another large scotch, Brassheim asked, "How much worse?"

Green took a nip of her own drink and placed it on the desk before her. "We've been led to believe there's the whiff of a Nazi revival. Smith, or Harrison, didn't take it seriously and... well, here we all are, sir."

Brassheim looked pained, but Green was distracted by the plaque on his desk which seemed to be rewriting itself before her very eyes and now read 'General Faulkner'. She looked up, slightly dazed, into the face of a completely different man. Equally suddenly, all memory of Brassheim faded and vanished from her mind.

The generals blinked at one another. Lieutenant Colonel Jonson was no longer in the room.

"Lisa?" asked Faulkner.

"Sir?" she replied, equally mystified.

"What the hell are we doin' here?"

Green opened her mouth to answer but none came.

AD1558 The Borderlands between England and Scotland

David, Lord Maxwell and Sir Nicholas Throckmorton huddled subconsciously. They had just witnessed a man walk from an inferno – a burning church no less – and take down one of their leaders with a mere thought. Just minutes later, a huge flying contraption had arrived in a roar of noise and fire, blue-white light lancing from its prow to strike unerringly for the cannon loops in Hermitage Castle's west wall. Once landed, it disgorged yet more of the newcomers, who collected around the form of Captain Baines like bees around their queen.

Maxwell gave Sir Nicholas a small tug on his sleeve, gesturing him away. They retreated a short distance from the mayhem of shouting and calling, and people speaking to and from small handheld boxes. It was all too much.

"Ah hope they can bring the lass back," was all Maxwell could manage. "Ah liked her."

Sir Nicholas merely nodded, overwhelmed. Eventually he replied, "From the dead?"

Maxwell swallowed. "Billy, come here, yer glaikit bairn!"

His nephew, usually so full of himself, joined them without comment, fear obvious on his face.

Sir Nicholas lightly touched Maxwell's elbow. Once he had his attention, he nodded towards Douglas. Maxwell followed his gaze to see his fellow Scotsman standing like a stone, just outside the circle attending to Baines, but with all his attention focused on the suddenly small body on the floor.

"Ah'd nae want to be in his way when he comes tae," Maxwell whispered to Sir Nicholas.

Once again, Sir Nicholas nodded. "His woman?"

Maxwell chuckled. "Ah ken it's complicated." They looked on.

"Your idea to keep her in the snow?" Dr Flannigan's voice rang out.

"Yeah. Was I wrong?" asked Gleeson, eyes full of concern.

Flannigan gave him a gentle pat on the arm. "It was a smart move, Commander. Gave us a little extra time to get here.

Gleeson and The Sarge had tried to resuscitate Baines with the APC's onboard defibrillator, but without success. Afraid of doing further harm, they decided to leave her in as cold an environment as possible and wait for the experts.

Flannigan took a large hypodermic from his ubiquitous leather doctor's bag and jammed it hard into Baines' heart to deliver a large dose of epinephrine. "Hit her again. Everybody, clear!"

Another jolt from the defibrillator shook her body. "Recharge. Again – clear!"

Flannigan breathed on his hands to get feeling back from the cold and leaned forward to check her jugular. "I've got a pulse!"

There was a whoop from the spectators followed by premature backslapping and congratulation.

"Shut up, will ya?" barked Flannigan. "I'm workin' here!" He leaned forward again, listening to her breathing. After a moment he sat back on his haunches, shaking his head. "I can't do anything more here. Get her into the ship and keep her warm now, before frostbite does irreparable damage. Move it – this ain't Happy Holidays!"

Another flurry of activity as Captain Baines was wrapped up, placed on a stretcher and quickly moved into the shelter of one of the *New World*'s escape pods.

Strolling briskly after, Flannigan felt someone grab his arm. He turned to give the perpetrator a mouthful when he found himself looking into the hard and completely expressionless face of Captain Douglas. "Dave?" His voice was soft, yet gravelly with contained fury. No further words were necessary.

Flannigan calmed immediately. "I don't know, James. I'll do all I can."

Douglas nodded. Dismissing his chief medical officer without a word, he turned towards the tracked personnel carrier.

"Here it comes," murmured Maxwell.

Douglas reappeared momentarily from the rear of the vehicle with an assault rifle strapped across one shoulder and a rocket launcher across the other.

Gleeson placed a hand on his arm, but removed it as if burned, so harsh was Douglas' glare. Without another word he set off east, through the dark and through the blizzard, towards Hermitage Castle.

Sir Nicholas leaned in confidentially towards Maxwell. "If the woman's life cannot be returned to him, forsooth he will settle for the Lady Elizabeth's."

"He cannae have gold, so he'll accept silver? Is that it?"

Sir Nicholas bristled slightly, but quickly realised the Scotsman's words for what they were – a comment to the captain's state of mind, not a slight. He nodded sagely.

Maxwell sucked his teeth. "Ah cannae see Jamie as a man who settles for second place. Can ye? Ah reckon he'll be more likely tae settle for the life o' the man who tried tae take hers."

Chapter 2 | Silver

Douglas stayed off the main track and approached the castle by skirting the river's edge. The walk was no more than half a mile, but he had almost completely lost daylight. The sky, so heavy with snow, showed no hint of moon or stars. It would soon be black as pitch in this valley. He quickened his pace. The northern bank of Hermitage Water brought him just south of the castle.

Hidden by an earlier earthwork, he debated what he should do next. His anger was such that he had never known before. It was all he could do to stop himself blowing the southern gate to kindling and rushing in there to slaughter every living soul.

He breathed deeply, years of training battling his emotions for control. *Ah've lost her. And Ah never told her... but then, told her what? What she meant to me? Damn the military. If Ah'd followed ma feelings what's the worst that could have happened? Ah'd have been forced to resign? Simple resignation, followed by a comfortable life in the twenty-second century with the woman Ah—*

A hand grabbed his shoulder. Rifle still around his shoulders, he balled his fists ready to punch and punch and punch anybody who came upon him from that hated pile. The face he was fixing to ruin turned out to be that of Sergeant John Jackson. "*Sarge?* What the...?"

The Sarge grinned in the gloom. "I met up with young Prentice, on my way over here, sir. I've got him scouting the curtain walls for entrances and surprise guests. I came straight on to where I thought you'd be, sir. Thought you might need someone to talk you out of it."

"Out of what?"

"Going in there and killing everybody, sir."

Douglas made to speak but subsided; he could not in good conscience deny it. Running feet slushed through the snow and Prentice slid down the bank to join them.

"So what do you suggest, Sarge?" asked Douglas.

"Sir, I know we're all fired up and our old Aprils[1] are going like good 'uns, but we need a plan. I also suggest, respectfully, sir, that you keep your assault rifle in reserve and use this." The Sarge handed Douglas one of a pair of Heath-Riflesons[2] he carried.

Before he could answer, they were forced to cover their ears as Flannigan's lifeboat roared overhead to the west, en route to the *New World* and her infirmary.

"Any change in Jill before you left, Sarge?"

"She was in a coma, sir." Feeling that more was required of him, he added, "Dr Flannigan's the best there is, Captain."

Douglas reached out for The Sarge's shoulder, both to reassure and steady himself as he muttered, "Ah know."

The Sarge cleared his throat into the awkward silence. "So, Adam, any sign of hostiles outside the castle walls?"

The Yorkshireman shook his head. "I think those stun blasts from t' ship-mounted cannon did t' trick, Sarge. Stopped them firing their big guns, anyroad. There's nobody about outside." When his superiors lapsed back into thoughtful silence, he prompted, "So about this lass – a princess, eh?"

Douglas smiled wanly. "Aye, and more besides. Boys, Ah think Ah have a plan."

The Sarge raised an eyebrow. "Front door, sir?"

Douglas' smile morphed into a wolfish grin. "Reckon it would be rude to burst in any other way – sneaky even, eh?"

"No one could call the Gleeson Manoeuvre that, sir."

---

1   'April' or 'April tart' is cockney rhyming slang for heart.

2   When first stranded in the Cretaceous, the *New World*'s crew jerry rigged their basic stun rifles to deliver a kick big enough to worry even a large dinosaur. Gaffer-taped together, they were initially more than a little 'Heath Robinson'.

"The Gleeson Manoeuvre?" Douglas repeated thoughtfully. "Ha, why not."

Baines had stared down at her own body for too long when a welcome distraction came in the form of Mario Baccini. The body, *her* body, was finally whisked away, leaving her temporarily confused by the fact that she had not been compelled to accompany it.

"Mario? What the hell is happening?"

"It's-a good to speak with you again, Captain. So many times I've reached out to you, but you were unable to see or feel me."

Baines extended her arm and *touched* her former engineer and wormhole specialist. "And it's good to see you, too, Mario. So good. But look – and I know this sounds self-centred – what's happened to me?"

Mario grinned. "It's complicated. There are a few others here who wish to say hi." Behind Mario were Private Andreas Paolo, the retired Sergeant Bud O'Neill and Dr Jamie Ferguson.

Even more surprisingly, hiding shamefaced at the back, was Dr Aabid Hussain.

"Commander," he nodded in greeting. "Ah, forgive me. I understand it's *Captain* Baines now. You may recall I missed your promotion. I'd have been there, of course, but you know how it is, the timetable just happened to clash with my getting murdered by Heidi Schultz."

Baines gaped. "It's all true? Beck Mawar, everything she's told us, all of it, true?"

Mario smiled his boyish smile. She had missed that smile so much, it struck straight to her heart – or at least to where her heart used to be.

"Beck is a special lady and, along with all of us, she will help you, Captain."

"But... but... why didn't you, you know, cross over, or whatever?"

"*When* we died, there was nowhere to cross over to. Look, it's a long story and we don't have time for it now. At the moment, just know that you're here, and we're here."

"Whoa, back up a minute! I'm *dead?*"

"Not yet."

"Not *yet?* Damn it, let me down gently, why don't you!"

"Remain calm, Captain. We're here now because you have unfinished business and will need our help to find your way back."

19

Baines blew out what used to be her cheeks while running her fingers exasperatedly through what used to be her hair. "Unfinished business?"

He gave her a knowing look. "The girl? In the castle?"

"Oh, that."

"We're here for you, Captain. Even Aabid wishes to add his force to ours by way of apology."

"*Does* he? Well, isn't that something? Still, I'll accept help from the devil himself at the moment!"

Mario's expression darkened slightly. "We don't joke about such things. We find it attracts unwanted attention. As the Bard said, 'more things in heaven and earth', et cetera, et cetera..."

"Yeah? Well, as the *bird* said, talk's cheap! I'm gonna go in there and sort him out! Let's go!"

"Get *him?* And the girl, Captain?"

"What? Oh, yeah, her too – come on!"

The heavy, iron-banded oak door, securing the castle's southern portal, was there and then it was not there. The detonation of the rocket vibrated through every stone in the not insubstantial place. Douglas looked at the stovepipe launcher in his hands with spellbound respect.

The Sarge winked. "Gleeson," he said, as if this covered everything. "Come on, lads. Let's hop it!"

The three men ran flat out towards the open portal. Needless to say, resistance was thin on the ground. What was *thick* on the ground, were the bodies of several stunned henchmen.

As Douglas jumped through the new hole in the wall, he caught a fleeting glimpse of someone he recognised and pulled up short, causing The Sarge and Pte Prentice to barrel into the back of him.

"Sir?" they asked together.

"Ah thought Ah saw... Och, never mind. Let's find the girl and get out of here."

Douglas was not having a good day. He had just left the semi-lifeless body of his best friend behind, and now he was losing his mind, too. He could have sworn Jill Baines had ducked out of sight just as he burst into the small courtyard. *Get a grip on yersel', man!* he upbraided himself.

The courtyard was a covered, cobbled area, lit with flaming torches in sconces along the right-hand wall. Douglas only knew the place as a gutted ruin, a tourist attraction visited as a child, but guessed that in this time there would be halls above them. The space felt more like an alley than the courtyard one would normally expect to find inside castle walls – probably because he now stood at the heart of what used to be a much smaller fortified manor. Heavy oak doors, set within arch-topped stone casements, sealed off rooms to the left and right. Directly ahead lay a third door. This led to a spiral stone stair, as Douglas found out when it opened to reveal armed men.

There is battle courage and battle terror, and these men were terrified, yet still they ran out, screaming hate at the invaders. All bore weapons, ranging from cutting swords to spears. Fortunately, none of the first wave bore anything ballistic.

Douglas, The Sarge and Prentice stood three abreast, raised their stun rifles and fired.

The old man steepled his fingers before his face, his eyes boring deep into those of the bridge crew and not least into those of Captain Aito Nassaki. He had taken the captain's seat for his own and was 'listening with intent' to their explanations regarding a complete failure to close the wormhole.

The female scientist his granddaughter had taken to calling 'Two' leaned in close to whisper, "Heinrich, I told you this might happen. The secant line the wormhole has taken cuts through the outer core. It is drawing power from, as far as we are concerned, a near infinite geothermal source."

Heinrich frowned at the familiarity, but perhaps it was to be expected. He was her first cousin, once removed after all. Of course, his granddaughter was unaware of this connection. Heinrich was a man who liked to keep everyone in little pigeonholes, only allowing them to mix when it suited his purposes – or when it was time to dispense with them.

"Dr Hemmings," he replied coldly, "I clearly remember instructing you to find any *definitive* reasons why the wormhole should not be opened. You failed. And now you have failed to close the wormhole, too. Have you any ideas about how to redeem yourself or this situation you and your colleagues have caused?" His left eyebrow rose slightly, but otherwise he was completely still, an island of deadly calm.

Two swallowed her indignation at this extraordinary accusation and stepped back. "At least we have a permanent link to Nazi Germany, do we not?"

"No, we do not!" Schultz slammed his fist down on the arm of the chair.

Two maintained a healthy caution where Heinrich was concerned, regardless, perhaps *because* of their familial relationship. However, her analytical mind took over for an instant, prompting her to ask for an explanation.

The old man's cold, grey eyes lanced through her, seeming to probe her brain directly. When he spoke, the silence on the bridge was absolute as everyone held their breath. "We have a permanent link to Munich in 1943. That is all."

Two's mind raced. Frowning, she dared fill in a blank. "No Nazi party?"

Heinrich's jaw clenched. "No."

Aito and Lieutenant Devon shared a glance.

The balding male lab coat known as 'One' forgot himself and spoke into the void, "What can this mean?"

"It means," snapped Heinrich, "that Douglas's gaggle of fools have unwound our timeline and replaced it with... *weakness.*" Bitter disgust twisted his face as he rounded on the scientists. "So, people, we shall need to weave a new thread to get the loom back on track. A mixed metaphor, but I'm sure you understand my point."

Heidi sat on a park bench alongside the River Isar. Stooped forward, hands cupping her chin with elbows on her knees, she stared blankly at the heavy flow. She had not spoken a word since storming from Hitler's apartment.

"Perhaps if I got you something to eat or drink?" tried Jansen, hopefully.

Heidi merely released a deep sigh.

"*Right,*" he muttered. "So what do we do next?"

Her voice was muffled by her chin resting in her hands. "Do whatever you want. We are stuck here. Get married and go and make babies or something banal like that."

Jansen was afraid to hope. "Y-you would like that?"

This time she looked at him, her eye twitching furiously. "Not with me, stud!"

He coughed with embarrassment, stifling it behind his hand. "Well, maybe we should go back to the museum – you know, to see if the wormhole is still there?"

She was about to bite back again, but realised she had nothing better to offer. "Fine. Let's go."

By this time there was quite a queue outside the Old Academy. Heidi strode to the front of the long line of tourists and rapped on the ticket office window.

"Hey! Who do you think you are?" snapped a burly man, until so recently at the front of the queue. Heidi ignored him, so he grabbed her arm and spun her round. "I'm talking to you, *Fräulein!*"

She looked up at him coolly, with no trace of alarm. "And you are?"

The man proudly pointed his thumb at himself. "Burnstein, Helmut Burnstein."

Heidi stared distractedly up and to the side, over his shoulder. The large man turned to follow her gaze. She dug straight fingers into his kidneys and twisted. Burnstein went down crying out. Heidi returned her attention to the kiosk. "I was here earlier. I no longer have my ticket but wish to come back in. I demand you open the gate. *Now.*"

The fracas soon attracted the attention of security. Jansen braced for trouble, but recognised the man as the guard they met just after stepping through the wormhole. "He will remember us," he pointed out.

Heidi turned. "Ah, you! Yes, *you* – come here! You will recall us from earlier, little man, yes?"

The young woman working at the tills looked to the guard for instruction. "I do, miss," he replied hesitantly, eyeing the large man on the floor, sobbing from considerable pain. "But I'm afraid you will still need to purchase another tick—" He stopped speaking immediately under the ferocity of her glare. "Maybe we could trace your ticket from earlier, miss?" he tried instead. "If you would be kind enough to tell us your name...?"

"Dr Heidi Schultz," she replied through gritted teeth.

The effect on the guard and the kiosk girl was immediate. Heidi fully expected her name to inspire fear in her inferiors – meaning everyone else – but the sudden look of sycophantic toadying that crossed the museum staff's faces was all new.

"Silly girl," the little man admonished the till worker, jovially. "We can't charge the lady to enter her own building, can we?"

Heidi and Jansen shared a look of surprise. Heidi rallied first. "You know me?"

"Of course, we all know *your* name, ma'am. You are Heidi, daughter of *Hans* Schultz. And if you will permit me, may I say you are even more beautiful in person than your publicity pictures portray." He smiled, opening the gate for them.

"*Publicity* pictures?" Heidi murmured dumbly as she and Jansen stepped through.

Completely forgetting he was there, the guard closed the gate on the still-prone Burnstein who reached out, only to get his fingers trapped in the hinge. "Aaargh!"

The guard frowned irritably and pushed the gate harder.

"AAARGH!"

"There we are. Now, please follow me, ma'am, and may I also say what a pleasure it is to be introduced to you."

"Introduced? I did that, did I?"

"Surely, ma'am," he wittered on. "The Schultzes are the most prominent industrialists and philanthropists in the Fatherland! There can scarcely be a museum, gallery or public building in the country that hasn't benefitted from your great benevolence and generosity. Of course, that's not even mentioning all your other charity and foreign aid work."

Heidi stared at the guard like he was a slug on her lettuce. "Foreign aid work?" she clarified with a creeping horror.

"Certainly." He smiled again. "Now, if there is anything else I can do for you, ma'am, anything at all, please be sure to let me know."

He strode away to move along some children who had dared to sit on a bench while looking at the dinosaurs.

Heidi was transfixed. Slowly regaining motor function, she turned to Jansen – who was having control issues of his own, wracked as he was with silent laughter. She raised a fist, causing him to make a feeble attempt to block any assault, but he was utterly at her mercy. Heidi lowered her fist, choosing to storm off instead. Jansen caught up to her as she passed the remains of the Spinosaurus that, in a way, had brought them there.

"I am glad you find this all so amusing!" she snapped.

He bit his lip and could not help slowing to look again at the paltry remains of such a majestic beast. After all, as far as his personal timeline was concerned, their all-too-close encounter had happened only yesterday.

Heidi slowed too. Despite the bottomless chasm of her disappointment regarding *this* Munich, she could not help but stand in awe of their achievement.

After a long, contemplative moment, Jansen asked, "I wonder if he recovered after you shot him in the nether regions?"

She rolled her eyes. Her faithful hound could ever be depended upon to ruin the moment. "Come!" she ordered, striding towards the nearby storage cupboard where their visit to 1943 had begun.

It was hardly fair, but then war seldom is. The first three men to rush Douglas from the doorway dropped like stones. The next man in line tried desperately to close the door, rather than burst through it. He fell too, jamming the door open with his body.

Douglas yelled, *"Charge!"*

The three *New Worlders* yelled an incoherent battle cry as they ran for the door before it could be fastened against them. The Sarge eyed the side doors warily, looking for unexpected guests, but none came. Douglas shoved the door fully open and immediately threw himself to the side. A crossbow bolt took a chink out of the stone casement, right where his head had been.

"Yes, watch that, Captain. These boys know how to shoot!" The Sarge advised. He opened the door to the left. It was in complete darkness. Activating the flashlight on his rifle, he called, "Storeroom, sir. No one to shoot at! Adam, check the other one."

Prentice did as ordered. "Another store, Sarge."

"Right," said Douglas, keeping the solid oak door between himself and any further missiles. "This is the only way in then. Strange layout for a main entrance, this place. Ah'm surprised we havenae encountered stiffer resistance, too."

"Our weapons and vehicles probably put t' wind up 'em, sir," offered Prentice.

Douglas nodded. "Aye. But now we have them cornered..."

"You're concerned about what traps they may have in place behind that door, Captain?" asked The Sarge. He stepped up to the door and pulled a small telescopic periscope from his fatigues. "Allow me, sir. Right. Hmm."

"Sarge?"

Jackson turned to his superior. "I think we need another plan, sir. There are about six of them crammed onto a spiral stair, all aiming crossbows at this door."

The three lapsed into silence for a moment, and then Prentice spoke. "I've got an idea, Captain."

"He's here, I can feel him!" Baines stated angrily.

"We can feel him too," Mario stated worriedly.

"This is a bad idea," Hussain stated moodily.

"Oh, *balls* to it!" shouted Baines egregiously as she kicked the door in. At least, that was what she intended to do. What she actually *did* was fall through it, without the need to open it first. "Damn! I've gotta get a handle on this!"

Ever helpful, Mario reminded her, "We're on a different plane of existence, Captain."

"Well, the quicker we deal with this jackbooted jackass the quicker I can get back to the 'plain old' plane of existence. Being bodyless is a bitch!"

They piled into the first-floor prison room[3] only to find it empty.

"She's gone," noted Hussain.

---

3   Second-floor by American convention.

"You're good," Baines drawled. "A better question would be: *where* has she gone? Has De Soulis stowed her some place other than the prison tower, or has the shady shade whisked her away elsewhere?"

"The shady shade?" asked Dr Jamie Ferguson – posthumously.

"Darth Casper," Baines elucidated. "Come on. Get into the spirit of the thing!"

"*That* was yer idea, laddie?"

"They're gone, aren't they? Erm, sir."

"Aye-yi-yi."

Sixty seconds earlier

Douglas was dragging the last of the stunned men away from the door when he was forced to leap aside.

"Look out! I've got a special delivery for 'em!" Prentice walked bandy-legged, carrying a wooden barrel acquired from the right-hand storeroom he had moments before checked for hidden assassins. He knocked in the timber lid with the butt of his rifle and rolled it through the half-open door. Snatching a flaming torch from the wall sconce behind him, he shouted, "Fire in t' hole!"

"Was tha' gunpowder?" screamed Douglas.

Prentice, his back to the door, grinned knowingly. "Aye. Barrel ought t' spook 'em, but there's hardly anything left in i—"

The explosion slammed said door into its stone keeps with a bias that acceded to no argument, launching Prentice at Douglas and sending them both sprawling across the cobbled floor.

Rooted in Anglo Saxon times, the English language has transformed, for many at least, almost beyond recognition over the last 1500 years or so. However, foul language seems to have evolved much more slowly[4]. Douglas was separated from his fellow Borderers by an extremely robust oak door, yes, but also by upwards of twenty generations. Yet the oaths that turned the air blue from behind that door were clearly understandable

---

4   If it ain't ******* broke, don't ******* fix it!

by him, a Yorkshireman and a cockney sergeant[5]. Furthermore, the lack of any warning to either party led to a not inconsequential amount of swearing from in front of the door, too.

The Sarge's lightning reflexes got him out of his comrades' path as they flew by. "That happened," he muttered, wiggling a finger in his buzzing ear. He reached down to help both men back to their feet.

Before he could check on their condition, Douglas shouted, "*That* was yer idea, laddie?"

"They're gone, aren't they? Erm, sir."

"Aye yi yi."

"You boys alright?" asked The Sarge.

"It looked empty..." Prentice trailed off under their combined glare, mumbling, "Well, there weren't much in it, anyroad."

"Come on!" bawled Douglas. "Before we lose the advantage!"

"I just hope we didn't lose the stairs," grumbled The Sarge, but he followed his captain faithfully.

On the other side of the door the stone was scorched black under their dancing electric torchlight. Splintered timber lay all around, but there were no bodies.

"Another surgical strike!" Douglas chuntered irritably to himself as he took the steps two at a time. He popped out into a torchlit antechamber. Four doors led away, one left, one right and two in front of them. "Where is everybody?"

"The prison tower's this way." The Sarge pointed to their left with his rifle. "Assuming Beckett's plan was any good."

Douglas sighed. "Och, *great*. You'd better lead on, Sarge."

Sergeant Jackson turned the iron ring. "Locked, sir."

Douglas turned to Prentice. "You like blowing the crap out of things. Make that lock go away, will ye?"

"They'll hear it, sir."

Douglas gave him a look.

"Right. Yes, sir. Cover your ears."

Douglas gave him another look.

---

5   Even after construction of the Tower of Babel was well underway, there were still certain words that could be understood by all. These were usually uttered when one of the builders caught his thumb between the hammer and the hammered.

Prentice winced. "Bit late? OK." He took his assault rifle and pumped thirty rounds or more into the door. A circle of oak fell out, taking the lock with it.

Douglas shook his head. "Yer no' a subtle man, Adam. Sarge – after you."

They ran down a darkened corridor. Near its end, they left the suspended timber floor behind, stepping back onto stone as they came to another pair of closed doors, and a vile stench. "Behind door number one?" asked The Sarge, arbitrarily gesturing towards the right.

Douglas nodded, levelling his rifle while Prentice watched their backs along the corridor. As the door creaked open noisily, the stink of decaying blood and urine assaulted them. "Oh, Turkish delight," The Sarge groaned. "It's a torture chamber. Looks like someone was having a jolly time at someone else's expense in here recently, too."

Douglas swallowed his disgust. "And door number two?"

"Ready?" asked The Sarge.

"Go."

They were no longer in a position to be surprised from their end of the corridor, so he flung the second door wide open, swinging his own weapon to bear.

The room was empty but for a small, three-legged milking stool. There was a latrine chute built into the west wall and a small slot in the northern wall for light and air. It was a grim chamber, but as The Sarge's boot struck a hollow note he realised there was worse to come. "Trapdoor, sir."

They looked at one another.

Douglas gave a slight shake of his head. "We have to check."

The Sarge bent to withdraw the bolts that secured the hatch in the floor. Tugging on an iron loop, the hinges creaked as he strained. The stench that molested their nostrils nearly felled them, but far worse than that was the moaning from the black pit below.

Jansen closed the storeroom door quietly behind them. The lights came on automatically once more. The slight distortion hanging in the air at the back of the room surprised them, providing clear proof that the wormhole had not, in fact, closed.

Heidi frowned. "It has been more than two hours now. Do you think they reactivated it, using the marker we left, to lock in the coordinates?"

Jansen had no answer, so he suggested, "Try the radio."

Heidi pulled her comm from a pocket, checked it was still set to analogue and spoke into the microphone. "*Heydrich?* Come in, *Heydrich*. This is Dr Heidi Schultz."

A crackle and, "*Dr Schultz, this is* Heydrich. *We are glad to hear from you. What is your situation?*"

Heidi raised an eyebrow. She doubted they were *glad*. "*Heydrich*, we are still in Munich, AD1943. Although, assuming *mein Großvater* has returned safely, you will already be aware that this is not the 1943 we expected. I assume you managed to reopen the wormhole as planned?"

"*Negative, Doctor. We have been unable to close it down. Your grandfather and his guards did indeed return safely, a little over an hour ago. However, we think the continuation of the open wormhole has something to do with the geology it passes through between Egypt and Germany.*"

"Geology? What does geology have to do with wormholes? Are they not *outside* our space–time?"

"*Apparently not so much, ma'am. Our science team now believes that if you create a wormhole next to a sufficiently potent energy source – say the molten core of a planet – you can experience cross-dimensional power bleed, or so I heard.*"

"How?"

"*That explanation is outside my skillset, ma'am.*"

"Get One on comms, immediately!"

"*Did you say 'One', ma'am?*"

"White coat, the bald one, whatever his name is – fetch him!"

"*Erm, I think I know who you mean, ma'am. Putting the call out now.*"

Heidi waited impatiently for a couple of minutes before her comm crackled again.

"*This is Reid speaking.*"

"Who?"

The comm crackled again but a sigh could clearly be heard. "*This is* One, *ma'am. Glad to hear you're safe. How can I help you?*"

"Everyone is glad, it seems. The wormhole has been open far longer than planned and is now exposed to a vast external power source, I understand. So all I need from you, One, is to know whether I will *still* be safe should I try and return to the *Heydrich?*"

A moment's silence. When One replied, his voice was quieter, as if he did not wish to be overheard. "*Of course, ma'am. I can* personally *guarantee your safe return trip.*"

Heidi's eyes narrowed, her instincts prickling. "Stand by." She turned to Jansen. "Did you hear that?"

He nodded. "Sounded like his 'guarantee' was for our ears only."

"I agree. He has no idea whether we can return or not, has he? If we arrive in one piece, his word is honoured. If we do not, then who is to know? No one would apportion blame to him."

A flicker of concern crossed Jansen's face as he arrived at the same conclusion. "So what do you want to do?" She appeared uncertain for a moment, so Jansen continued, "I have an idea, Doctor."

"Speak."

His lips twitched with the beginnings of a smile. "I take it the Heidi Schultz that guard mistook you for was a relative? A great-great-great-great-grandmother, perhaps?"

"Yes, give or take a great! Heidi has always been a popular name in my female line – arrive at your point!"

"OK. Well, chances are, there's a strong physical resemblance between you and her – that guy was fooled anyway, and so was the girl at the kiosk. Now, you remember that young blonde we held from Douglas' crew some weeks back? The pretty one captured by Del Bond? Her name was Rose Miller, I think."

Memories of Heidi's time with Tim Norris flooded back, along with his eventual betrayal of her trust. She soured. "Yes. *And?*"

"Remember Bond trussed her up in that evening dress – the little blue number with the split all the way up to her—"

"I suggest we return to your idea!"

His grin broadened. "Reckon you could get into it?"

"De Soulis is in there," said Mario. "In fact, it seems pretty much everyone is in there. He has a token watch, chattering their teeth up on the battlements, but that's it. Hard to believe after those explosions from downstairs."

"Hmm," Baines agreed thoughtfully. "That was James breaking down the door, I saw him. I think he saw me too. Is that possible?"

"Some people see us," offered Bud O'Neill. The other spirits nodded agreement.

"James has never mentioned such a thing to me?"

"The thing is, Captain, people, especially people with a reputation to uphold, seldom go around telling everyone they've been visited by the dead," explained Mario. "We get-a used to it. Of course, it may be that his connection with you is simply stronger?"

"Or it may be that *she* is," added Hussain.

Baines stared at him. "What do you mean, Aabid?"

"Simply that our physical forms are long gone. Yours, on the other hand, is still at least partially working. Our bodies are like a power source. Comparing our physical bodies to our souls is like comparing a power cell from a lorry with a watch battery."

"You think she could take him?" asked Jamie Ferguson.

Hussain shrugged. "Maybe she could at least send him away, until someone can find a more permanent solution for dealing with him."

"Hey, I'm still here, you know. Well, sort of," Baines felt the need to point out. "What are you talking about? I could take who?"

"Rotmütze," Mario supplied. "Or 'Robin Redcap' as he likes to call himself these-a days."

"The one who killed me?"

Mario had the decency to look uncomfortable. "You're not actually *dead*. At least, not completely."

"Oh, thank you! So I'm on a day pass – how does this help us?"

"It means," Hussain rounded on her, "that you are much more powerful than we are. Of course, if you're not willing to use that power..."

Had her spirit required air, she would have sighed with annoyance. "OK. Let's remember I'm the new kid here. You guys will have to tell me what to do."

"It's not that simple," said Mario.

"Don't get in the way of what needs to be done!" snapped Hussain.

"She has to know!" Mario retorted. "Look, Captain, you are in, er... sort of a coma. There may be a route back to your body for you – back to your life. However, if you lose this fight..."

"I might die?"

"Again," Hussain stated flatly.

Baines glared at him. "Whose side are you on... this time?"

"Oh, *touché!*"

"Please!" Mario cut in. "It's your call, Captain. He's just through that door."

"We may have other considerations any second now," added O'Neill. "Captain Douglas and a couple of other guys are heading here, too. They're getting ready to face off against De Soulis and his men, barricaded in the great hall, but they won't have any way to defend against... *him.*"

Baines sighed – it was a hard habit to quit – and held up her hands. "OK, so decision made. I'm not letting anything happen to James – or the others, for that matter."

"You love him," stated Ferguson.

"I *what*, now?"

Ferguson smiled knowingly. "You can't hide your feelings from us on this plane, Jill."

Baines frowned. "Then it's time this plane hit the landing strip – I'm gonna need to pick a little something up from the duty free for my nerves after all this! Let's do it."

Using her new skills, she put her head through the door to see what lay beyond. In the far corner, she caught a glimpse of De Soulis' cloak disappearing down a very narrow spiral stair hidden behind a tapestry. Four men forced a young woman down after him. She was dressed in a fine, if dishevelled, dress and cloak.

"So that's soon-to-be-Queen Elizabeth. Son of a... *He's running away!*"

Heinrich Schultz stood at the promontory's edge, the *Heydrich* and her wormhole behind him. His bodyguards stood at full alert but kept a respectful distance, leaving him alone with his thoughts.

The sunset over the North African Delta was bewitching as always. The fiery disc glowed pale and unnaturally large as it kissed the tops of the mountains some miles west; a peninsula reaching out into the sea like the arm of a protective parent around the bay.

Although appreciative of the view before his eyes, the real work was going on behind them. What was his granddaughter up to now? He had fashioned her into a cold, lethal weapon for sure, but she occasionally exceeded even his expectation. His emotions, while always under control, were becoming ever more erratic where she was concerned. He felt pride at what he had achieved with her, of course, but there was also – and he could not deny it – dread.

She was like the sun that dipped towards the horizon; beautiful, full of life and power, but he knew only too well that such power tended to burn so brightly that anyone standing close would do well not to be incinerated.

Such schemes she had – perhaps even reaching outwith his own. Of all the things she might have requested for her elongated stay in 1943, she had asked for an evening dress, a black-tie suit for her guard dog, and a small vial of cyanide.

So mesmerised was he by the vista before him, and the depth of his thoughts, that the screeching took a moment longer than it should have to penetrate his mind and engage reaction. The sound came from above, and from many tiny throats.

Heinrich naturally raised his arms to protect his head. Where the hell were his guards? Napping? He soon saw the truth; they were at the heart of a maelstrom. It was as though they were cloaked in leather, barely a square inch of them remained visible through the flapping ferocity of their attackers.

For the second time on this hill, Heinrich ran for his life. Being chased by a full grown Spinosaurus had pushed him to his limits, but there had been only one – and Heinrich had begun his charge well out ahead. These miniature killers were no more than a metre across the wing, but they were quick as sight – moreover, they were many. Many, many.

The sky behind him was thick with them, hundreds at the very least, their leathery wings brown from an equatorial sun while their bodies were clothed in fiery red, downy feathers. Rather than the beak of a bird, they sported long, red and black snouts, filled with sharply serrated, and distinctly dinosaurian teeth.

The old man did not know what species they were, nor did he care. What he *did* know, was that he had absolutely no chance of reaching the safety of the *Heydrich* before they had him, and in such numbers that he would be shredded before help could arrive.

The screaming from his three guards ceased abruptly. It happened, and was over, so fast. The feeding frenzy around his men filled the air with blood beaten to mist by flapping wings, as savage teeth stripped their bodies with the efficiency of piranhas. At least half a dozen of the deadly pterosaurs were already attacking Heinrich, too; diving, slicing attacks that left his arms and head bloody. He had only one chance. His granddaughter had kept everyone so busy with her schemes that no one had yet reclaimed the escape pod he used to flee the *Sabre*, Captain Aurick Hartmann's ship, just moments before Del Bond destroyed it and himself, along with Captain Emilia Franke and several of her crew in a single act of treachery.

It seemed an age ago now, but he had no time to dwell. He yelled, "Unlock!" After taking another breath on the run, he followed up with "Open!" His prayers answered, the hatch in the side of the little craft slid open with a hiss of hydraulics.

The tiny, winged predators certainly put the terror into pterosaurs; it was almost as though they knew he had a plan to escape them and began diving for his legs, shredding the combat fatigues he still wore.

Time seemed to slow for Heinrich, an almost dreamlike state shielding his higher brain from the electric shocks of agony. Thoughts barely under his control, he was glad he had not bothered to change after his return from 1943 – he would have hated to sacrifice one of his exquisitely crafted suits to these foul little creatures. His legs were failing too. He could tell. Yet his mind was somehow dulled, making the damage he suffered, and the pounding of his slowing feet, feel more like the shuddering vibrations of something happening *next* to his body, rather than to it. Just metres away from the open hatch, he was almost completely ballistic now, his legs freewheeling without power. All vision blurred, further impaired by blood coursing down his face from a ragged scalp wound. He was a dead man, surely, but it no longer seemed to matter. If this was the end, he had his acceptance. In fact, it seemed all that was left to him.

"This was a good idea, Ben."

Heidi actually smiled at him. Jansen hated the fact that, on the rare occasions she treated him like a human being, he always felt so *grateful* – he almost wished he had a tail to wag. In moments of introspection, he wondered whether he had been in some way 'programmed' to follow her – with the Schultzes, one never knew. She was, of course, one of the most beautiful women he had ever seen, there was no doubting that. He could only bring himself to take his eyes off her because, knowing Heidi, he would probably lose them otherwise. Though he was often tempted to risk just the one, he constantly struggled to explain the hold she had over him.

He did not love her. How could he? Her beauty was a mere façade for a twisted soul, like the reflection granted by a house of crazy mirrors. He had been safer with the Carcharodontosaurus that almost killed him a few days ago – at least he always had a chance of outwitting that kind of monster.

No, Heidi's lure was a puzzle, an internal struggle he could not quite get to grips with. Perhaps he did not want to? It was a thought. Quickly followed by another, as he sneaked a surreptitious glance. Heidi always dressed with a soldier's lack of modesty. What if he met another Heidi from this time? *Two of them... Wow!*

"Well?" She broke into his thoughts. "How do I look?"

Startled, his mind raced. *Sweet Jesus. If I tell her what's on my mind right now, I'm dead!* With any other woman this would have been mere metaphor. As he found his voice, courage completely deserted him. "Very nice, ma'am. I'm sure they'll be suitably dazzled by the glamour of that dress. Just what we need to impress the natives."

She seemed content with that. "You scrub up quite well yourself, Ben. Perhaps we should do this more often, hmm?"

Oh my God! Think about something else! I'm in the kitchen – no, the launderette! Yes, that's it. I'm in the launderette and, and, and, while I'm waiting, I'm field stripping my rifle for maintenance, too. Nooo! DON'T THINK ABOUT STRIPPING!

"Ben? Are you alright?"

Jansen tried to speak and began coughing. "Just something in my throat," he croaked. "So, we may not have plugged straight into Nazi Germany, but surely the possibilities of this time make it a palatable second prize – wouldn't you say, ma'am?"

Heidi smiled again. Showing her perfect teeth, she nevertheless had an air of something wholly carnivorous. "Yes, we may yet take gold. And it all starts this evening. Who's a clever boy then!"

Chapter 3 | Show Time!

With the trapdoor raised, The Sarge shone his rifle's torch down into the hole below, bringing the full horror to light. The pit drank in the semi-fresh air from the cell above, returning a ghastly stench that caused the three men to turn away and gag. The damp alone made it hard to breathe, but carcinogenic mould was the very least of it. The tiny chamber was little more than an airless, lightless, vertical shaft built into the monolithic stone walls of the tower. It was clearly a place where people were cast down and left to rot.

"Oh, my God," Douglas muttered, in disgust yes, but more at what he saw than what he smelt. Three ragged and bloodied children huddled together, filthy, in the dark. The remaining bedrock floorspace was taken up by a further three semi-decomposed corpses. The children blinked up at him, too terrified to move or make a sound. *The poor wee wretches are probably praying we think they're dead, so we'll leave them alone. How could* anyone *do this?* He dared not voice his thoughts aloud, fearing that any exertion of his throat might cause him to either vomit or burst into tears. Never had he been so disgusted by his fellow man.

"I saw a ladder in the next room, sir."

The Sarge's voice was so subdued, Douglas barely recognised it. He nodded, still not trusting his own.

Within moments, Jackson returned to lower the ladder into the stinking pit. The children pulled in even more closely together.

Douglas watched Prentice wipe an angry tear from his eye before returning to his vigil at the corridor's end. He knelt at the edge of the hole. "Ye can come out now, we'll no' harm ye."

Three grimy faces looked up, blinking wide-eyed and silent.

Passing his weapons to The Sarge, Douglas began down the ladder. His heart almost broke as he heard the children whimper in fear and distress at his approach. Stepping off the bottom rung, he turned to appraise them. Two boys and a girl. She was clearly the eldest but could be no more than seven or eight. The boys were seemingly of an age, perhaps a year or two her junior. They were so filthy it was hard to discern anything more. There was also something behind them. Douglas wondered what it could be they were trying to hide.

"Come now, let us help ye." He spoke gently, giving the local accent of his early years full rein so as not to scare them further. "Ye're safe now."

He reached out and they flinched to the side as one, revealing what they had been hiding. With the children out of the way, the torchlight from above illuminated the body of a man, his remains little more than a bundle of skin and bone, wrapped in bloody, faeces-smeared rags. Douglas closed his eyes against the sight. The poor wretch was beyond any help he could provide, and that was probably for the best, so badly tortured was his body.

Douglas' disgust, even his pity, was shoved aside for a moment by the brute force of his anger. He had to fight hard to keep his temper under control; the three lost and broken youngsters were timorous enough as it was. It did not take long to realise that getting them out of the hole was about all he could do for them for the moment. The man, and the remains of those other poor souls, would have to stay where they were until the castle was taken and held. He knew it was only a matter of time before Commander Gleeson used his 'initiative' and blew the place to hell. Part of him would happily see it happen too, after this; tragic loss to history or no. However, dwelling on it was a luxury he could not afford right now.

He returned his attention to the children. They clung to one another with a wordless desperation that tore at his soul. Getting them to unclasp and straighten up was like trying to pry open a spring-loaded deckchair one-handed, but eventually he managed to part them. Encouraging them to climb towards the waiting arms of The Sarge took even more convincing, but eventually all three huddled once more in the corner of the comparatively humane holding cell above. It was far too dangerous to let them run around the castle and Douglas could spare no one to take them out at this time.

He caught The Sarge's eye. He knew that look – it was the 'blue touchpaper' look. Someone was about to wish they had never been born.

Patricia Norris sat in her wheelchair, holding Baines' hand. "You must come back to us, Jill. We need you, need your strength. And I still need to thank you for getting me back to the ship after I was shot. Without you, I—"

"How are you feeling, Patricia?" asked Dr Dave Flannigan, gently. "You've been sitting there a long time."

Patricia gave a tired smile. "Hi, Dave. I didn't hear you come in. I'm OK. I'd like to stay a little longer, if I may. I don't know if talking to Jill can help, but it's all the help I can give."

"I understand. We've all heard about the studies that suggest talking to coma patients – about it reaching them at some level," he sighed. "Besides, I'll take any edge I can get, right now."

"No luck in finding the cause of her condition?"

He looked a little shifty. "Not as such."

Patricia turned to study him fully. "Dave?"

He pulled up a seat and sat heavily. "*Some* people think that this is a spiritual problem, rather than a physical one. I told them to go ask Mother Sarah to pray for her, but otherwise I couldn't help with that."

"What did Sarah say?"

"Yeah, that's the thing. She was more than happy to ask for God's help, naturally, but our priest believes it's a *physical* problem – you gotta love it!"

"But you're not sure?"

He leaned in close and conspiratorial. "Now, you know I'm not usually one for hocus pocus, but I gotta tell ya, there's somethin' weird goin' on here."

Patricia frowned. "How so?"

"Oh, I dunno, perhaps it's just that I can't find a damned thing wrong with her – she's just... out to lunch!"

"But you can't really believe she's 'ghosting' around, can you?"

He grunted and gave a wan smile. "I know this is gonna sound crazy, but sitting in my office a few weeks ago, I received a message. Didn't realise who it was from at the time. I was later told it came from Mario."

Patricia searched her memory. "The young man who was killed right at the start of all this, when the wormhole drive exploded?"

Seeing her expression, he held up his hands in a placatory gesture. "Yeah, I know. You don't gotta tell me how that sounds. But when Beck Mawar explained it all to me, she... she *knew* things – things only Mario could know, things she certainly couldn't have found out in any normal way – at least that I could see. What? You think I'm crazy?"

"No. Not as such."

"Not as *such?* Gee, thanks."

Patricia giggled and immediately took a sharp breath, holding her stomach.

"You OK?" Flannigan reached forward, suddenly concerned.

Patricia took a deep, slow breath this time, as she waited for the pain to subside. "It'll pass."

"Hey, don't go splittin' your sides, now."

She tried not to laugh. "Don't!"

He grinned. "Sorry, that was a cheap trick."

She grinned painfully back at him. "So what are you going to do for Jill? Feed her a broad-spectrum antibiotic or begin a séance?"

It was Flannigan's turn to look pained.

"So what now?" asked Baines. "We know they're all holed up in there and De Soulis is getting away, but I can't even turn a door handle right now – how am I meant to fight? Do we just stand around outside and hope they order up a séance or something?"

"You should try and relax, Captain," said Ferguson. "Centre yourself."

"What can I say? Being dead hasn't agreed with me!"

"You're not technically dea—"

"So it hasn't *taken!* I still can't even turn a door handle, so how do I protect James and the others, and get rid of Robin Redneck?"

"Redcap."

"Whatever."

Mario looked around his spiritual compatriots with concern. "You really must try and calm yourself, Captain."

"Why?"

"Because, if you become overwrought you might awaken too early, and we'll lose any chance we have to send him away."

Baines frowned. "What? You're saying that if I get angry, I return to my body?"

Mario shrugged. "It's-a possible. If returning *at all* is possible. Look, I'm truly sorry, Captain. All I can say is, you're our best chance, but we can promise nothing. None of us have been fortunate enough to *be* in your situation."

That gave her pause, and when she spoke her words came slowly, thoughtfully. "But don't I *need* my body's power to do this? And if the only thing linking me to *me* is my anger, then how do I bring this power to bear before I pop back to the real world or, or... *wherever?*"

Mario smiled warmly. "Remember when you dragged that massive black warship over the edge of a promontory, back in Cretaceous Patagonia?"

"You were there?"

"I was. We were all with you."

"OK, I think that's comforting, in a sort of late-night ghost story kind of way."

His grin broadened. "When you destroyed the enemy's warship, against all odds, what was your thought process?"

Baines looked around their faces hoping for inspiration but found none. "Erm... *wing it?*"

Prentice walked unknowingly through the bickering spirits to fire upon the lock. The door would not move. "Most likely it's heavily braced from t'other side, sir. They've barricaded 'emselves in."

Douglas pulled Gleeson's rocket launcher from around his shoulder and fed one of his two remaining shells into the pipe. "Stand back, laddies."

"*Sir?*" asked The Sarge in some alarm.

"How far back?" asked Prentice.

Douglas reconsidered. "Right. I suppose we'll be able to see this door from all the way down the corridor. Perhaps Ah should fire from the prison cell."

The Sarge gave a look of misgiving.

Prentice shrugged. "Better than standing here, sir."

Douglas shook his head. "It'll have to be enough. They know we're coming now."

Seconds later, they were back in the prison cell.

Doulas hid behind the door jamb to aim the launcher. He closed one eye, focusing on the door at the far end of the corridor. "Tell the bairns to cover their ears."

"Erm, are we going to be OK standing here?" asked Baines, tremulously.

"There's no cause for concern, Captain. You won't feel a thin—" Mario never got the chance to finish his consolation before the oak door barring the way for Douglas' team exploded into fire and fragments.

Baines wore an expression of abject horror.

"See?" asked Mario, with a calmness that bordered on the absurd.

"Why aren't my ears ringing?"

"You don't-a have any."

"Good point."

Douglas charged down the corridor, not willing to give De Soulis and his men time to recover. The three *New Worlders* burst into the great hall with stun rifles blazing, no time for questions. Five men were down already, moaning from shock and shrapnel after the bang. A further three went down from their fire, while fifteen or twenty more hid behind long wooden trestle tables, with the grand fireplace behind them.

In the darkened room, the fire blinded Douglas – as it was meant to. His enemies were experienced fighting men, after all; were they stupid, they would already be deceased fighting men. He dove behind a group of large barrels – hoping they contained ale and not gunpowder – just as a hail of crossbow bolts turned them into wooden porcupines. What leaked from them was small beer[6], from the smell. *Not surprising if*

---

6   Of low alcohol content, 'small beer' was drunk by all, as a safer alternative to water.

they expected a siege, thought Douglas. *De Soulis wouldnae want his men legless from the good stuff – and talking of De Soulis, where is he?*

The Sarge, with a luck that ran alongside the skill of only the very best warriors, had evaded the enemy's attention altogether. After a dive and a forward roll, he regained his feet to snatch one of a pair of Norman kite shields from the wall. Painted with what he assumed to be the De Soulis coat of arms, they were obviously centuries old and placed for display, but as he hunkered down to wait for the bolts to cease, he hoped they were more than ceremonial.

Prentice, having brought up the rear, now filled the hall with a withering fire from what was left of the doorway, using its stone jamb for protection.

"Give up *now!*" bellowed Douglas. "Or we'll blow ye all to hell!"

Not really expecting that to work, he was more than a little surprised when the loud chuntering of discussion reached his ear, rather than the thuds of another volley hitting his barrel. He was already soaked.

"Well?" he called again, against hope.

"Who are ye?" a rough, brutal voice came back.

"The name's Douglas. Captain James Douglas."

"What promises can ye give?"

"Throw out your weapons and the warriors among ye can go free – unarmed o' course."

"The warriors?"

"Aye," Douglas shouted around his barrel. This had been too easy so far; he could hardly believe it. "But De Soulis and yer jailers stay here!" It was worth a try.

More disgruntled chuntering. Douglas tried to pick out distinct conversations, but it was difficult, especially when a voice whispered forcefully right next to his ear, "*He's gone, James, and he's taken the girl with him!*"

Douglas jumped hard enough to set his barrel rocking. "What the... *Jill?*"

"No. The name's Donald. Ah'm captain here," the man behind the barricade shouted back.

Trying to regrasp the greasy rope unravelling from around his sanity, Douglas called, "Right, Donald, o' course. What's yer answer? Ye know we can kill ye all, or ye can give me De Soulis and his jailers, and the rest o' ye walk free! My word on it. What's it to be?"

Various latches[7], swords, spears and even a couple of daggs[8] came over the top of their barricade. "We surrender."

Douglas, his eyes now acclimatised to the shadow and firelight, caught The Sarge's eye. Jackson could only shrug back at him. Clearly, he could hardly believe it either. "Ye can come out, Donald. Ye'll nae be harmed."

A dozen castle guards came out with their hands high while another four stepped out holding a couple of kicking, struggling men in filthy leather aprons.

Douglas smiled with satisfaction, but little humour. No true soldier could stomach torturers. *It seems these boys are no' so different from us, after all.* One of the men wore armour and a helmet of superior quality to the others. "Donald?"

"Aye. Will ye let ma men go, Captain?"

"Where's De Soulis?"

"Sir William left a wee while ago with that English lass. Ah dinnae ken where he took her – only that he left us tae face ye, and yer muskets that shoot killing light."

Douglas searched the man's face for a lie but saw none, only a measure of contempt for his own superior. "Yer men are no' dead, Donald. They're knocked out. Was he alone with her?"

Donald shook his head. "He took four o' ma men 'n' his pet torturer wi' him. They will hae left on horseback. He was furious that ye blew up his wee kirk[9]." Donald could not quite conceal his smirk.

Douglas returned his smile. "So these two are his jailers?"

"Aye, Captain. Two o' them, at least."

"And ye still have men up on the battlements?"

Donald looked disappointed that Douglas knew of them. "Aye," he admitted with a sigh. "Just the four. Will ye keep yer word now, James?"

"Before Ah let ye go, answer me this – why do ye serve a monster like De Soulis?"

"It's safer in, than oot, ye ken? Many o' us hae families..."

Douglas nodded. After seeing those children and the bodies, down in the hole, he understood only too well. He was about to accede when

---

7   Crossbows favoured by Scottish and Borderer archers.

8   Early, heavy, single-shot wheel lock pistols.

9   Church, in Scottish and Northern English dialects.

a squeal of electronic feedback and a preternaturally loud voice came from outside the castle walls. *"Alright, you mangy baggers. I'm gonna need you to surrender and come out now, unarmed and with your hands in the air. Otherwise, I'm gonna blow a hole in the ground so big under ya, that they'll be picking up your teeth in Melbourne! You've got one minute – and I never was great at counting, so don't push the envelope!"*

Douglas snorted, shaking his head.

"Yer men?" asked Donald.

"Aye, that'll be them."

"Whit tha hell's bells is he talkin' aboot?"

Douglas threw back his head and laughed. "Ah'll free your men, Donald. Just let me sort this out." He sobered quickly. "De Soulis badly hurt one of ma people. Commander Gleeson out there was very fond of her, so Ah couldnae guarantee yer safety if ye left right now. Ye ken?"

"Thirty seconds or it's boom time, ya stinking mongrels!"

Douglas frowned. "That was ne'er thirty seconds. Hang on, Donald, while Ah stop him blowing us all over the moon!" He strode to one of the small windows in the west wall of the Douglas tower and threw open the shutters – taking care to stand well back. "Commander?"

Another squeal of a public address system feeding back and, *"Captain Douglas, is that* you?"

"Aye, who did ye expect? We have everything under control here now, Commander, but it was good of ye to stop by! Send in six armed men through the south gate – ye'll find it open, what's left of it – and stand down those explosives!"

"Good on ya, Cap! I'll send the boys in. Is there anything else I can get for ya?"

"Apart from roast beef and Yorkshire pud? Aye. Ask Meritus what kind o' sensors his contraption carries, and get him to start scanning for five men and a woman, probably on horseback."

Baines felt him before she saw him – Rotmütze. "Oh *crap!* And it was all going so well." She, along with her ethereal companions, turned to see him standing by the doorway with his arms crossed, a cocky grin on his face. It was a look Baines wanted to hit until he stopped twitching.

She glanced around. It seemed Douglas and the rest of the *living* could not see him. "So, Robin, do you mind if I call you Bob? You can hide yourself from us— *them*, then?"

Heat seemed to sear the air around him. "Oh, you don't know the half of what I can do, Jill. Perhaps you'd like to say a quick goodbye to your friends here, before you join them in the forever?"

Roar! He could hear it coming closer, even over the deafening screeches of those devilish birds. Several large animals were calling out, their harsh, bloodcurdling cries splitting the air. The *Heydrich* was yet to respond. It felt like many minutes to Heinrich, although only seconds had passed.

He lay across the threshold of his erstwhile escape pod with just enough faculty to stop himself from ordering the hatch to seal. It would have chopped him in half. It was hard to tell for sure, he was so numb, but he believed the attack on his legs had ceased. One of the small pterosaurs had flown into the lifeboat ahead of him to flutter and screech wildly. Believing itself trapped, it clawed and snapped at the forward screen in an almost demented rage.

"Ha!" was all the ire he could manage at the creature's stupidity. However, there was clearly something else going on that he, too, did not understand. He was losing a lot of blood but managed to raise himself from the ground on one elbow.

Then he saw them. Three of them. He even fancied he could put a name to them: Bahariasaurus ingens – his granddaughter's third choice if the Spinosaurus failed to lead them through the wormhole. He began to chuckle and then laugh, which gradually turned into a coughing fit. It all seemed so ridiculous now. His whole plan, all in ruins and him, about to be eaten by Heidi's runners-up – or *was* he?

Taking several deep breaths, he forced his prodigious mind to focus one last time. The bahariasaurs were snapping after the pterosaurs. It was like watching sharks attacking a shoal of fish. It lasted only a few seconds before the flyers remembered their advantage, forgoing the scraps from their kill. They burst into the air, a livid migration, but the theropod giants' muzzles nevertheless dripped with blood and body parts, speaking to their successes.

Heinrich watched, captivated; he had regained his senses only to find that he could not move his legs. *The blood loss must be more severe than I guessed,* his woolly mind filled in the details.

The dinosaurs were still mopping up the dead and dying pterosaurs, following their brief altercation, but he knew they would make short work of that – then they would notice *him.* Two of them were at least twelve metres long, the third slightly smaller. They were huge and terrifying certainly, yet comparative lightweights next to some of the other predatorial super fauna inhabiting this continent. He guessed that they probably weighed in at no more than a third of the mass of the largest of the carcharodontosaurs or spinosaurs, and this made a difference. They lacked the power, but were *oh* so much faster.

"No..." he groaned. Reaching behind to grab the edges of the lifeboat's hatch, he pulled with all the life force remaining to him. Gradually, he began to slide.

In the near distance he heard the hydraulic hiss of the *Heydrich*'s ramp lowering. His people were coming – perhaps there was yet a chance. The thought bolstered his final efforts. As he slid through the dust and sand painfully, and painfully slowly, the thunder of heavy, running feet made him look round. He had been spotted, but by the wrong side. "Oh, *damn!*" he cursed weakly.

One of the bahariasaurs had indeed seen him and was bearing down. He had seconds. Dragging his legs over the threshold with his hands, one at a time, he heard the roar of a powerful diesel engine from the direction of the *Heydrich.* This seemed to unsettle the dinosaur, causing it to slow. It stood over the old man, while turning to stare out towards the huge black spaceship and the alien sounds coming from it. Blood dripped from its jaws to spatter the sand around Heinrich's feet and legs. Still glad that he had not changed into a nice suit, he stole the moment to drag his remaining foot over the threshold.

Bahariasaurus sensed his movement and snapped for him, hunting again. Its huge eyes burned into the old man's. "You won't win that game with me, my boy!" Heinrich chuckled gently. A crash, off to his left, saw several of the scrubby trees and bushes that grew on the plateau flattened, as a tracked vehicle smashed them down.

While the huge animal was distracted, he cried out, "Close hatch!" The machinery obeyed his command instantly, but not before he glimpsed the dinosaurs taking flight from the APC. "*Now* they come to save me!" he managed before the sliding door hissed closed with hydraulic finality, sealing with a *thunk*.

Crawling across the carpeted floor to the cabinets opposite the hatch, he popped a soft-opening drawer. Feeling around with one arm, his fingers closed around the thing he sought. "Ah, still there. Excellent."

Sealed away from the outside world, their enclosure fell immediately silent. Trapped, the pterosaur heard Heinrich's voice over its own panicked shrieks and diverted all its attention towards the source. Eager to take out its fury on the only other living thing within its suddenly shrunken world, it turned and dove.

"Hmm... I would have expected nothing less, old chap." Heinrich fired the nine-millimetre pistol retrieved from the drawer. The little animal fell from the air to land by his side. It was not dead, rather flapping one wing ineffectually as it spun bloody circles on the carpet.

Heinrich watched it suffer impassively. "Yes, I feel your pain, little one."

The Old Academy's manager had seemed only too keen to arrange rooms for such honoured guests at a nearby five-star hotel, along with a car and driver for their convenience.

Before leaving Cretaceous Egypt – back when the possibility of making it to 1943 had seemed such a long shot – Heidi remembered impressing the need to believe in the righteousness of their cause upon her 'white coats'. In short, she had told them to trust in their destiny. She had barely believed it herself at the time, had simply used the speech as a device to bolster her own waning confidence while reiterating the importance of their work to her science staff.

That was then.

Now it seemed that destiny was indeed *everything*.

Hitler's famous final meeting of the party at the *Löwenbräukeller* in Munich on the 8th of November 1943, could no longer take place in this timeline. However, after subtly pumping the museum's manager for news, she had found out there would still be *a* meeting of the party. This provided Heidi with an opportunity, further strengthening her belief that there might be more than blind luck at play here. When she found out that 1943's Dr Heidi Schultz had been slated as a guest speaker, she was sold. Moreover, the other Dr Schultz would be stopping by the Old Academy Museum prior to the engagement – apparently, her namesake was donating a painting or some such. Heidi cared little for the details. All she cared about was the opportunity this coincidence, if that was all it was, presented. She would use it and build upon it.

Jansen's semi-formed plan involved impersonating the Heidi Schultz of this time to garner support, resources and information at the highest levels. It was an interesting idea, particularly as it came from the mind of a mere minion, but as such, it typically lacked audacity and vision. It was 'daring light', but that was fine, because she would bring the expansion pack that would upgrade it to 'derring-do'.

After an evening and a day's planning, she had nevertheless thought it best to leave Jansen in the dark regarding her planned *coup de grâce*. He had an occasional habit of lapsing into morality that was most vexatious.

Heidi waited calmly, just inside the museum's grand entrance. Presently, a motorcade of three limousines and a van pulled up outside. Several very serious-looking men wearing black suits with earpieces poured out of the vehicles to run about, checking their surroundings for threats. Another retrieved a large, flat box from the van. A metallic slide, followed by a boom, rang across the square as the van's side door slammed shut. With the area deemed secure, the rear door of the second car was opened and out stepped an arresting blond woman in an evening dress of shimmering gold.

To Heidi, waiting in the wings, the idea of waiting for someone else to open the door seemed quite absurd, not to mention the fact that *she* would rather have driven herself. However, she noted carefully the customs of this time and place, as she slipped further into the shadows.

"It's fully dark now, can we please make our move before my joints are completely frozen stiff?" Allison Cocksedge never admitted to anything, but were she to make an *allowance*, she might grant that she was not really cut out for this type of thing. She was not a soldier, after all; she was not an athlete, nor an outdoorswoman, she was not even a rambler. She *was* out of her depth and in the company of someone who, by similar degrees, was out of her mind. "You're enjoying this, aren't you?"

The accusation bounced off Erika Schmidt like a request for a voluntary tax audit. She replied without even looking round, "It has been so long since I got out of the office." She continued her study of the bastle[10], nestled in the glen below them. Lowering her stolen binoculars, she added, "However, I agree. We should go now. They will no longer see our approach."

"Thank you!" Cocksedge replied to the universe at large. Stiffly, she slipped and slithered down the slope after her companion, who it seemed *was* cut out for this type of thing. They pushed their bikes to avoid the danger of riding in the dark without headlamps. Guided only by a dull, red pinprick of firelight, flickering from one of the structure's windows, they trudged through the worsening snow. Pretty soon they would be in the dark heart of a blizzard and Cocksedge very much wanted to avoid that. Consequently, she had no choice but to pin all their hopes on her psychotic sidekick securing the keys to their new situation. She could only imagine what it would be like to pitch their tent in a full-blown snowstorm at night. She would have shivered at the thought, but that would have meant stopping shivering first, to show dynamic range. When it came down to location, location, location, she preferred ones that were inside, it had to be said.

Thirty paces from the entrance to the bastle, Schmidt raised her fist as a sign for Cocksedge to stop. The daylight was completely gone now, and Cocksedge missed it. Fortunately, crashing into the back of Schmidt's ride worked almost as well. "You could've—"

"Shhh! Silence!" Schmidt whispered just above the howl of the wind. "These people will be far more attuned to the world around them than modern city dwellers like you. They will hear and possibly even *smell* us if we are not careful. That is why I have chosen to stop downwind and at this distance."

Cocksedge's face screwed up in annoyance. She was elated to have such a capable companion, but preferred all such people to be

---

10 Bastles are defensible, thick-walled, stone farmhouses commonly found in the Scottish borders.

working for, rather than alongside, her. The idea of a partnership was new territory and came about as naturally as genuine gratitude. "So what now?" she hissed.

"Wait here."

"*Huh,* didn't see that coming!"

Schmidt kicked down her bike's side-stand and walked up to the solid-looking front door on the ground floor of the also very solid-looking stone building. She rapped twice.

A small trapdoor opened in the door above – a door with no obvious access from the ground. Schmidt noted this as most likely a simple, yet effective, defence mechanism. "Who's there?" asked a gruff and distinctly unwelcoming male voice.

"I am looking for a bed for the night," answered Schmidt.

"Show yersel'!"

"And how am I to do that? Do you have porchlights?"

"Step back!"

Schmidt did as instructed.

"Turn yersel' aboot!"

Hoping she had understood correctly, she spun slowly, arms raised, eventually facing the man above once more. In the time it took to turn away, an arm bearing a lantern had appeared. Held by a handle at its conical top, the cylindrical box housed a candle, heavily guttering in the wind. What little light it cast came from myriad patterned slits cut into the lantern's metal sides.

The door above opened and a man leaned out, leering down at Schmidt. "If 'tis a bed ye'll be wanting, Ah reckon we kin oblige ye!" The lascivious undertone in his words was unmistakable and hardly surprising to Schmidt. Very few men could rebut her charms, but this would be a tough one to play along with. Even from a metre above her head, his high body odour penetrated the storm on a gust of rapidly cooling warm air from inside – offering grievous insult to her delicate nose. He had to be in his fifties. This did not concern her, but his fifty or more years had clearly been hard and rough ones. That, combined with a lack of hygiene or personal grooming, gave him all the charm of a hedge growing from a broken drain – she had no wish to pluck its fruit.

She fought the urge to recoil from a man whose sex appeal had been appealed. Instead, and despite the weather, she offered him a smile that, to a man of his standing, must have seemed like an angel had just fallen out of the sky. "Please let me in. I need warming up, yes?"

A wooden ladder appeared at the now fully open first-floor door, crunching into the snow with alacrity. Schmidt gave it a quick shake to check it was secure and on a firm footing before beginning her ascent.

As she climbed closer, the man wiped drool from his beard, quite obviously in a state where he simply could not believe his luck. It transpired that the notion was a correct one. He reached down, to help her in as quickly as humanly possible. Leaning forward, his posture was perfect for snatching out of the open doorway, and this was exactly what happened next. Unfortunately, he hit the snow where it was thinnest, so that his three-metre swan dive pitched him headfirst into the frigid earth with a crack. He did not move.

Schmidt leapt lightly inside. The single room was surprisingly small compared with the building's outer proportions. She chalked this up to solid defensibility – a good thing. A large stone fireplace, with an iron cauldron suspended above the hearth, lit and heated the abode. Four sleeping pallets were arranged two on each side. Three of them were occupied.

From under a sackcloth blanket, hiding from the ferocity of the freezing wind, came another male voice. "Faither? *Da?*"

"He is checking the depth of the snow outside. It is less than he hoped, I think," replied Schmidt.

All grogginess was suddenly cast aside with his blanket as the young man jumped from his bed, calling out to the other recumbent forms in the room. Before anyone else moved, he snatched up a spear from the wall and ran for the intruder.

Schmidt stepped to the left, but not too quickly, leading the running man's weapon. As he lunged to strike, she jumped right with the grace of a gymnast, allowing him to pass, and with the lightest kick in the rear, he too was dispatched out into the night with a cry of surprise.

The second young man gave a wordless, animal cry of fury and ran at her brandishing a roughly made cutting sword.

Schmidt cast about for a weapon; even with her looks, guile was no longer an option. The other person in the room was a young woman who clutched a blanket to her breast, but remained otherwise motionless, eyes wide in terror. Automatically, she assigned the girl a low threat level.

On the other hand, the young swordsman was clearly cut from the same cloth as the other men. He lunged, all anger and language. Schmidt skipped backward, allowing the sword to sweep in front of her stomach. Following up with a dive and roll to his right, she regained her feet lithely, facing back towards him once more. Now standing in front of the fireplace, she helped herself to an iron poker. Not the last word in fencing equipment, but it had the dubious benefit of matching the calibre of her opponent.

He came on again, swinging violently, his weapon for slashing, not stabbing.

Schmidt's poker was made for neither, but it was, at the end of the day, an iron bar with a pointy end, so she felt confident of making it work. However, the more she evaded, the more he seemed likely to suffer injury from his own rage, requiring little input from her. Indeed, just as that thought flashed through her mind, her adversary created an opportunity.

Having smashed almost every stick of furniture in the place with his wild slashing and lunging, he decided on a change in tactics. Lifting his sword overhead, he ran straight for her.

Schmidt's footing was restricted by hearth and debris, so she raised the poker ready to parry, hoping it would carry the blow without bending. It was never put to the test. The man's ferocious overhead swing lodged his blade firmly into the oak collar-tie of the kingpost truss supporting the roof. His effort was such that he continued forward, even after the sword was jarred from his hands, straight onto the point of Schmidt's poker.

The shock in his eyes registered before the pain of being gut stabbed. Schmidt did not give him the luxury of suffering, she simply twisted and pulled. The young man instinctively brought his hands together over the wound in his belly, staggering forward as she swished the poker across his throat. The point was not sharp, but the speed and the weight behind the thrust ripped across his Adam's apple, dropping him to his knees and then – with a little help from Heinrich Schultz's personal assistant – face-first into the fire.

Schmidt walked towards the door, but remembering the building's fourth occupant, turned back once more. The girl had neither moved, nor even cried out. While she pondered the strangeness of this, a bellow of rage came from behind her. Ducking instinctively, Schmidt spun to face this latest challenge when the bloodcurdling cry turned to sounds of shock and alarm.

Before Schmidt could bring any of her prodigious fighting skills to bear, the other young man she had so recently helped outside was travelling sideways, from a toppling ladder. He hit the snowy ground with a *whoomph* and an oath. Schmidt unbent her legs from a fighting crouch to approach the doorway with caution. From outside, she heard a loud *crack* and, "Oh, no!"

Schmidt frowned. 'Oh, no' did not seem like these men's style at all, and in any case, the voice had been a woman's. "*Allison?*"

"Yes."

"What is wrong?"

"I'm still down *here!*"

"Is that man coming round? Do you need my help?"

"Erm... I don't think so, it's just that after pulling him away from the wall, I needed something to subdue him with. And now I think I've broken the damned ladder on his head!"

"I see, but I too have problems, I think."

"Oh?"

"It smells very badly of burning hair up here."

Chapter 4 | Castles and Kings

It took more than twenty minutes to die. It may have been vicious, monstrous even, in life; yet in death, it could be considered pitiable. Heinrich felt no such pity. It was not the fact that the diminutive pterosaur had tried to kill him – as far as *it* was concerned, his death was necessary, he understood that well enough. It was more that, by training and will, he had stripped all such useless emotions from his psyche – if they had existed at all. He was once again the only living thing within his tiny world of advanced alloys and ceramics; that was what mattered. At least, that would have been his usual response. Currently, his lack of feeling was born more out of external circumstance than any sort of mental regime. His vision blurred at the edges. Out on the periphery of thought came realisation. He was *still* dying. *Where are those fools?* he thought blearily.

When several stout knocks rang on the outer hull, hammering out a decidedly human little rhythm, he was not completely sure they were real. Part of his mind suspected that another part of his mind might be hallucinating. *Possibly.* Nevertheless, and showing typically subliminal Schultz foresight, he had closed the hatch without locking it, assuring his safety. Voice command was now the only way to reopen the ship, and as his life was not playing out across millions of screens all around the world for the entertainment of others, he doubted the dinosaurs would instantaneously and entirely independently develop a parallel English language – even with the way his luck was going this evening.

However, when the hatch opened, seemingly on its own, his assurance did waver just for a moment, forcing him to wonder whether he was saved or had simply *been* saved, for afters. Eventually, his befuddled mind rejected the idea of Disney dinosaurs popping round for dessert. Helping hands were not their style, after all, ergo the former seemed more likely. *Yes,* he thought wearily, *so glad I didn't change into eveningwear.*

Two litres of type O-positive later, Heinrich awoke to the smell of disinfectant in the *Heydrich*'s small infirmary. Immediately, his eyes narrowed, and he demanded, "Why was my rescue so delayed?"

"Please try to relax, sir," a nurse comforted, plumping his pillows so that he might sit up.

"Never mind that!" he snapped ungraciously. "Fetch my tablet!"

"You're not due any medication for another hour, si—"

"My computer!"

"Of course, sir. Sorry, sir."

"Imbeciles!"

From nought to surly in 1.8 seconds, he glared balefully at the spare blood bags his nurse had been clearing away – before he had shooed her away. Type O-positive, the most *common* blood group. He soured further, hating the fact that he, Heinrich Schultz, belonged to such a vulgar clade. He periodically donated his own blood for personal storage, as security against a time when he might need it. Unfortunately, those stocks had been destroyed with the *Eisernes Kreuz.* He could only hope that his transfusion had come from a suitable donor. His scowl deepened as he vowed to investigate the matter later, and if he did not like what he found, the officer in charge might well find themselves in the market for a transfusion, also.

The nurse's return interrupted his fuming. Snatching his tablet from her hand, he switched it on while metaphorically switching *her* off. He called up the reports and head-cam videos from his recent rescue. From what he could glean from the clips, cut together for posterity – they seemed of little value otherwise – there had been many minutes of running around and shouting, while a number of rather confused-looking dinosaurs angrily snapped at anything nearby until they were eventually driven away.

He sat back, shaking his head. "Shambolic," he muttered disgustedly, but he could see no evidence of hanging him out to dry, so he chalked it up to incompetence rather than treachery. Had he been home, heads would have rolled. As it was, he would have to settle for giving his officers and NCOs a stiff talking to.

That would have been that, had he not noticed an alert flashing at the bottom right of his screen. This was the first time the tablet had been activated since his return from an abbreviated trip to 1943. It seemed the program he had left running aboard ship in his absence was now demanding attention.

He opened the application. Anger coursed through his veins quicker than the cut-price plasma had, and the act of clenching his fists to slam them down on his lap caused several of his slash wounds to burst their sutures and butterfly plasters. "*Damn* them!"

The Old Academy's manager controlled his bafflement well. From the shadows, Heidi smirked as he introduced himself to a striking young woman who bore a distinct and disquieting resemblance to herself. It certainly had the man confused and second guessing himself. Especially as he had ordered no armed security to chauffeur her around. She could almost hear him thinking, '*Is that her?*'

As destiny would have it, *this* Dr Schultz had requested a private meeting to hand over the painting she was about to gift. Apparently, two public engagements in one day were more than she was willing to countenance. Heidi could certainly sympathise there.

The manager, one Wilhelm Weber, ushered her away while one of her entourage carried a large, flat box after them.

Heidi took a parallel route around the back of what she could not help but think of as *her* Spinosaurus remains – life-size colour photograph of a proud Ernst Stromer, side by side with a giant spine, notwithstanding. The colour imagery was yet more proof, had she needed it, of how much more advanced was the technology of this timeline compared with her own 1943. She shook her head; this was not the moment to ponder Douglas' meddling.

Her ancestor was making polite conversation with Weber, in German. They were clearly discussing some of the exhibits, so she had no problem in getting ahead of them.

She waited impatiently while they dawdled and droned on about art history and the important part charitable institutions played in its continuance. Listening to her 4th-great-grandmother was surreal and disturbing to Heidi on many levels. Aside from the natural creepiness of eavesdropping on family from another time, she was alarmed by the apparent political stance these Schultzes seemed to have adopted. Could it be a ruse to garner popularity? That had certainly been done before, but that was not the *Schultz* way – at least, she had always believed it the case. It made her uneasy. *It's time to bring these proceedings to a close.*

"*Herr* Weber," she said, stepping out and startling them. "You seem to have begun without me."

Weber's jaw dropped. All he could do was stare from one to the other while his scrambled mind hammered and banged to bend thought back into language. "*You?*" he managed at last.

"A rapier sharp observation, Weber," Heidi sneered.

As Heidi would have expected, her 4th-great-grandmother recovered from her surprise first. She looked Heidi up and down with approval before asking, "Dear Wilhelm, who is this astonishingly beautiful young woman?"

That was the final straw. Being 'checked out' by her 4th-great-grandmother made Heidi's skin crawl like a zombie rebirthday party.

Not sensing this, 1943's Dr Schultz stepped closer, running her finger along the single sleeve of Heidi's off-the-shoulder evening dress, surreptitiously sliding her arm around her waist. "What a beautiful fabric. *Darling,* you simply *must* let me have your dressmaker."

Heidi gulped, stepping away in horror.

The carrier of Dr Schultz's painting was obviously more than that. Reading Heidi's body language as offensive, he carefully leaned his valuable cargo against a wall and reached inside his evening jacket. Before he could pull out a weapon, Jansen materialised from the background to cock his own pistol right next to the man's ear. The bodyguard swallowed, allowing his gun to be confiscated.

Jansen seemed to have brought a silencer with him. Ordinarily, Heidi would have approved of this; she was always pleased when her pet showed initiative. However, still reeling from – she was not sure whether to think of them as 'ancestral' or 'incestral' – advances, she stepped awkwardly towards the door of the storage cupboard. "In here," she ordered, stiffly.

They filed in, Jansen once more bringing up the rear and securing the door.

"I have a story to tell you, Great-grandmother." Heidi relished the look of afront this comment generated. "I am sorry, Weber, but you will have to hear this too, along with...?"

"Ulixes," murmured the disgraced bodyguard.

Heidi raised an eyebrow. "Useless would seem more appropriate," she replied ruthlessly.

The man's brows knitted angrily. "It means 'full of wrath'."

"Ha!" Heidi handed her 'guests' a glass of the most expensive champagne their hotel carried. Pouring a separate one for herself, she raised a toast, "To family."

"Er, w-why are you sorry?" asked Weber.

Heidi smiled blandly.

"And, and why isn't he drinking?" he tried again, nodding towards Jansen.

"He's driving. Ben, turn up the lights."

Fully illuminated, their prisoners noted the shimmering wormhole and froze. "What is that?" asked Dr Schultz, tremulously.

Heidi explained.

After a protracted silence, Dr Schultz asked again, "And through... *that*... my descendants are waiting to show me the *future?*"

"Not exactly."

"But I never even wanted a family!"

Something did indeed seem a little *off* here. Heidi's eyes narrowed as she replayed the last few minutes through her mind. "For what exactly did you receive your doctorate?"

Dr Schultz blinked. "Why, sociology, of course, it's public knowledge, but I do have a degree in art history, too."

Heidi's eyes narrowed further. "You have siblings?"

"Yes, I have a brother in the military."

The way ahead began to clear for Heidi, and she glanced to Jansen. "Perhaps we were too quick to arrive at our conclusions, Ben? *Perhaps,* this is my great-great-great-great-grand-*aunt* Heidi?" Refocusing, she asked, "Your brother, does he have a family?"

"I do not know. I have not spoken to him since our father died. His beliefs are contemptible. Until he comes around to my way of thinking, I want nothing to do with him."

"Your father is dead?" asked Heidi, picking out what she considered to be the important point from the woman's prattle. By contrast, Jansen caught the first glimmer of a through-line, connecting all the dots on the Schultz family tree.

"Erm, yes."

Heidi's expression completely reset, and she downloaded a smile. "Excellent!"

This time it was 1943's Dr Schultz's turn to look horrified.

"Please," Heidi encouraged jovially, "drink up!"

Rotmütze moved without seeming to move. *I'm trapped in a horror film,* thought Baines. She knew she should be genuinely afraid, though she barely felt anything. The knowledge of the task before her was still there, but as if viewed through glass. All sense of righteousness, morality, duty, more like the memories of feelings, rather than the sharp sting of real emotion. *Come on, Jill, no time for philosophising.* As she thought it, another memory surfaced – Del Bond. How he had hidden his true identity and taken all their loathing and punishment on the chin, right up to the point where he sacrificed himself to save them all from the Schultzes and their madness.

Who'd have thought I'd be looking to Del Bond for a role model at a time like this? And what happened to his *spirit?* Had she any, her breath would have caught in her throat.

Rotmütze's approach was slowed. She had no way of knowing, yet she knew – this was down to the efforts of Mario and the others, efforts that were taking everything they had, efforts that, ultimately, were failing. *Time for me to pile in!* She ran at him.

Although she felt nothing in the literal sense, the pain was exquisite. In her current state, she could hardly ascribe it to being burned alive. Burned to death seemed a better fit. She cried out.

Rotmütze was still pushing, moving ever closer to Douglas – who was quietly celebrating his taking of the castle without a single life lost.

He chatted with The Sarge and De Soulis' guard captain, completely unaware of the struggle taking place in the very hall where he stood. Meanwhile, Baines planted herself between the twisted Nazi shade and the man she loved. The truth of that, far from setting her free, seemed to have sealed her fate, but she would not give an inch.

Rotmütze rammed forward – a psychic and physical shove. Baines felt Mario, Bud, Jamie, Paolo and Hussain disperse. Theirs was not exactly a second death; they were simply dew on a summer's morning. She had known this creature to be strong – its sense of power was unmistakable – but now she stood alone, the realisation of just how overmatched they truly were came home. He had the strength of the whole world's fear and superstition to draw upon. Beck had been right. Now Baines believed, believed it all, and it *was* too late. That was when she heard the voices. A small part of her mind, not completely dedicated to stopping this monstrosity from killing her friends, screamed at the universe in despair, *Great! I'm dead and now I'm hearing voices – what else have you got to throw?*

The voices were those of women. It sounded like two of them... and they were bickering.

"Let me in, yer sour-faced old boot!"

"How dare you!" Cocksedge shouted from the small hatch in the first-floor door. "You can stay there and freeze until you—"

Schmidt gently pulled her aside from the hatch so that she might speak through it. "We have a proposition for you."

"Ah'm aff tae murdurr ye! Ye hear? Ye glaikit witch, ye!"

"Tush, tush, tush," she replied with a calmness that drove the young Johnstone, outside in the snow, to murderous insanity. "You could be *rich,* if you play the game, yes?"

That piqued his interest. The shine of greed dousing the fiery anger in his suddenly beady eyes, he calmed and allowed her to continue.

"You have many clan members nearby, yes?"

"Aye. *Many!*" he replied threateningly.

"Good. Go and find your leaders and tell them we wish to make a deal. Here, you may show them this."

A small plastic bag with a resealable top dropped onto the snow at his feet. He picked it up with a nervous curiosity. "Whit's this?"

"Gold dust."

That certainly grabbed his attention. "Whit sort of a deal?"

"One where they kill the people we want dead and steal what we tell them to steal. In return, we will pay them in gold and other precious commodities beyond your imagination."

He grinned toothily, seeming to forget the body of his father, now half covered in snow at his feet. "Ah cannae go on a neet like this."

Schmidt gestured with a jerk of her head. "There is a barn over there, boy. Perhaps the cows will not mind your smell. You can fetch your clan leaders or elders, or whoever you people look to for leadership, in the morning. Now get from my sight!" With that, she shut the hatch, leaving young Johnstone turning the plastic bag over and over in his hands in wonderment.

In the warm, firelit bastle, the girl had made neither sound nor movement since their attack; she merely stared. Cocksedge picked up an overturned stool and sat by her side. Slipping effortlessly into her 'full politician' mask, she arranged every facial line and feature to say: 'We're listening to *you* and after taking on board *your* needs will determine an effective strategy, enabling us to move forward *together,* equitably obtaining all the things that we need to support *you*'. Later would come words like 'efficacy' to demonstrate, or at least sublimate, that ten percent success was by no means ninety percent failure, but she would get to that in due course.

Honest, animal instinct backed the girl further up the wall.

"Be careful she does not possess a knife," Schmidt remarked wryly.

Cocksedge surreptitiously removed the stool a little further from her new constituent, while her smile remained fixed. "Why don't you tell us your name, my dear?"

Tight-lipped, the girl continued to stare.

Cocksedge tried again. Tearing open a Velcro pocket on her waistcoat, she took out a chocolate bar. "Would you like some of this?" She opened the top and took a bite. "Mmm, caramel."

Perhaps unsurprisingly, caramel curried about as much favour as, well, *curry,* to a sixteenth century British girl. So, talk having failed, Cocksedge torqued up her smile instead, stretching forward to offer the bribe.

At first, it seemed the girl would not be cajoled, but then her arm lanced out suddenly from beneath the blanket, snatching the confection out of Cocksedge's hand. Rather than eat it, she instantly squirrelled it away inside a fold of her dress.

Cocksedge's mouth opened in astonishment. "That might melt... there... erm, never mind."

Schmidt called across the small living space, distracting her, "Look at this." She held open a lightweight, emergency rescue blanket, made from a silver foil material that was clearly not of this age.

"That's mine!" the girl spoke, surprising them both.

"This was your father's *bed?*" Schmidt used the word for lack of a better one.

The girl nodded.

"He stole it from you?"

Another nod.

"You took this from the visitors you met, earlier today?"

She shook her head.

"No?"

"Was given it."

Cocksedge soured. "Isn't that just like them?"

"I thought," Schmidt spoke wryly, "your political party were all about taking from the rich and giving to the poor?"

Cocksedge looked at Schultz's aide as if she were an idiot. "You cannot *serve* 'the people' as one of 'the people' unless you first rise *above* 'the people'," Cocksedge over-punctuated – wearying the ears of the inverted comma bunnies almost as much as Schmidt's own. "It was my *duty* to—"

"Lady Natalie gave it tae me." The girl interrupted her speech.

Schmidt approached menacingly, showing the underside of politics. "Tell me what is your name, this instant, girl, or I will extract the information I want through pain."

"Aila, m'lady," she answered, shrinking back still further.

"That's a pretty name, my dear," oozed Cocksedge.

Schmidt rolled her eyes, but nevertheless returned to the girl her blanket, who wrapped it about herself immediately as if it offered protection from more than just the cold.

"Allison, we must plan our next move."

"And what exactly *is* our next move, Erika? We've taken a fort, or a house, or a stone shed, or whatever this muck heap is. I wanted to make a clean getaway and start again, far from here. It only makes sense that we—"

"No!"

Cocksedge gaped, outraged by the interruption but far too afraid of her colleague to gainsay it.

"We must not stray too far from the *New World*," Schmidt explained. "There is much inside that could make us very, very comfortable in this time, and rich."

"And Douglas' rabble?"

Schmidt smiled mirthlessly. "We must gather forces to us, so that for him, coming after us is simply too much trouble."

"With the weapons *they* have? Erika, you can't be serious. Douglas, or that loopy Australian, could swat us – and our brick shed – like a housefly!"

"Indeed, but will they spill a river of blood to do so, Allison?"

"What do you mean?"

"Douglas, and his gaggle of do-gooders, will try to protect the timeline at all costs, and especially these people's lives. You yourself could theoretically disappear if one of your ancestors were to be killed here – at least if they died before breeding."

Cocksedge's mouth pursed. "Do you have to put it like that? I'll have you know, I come from a very prestigious line of—"

"You understand my point," Schmidt overrode her objection, witheringly. "If we band people to us, using *money*, we can strike at them, but they cannot – or more accurately, *will* not – strike back, yes?"

Cocksedge absorbed the point. "Very well. What about this one? Her ears have been flapping all the while we've been discussing this." She pointed at the girl, who drew in a sharp breath, anxious once more.

Schmidt gave a casual wave of her hand. "We keep her. Following on from your astute observation earlier – someone will have to clean up this dung heap."

"Sarah! We have to do this – and *you promised* to help."

"Alright, alright, Beck. There's no need to get all accusin'! And I only said I would try, as long as you promised not to go searchin' the land to lasso a couple o' clerics! Heaven only knows what could happen to a girl alone out there – especially one foreign to these lands. Mr Beckett made it quite clear that we—"

"Sarah!"

"Alright, I'm a-comin', I'm a-comin'. Now, I think we start here, and you have to read these bits here. OK?"

"Got it."

"Right. You know, perhaps we should wait until we actually kno— Alright, *alright*. I'm just sayin' we're meant to have the seal of a bishop before attempting this, and secure a full mental health check of the victim – I'm feelin' like I need one of those myself for agreein' to help you! We're also meant to be *with* the vic!"

An exasperated sigh. "*Sarah!* You know they wouldn't let us in. Could we please continue?"

"Are you sure this is the right one, Beck, huh? The rites have been updated a whole bunch o' times over the last five or six centuries, you know?"

"Yes, I'm sure. He's drawing power from this time, so we must fight him *with* power from this time. Now come on, *please*. You've already blessed us and asked Saint Michael to defend us, so can we please get on with it?"

Another sigh, this one of disbelief mingled with resignation. "OK. Here goes. *Crux sacra sit mihi lux.*"

"May the holy cross be my light."

"*Non draco sit mihi dux.*"

"May the dragon *never* be my guide."

"Dragons? Seriously?"

"Sarah! We just spent the last three months living with them! Would you just read the damned text!"

"*Child!*"

"Sorry, sorry. I apologise. We just *really* need to help our friends. They're in extreme danger. Sarah, *please...*"

It was like a buzzing migraine wrapped up in a nightmare within Baines' skull. She could hear the voices, but in the manner of a badly tuned radio. It was really irritating. However, the effect on Rotmütze, even over such a distance, seemed profound. Clearly her proximity –

or her spirit's proximity – to him acted like a conduit for the power. A narrow conduit, perhaps, but she would take anything she could use.

Rotmütze cried out in anguish, looking into Baines' eyes with the light of murder in his own. "How dare you try to..." He gritted his teeth, all his strength suddenly split between pushing her back and fighting disintegration.

The prayers lapsed once more into squabbling. His eyes flashed and with a huge push he overwhelmed Baines.

The monster was now mere feet away from Douglas' defenceless back. She screamed. This *thing* threatening James' life, lacking even the honour to face him, filled her with rage, but she was powerless to act, even to warn.

Rotmütze grinned savagely and reached out a hand towards Douglas – through him – as if clutching for his heart. Douglas stiffened. Giving a strangled cry, he fell to his knees. Before The Sarge or the other man could even react, the demon snapped their necks at sickly, unlifelike angles, causing them to collapse onto the oak floorboards with him.

Baines could not tell if her scream was within or without. James gone. The Sarge – another pillar of her world – gone. Rotmütze's laughter seemed to ring from every surface, from every direction and all she could do was stand, paralysed, and look on. Although denied the full emotional range of her living self, she felt her spirit quite literally break at that moment. Even when trapped, potentially forever, in the Cretaceous Period and facing a massively superior, ruthless enemy, never had she imagined such despair.

"*James!*" Darkness claimed her, she had no idea for how long, but when she eventually opened her eyes, it was to see Douglas standing once more, several metres away, talking quietly with Sergeant Jackson and De Soulis' guard captain.

Baffled, she turned to find herself practically nose to nose with Rotmütze, his laughter grown maniacal. Baines, still within his clutches, checked over her shoulder, terrified as to what she might see. However, Douglas was still there, alive, and for the moment, in one piece. When she faced Rotmütze again, it was with a fury to match her earlier despair. "*You* son of a bitch! None of that was real!"

Rotmütze could barely speak past his guffawing. "Ah, Jill. I know it's rude to play with one's food, but the look on your face when Douglas died made my aeon!" He calmed gradually, still chuckling.

"Still, all good things must come to an end, and now it's time to finish this. Perhaps I will kill them in a different way this time, eh? Wouldn't want to bore you with a repeat performance, would we? I shall kill your friends and... *no*... I sense Douglas is much more than that to you. This is good, excellent, in fact. I shall kill him last and most painfully. Then it will be time, I'm afraid, for you to *actually* die!"

The light of evil in his eyes made her shudder, cutting even through her rage. On the periphery of all senses and sensibilities, she heard the women's voices in her mind's ear cease their bickering. Working together now, they sent words she did not understand out into the ether.

Rotmütze looked as though he might explode, the fire in his eyes turning instantly from hideous glee to terror for his own sake. He leapt for Douglas, and Baines leapt after him, pouring all her fury into the lunge. She felt an immediate and shocking connection. She lacked the time to understand this transition from energy-saving to supercharged. All she knew was that she felt *strong,* and she knew just what to do with that strength. Something was leeching Rotmütze's power by similar degrees. Whether this was the same 'something' as previously, or another force entirely, she neither knew nor cared; she simply attacked...

"Jill? Jill, can you hear me? It's Patricia, Patricia Norris. You're safe now. Oh, Jill, I'm so glad you're awake. Hang on, don't you go anywhere. I'll call someone. *Dave!*"

Baines heard a weak voice nearby call out for Dr Flannigan. "Wha'?" she managed.

"Hey, Jill!" greeted a man's voice a moment later. "So glad you're back with us! You're a hell of a fighter!"

"*Dave...?*"

"Yeah, it's me, Captain. It's so good to—"

"Noooo! Not yet! Not *yet!* Send me back!"

"Dr Hemmings, you will perhaps explain to me why you actively tried to shut the wormhole down?" Heinrich sat up straight in his bed, glaring at the whitecoat before him.

"You asked us to find a way, Heinrich."

"Do not take me for a fool, Anne! You were trying to shut that wormhole down from the moment we stepped through it. Was this some sort of mutiny aboard my last ship? Or was it merely a personal excursion of your own? Family or no, your life depends upon answering my question, so think carefully – *why* did you attempt to maroon me in 1943?"

The scientist Heidi had dubbed 'Two' stared impassively at the old man.

He nodded, only slightly, showing approval for her bearing.

Two knew it would cause a complete faeces storm if she told the old man of the crew's agreement to get rid of the Schultzes forever, but worse than that, if she did, any further attempt would be hamstrung before it began. She spoke slowly at first, gradually speeding up as if simply wishing to be done with the ordeal. "Heinrich, you ordered the execution of my daughter – my *daughter!* You sent your creatures to track her down and the only reason she escaped was because the *Last Word* had already departed for the Cretaceous."

"I did not kill Lieutenant Elizabeth Hemmings. She was killed when Captain Douglas escaped, or so I have heard – perhaps he is your man—"

"Do not take me for a fool, either, Heinrich! We agreed that her husband was to be removed. Her decision to marry him was... an *aberration*. But you sent assassins after my Elizabeth, too!"

Heinrich's colour rose, a rare occurrence. "She betrayed me!" he spat. "She gave up our plans to the American secret services."

"They never acted on any such information—"

"Do not mistake the incompetence of government agencies for loyalty, Anne! She betrayed me—"

"And you betrayed me! And our family! This whole venture would not even have been possible without me! I made it work! *Me!* Not that white-coated wantwit you placed in charge of our research department."

"It would not have done to show favour. Besides, despite his natural tendency to hand-wring and cower, Dr Reid has actually done some sterling work under me. He—"

"Takes *my* ideas and presents them as his own! OK, I'll admit, he's not a complete fool, but you owe me, Heinrich. And you repaid me by ordering a hit on my daughter – and don't bother trying to pin this on Douglas. I've read his file, he would rather cut his arm off than hurt a young girl like that, especially if she was trying to help him, and after what we did to her, I don't doubt that was exactly what she was doing!"

"Exactly! Treachery!"

"Oh, *please!*" Hemmings shook her head with derision. "*You* are going to preach a sermon on *treachery?*"

"Very well," Heinrich spoke icily. "So where do we go from here?"

She looked thoughtful for a few moments. "What do you suggest – kiss and make up?"

"Hardly, but you can begin by telling me, was this your idea or was there conspiracy?"

Hemmings stuck out her chin belligerently.

Heinrich raised his voice once more. "*Was there conspiracy?*"

"There was... none."

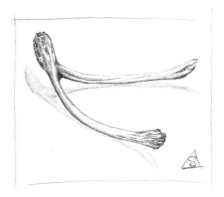

Chapter 5 | If Wishes Were Tyrannosaurs

Geoff Lloyd leaned against the wall to get his breath back. He could walk across the ward now, aided only by sticks. It was not much, but it was progress. He opened the hatch and hobbled over to the couches that served as an informal waiting room for the infirmary within the main hangar.

He had no sooner taken a seat to watch the world go by when he heard the voice – *her* voice. "You are not allowed out of the infirmary, you silly man. Get back in here!"

Lloyd rolled his eyes. "Matron, I haven't seen anything but that damned infirmary for as long as I can remember. Leave me alone!"

"*Nein,* you must come back inside now. Those are the rules."

"So sue me!"

"I will inform Dr Flannigan of your insubordination and he will stop your treatments!"

"Ha! We're not on Nazi world now, *gnädige Frau!* I'm here on the personal order of the Almighty Douglas – captain, pilot, leader, do-gooder to the stars! He won't let me die, it's a point of honour for him, so good luck with that!"

"We shall see!" Matron turned on her heel and stormed away. Lloyd watched her with a self-satisfied grin on his face as he imagined the ear-bending about to descend upon Flannigan. There would be a price to pay, but to hell with it.

Reseating himself more comfortably, he let out a sigh of relief. A hot beverage appeared before his eyes. He looked up in surprise to find young Tim Norris holding out a steaming mug of coffee. Lloyd took it.

Tim sat. "I don't know if that's any good – I don't do coffee."

"Well, thank you anyway," Lloyd raised the mug in mock salute and took a drink.

"Does it taste like crap?"

Lloyd winced slightly. "No, not at all. It's actually worse than that." He grunted, leaning forward to place the mug on the coffee table.

Tim grinned and Lloyd, despite himself, grinned back. "So what can I do for you, young man?"

Ever thoughtful, Tim took his time before answering. "If you could change everything that's happened, would you go back? To where we started in Patagonia, I mean?"

Lloyd tilted his head slightly, scrutinising the teenager. "I take it you would?"

Tim nodded. "I think so. Would you?"

"I've no urge to return to the dark side – if that's what you're reaching for? Don't tell me you wish you were still with that mad German bitch?"

It was Tim's turn to wince. He hated Heidi, of course, but it was more complicated than that. She was, at the end of the day, family. Moreover, he genuinely believed that he had begun to get through to her. It seemed unlikely he could have turned her completely; she was a creature of their grandfather's making in a way that he could never be, but now he would never know.

"You *do*," Lloyd spoke slowly, stroking his stubble. "Fancied her, did you? Ha! She certainly had the looks – I can't deny that, lad. Filled your boots, did you?"

Tim shook his head, horrified. "It's not that! She's my..."

"She's your what?" Lloyd interrupted, snagging something interesting – better yet, *secret* and interesting.

"She's, or at least she *was,* my... my..." he reached for inspiration, "my *jailer.* Anyway, this has nothing to do with her." *At least, I don't think it has,* he added in the privacy of his own head. "It's more that I felt *alive* there – worthwhile, even, you know?"

"There was a certain purity to the place, I'll admit, but surely you're better off here, eh? Among humans?"

"Yeah, *right!* So, assuming we're stuck here, what do you intend to do?"

The teen's youthful confusion almost touched Lloyd's heart. Almost. "I dunno, lad. I've been thinking about just that a lot lately – as I stared at the hospital ceiling, you'll understand. I dare say I could make a life for myself here, at a push."

Tim nodded, absently. "Well, you'll know a heck of a lot more than anyone else alive out there, so that's a good start, surely?"

Lloyd stared at him. *Out of the mouths of babes,* he thought, once more picking up his mug. "Cheers." He took a second swig of coffee before remembering how filthy it tasted. He coughed disgustedly, catching the flap of a white doctor's coat from the corner of his eye. "Oh," he chuckled, "here comes trouble."

Dr Flannigan strode to stand in front of Lloyd, red-faced with his fists on his hips.

Lloyd looked up at him, a smile twitching his lips. "Dave – you look all riled up. Don't tell me someone's ruined your evening, eh?"

Tim surreptitiously slipped away, muttering something about fetching his mum.

"I hate it here!" Tim slumped in his chair, sullen. "I'm sorry, Mum. It's just that I – and I understand that I might be alone in this view – *miss* the Cretaceous. Since we lost Dad, it's the only place I've really felt that I belonged."

Patricia smiled with understanding, and a little sadness, from her wheelchair at the end of the teens' favourite table in the Mud Hole. She reached out a hand to take her son's. "Come on, Tim. That's not like you. We always make the best of it, don't we?"

He still had not told Patricia about his familial relationship to the monsters who had orchestrated the entire mess they were living through. He was equal parts afraid that the shock might kill her and that it was only a matter of time before some idiot spilled the beans unthinkingly – and by idiot, he meant Woodsey.

However, on the plus side, his mum was alive and for the first time, out of hospital. His black mood faded, a smile creeping across his face to break the spell. "I'm really glad you're better."

"Not quite better, but I'll agree to *mending*." She covered a yawn with her hand.

"I'll get you back to the ward when we've finished these drinks, Mum. It is getting late."

"Even if it's only a visit, it sure is great to see you outta the infirmary, Mrs Norris—"

"*Doctor* Norris," Rose hissed, interrupting her boyfriend.

"Oh, yeah. Sorry. *Doctor* Norris. We've all been real worried about you."

"Yeah, me dad sends his best, too."

"Thank you, Henry. Thank you, Woodsey. And, Henry, don't mention it. I was proud to be Mrs Norris then, and still am – he was my love and my best friend."

Tim squirmed, embarrassed. "*Mum.*"

She smiled again at him, squeezing his hand even tighter.

"I see you're regaining your strength – could you not break my fingers, please?" He took back his hand, shaking it theatrically.

"So what's wrong with this place?" Patricia asked, looking around all of Tim's friends for opinions. "I haven't seen any of it yet, but I hear it's very beautiful."

"I like it," said Woodsey. "Tim's just wimping out because he lost a snowball fight!"

"*I* lost it? You were crying!"

"Now steady on, mate!"

"Boys, *boys!*" Patricia chuckled. "What do you think of it, ladies?"

"I love it! Especially the snow," said Clarrie, brightly. "But I miss the Cretaceous too." She sneaked a sly, sideways glance at Tim – of which he was completely oblivious. "I found happiness there, for the first time in my life."

"You're right, Dr Norris. It really is pretty here," Rose added, "and the air is nothing like back home. We got so used to going everywhere in masks we'd forgotten what it was like to just breathe deeply – and not cough yourself hoarse or risk a trip to the hospital! The Cretaceous was nice too, but a little too hot for me. Not to mention dangerous!"

Clarrie sighed as she strolled down memory lane. "It's a pity we never got chance to go sunbathing there, before we left."

Henry looked Rose up and down. "Hmm."

Rose spotted this. "Are you OK?"

"Hmm," he replied dreamily. "I was just thinking about bikini—about *back in* the good old Cretaceous... you know?"

"I think you guys are missing the Brontosaurus in the room, here," Woodsey butted in. "This place may not have Wi-Fi, or Amazon, OK – nothing's perfect – but everything, *everything* there tried to kill us."

"Not everything," Tim objected. "What about Mayor?"

"Yeah, right! We met one small hypsiloph... one small hypsil... topho...polo. *Damnit!* One little guy! We met one little guy that didn't want to kill us, OK! I wouldn't call that a great place to visit, dude."

"And I think you'll find the Amazon *is* here, by the way," Tim was unable to prevent himself from correcting. "Both the river and an infinitely bigger rainforest. But that's beside the point. If we *lived* in the Cretaceous, rather than just visited the place for little while, we'd get used to it," he tried again, earnestly.

"Get *used* to it? You're confusing ten-ton monsters with car thieves and drug addicts, mate. And people only *say that* because they've got nowhere better they can move to! Even if we did *acclimatise* to living in a fortress, cowering behind locked gates, what kind of life would that be?"

Tim struggled to find an answer, so he settled on, "You're just so negative these days."

Woodsey spluttered while everyone else burst into laughter.

"Good morning, gentlemen, and lady," Major White greeted. "While everyone else is getting themselves acclimatised, our job is to figure out a way to get us the hell outta here!" His shoulder still in a sling from an unlucky collision with a stationary lorry, during their re-entry to real space, he nevertheless gestured with his good arm for the others to take their seats. "I've had Mary lay on a few refreshments, as I doubt any of you have had time to grab any breakfast yet."

The bleary-eyed nods and groggy good mornings confirmed his suspicions. He grinned his lopsided grin. "I can just feel the positivity charging the air in here already – I can't wait to soak it all in!"

A few chuckles and generous amounts of caffeine eventually got the scientists and engineers talking. Jim Miller, Satnam Patel and Samantha

Portree spoke for the science staff, whereas Hiro Nassaki, Sandip Singh and Georgio Baccini represented the *New World* and her crew. With all their available captains so abruptly *un*available, White chaired the meeting.

"OK," he called them to order. "The *New World* is totalled, so we can't fly outta here to open a wormhole either forward to 2112 or any place else. Other options – go!"

After much clearing of throats and adjusting of seats, Hiro finally spoke out, "I've been thinking about taking our jerry-rigged wormhole drive out of the ship and just, well, *opening* a wormhole."

"As have I," added Patel. "It is an insane idea, almost guaranteed to get us killed."

That certainly killed the conversation stone dead.

Eventually White said, "That's a little 'glass is half empty' isn't it, Satnam? Is there *no* merit in this?"

"Certainly," replied Patel, in his clipped English. "It might even work, but I doubt any of us would survive a trip through a wormhole unprotected."

"My brother did wonder whether such a thing might be possible," chipped in Georgio.

With all eyes suddenly upon the young Italian, Patel asked, "And what did Mario think the likely outcome would be?"

"I never asked."

Uproar.

"Well, *you* all think it's a stupid idea, too!" Georgio barked back. "Who saw all *this* coming?"

Into the sudden silence, broken only by further clearing of throats, Singh asked, "Could we fly a ship through it then? Just a small one. We've freed up access to the shuttle now."

"Hang on, Buck Rogers[11]," Hiro interrupted. "This isn't even on the drawing board yet."

"Hiro is correct," agreed Patel. "And even if our wormhole drive *was* ready, it has never been used like this before. We may only get one chance to jump. So, even assuming everything worked, how many people could we take with us in the shuttle? Thirty? As sardines?"

"OK," said White. "What about spacesuits? Could we manufacture enough for everyone?"

---

11 Although Singh was the classic sci-fi nut, by AD2112, there remained very little that had not been remade at least thirteen times over.

"Of course," Jim Miller replied brightly.

"That's great—"

"If we had a couple of years development time and access to materials from all over the world!"

White glared at Miller, a little deflated. "Oh."

"We don't actually *know* that wormhole travel is unsurvivable without a ship," countered Hiro.

"Are you offering to trial it, then?" asked Singh, caustically. "And is 'unsurvivable' even a word, for that matter?"

"Look, I'm just saying that, theoretically—"

"*Theoretically?*"

"Gentlemen, gentlemen," White interrupted. "Is there any way it can be *proven?*"

"None," stated Patel, flatly.

White looked at him askance. "You're really not wearing the team colours this morning, Satnam."

"I'm sorry, but there it is. Even if we sent a mouse through—"

"A *mouse?*" exclaimed Singh.

"We could send it with a radio," offered Portree.

"And what?" Hiro rounded on her. "Ask him if he just *squeaked* through? Maybe we could bribe him with a little cheese, perhaps? Tie it to the end of his tail to make sure he went all the way!"

"I'm just *saying*—"

Once again, White butted into the raised voices as gently as he could. "Please, everyone. Let's forget the mouse, OK?"

"I take it back," said Miller.

"Jim?"

"We *would* have enough material to build an experimental spacesuit for a test-mouse."

Raucous laughter.

"Alright, *alright,*" White broke in again. "So what about a volunteer?"

Silence...

Forsooth, what I would not give for a way to leave a message behind for Sir Nicholas. For I feel sure he doth follow me and must believe it.

May the Lord hold further snow, ere it covers our tracks. Bess rode a chestnut pony, her hands tied to a copper-alloy pommel. After several attempts to pull free, the iron rivets held it, and her, fast to the saddle. The pony's bridle was roped to her hated, rat-faced jailer. A vile creature who became ever uglier with the growing daylight.

She had little or no idea where she was. Dawn had passed and they were well into the first hour[12], so at least she could gauge her direction by the sun. The morning was bright, blue and crisp, over a landscape still blanketed with overnight snow. It gave an impression of purity that belied her situation. Their journey through the dark and the storm, the previous evening, would have been arduous, unpleasant and dangerous, even in good company, but De Soulis and his closest minions made the ride literally diabolical for Bess.

However, with a sun in the sky and visible, she now had a bearing; they were travelling north. It was almost impossible to know for sure how many miles they had covered since leaving Hermitage Castle. She guessed not more than ten, so slow had been their progress. De Soulis had taken drovers' trails up and over the hills, traversing the very worst of the weather to reduce any chance of being followed.

Bess knew from the scarce maps of the area, so well-thumbed during her time at Bishop Tunstall's castle in Durham, that there was very little between Hermitage and Hawick. Furthermore, she could not imagine why De Soulis would wish to take her there.

She closed her eyes, rummaging through the maps one more time in her mind. There was a tower – more specifically, one of the fortified tower-houses, favoured by the Scots – just south and west of Hawick, she felt sure of it. Could he be taking her there? The fluid politics and interfaction fighting within the region was dizzying, leaving her no way of knowing.

---

12   In early November 1558 within the borderlands between England and Scotland, 'well into the first hour' would have been around 9am. Most of northern Europe, at the time, counted days from sunrise to sunrise. Naturally, the seasons must have made this rather complicated, but luckily, they did not have to rely solely on old Sol; they also used the stars. Astrology could be used to gauge the time – as well as affecting usefulness for horoscopes. However, if, heavens forbid, even astrology proved inaccurate, there was always the canonical clock. Church offices divided up the twenty-four-hour day into eight services: matins, lauds, prime, terce, sext, none, vespers and compline. Sext was always the sixth hour of the day, counted from dawn, and vespers was always at sunset, which naturally also varied with the seasons. However, by 1558 in Britain, these 'offices' diverged. The Protestant church now observed their own variation, and the *post* reformation Catholic church also changed its practices. In the absence of a digital watch, Bess decided to stick with the sun.

A sinking feeling threatened to overwhelm her once again, but if that were indeed her situation, then she would know it. "Where art thou taking me?"

Despite the imperious tone of her demand, De Soulis turned casually in the saddle and merely flashed a grin, his animalistic canine teeth showing over his lip. Her rat-faced jailer chuckled nastily. "Ye'll find out soon enough, lass."

"Have a care, stinking cur! How darest thou address one in the familiar!" she snapped, furiously.

He made a show of touching his cap. "Forgive me, yer *majesty!*" He continued to snigger, as if he had just discovered something endlessly entertaining.

Bess knew that it could be only a matter of time before the region was awash with tales of Sir William de Soulis and his ousting from Hermitage Castle by a band of outlanders. He was such a brute that she was consequently forced to surmise that these lands must also be filled by people with a score to settle, too. Would that increase her chances, or would mere proximity to De Soulis bring death or worse down upon them? He did not appear overly concerned. In fact, she rather feared he had a plan up his ravelled sleeve – doubtless of the nefarious sort.

Either way, it seemed she was about to find out. Their way ahead was blocked by a horseman, but before she could discern any detail, the horseman became *horsemen* – thirty of them.

"Going back to the mouse," Georgio hazarded, among a most inappropriate gale of catcalls that forced him to raise his voice. "Do we even know if a radio signal, or indeed anything, can travel both ways through a wormhole? It was theorised, but...?"

Patel frowned. "Are you suggesting two-way travel?"

"Why?" Singh asked, fatuously. "In case we end up in the wrong place and want to go back to try again?"

Georgio bridled. "I'm guessing that-a were it the case, *you* would be the first to want to do exactly that!"

Singh bridled. "It's a wormhole, not a skirting board! Whether your *mousestronaut* can—"

"What's your point, Georgie?" asked White, cutting them off before their spat developed into yet another row.

"It occurred to me, if it's OK with *you*, Sandip," Georgio elaborated, "that we might try sending a camera through to see, not only what is there before we step through, but also, whether a signal *can* return."

White clapped his hands together. "That's a brilliant idea!"

"Yes, I stole it from an old TV show."

"And did it work?"

"Major," interrupted Patel. "Whether those actors travelled one way or both ways through a wormhole hardly matters. They could have used wormholes for waste management for all the help that gives us."

"Right," agreed White quietly. "What was that show, again?"

"Major!"

"Yes, of course. Well, I say we give it a go, people. What resources and how long will you need to make this happen? James will want to know as soon as he gets back. And I understand that Jill is awake and recovering, thank God. So she'll be after me for a report, too, as soon as her head's off the pillow."

Patel and Hiro eyed one another. "Several months," said Hiro.

"Several?" asked White.

"At least two, I think," replied Patel.

"Great!" White rubbed his hands together excitedly. "So, we're here for Christmas!"

Douglas awoke with the worst and most ill-deserved hangover he had ever had. "Ah've nae touched a drop."

Meritus spoke into his bleary thoughts, "*James?* You've been out for the count for hours – we couldn't rouse you."

Douglas croaked, cleared his throat, and tried again. "What happened?"

"We don't know. You were talking with the captain of the castle guard, and you just collapsed. I mean, we knew you were under a great deal of pressure – you'd had a hell of a day, what with Jill and all – so we hoped it was just fatigue. We called Dr Flannigan and he told us to make you comfortable – said he'd return as soon as he was sure Captain Baines was out of danger."

Douglas groaned as he massaged some life back into his stiff neck. He took a brief look at the rough wooden bench on which he had passed the night, noting his jacket on the floor. "Comfortable? Remind me never to accept an invite round to *your* house, Tobias."

Meritus laughed. "Sorry about the jacket. We made sure it stayed over you for most of the night, I promise. Besides, we had a good fire going in here. So what happened? Was it the sudden heat after being in such freezing conditions?"

Douglas kneaded his brow. "Ah don't know. Ah didnae faint, if that's what you're suggesting." He frowned in thought as a memory surfaced. "Ah heard Jill. It was like she screamed."

"Well, like I said, you'd been under a lot of pressure—"

"No, no. It wasnae like that. It was more like a... a crisis apparition! Ah heard her earlier too. She told me De Soulis had left with the lassie Elizabeth. Once the men here surrendered..." He floundered, unable to recall more. "Is there any news on Jill?"

Meritus beamed. "She's awake."

Douglas' colour returned, almost at once. "That's the best news Ah've had since we landed here."

"Crashed."

"Thanks for reminding me."

"It was no picnic for me either, James. I thought I'd died in that crash."

Douglas brightened, stood, wobbled and held on to Meritus. "Well, yer no' dead, Tobias, and it seems naebody else is either – thank God!"

Meritus steadied him. "So what now?"

"Now, we go and save the next Queen of England. Never thought Ah'd say that! How's the weather doing?"

"Sunny, snowy, beautiful. Reminds me of the foothills to the Rockies, back home."

"Aye. Ah'd forgotten ye came from Canada. Your accent, or lack of, doesnae give anything away. Ah was disappointed when your country was asked to leave the Mars Programme – if *asked* is the right word. Ah know Canada made the decision to leave, but as Ah understood it, not without a push.

"Anyhow, if we get ye back one day, maybe things will be different." He brightened. "Aye. If ye took a ship over there now, ye could practically have the place to yourself, man!"

Meritus chuckled. "Yes, it's a strange thought. But what would I do without this 'carnival' of ours to worry about?"

"And it's good to have ye on board! Now, let's see if we can find some eggs or something, before we go. Ah feel – as a good friend of mine puts it – like the plug's been pulled out of ma bath!"

Meritus smiled, glad to see Douglas returning fully to himself. "I'm sure we'll find you something. Gleeson has ordered some dirt bikes to be flown over – I suppose the time for clandestine operations has passed, eh? Apparently, this De Soulis guy has enemies—"

"*No?*"

"S'all true, mate!" Gleeson interrupted, surprising them and stamping snow from his boots. He approached, bearing a rough wooden bowl upon which several somethings sizzled. "Glad to see you vertical! The way we get through captains here, I'm glad I took the 'sort of' promotion, just to get the bullseye off me back. What Merito was saying is true though, Captain. The bloke does have enemies. And now his blood's in the water, practically everybody's after him."

"How do we know this?" asked Douglas.

"That Captain Donald's not such a bad bloke when you get talking to him. And one of his guys has fried a few snags up for us all – so watch you don't miss out, mate. Would you believe it, turns out Donald's a bit of a larrikin, too – although ya can only understand about half of what the bagger says and that's a bladdy oath." Douglas and Meritus shared a look. "Still, I'm glad I didn't have to blow him to hell and back. He told me the peasants were out before dawn looking for De Soulis."

"Peasants?"

"Yeah."

"Are we allowed to call them that? It doesnae feel very respectful."

"Yeah, no worries, mate. It's 1558, ya see? Politically correct here, means your team winning – and by winning, I mean killing all the other baggers and bringing home their gold. Anyway, they tell me it's less offensive than serf – they really don't like being called that in these parts. Now, me? I thought surf was all about waxing up your board and catching a few heavies before a barbie and a brewski, but, hey."

Douglas frowned. "An interesting take on Renaissance politics, Commander."

"Nah, mate. It's just the same as ours. Only difference is, these blokes are helping themselves without bothering to pretend they're not. It does make it easier to foller."

"Perhaps you're referring to our Ms Cocksedge?"

"Yeah. Her and all the other baggers."

"Hmm. Ah vaguely remember Mr Beckett telling us that Elizabeth will free the last serfs in England just a few years from now." He frowned some more. "Pity it took another two and a half centuries to cross the border! So, what have the – shall we settle on 'locals' – managed to find out?"

"The snow was heavy overnight, Captain. Even so, one of the valley's shepherds came across tracks in the snow that were preserved – in the lee of some trees after the wind changed direction, or some bladdy thing. These old-time guys are real good at all that stuff. Anyway, they were heading north."

"And we know that was De Soulis, how?"

"We don't, mate. Just that the bloke reckoned there were about half a dozen riders on good horses. S'all we've got."

"Then it'll have to do." Douglas grabbed one of the sausages from Gleeson's wooden trencher with a wink and stuffed half of it into his mouth. "Let's go," he spoke around it.

"Help ya bladdy self, mate, why don't ya! Anyway, I can't go yet, me bikes haven't arrived."

Douglas thought for a moment. "Wait for your bikes, then leave six men here to hold the castle. If they patch the door Ah blew off, they should have no trouble – not with our weapons. Ah'll take the APC with Captain Meritus, The Sarge and Ah'll need Corporal O'Brien, too – she's got a knack with that thing. Ye'll soon catch us up. Ah'm no' leaving the lassie in the hands of that madman any longer than necessary. Everybody got it? Good." He turned to leave. "Oh, and just one more thing. How are those wee bairns we pulled out of the hole?"

A cloud passed across Gleeson's face; a look shared with Meritus. "They're alive and we've cleaned 'em up a little and fed 'em, but as for long term..."

"Aye. Ah'm guessing, and hoping, the people here will be tough. At least they're safe now. Do we know from where they were taken?"

"Donald thinks he knows the village. With your permission, he's willing to take them home. He told me De Soulis used his 'favourites' for missions like that. Real sweethearts to a man. We have two of 'em waiting in the prison tower."

Douglas' frown of concern darkened. "They're the ones who did all... all *that?*"

"They say not. Donald says otherwise. De Soulis has others with him, but these two were part of it – no mistake, mate. So what are your orders, Captain?"

Douglas' eyes hardened. "Down the hole with them. It'll do until we can find some local authority to hand them over to. Perhaps Maxwell would be willing to take charge?"

"I'm sure he would, if you just want them left to rot!"

Douglas shrugged. "Well, when you live by the thumbscrew, you die by the rack! Let's move."

Heidi collected the champagne glasses from Weber and the bodyguard. "Drink up, *Aunt*."

Heidi's ancestor took a nervous sip.

"You can do better than that. Tip it back. Very good." Heidi took the remaining glass and forced the men through the wormhole. "And now you, *Doctor*."

The woman had clearly led a pampered life and looked terrified, but she was not stupid. Jansen suspected she was yet to swallow the champagne, so he shoved her through the wormhole. It was tough love, but the way he saw it, she would stand no chance at all if she disobeyed her 4th-great-grandniece.

"Excellent!" Heidi raised an eyebrow. "What an absurdly simple way to dispose of garbage. Now we will leave via the back entrance to summon our own driver, who will take us to the *Löwenbräukeller*." She turned to Jansen with a cruel smile. "We may yet see all of our wishes come true, Ben. Good work."

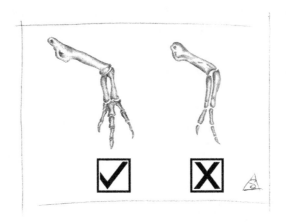

Chapter 6 | The Next Big Thing

Heinrich Schultz appeared outside Hemmings' cell, leaning on a walking stick. "How are you finding the food, Anne? Whilst I was enjoying these facilities, I was quite partial to menu item 3b."

"If you're just here to gloat, Heinrich, please save it for the help. They're far more in awe of you than I."

"On the contrary, my dear. You have proved yourself far too dangerous to be allowed to run free, but I nevertheless thought you might enjoy an update on the mission and my granddaughter's progress."

"*You* are keeping *me* informed?"

He smiled coolly. "It's the personal touch. We have a visitor, it seems. All the way from 1943 – three of them, in fact. Unfortunately, two of them are dead, but perhaps unsurprisingly, *our* ancestor had the sense to spit out the poison Heidi forced her to imbibe, the moment she stepped through our side of the wormhole. She's rather sick, of course – that would be the minor dose of cyanide poisoning, but she will make a full recovery."

Hemmings stared balefully from her cell. "And why should this interest me?"

"Oh, Anne, let's not be coy. A living, breathing person from Munich in the autumn of 1943? And my great-great-grandaunt, no less? You expect me to believe you have no interest in seeing her? In *studying* her?"

Hemmings' stare turned to a scowl. "Fascinating."

Heinrich chuckled jovially. "Come now, wouldn't you like to at least meet her?"

Leaning back in her seat, Hemmings wondered what his agenda might be. There would be one, she did not doubt that. *Time to put him on the back foot, instead, see how that changes the dynamic here.* "Heinrich, have you continued to take readings from the wormhole?"

He hid his surprise at the turn in their conversation completely, but Hemmings knew it was there. "We continue to monitor—" he began.

"No," she interrupted, relishing his confusion. Like the proverbial duck, his plumage showed not a feather out of place on the surface, but she knew all hell was breaking loose below the waterline. "What I am asking is, have you *measured* the wormhole?"

His bonhomie faded instantly. "Speak."

"When I urged you *not* to proceed with this plan, from this location." She held up her hand to forestall Heinrich's protestations. "Let's not waste one another's time, cousin. I *did,* and you ignored my warnings. I could not prove it prior to commencement, but I suspected that a wormhole passing through such a vast power source might begin to feed off it, supping enough energy to stay open for a very long time, perhaps even indefinitely. More worrying still, such a wormhole might also continue to grow."

"*What?* You proceeded with this plan knowing—"

She interrupted him again – she had nothing to lose any more. "Spare me the rhetoric! I suspected there might problems, unforeseen problems, and I *warned* you. But you were not interested in my speculations, were you? So I ask again, have you measured the wormhole's physical dimensions in our space–time?"

Heinrich's expression hardened to ice. Without another word, he stormed from the brig, his tapping stick ringing off deck plates all down the corridor until the hatch automatically sealed behind him.

Hemmings grinned with satisfaction. She had not the faintest idea whether the wormhole really was growing – although it remained a distinct possibility. No, her effective vetoing of his 'big news' was a tiny victory, nothing more, but she would enjoy it, nonetheless. The knowledge that she was alive only as long as Heinrich believed she might prove useful, was actually freeing. Of course, if she were right, it could spell disaster for her, but as it would also spell disaster for every other living thing on the Earth, she could sit back, content in the knowledge that it was no longer her problem – perhaps she might even try '3b' from the menu.

4000 kilometres north-west

"No, no, no!" snapped Commander Coleman. "We're going round in circles. We need to get the pipeline much further out into the lake. Otherwise, we'll run out of water every time there's a drought! And can you think of a worse time to run out of water, ladies and gentlemen, huh?"

Her engineers were nonplussed. One dared raise a hand. "Have you seen the monsters in that lake, ma'am?"

"We're in Britain – everything's smaller here. We'll cope."

"If we were *actually* in Britain there wouldn't be damned great water monsters with huge teeth and flippers out there in the lake!" the man retorted angrily.

"Well, there *was* Nessie—" another man ventured.

"*Shut up!*" they told him together.

Coleman held up a calming hand. "Look, I'm not saying this won't be dangerous, but we *need* water. This is not news, people. We need it, our crops need it, and you know we have showers on this boat, right? Let's see a show of hands – who would like to get them working, too?"

Disgruntlement and chuntering.

"We need a better delivery system," her antagonist tried again. "OK, we managed to fix up two of the inflatables from stores, but would *you* want to go out on a lake full of giant crocodiles, and who knows what else, in a forty-year-old rubber dinghy?"

"So what we need," Coleman continued the thread, "is a distraction?"

"No. What we need is a heavily armoured submarine!"

"Come on, Dr...?"

"Alba."

"Oh, how ironic."

Dr Brian Alba stared at her. "For why?"

"Never mind. Look, we can't build a submarine, but we can distract the animals away from where you're working, can't we?"

"OK. Let's say you can, Commander. You distract the crocodiles – great. Now what about those hideous, giant killer birds nesting on our roof, hmm? Got an idea for distracting them too? Because your plan, so far, seems to involve us riding our small rubber boats through the middle of a death-from-above and death-from-below sandwich! Did I miss anything?"

Coleman frowned stubbornly. *How would Heidi handle this? She would shoot him. Hmm. Tempting, but that won't help us lay pipe. Ah-ha, got it!* "We need a shark cage!"

Alba sighed, throwing his pen down on the table in front of him. "Fabulous."

Coleman genuinely believed her epiphany deserved more enthusiasm than that. "What's wrong with my idea? You got a better one?"

"No, Commander. It's not that your idea is *completely* idiotic—"

"Oh, *thank* you."

"We could probably work something up from stores, given a little time. We have oxygen. It's what we *don't* have that's the problem."

"Meaning?"

"*Meaning* any way of moving it to where we need to work. Any idea how we address that? Or are we back to rubber boats and certain death, again?"

"Dr Alba, what exactly are your credentials?"

"I have PhDs in both Irrigation Engineering and Marine Engineering—"

"THEN WHY THE HELL ARE YOU ASKING ME?" Coleman slammed a fist down on the table before her. "*Now* look, you've made me spill my coffee! Make this work, Alba. I have to inspect the crops our agricultural team are trying to keep alive with their *small* pumping equipment. A heroic effort but doomed to failure, I'm sure you'll agree. We need a solution, or we'll lose our food."

"Their hoses are good for keeping the avians away," he replied moodily. "The stinking things don't like being water pistoled, I hear."

"We could build a scarecrow to do that!" she retorted. "What we need is a way to move vast quantities of water right to the back of our plantation. And on that note, ladies and gentlemen, I'll leave it in your capable hands!"

The limousine pulled up in front of the *Löwenbräukeller.* Resisting the impulse to jump out, Heidi waited impatiently for their driver to open the rear door. She stepped out into the well-lit and usually pedestrianised area immediately before the venue. Jansen followed out of the car to stand by her side.

Two barriers, made from thick red rope drooped between black posts, forged a pathway into the building. Standing before the barriers were two lines of security personnel, arms linked to hold back the crowds of party followers to either side. Above the ornately carved portico were two large flags. The first was the *Bundesflagge,* the second was plain red and bore a central, flaming torch motif, in black. Heidi had never before seen the emblem.

Electric lights dazzled them; a condition worsened by the near-constant salvo of camera flashes. Hanging from the portico was a huge red banner, underlit for all to see. The normally catlike Heidi Schultz almost staggered. It bore the name 'International Socialist Party' in large black letters, while underneath was a huge, stylised logo, which read 'iNazi'.

"I do not believe it..." she muttered, her voice husky with shock.

Jansen nodded his agreement. "I know, Apple must be loving this!"

A broad, white-toothed smile backed by an expensive suit trotted down the centre of the pathway to greet them. "The stunning Dr Heidi Schultz! Thank you so much for coming," the man oozed. "May I say, you look even more gorgeous than your pictures would have us believe. Wow! Look at this *dress,* ladies and gentlemen – isn't she wonderful?"

Ashen, Heidi turned to Jansen. "I am in hell."

Britain, 385 years earlier

"Sir Walter," De Soulis greeted jovially. "Ye got ma message."

At the head of thirty heavily armed horsemen, rode a young boy. He reined in directly before De Soulis and gave a small nod. "Sir William. Aye, Ah got yer wee note. Ah take it yer messenger couldnae read?"

De Soulis shook his head, negative. "The message was far tae important tae run the risk o' rumours abounding."

"That's whit Ah thought," the boy replied. "But ye'll ken that Ah had tae put him oot o' tha world anyway."

De Soulis' forced *joie de vivre* faded utterly. "He was one o' ma most reliable men."

"Aye." The boy's reply was as noncommittal as it was unemotional. "So ye'll be looking for a fair profit tae offset tha loss noo – will ye no'? Is that tha merchandise?" Holding onto the reins with his left hand, he pointed at Bess with his right.

De Soulis nodded, suddenly far less sure of his position.

Bess glowered at Sir Walter. A boy of maybe thirteen, his harsh dialect could not disguise the weakness in his voice, nor its undulation from a husky, sore-throated man's, to a squeaky, rasping boy's. "Ah'll give ye a fair cost – if tha mare is whit ye say she is."

"You insolent dog!" screamed Bess.

In no way cowed, the boy actually smiled. "That's tha Tidder[13] temper we've heard a' aboot, eh?"

Bess straightened to stare the boy down. "And you will be Sir Walter Scott – the *younger*," she sneered.

Some of the horsemen sniggered but stopped immediately when the boy's eye fell upon them. He reddened furiously. "Ah'll give ye a bag o' gold and a bag o' silver for the mare – tak' it or leave it!" He threw the bags of coins at the feet of De Soulis' horse contemptuously.

"Ye insult me, sir!" bellowed De Soulis, nevertheless dismounting.

Sir Walter's temper calmed as De Soulis lost his. When the boy spoke, he spoke quietly, almost conspiratorially as he leaned down from his mount. "We have ye here, Willie. Ah could just tak' her and give ye *gun dad idir*[14]. Ah'll up ma offer tae five in gold, but Ah want Hermitage, tae."

"*What!* Impudent pup! Ah'll have yer head for this!"

"Hermitage is mine!" retorted Sir Walter. "Ma family's from tha time o' Archibald, Fifth Earl o' Angus!"

"He was a traitor who sold us oot tae tha English!"

"Oh, aye!" The boy laughed. "And whit the hell are *ye?*"

---

13   The Tudors were originally from Wales, where the name was spelt (among other variations) Tudur (pronounced Tidder) or Twdwr (pronounced Tewdor). Sir Walter uses a Celtic variant of the pronunciation that would perhaps not have been uncommon for the time or location.

14   Gun dad idir – Gaelic for 'nothing at all'.

De Soulis reached into his cloak and pulled out a small bag filled with a secret compound. "Ye'll eat those words when the demon comes!"

He made a show of uttering a few words in a language none but he understood, and cast the compound to the ground in front of Sir Walter. The dust exploded with a multicoloured flashbang, causing several of the horses to rear. "Robin Redcap, Ah summon thee..."

The ground began to rumble beneath them, and they all heard a monstrous growl from the south. De Soulis grinned as some from the back of Sir Walter's group began to break away, galloping north.

"Cowards!" the boy screamed. "Ah'll hang ye oot f' tha crows!"

Bess would have been thrown, were she not tied to her mount. Around them, all the horses began bucking and whinnying. Several men were hurled from the saddle while the rumbling grew louder.

De Soulis began to wonder just what he had summoned. "Wally! Bring the girl and follow me!" He snatched up the bags of money from the ground, somehow managed to jump into the saddle of his panicked horse, and turning south-east, spurred away.

The hated, rat-faced jailer pulled on the rope attached to the bridle of Bess' horse and shot off after him, dragging her behind. Her mount instinctually followed the horse in front, happy to be at gallop and heading away from the terrifying rumble coming from behind.

Heidi followed the grinning suit, and walked between the parted crowds in a 'Mosesian' daze – all the while expecting the two sides to crash back in about her, drowning the outrageous imposter with adoration. Just as they reached the doors, one waving, nameless face spiked into sharp relief. Clawing at her wits, she manged to snag their host's jacket. "Bring me that man. No. *That* one. I want him inside – he can help me with my presentation."

The grinning fool bent close to catch her words above the roar of the crowds before giving her a theatrical thumbs-up. A security flunkey was summoned and a middle-aged man with a black pencil moustache was snatched from the crowd, with some alarm, and propelled inside.

Once they too were inside, the doors closed behind them. The noise levels fell dramatically as their host turned to Heidi, offering the curt nod and heels-click of a military salute. "Welcome, Doctor. I am Martin Bormann, head of the party chancellery. Please forgive the theatrics out there – we must provide the people with their carnival. I'm sure you understand."

Heidi stared. She knew that name well, but everything here was so upside down, she was at sea. Not trusting herself to speak yet, she merely extended her hand, allowing Bormann to take it and bow, as if to kiss. She noted that he did not actually make contact, and that was the first thing to happen this evening that she approved of.

"Many of us are very excited to hear your speech, Doctor. It should be quite an evening."

"It already is," she remarked quietly. Remembering how inclusive these people were – at least on the surface – she introduced her faithful hound. "Martin, this is Benedictus Jansen, my aide."

Bormann took the measure of the large, squarely built 'aide' and nodded greeting. He fondled a small pip on his lapel twice. "Of course. Welcome, Mr Jansen. My, what a big fellow you are." Then, as if on reflection, he fondled the pip for a third time. "Dr Schultz must feel safe indeed, when aided by yourself. Please, if you will all follow me?" He smiled blandly at the man snatched from the crowd. "Mr Hitler I already know, of course."

"You do?"

"Indeed, Mr Jansen. Mr Hitler painted the signs outside for us, didn't you, Adolf?"

"*Ja,* I did. In between jobs, that is. Not that I can't pay my rent, of course," he added quickly. "May I ask why you, er... *invited* me inside, *Fräulein?* In case you have not realised, I have, in fact, now paid you."

"What?" she demanded imperiously.

"*Meine* rent, *Fräulein.* That is, my *arrears.* You own the building in which I reside – along with half of the city, so I'm sure this is easy to forget..."

She stared down her nose at him. "Be quiet, Adolf. When I need you to speak, I will give you something to say." Heidi pointed, and Hitler walked, hangdog, following Bormann along a corridor. They quickly passed the main hall, continuing down towards the administrative heart of the building.

Bormann opened a door for them. "After you, Doctor, and you, Mr Jansen."

Heidi took a step forward when all her danger senses screamed for her to stop. A heavy arm reached out, but she was already moving, spinning the man's arm in a windmill aikido motion to lock his elbow, twisting the wrist so the hand pointed up at the ceiling. He cried out in surprise and alarm. Another arm reached around her neck from the other side of the door. She had been expecting that, too. Tensing her neck muscles, she made a vicious lefthanded chop, snapping the elbow of the first arm backwards while dropping all her weight forwards and down. The man who had grabbed her from behind was pulled forward and off balance. Heidi let go the first attacker's broken arm and reached between the legs of the second with her right hand, and that was when the screaming began.

She located a couple of 'pressure points' almost immediately, and then *dislocated* them. Pulling her arm upwards in a lightning strike, she made a hammer-fist on the way and smashed it, backhand, into the man's nose with all her wiry strength. He jerked backwards in a claret fountain, once again off balance. Automatically, he stepped back, so as not to lose his feet. The space thus created between them gave Heidi the opportunity to mule kick him across the room. Spinning back to her first opponent, she found him on his knees, sobbing, holding his right arm with his left. He may have no longer been a threat, but he had attacked the wrong woman, and she side-kicked him, supple as a dancer but with all the power of a fighter. Unfortunately for him, she also struck with the heels of a female after-dinner speaker. Doubly unfortunate for him, she was Dr Heidi Schultz, and the four-inch heel stabbed straight through his eye, pinning its jellied core to his hindbrain.

She glanced at Jansen. "And *that,* Ben, is what the split in this dress was designed for! Feel free to help out at any time."

Jansen pushed Bormann into the room at gunpoint. Hitler tried to make a bid for freedom, but Heidi's aide collected him, too, in the crook of his arm to spin him round and back through the door after Bormann. "I thought it best to leave you room, ma'am." He looked down at the dead man with some distaste. "I'd have hated to get in your way," he murmured.

A woman screamed and Heidi spun again, bloody and savage – but then froze.

For the second time today, it felt like she was looking in a mirror.

Jansen pushed Bormann into a chair and stepped quickly across the room to grab yet another Heidi lookalike. He threw the girl into the seat next to the party chancellor.

"Are you sure you can manage that girl all by yourself?" Heidi asked, drily.

Jansen gave a sarcastic smirk, but before he could riposte, the mule-kicked attacker got back to his feet, bellowed in animal rage, and ran at them, his face a snotty, bloody mess. Heidi calmly relieved Jansen of his pistol and fired. The silencer dealt with the noise and the bullet dealt with the man. A small red dot appeared in the middle of his brow, while the back of his head sprayed the wall behind.

Heidi looked at the pistol in surprise. "Hollow points?"

Jansen winked.

She gave him the gun back and removed her shoe, wiping the blood from the heel on the expensive suit worn by the closest of a pair of particularly well-dressed corpses.

Bormann cried out in horror, "Who the hell *are* you people?"

Slipping the shoe back on, she straightened. "I am Dr Heidi Schultz, but not, I think, the Dr Heidi Schultz you were expecting, hmm?" She leaned forward, placing her hands on the arms of his chair. Bormann cowered as far back into the seat as he could, crawling up the sides while she whispered intimately into his ear. "*That* Dr Heidi Schultz is gone – quite dead. So let us just say, I am *the* Dr Heidi Schultz."

Coleman watched the tracked personnel carrier with pride as it pushed a large, redundant water tank out onto Crater Lake. The tank came from the now-cannibalised *Last Word,* during Heidi's last trip to Patagonia. Engineered to be both lightweight and strong, she hoped it would be tough enough to fend off any bites or clawing from their aquatic neighbours.

Her scientists had worked through the night to pull everything together, had even experimented with the idea of converting the tank into a basic submarine, but their final solution turned out to be much simpler. Empty, the tank floated with enough displacement to carry many tons. From there, they simply had to build a cage and come up with a method of propulsion. This came from a couple of the USS *Newfoundland*'s remotely operated vehicles. The little ROVs, kitted out with cameras and underwater microphones, were fully equipped for aquatic search and rescue. After a little renovation, their small, powerful impellers, used in tandem, would soon be towing the empty water tank like a huge buoy, with the cage suspended below.

The APC reached maximum depth and one of its occupants began to feed out slack on the ropes that would tie the whole contraption to terra firma. Gradually, the driver backed out of the water to collect their homemade 'shark cage'.

Dr Alba, and a fellow engineer called Harry Bismarck, wore air tanks on their backs and carried powerful lamps as they waited inside the cage with understandable trepidation. The cage was mounted onto a flat trolley with six solid, non-buoyant rubber wheels; one of several trolleys used to move heavy equipment around the Rescue Pod's hangar. Also attached to their cage was a large steel cap secured about the end of a coiled medium-density polyethylene pipe. 150 millimetres in diameter, the pipe was much too heavy for the ROVs to tug on their own; there would be far too much drag. However, the momentum created by the floating water tank's mass under power would unroll the coil easily.

The ropes from the 'buoy' were tied on to the cage and further ropes now secured it to the APC. The driver offered the vehicle up gently behind the trolley and pushed the whole construct out into the lake. The tiny remote submersibles took up the slack and once the APC again reached its maximum depth, the lumpy, uncomfortable ride across the lakebed suddenly became intolerable for the cage's occupants.

"For crying out loud!" Alba shouted into the comm within his visor.

Coleman allowed herself a self-satisfied smirk. Alba may be a royal pain in the backside, but she had to admit, he was acquitting himself well now. The problem they faced was the ever-lowering tideline. When the *Newfoundland* first landed, one of her rear stanchions had been more than twenty-five metres out into the lake. Several weeks under the burning British sun[15] had left her high and dry as the lake drained away or evaporated, with nothing to replenish it. The rains would come, but probably not in time to save their crop. This had to work, or the future she hoped for would be replaced by starvation.

---

15 British readers are respectfully requested to suspend their disbelief at this point, and not to look out of their windows.

The ROVs had been sent out the day before to collect core samples from the lakebed. Under a microscope, the constituents making up the soil showed that the bed, just a hundred metres off the current shoreline, never dried out. Ergo, that was how far their new pipeline must reach to irrigate their fields all year round.

The lakebed was shaly, with aggregates varying in size from a few millimetres up to boulders. Alba and Bismarck's ride had been far from smooth, but once they reached the maximum depth for the tracked vehicle, the unstoppable momentum of their floating steel buoy had taken over.

From a jostling, rolling motion, they were suddenly snagged and tipped forward. The ropes connecting them to the floating tank were necessarily secured to the upper half of the cage to prevent it from getting stuck. The downside was that they were now being dragged and bounced off every rock in their path. Worse still, Alba knew that when the APC pulled them back out, they would have to do it all again, in reverse.

Holding on to the bars was all the men could do to steady and prevent themselves from being brained against the sides of their cage. Gritting his teeth, Alba accepted this with ill grace, and when things became even worse, it was a surprise, and yet no surprise.

The muted bumps and bangs, as their cage crossed the lakebed, took place in almost complete silence for the humans – aside from their own heavy breathing and occasional swearing in their earpieces. They were uncomfortably outside their habitat. However, for creatures finely attuned to the merest vibration through water, it was quite a different story.

Alba was already harbouring a secret dread. *Where the hell are they all?* He had expected all kinds of attention from the inhabitants of this prehistoric, underwater world, but they had hardly seen a fish. *This is bad.* He did not even want to pass on his suspicions to Bismarck, should his words be made flesh. Having personally seen many large mosasaurs out on the lake, there were still other denizens he had only heard stories about – but as with all stories, there is always another chapter.

The sudden and shocking *clang,* both men certainly heard. With the slight delay of life underwater, they were hurled to the back of their cage. Reaching out to the sides and each other, to save themselves, they saw an enormous head strike and strike again at their makeshift refuge, savaging the bars before them.

From the shore, Coleman knew they were in trouble. It was less the vibration through the tethers than the astonishingly foul language through the comms. "Alba? Bismarck? What's happening?"

The response from underwater went something like: *static, bang, static, cursing, static, bang,* "*HEEELLLP!*"

"Get them out of there!" she screamed. "Take up the slack – back them out!"

Her orders caught on quickly, with further shouts down the line reaching the driver. Almost immediately, the APC began to reverse out of the gently lapping waves, ropes pulling taut as the vehicle backed away. The serenity of life above the waves was only belied by the rise in pitch of the APC's diesel engine and the occasional slip and skip of its tracks. Invisible resistance was clearly slowing the cage's retrieval. Coleman raised her command centre on the *Newfoundland*'s bridge. "Get me a feed from the cameras aboard the ROVs – on the double!" she snapped without preamble.

Alba watched in a horrified 'slow time' as the front of their cage was disassembled, bar by bar. The terrifying stories had fallen woefully short of the mark as far as he was concerned, and he was sure Bismarck felt the same way – it was the first time either of them had ever seen the dreaded rogue Sigilmassasaurus.

Cocksedge shook Schmidt hard. "Erika, wake up! There are dozens of horsemen outside! What should we do?" She sat down on a stool, wringing her hands in panic while her partner sat up on one of the sleeping pallets, stretched languidly, and swung her legs around to the floor.

"Calm yourself, Allison. We asked them to come, remember?"

Schmidt's emotional poise only increased Cocksedge's edginess. Did she not understand the danger they were in? The young woman's composure was as complete on the outside, too. She had moved from beatific slumber, to standing, completely sorted and stunning, in the time it usually took Cocksedge to unstick her eyelids. *Damn her!*

Taking a breath, she asked, "Do you really think we can control these animals?"

"I do." Schmidt's smile would have out-enigmatised Lisa del Giocondo, had she not been sixteen years in her grave by 1558.

At the risk of becoming the 'Moaner Allison' by contrast, Cocksedge's mind painted only a picture of pure disaster as she fumed in silence. Deeply afraid for her own wellbeing, she knew how much she needed her statuesque companion, but was sick of being the one always outside her comfort zone. Having skipped from university to Parliament, bypassing the real world entirely, her working triangle of envy, greed and treachery had supported her ambitions thus far, but she lacked instinct for situations like this.

Unaware of Cocksedge's dilemma, Schmidt walked casually to the door. The tall blonde stooped slightly to open the small hatch mounted at chest height.

Cocksedge took deep breaths, listening hard to her inner voice, and as daylight lanced into the smoky bastle, it brought with it the light of epiphany. Envy subsided. It was time to let the triangle stand on treachery. She painted on a smile. "Erika, darling. I think I may have a way of securing everything this world can provide."

Schmidt's eyebrows rose in question, but Cocksedge merely patted her on the hand. "Follow my lead, dear." She looked out over what she deemed to be a mangy band of miscreants. Young Johnstone stood at the front of the pack, glaring up at her. Some were dressed more outlandishly than others, singling them out, she suspected, as local nobility.

"Who commands here?" she asked, ministerially.

A young man, not out of his teens, spurred his horse forward, knocking the bastle's previous tenant aside. "Ah'm Sir John Johnstone, Marquis of Annandale, and who tha hell are ye?"

"I am All— *Lady* Allison Cocksedge, *Member* of..."

The raucous guffawing prevented her from continuing or even being heard.

"What are you laughing at?" she screamed, indignantly. "*You...*" She looked around to their captive, the young girl Aila, for a clue as to how she should cast a suitable insult. "You stinking *knave?*"

Aila shrugged and so did Cocksedge. She had no idea what that meant, but it seemed to catch the young lord's attention.

"Wha'! Ah'll burn ye oot, ye rancid witch!" he bellowed, red-faced. "Fire arrows!"

His men made ready immediately.

"Your diplomacy is not going so well, it seems," muttered Schmidt.

"Lord Annandale," Cocksedge tried again, calling out over the din, which quieted with a wave of his hand. "*Sir John,*" she continued unctuously. "We seem to have started off on the wrong foot. Let us begin anew. We have much to offer you and crave only your manly protection in return." She gave Schmidt the merest wink to show confidence.

"Show me tha woman!" Sir John shouted.

"I *am* a woman, sir—"

"Tha other one!" he cut her off.

Cocksedge's expression curdled like a bulldog chewing a hornet.

Schmidt opened the door fully to reveal her majesty to the mere mortals below, several of whom almost fell from their mounts. The wide-eyed lust on Sir John's greedy face forced Cocksedge to remind herself that power was power, and it was small matter to her how she came by it. In fact, the more her devious mind worked on their predicament, the more she realised that, blinded by Schmidt, these fools might leave her free to propagate all manner of chicanery under their very noses.

"Yes," she called out, commanding. "We have *much* to offer. Gold, technology and—"

The interruption was manna from heaven. From the north came the unmistakable rattle and boom of what could only be heavy machine guns. Cocksedge smiled at Schmidt, who frowned questioningly.

"You hear that, Sir John? Gentlemen? That is the sound of the most fearful cannon you have ever heard. It can fire more than a thousand exploding shells every minute!"

Schmidt looked impressed.

Cocksedge leaned in to the younger woman, conspiratorially. "I sold a few to a foreign power, some years back. Strictly under the counter, of course – in line with our policy of disarmament. I have to say it was a most lucrative deal, and with the treasury paying all the costs, what was a girl to do?" She smiled craftily when a cry swung her attention back towards the men outside.

"Devilry!" shouted Sir John, clearly shocked and at a loss. He looked around his men, most of whom, lacking their previous bravado, were backing away.

"It's witchcraft, Sir John," one of his lieutenants stated.

"No!" shouted Cocksedge, opening her arms wide as if to embrace them. "It's the *future,* gentlemen. And it can be your future, Sir John – or should I converse with Lord Maxwell?" It was a complete shot in the dark; her only link to the Maxwells was through Captain Douglas, but she bet on Johnstone not knowing that. She was right.

"The next shots willnae miss!" Douglas bawled across the clearing. "Who's in charge here?"

The young Sir Walter Scott picked himself up from the floor, straightening his attire indignantly. "Tha' would be me!" he spat.

Douglas looked around the other men's faces. "The bairn? *Seriously?*"

"Strong work," Meritus muttered in his ear. "Ever thought about the Diplomatic Corps?"

"*Ah'm* the one who keeps our little triumvirate's feet on the ground," Douglas answered out of the corner of his mouth. "Jill was always better at this sort of thing than me." He sighed. "Ah wish she was here."

The boy strode over to the APC, his face red with anger. "Ah'm the laird here. Ah've taken eyes for less, auld man!"

Some of the fear had left Sir Walter's men, once the steel monster disgorged ordinary, mortal men, but they still crossed themselves – a habit long transcending any shifts in religious denomination – and kept their distance.

Douglas smiled down at the young lordling standing, legs braced apart, before him. "Ye've courage, Ah give ye that," he placated. "We're here for Sir William de Soulis. D'ye know him?"

Sir Walter gave a sideways look, full of guile.

Ah suppose they grow up quickly round here, Douglas thought. *The ones that grow up at all.*

"Aye, Ah know Sir William. He has something o' mine."

"Does he? Well, he has something of ours, too. He had a girl with him, about mid-twenties – red hair?"

"Aye, Princess Elizabeth."

That pulled Douglas up short. He looked to Meritus for ideas.

"What makes you say she's a princess?" Meritus asked, trying to deflect the boy from the truth.

"Half the folk in thae hills ken by noo. Ah paid De Soulis for her. A bag o' gold 'n' a bag o' silver. She's mine."

"Now you listen here, laddie!" stormed Douglas, grabbing the teenager by his tunic. "Ah need to know where he's taken her, and Ah'm nae in the mood for games!"

One of Sir Walter's men raised a crossbow but crumpled to the floor before he could even take aim. "Next one of you little Herberts who tries anything like that," The Sarge growled from the personnel carrier's top hatch, "will be joining your mate here, on the ground." He readied his Heath-Rifleson for another shot.

The arrogance in the boy's eyes turned to fear, and for a moment, Douglas felt shamed. After all, they controlled thunder, lightning and the very forces of nature – or at least that was how it must have appeared to these locals, and their young laird. Then he remembered they were Reivers. Regardless of his youth, the boy must be tough as nails and doubtless capable of who knew what. "Tell me, laddie," he snarled menacingly. "Where did De Soulis take her?"

"Follow those tracks," Sir Walter replied quietly. "And dinnae think Ah will forget this, auldjin."

Douglas followed his gaze and let the boy go, smoothing out his tunic. "And Ah'll remember ye had the good sense to help me, when it really mattered. *Let's move out!*"

"Drop the pipe!" screamed Alba from his corner of the shark cage. "Drop the damned pipe!"

"It's your side!" Bismarck screamed back at him.

"Of *course* it is!" Setting action to words, he released the catch that secured the end of the pipeline in place. It dropped the metre and a half to the lakebed, disappearing into the maelstrom of muck dredged up from the bed by Sigilmassasaurus' frenetic efforts to reach them. "I think it's down. I can't see!"

Bismarck cracked a couple of light sticks, breaking the inner glass tube and shaking them, to allow the diphenyl oxalate and fluorescent dye to mix with the hydrogen peroxide solution. He cast them through the mirky water as one might throw a frisbee, right into the face of the dinosaur. The savage crocodilianesque head, darting left and right, huge jaws wrenching at the bars, was now lit up in flickering green monochrome through the billowing muck and sand all around them. Both men screamed again.

"Harry! What did you do *that* for?" Alba cried, breathlessly.

"So we could see."

"I don't *want* to see!"

"I thought it might scare it away."

"Great job – now it can see *us!* What's your next trick – smear us with lamb's blood?"

"You really want your last words to be sarcasm?"

"*Yes!*"

The cage bounced and rocked from side to side with one ferocious attack after another.

"Aaaarrgh!" they screamed together.

The ropes attached to the rear of their cage were mounted low down, to prevent it from falling. No force in the lake could prevent the relentless tug of the tracked vehicle on the beach, so getting stuck was never a concern. However, as they were dragged backwards, they smashed into every rock in their path, throwing the two men all over the cage – often dangerously close to the gnashing jaws of the world's most literally draconian pool attendant.

From above the waterline, Coleman could see the APC backing out of the water, ropes taut, while the water tank they were using as a buoyancy aid was also dragged back across the lake with enough force to create a bow wave. The small ROVs – hideously overmatched – brought up the rear, bobbing and slewing in a vain attempt to maintain their position. *That* was alarming. What was terrifying, were the flashes of the monster that broke the surface while it fought to drag her men out of their container and down to the depths.

Following quickly on the heels of that terror came the shocking realisation that the venue for this spectacle was about to change. Unlike the predatory mosasaurs[16], so numerous in the area, Sigilmassasaurus was quite comfortable on land, too.

The cage broke the surface first, chopping white water as it came on, gaining speed. The ropes attached to the front of the APC slackened unexpectedly. Uncertain, the driver began to slow when the cage and its terrified occupants lifted clear of the water altogether, on the crest of a wave. Despite their masks, the men's screams could be heard clearly as Sigilmassasaurus shook their container in its jaws.

The drag of the water lost its hold quickly as the giant spinosaur lunged from the shallows. It swung the cage around, launching it up the beach in a flat trajectory.

Rather than sarcasm, Alba's actual last words turned out to be the four-lettered kind.

"Where are the rest of your party leaders?" asked Heidi, standing with arms crossed and legs braced in a wide stance – a heroic posture more befitting a Germanic rock star than a beauty in evening dress.

Jansen stood to her left, once again covering their prisoners with his pistol. Before her, in three stylish office chairs, sat their erstwhile *maître d'*, Martin Bormann – head of the iNazi party chancellery; a beautiful blond girl named Christina Müller – who bore a striking resemblance to both Heidis; and, of course, Adolf Hitler.

"*Well?*" she prompted.

"They opted to arrive later, in case..." Bormann tailed off under the blowtorch of her glare.

"In case?"

"Well, you know, in case anything went wrong with our plan. They would arrive just in time for a meeting of the party, or..."

"*Or...?*"

"Or to condemn an act of terrorism that could in no way be attributed to them. That's why this building is so empty right now. They would

---

16   At a glance, mosasaurs were crocodile*like* predators, aquatically adapted with four large flippers, rather than the legs of terrestrial archosaurs. However, the mosasauria were not directly related to crocodiles and may have actually been a sister clade to Serpentes (snakes). What Dr Brian Alba would not have given for a ladder!

naturally propose a charity ball, inviting the great and the good, in honour of Dr Heidi Schultz – whom the public loved, believing her to be a great philanthropist. They may even have suggested a public day of mourning – that sort of thing."

Heidi glanced at Jansen. "If the now-deceased Dr Schultz was so beloved, why was it necessary to have her assassinated? I assume this girl was meant to, at least nominally, take her place, yes?"

Bormann nodded. "She had access to the Schultz empire and all its resources and wealth—"

"Empire?" Heidi interrupted. "I like the sound of that."

"Yes, indeed. Well, her brother, Hans – named for their father – is a colonel in the 'hiking and scouting enthusiasts club' we laughingly call an army these days. There was a family falling-out, before the old man died, and the favoured son lost out to Heidi."

"Sounds familiar. Go on."

"She was not unintelligent. She *chose* to live the playgirl lifestyle. I regret her choices – they made her little more than a useless icon. Most of the charitable works attributed to her were conceived and executed by others with her consent – she loved the adoration of *her* public, you see?"

"I believe I am beginning to. So for this you wanted to kill her?"

"Not exactly. There's a bit more to it than dislike or jealousy. You may not know this, but our country, our world, in fact, is at a crossroads. We have made our planet a wonderful place of beauty and opportunity. But by sharing all that we have, all that we are, we have somehow made enemies."

Heidi frowned. "How?"

"No good deed ever goes unpunished," he said wryly. "By sharing our technology freely and diminishing our ability to defend ourselves, we have placed our nation in harm's way. I mean, why do we need a vast military? All we do is help people all over the world, so they must love us, right? Wrong. Many of our leaders don't see a problem when other nations we have helped use the knowledge *we* imparted to build arms and forces that could be turned against us. Our knowledge and technology must seem threatening, after all, they have the right to defend themselves – and on, and on the arguments go. However, some of us are looking out into the world and seeing armed camps forming, and if we're not careful, the Fatherland may simply provide a useful venue where they can sort out their differences – destroying our beloved country in the process."

"Fascinating," Heidi remarked drily, remembering the history of her own timeline. She pulled up another seat. "Truly fascinating. One can almost hear the French breathe a universal sigh of relief."

Bormann frowned. "The French?"

"Never mind. So your plan was to remove the great philanthropist, Heidi Schultz, and replace her with a more militant model?"

"Not just her. There are others, too."

Heidi began to laugh. She could not help herself; it was all at once so insane and yet so comfortingly familiar. "Well, it seems you have what you wished for, *Herr* Bormann. However, a shocking behavioural change in one of this nation's richest celebrities would surely not go unnoticed. Once out in the open, what did you actually intend to achieve by this?"

"We intended—" He began again, "We *intend* to secretly rearm and revitalise our space programme. That is where our future lies – out *there.*"

Heidi shook her head ruefully. "Colonising other worlds, and in 1943 – remarkable. But moving so much wealth within our own borders will surely also not go unnoticed."

Bormann held out his hands, palms up. "True, but we have to do *something.*"

She lapsed into thought. The Nazi movement, the Third Reich – none of it had come to pass during this timeline. There had been no Great War. In fact, despite their pathetically executed failed execution, these were largely good people – she could find no other way of describing them – but even when things pan out so differently, human nature always seems to find a way to debase itself in bloodshed and warfare. Written into the laws of entropy, order always tends towards chaos; inevitable to the bitter end, and for the first time, Heidi was beginning to feel at home.

For many, this train of thought might have caused deep depression, but Heidi was a Schultz, cut from the original mould, and not part of this cuddly world Douglas' interference seemed to have created. What *she* saw was nothing less than an opportunity for unlimited *power.*

In a flash of inspiration, she began, "I may have a way to fund our efforts, without drawing too heavily on our nation's resources."

Bormann looked up sharply. "*Our* efforts? You wish to join with us, then?"

She saw the hope in the man's eyes – it was pathetic, but she could use it. "Why not?"

"And the money?" he asked, tremulously.

"You must still have some people in this world who, shall we say, live outside the normal rules and regulations, yes?"

"You mean criminals?"

"More importantly, rich criminals," she elucidated. "The sort of people who will pay any amount of money to possess something extremely rare. Regardless of the laws put in place to protect and hold those items in public ownership. You have such people?"

He nodded.

"Do you have *access* to such people?"

Bormann grimaced uncomfortably. "We could probably open avenues of communication, if we *had* to."

"Trust me, you have to. I wish to set up an auction for four of the rarest items on Earth. Can you do this?"

He shrugged. "Possibly. But we will need billions of dollars to achieve our goals, and top-secret development facilities safe from prying eyes. How do you propose we accomplish all this?" His eyes narrowed. "And what *are* these items of which you speak?"

She smiled coolly. "*Living* dinosaur eggs."

Bormann released a bark of laughter, but glimpsing the bodies on the floor, sobered quickly. "Forgive me, but you can't be serious."

"I am always serious, *mein Herr.* Ben, tell these people how serious I can be."

Jansen cocked his pistol, aiming at Bormann's head. "*Very* serious, ma'am."

"But it's impossible, Doctor. I mean, our scientists have theorised about genetically engineering—"

Heidi cut him off with a hand. "No. I am not talking about dinosaur kits extrapolated from rocks and the DNA of their descendants. I have real—"

"Ahem," Jansen interjected.

"*Will* have, *real* dinosaur eggs," Heidi completed, barely missing a beat. "Still warm from their mother. What would *they* be worth? And don't forget that a properly incubated egg is far more than a trophy or a paperweight. Some rich recluses enjoy populating their estates with lions, tigers and bears." She allowed a tinkling, girlish laugh. "*Adorable.* Now, how much would those same billionaires pay to guard themselves with giant theropod dinosaurs, I wonder? Trust me, those eggs could quite literally be 'the next big thing'."

Even in a time and a land where big things were commonplace, there really was nothing that could truly prepare one for standing in the path of a charging spinosaur. Under the baleful, reptilian gaze of a nesting flock of Ornithocheirus, Coleman looked around for somewhere to run. Her guards opened fire with assault rifles. Their tiny bullets would add up eventually, even for a behemoth like Sigilmassasaurus, but it was all too little, too late.

Alba and Bismarck lay still, inside the broken cage. She truly hoped they lived, but had more pressing concerns at that moment. Her men were standing their ground. *Bless them,* she thought as she hollered in disbelief, "*Run,* you damned fools!"

The dinosaur was on them in a moment, taking one to the ground with a huge, taloned foot, while its head bobbed with unerring aim to snatch another in its jagged teeth. The *pop-crack* sound as the man was bitten in half turned Coleman's legs to water. *This is it. After all our cleverness and hard work, this is how it ends.*

"Run, ma'am," her last guard screamed as he fought with his weapon. It seemed to have jammed.

Probably all the flying dust and sand, the thought popped into her head, leaving her body in a treacle-slow dream. *This was how Nassaki got it, but he survived. Might I?*

The last guard gave up, actually throwing his rifle at the bloody, grinning maw overhead, while a woman scrambled over the APC, desperately trying to cut the ropes tying them to the cage. Coleman saw they were too far away to help, and they had no guns on that vehicle. However, the word *cage* snagged at her mind, tugging for her attention.

Spinning round, the cage was near, but it was broken. Her mind was porridge. Thoughts formed, but with all the detail of plasticine men. The cage was within reach, but it was *broken*. Round and round again in her head – why was that important? Reaching a decision, she ran for it, hoping her thoughts would catch up. Fortunately, for the times when fear saturates the conscious mind, there is instinct.

Coleman dove through the bent and broken bars of the cage, falling upon Alba and Bismarck. A part of her mind she barely understood at that moment, registered groans from each of them. This *felt* like a good thing, but it would have to be sorted through later. Her driving concern was currently the ground – it was going away.

Forgetting her new rank, Coleman swore like a sergeant. Three metres from the ground, Sigilmassasaurus held them in its mouth like a dog toy. Placing a protective arm in front of each prone man, Coleman edged back into the cage, with all her might fighting to prevent them from spilling out. With foresight, the welders had fitted all six sides of the cage with mesh, as well as the main bars, before attaching it to the wheelbase. The six-wheeled trolley now hung from the bottom, swinging, attached only by one tortured length of box-section steel. Had it not been for the mesh, she and the others would have lost their limbs in the roll and tumble.

The dinosaur was staring at her. Just a metre away. It was the most incredible experience of her life. *Just please, God, don't let it be the last!* Also incredible, was the eye-watering stench. Large carnivores often exude a ripe odour, but when their diet is mixed with fish in various stages of life or decomposition, the effect is truly memorable. Coleman threw up.

Sigilmassasaurus did not seem to mind.

Is it trying to work out how to get to us? She pondered, wretchedly.

The gears within its brain were turning before her very eyes, putting her in mind of a caveman frustrated by a tin of beans. "OK, genius. What now?" Although, *she* was one to talk. Surrounded by her brave and – it had to be said – loyal guards, she had not bothered to arm herself. She would not make that mistake again – hopefully through preparedness, rather than finding herself in the funereal way. Still, small arms had not saved those poor men.

"Ally?"

Coleman turned towards the husky, pain-wracked voice of Dr Alba. "Brian?" she whispered. "You picked your time to wake up. Keep *very* still."

"Ouch. Was I knocked out? Everything hurts."

"*Shut up!*"

The dinosaur snorted and the barrage of fishy bogies left both conscious cage passengers staring at one another, in a shared misery that denied any possibility of speech.

"That's it!" shouted Alba. "That's my ceiling! And I dare any man to call it his floor!"

He pulled the air tank from around his shoulders and picked up a large adjustable spanner trapped within the mesh on what was currently the bottom of their cage. The giant theropod snorted more gently, huge eyes following the tiny monkey, with his monkey-wrench, around his cage. Alba laid the air tank before its face and smacked the small valve at its top for all he was worth. The explosion coincided with the roar of a massively powerful diesel engine from somewhere off to their left.

The small air tank slipped elegantly between the broken bars to hit the dinosaur in the tender flesh on the roof of its mouth. "Bullseyeeeeee!" Alba's shout rose in pitch to fall in with Coleman's scream – even Bismarck began to moan as the cage dropped.

Expecting a thud and serious injury, they were surprised by a loud *clang*. Sigilmassasaurus had dropped them – that part of Alba's plan had worked – but it had dropped them in the path of the speeding armoured vehicle. Injury was to follow.

Consciousness returned slowly, which was odd, because the pain struck Coleman like lightning.

"Ah, you're awake."

Coleman took a while to realise who was speaking. "Brian? Ah, ah, *ahhhowww!* Ooh," she whimpered. Turning her head caused a second outcry. Before she fell back with an agonised sigh, she noted Alba sitting up in the next bed, reading. They were clearly in the *Newfoundland*'s surprisingly tidy sickbay.

"It's OK, I'm alright," he said. "Don't worry."

Talking hurt her, and this was probably for the best, as it prevented her words from hurting him.

"Bismarck's going to be OK, too. Funnily enough, despite all we went through, your injuries were actually the worst. Well, apart from those dead guys, of course."

"*Funnily?*" His matter-of-fact manner was fast becoming a matter of fulmination for Coleman. She could feel it brewing within. "What happened?" she croaked, choking back her simmering annoyance.

"After my master stroke with the oxygen? The cage fell, and that horrible thing ran away, and—"

"What happened to *me? Idiot!* Ow, ow, *ouch.*"

"Oh, just a couple of broken ribs. There's a doctor around here somewhere. He's not the best – Heidi took those – but don't worry, I saved us, and you."

"I'm OK, too," she spoke the lie through gritted teeth. "Thank you for asking!" Seething, she thought it would be less painful to change the subject. "I don't suppose you managed to attach the grill and filters to the end of the pipeline, before the attack?"

"Honestly, is that all you care about, Ally?"

Coleman attempted a turn onto her side, which ended in another cry of defeat. "Is that... all *I*... Why, you self-centred, petty little man! I can't believe you... Oh, never mind – *did* you?"

"Did I what? With all your ranting, I've forgotten your question – if you had one."

"Did you place the grill and filters over the end of the pipeline?"

He closed the tablet he was reading from, to place it on a bedside table as he lay down, drawing his blanket up comfortably to his chin. "You know, in all the excitement, I must have forgotten to look."

"*Brian!*"

"Of course we didn't fit them – we were attacked! Now if you don't mind, Ally, I've been told to rest. I too sustained an injury, you know. I bent my finger right back in that crash."

Chapter 7 | The Widdershins Rig

Charging through the Scottish Borders on galloways, De Soulis and his men followed in the tracks of their forebears. Meritus' armoured transport pursued them, untiring and relentless; even so, galloway ponies remained the fastest, most effective means for getting away through the hilly Scottish border wilderness. Incredibly tough, they carried their masters mile after gruelling mile before requiring rest.

After an arduous morning, they holed up in a small copse, high up in the hills. De Soulis stared out to the south, his expression darkening. They were not far from Hermitage. Should he chance going back there? He had no way of knowing whether his men had managed to defend the castle, surrendered it, or fallen in the process. Should he try and summon Redcap once more? The sub-creature would have the information he needed, certainly, but would he help? Indeed, he seemed to have made himself altogether scarce. When summoning him for the first time, De Soulis had used a spell from long gone days, written specifically to *bind* a demon and force it into servitude, but Redcap had proved *so* strong. Once fully materialised, he had simply overwhelmed his unsuspecting master.

De Soulis disregarded the idea. Instead, he considered sending one of his remaining men ahead, but then, if that fellow failed to return – for whatever reason – he would learn nothing. More to the point, there were only four of them left. Five, including himself, and then there was the girl. He had lost much, potentially everything, in fact, but if he could just get her to the right buyer...

His thoughts of wealth and vengeance were interrupted by a distant growl. The steel monster, dogging their trail all morning, had caught up with them again. It always seemed to know where they were, never mind how far ahead or how well they hid. It was another power beyond his ken – and it *terrified* him.

"Do we remain hidden or flee, master?" asked the rat-faced jailer.

"We cannae rely on our hiding place, Wally. This monster can sniff us oot."

"Our ponies need rest, Sir William."

"We dinnae have the luxury. Besides, it's doonhill from here. Mount up!"

From high on the south-eastern slopes of Wyndburgh Hill, the riders looked out over a slight bowl leading up to a ridge conjoining two nearby hills. The gap between the peaks revealed Whitrope Burn[17]. Occasional pools twinkled in the morning sun as it carried away the early meltwater. The lower slopes were forested, but De Soulis knew Hermitage Castle lay directly along his line of sight, and would be visible were it not for the hulking shoulder of Hermitage Hill in the way. At least, that was what he hoped. In truth, he had no idea what he would find there.

The betrayal of Sir Walter had changed the whole playing field; that, and his inability to shake the devilish monstrosity that pursued him. He felt a natural calling for the strong stone walls of Hermitage – ever his salvation – but within this changed reality, and against such powers, his last bastion would be more likely to trap him than save him. The Scott family had coveted De Soulis' lands ever since their ancestors lost them, three generations ago. Even so, he had believed the capture of England's future queen would bridge their differences, for a little while at least. He would rather see Hermitage back in the hands of the Crown than be stolen by that young rogue – no less dishonourable, granted, but far less embarrassing.

No, after all he had witnessed in the last twenty-four hours, he knew Hermitage could not keep the outlanders at bay. Consequently, returning was a gamble, but he could see no other route. He had to

---

17   Burn: common name for a watercourse in Scottish and Northern English dialects – typically a large stream or small river.

secure fresh horses. After that, he would take his chances across Johnstone territory, in the south-west of Scotland. His prisoner would surely have value there. If even that failed, he would just have to consider her a hostage and try his hand against England herself. All he needed was a place to hold out. Surely Queen Mary of England could not last much longer, and when she was gone, his prisoner would carry a price tag large enough to assuage even his appetites. They were far in the north, yet stories reached them that Mary was not long for this world. Yes, his problems would be over, once Mary was dead.

While De Soulis planned and machinated, his stallion loped more than trotted, its short, sturdy legs eating up the miles as they approached the ridge. The roar of the beast hunting them echoed and bounced around the valley long before it came into sight. Clearly, its master believed stealth unnecessary – that he could run them down in good time. The roar and the smell of diesel fumes on the prevailing north wind upset the horses more than the clash and screams of battle. Hardy Reiver ponies were bred and trained for that, but this was different – unnatural. De Soulis shared their nebulous fear of the unknown, though his was crowned by the knowledge that they really *were* after him.

Gaining the ridge, he reined in to scan the landscape ahead and below. The way down seemed clear as far as Whitrope Burn, but the forests in the lower valley could prove difficult to traverse by horse. The Reivers knew tracks through well enough, but forests presented ideal opportunities for ambush; lesser-known paths would mean dismounting and cost them time.

The monstrous roar peaked and attenuated behind, as the wind gusted and changed direction at random. However, De Soulis felt sure the steel beast was gaining on them.

"Get down off the ridge!" he shouted, matching words to action.

The six horses plummeted, breakneck, down the other side. The great, heavy destriers favoured in the south would likely have fallen, killing themselves or their riders, but though the gradient was steep, the surefooted galloways were at home. They carried their mass and that of their riders expertly, always balanced, always certain, until the slope at last began to level out.

Once over the ridge, De Soulis could no longer hear their pursuit, but as they galloped towards the rapidly approaching treeline, knew he had just minutes to reach a decision – speed or stealth. A sixth sense gnawed at him, also, warning of danger, perhaps the greatest he had ever faced.

He could do nothing but run from the machine that chased them, but there were other perils in these lands, especially now. If they dismounted, to pick a secret way through the forest, the machine would catch or even overtake them, cutting them off from his castle. If they charged down the wider tracks – assuming they were able to avoid an ambush – they would reach Hermitage first, but would he be able to gain entrance? Or would he simply find himself trapped between his stone walls and that steel beast?

De Soulis had experimented several times with scrying, but the art eluded him. Exasperated, he knew he needed Redcap.

Once inside the treeline, he allowed his horse to slow to a natural canter before reining in. Several hundred metres into the forest, his men drew up behind him.

"The Rig?" asked Wally.

De Soulis nodded. A hidden path forked to their left, all but invisible unless one knew it was there and actively sought it. De Soulis jumped out of the saddle and led his pony into the heavier brush, his men, and the reluctant Bess, following.

She was helped from the saddle, though her hands remained tied and bound to the pommel. She was allowed just enough slack to walk alongside her pony, while Wally tied the animal to his own and led them together in semi-single file. Dragged alongside their mounts, Bess worked to loosen the bindings as every twig and thorn tore at her. The tough, barrel-chested pony at her side walked slowly now, but seemed otherwise oblivious to her discomfort.

Desperate to create an opportunity, Bess' mind raced to come up with a plan, any plan, to escape her situation. Frozen by the north wind's bite and the tightness of her bonds, her hands had lost all feeling. She briefly wondered whether the sweat, lathering her pony's flanks, might help lubricate her wrists in order to effect an escape, but there were a further three men right behind her on the path. Besides, escape through the trees looked near impossible, even if she could free herself. Frustrated and afraid, she called up the line, "Where art thou taking me, Sir William?"

De Soulis ignored her, speaking to Wally, "Keep her quiet. Ye ken?"

Her vile jailer grinned and patted his pony by as he pulled a long knife from the scabbard at his belt. As she drew up in front of him, he placed one finger to his lips. She got the message.

Progress was slow, the path hardly used and hopelessly overgrown. All sounds of pursuit seemed to have died, though De Soulis suspected they were not far behind, their movements muted by dense woodland and the swaying of a hundred thousand leafless limbs.

Bess suspected the path would be impassable with horses by summer, so close must the foliage reach across the narrow way.

The better part of an hour had taken them no more than half a mile when the path opened out into a rough clearing. It could hardly be said that the area was maintained, yet there were signs that the forest had been fought back at least a handful of times in recent years.

De Soulis tied his stallion off to a branch, awaiting the others.

Bess entered the clearing, bashed, scratched and bruised, revelling in the opportunity to step just a few inches further away from her pony. She loved horses, but after their pell-mell ride, the little fellow's body odour was hard to abide, mere inches as it was from her nose.

Small for a horse, it nevertheless blocked her view almost completely. At fourteen hands, it was taller than she, even at the withers. Only when Wally tied his own pony next to his master's, did hers dip its head to graze. The spartan canopy kept the snow at bay around the edges of the clearing and as the pony munched on yellow-brown winter grasses, she was able to glance over its neck.

By her reckoning, the clearing was perhaps twenty poles[18] in diameter. However, its most striking feature was the stone circle at its heart. Eight standing stones, with a ninth fallen flat, lay in a slightly oval configuration. Most were broken and eroded by the centuries. Only two stood out as nearly intact; one as tall as a man, the other perhaps at chest height.

Bess knew of many such places; these isles were practically littered with them. However, she could not guess at the monument's age, sure only that it had been left by 'the old people', long before the written word had reached Britain.

De Soulis knew it as a place of power – he had used it to great effect in the past. The DNA of his victims was soaked into these

18   Approximately 90m

stones, for those with eyes to detect and minds to understand such things. In fact, all his most potent rituals had been performed here, and that gave him hope.

"Make sure the lass is tied securely," he barked.

In response, he heard only laughter – low, cruel and mirthless. The lone male voice from the woods was quickly joined by many more, seemingly all around them. De Soulis recognised the tone; none knew it better. It was the harbinger of torment.

Out of the trees they came, running, jumping, screaming and calling out, in gleeful expectation. De Soulis' heart sank. His abandonment of Hermitage was a story that could not be contained, he understood that, but had nevertheless expected at least a few days to make good his escape. Once liquidated, his merchandise would have encumbered him no longer, enabling a return in triumph to new and unprecedented powers. Such reach he would have had, but now, all he could do was guess at his betrayer; his castellan, perhaps, or others among his former retinue. He vowed that, if he survived this, they would pay a heavy price for it.

However, survival was looking increasingly unlikely. The force surrounding his meagre entourage were mere peasants with not a warrior among them, but that hardly mattered. They were all armed with fearsome-looking farm tools and were several dozen to his five. Numbers alone would tell.

De Soulis quickly moved to the centre of the stone circle. Immediately, he began an elaborate incantation, throwing several of his compounds to earth. As they impacted on the ground, each erupted with bangs and multicoloured flashes.

The locals were a simple people and stayed outside the ring of stones, but did not back off further. Once their group had amassed fully, they began to circle *his* circle, in a sort of eerie widdershins standoff. Fear of his archaic spellcasting and pyrotechnics, combined with their superstitions about crossing the circle of stones set in place by the ancient folk, kept them at bay for now.

They believed the ring to be a gateway. Over the centuries, tales of faerie, borrowed, warped into dire warnings of demonic hellfire with the telling.

Even knowing this, De Soulis felt sure their superstitious caution would not last. Not this time. One would find his courage, the others would follow, and that would be the end of it, for he recognised something new in these beaten and ravaged people – defiance. They had him. Doubtless, they expected to lose people, but they had him.

Stories had long abounded throughout his lands, relating how his mastery of the dark arts was such that no normal weapon could kill him, and no rope could bind. He knew the stories – had started most of them. They were like armour. He prayed they might save him still, but then a second wave of his long-suffering people entered the clearing from the south, and De Soulis felt his legs give way beneath him. With sudden, stark realisation, he understood that the men from the villages under his thrall had merely been sent to ensnare him – their task to keep him there, and now came the women.

They arrived by a slower, more circuitous route, less steep and utilising wider paths. Three dozen or more of them pushed and pulled a large cart with a brace of oxen in the lead. Several children ran around and ahead of them, screaming with excitement as if they were on their way to a fair. Upon the cart sat a huge cast iron cauldron, bound with thick ropes, along with something else. De Soulis could not make it out. It looked like a block of mangled metal.

Broken swords? he mused, but then, swords cost more than houses, so where could these peasants have possibly amassed such a pile? As they grew nearer, he recognised the load for what it was, and his blood turned to ice. At last, he understood their full intentions.

Walking in line and in time, the women sang. The tune was simple, its harmonies effortless; yet their voices haunted the afternoon air like a stitch through time, gently binding them to another age as it lay dormant just beneath their own. On any other occasion, theirs would have been a mere folk tale – a local story brought to life in song – but as the sun began to sink in the west, De Soulis felt its ancient magic amplified by the stones. The villagers, *his* villeins and farmers, were simply unwitting components of a spell. Without concept or design, its only purpose was balance. Yet within those simple repetitive rhythms and phrases, he recognised the cadences of his own circle, closing. He was trapped. They had his body, and now they had his soul, up at Ninestane Rig[19].

---

19 Nine Stone Ridge from the old border dialect.

Douglas glared at the monitor before him. "Where the *hell's* he gone? How could we have lost his trail so completely? We were all over him!"

Meritus leaned over his shoulder while they were stationary. "Let me see. Nothing on infrared, no sonics – at least not that would account for half a dozen riders. The forest is interfering with our instruments. Too many destructive frequencies." He sat back, blowing out his cheeks. "Be nice if we had a few satellites up there, wouldn't it?"

"Can we sniff them out?" asked Douglas.

Meritus snapped his fingers with epiphany and leaned across once more. Several menus later, he brought up the air quality sensor array. "Right, this system runs permanently in the background – it's kind of a safety feature that sounds an alarm if the air outside becomes toxic. It can also filter for almost any chemical composition, if programmed to search for it – that is, what our natural olfactory system would recognise as a scent. Or perhaps stink might be closer to the mark."

"So, we can scan for individuals?" O'Brien asked, ever more impressed by her favourite toy. "I've noticed these old-timers haven't discovered shower gel yet."

"Technically, yes," Meritus explained, "but we would need a lot more sampling to be sure of who was who. Simpler to look for the horses, I think. The air is extremely pure in this time, and as we've been nowhere near any fires or settlements, we can filter for the strongest scent our equipment has detected since the chase began. It records everything. Look, I can even split it into time frames... hmm, yep, there it is!"

Douglas frowned at the screen. "So this is background – *fresh air*, if you will." He pointed at a set of rolling sinusoidal waves in shades of blue. "And these reds are the horses?"

"Yes. Horse sweat."

"Lovely," O'Brien drawled.

Meritus grinned. "Do you also see these other frequencies cropping up, intermittently? The ones I've picked out in brown for you?"

They nodded.

"Horse manure!" Meritus stated proudly as if revealing a trick.

O'Brien gave Douglas a secret look, before answering, "Nice touch."

"OK." Douglas motioned for Meritus to move it along. "Colour me impressed—"

"Not in brown, I hope," O'Brien murmured, interrupting him.

"*Thank you,* Corporal. This is great, but how do Ah turn these sine waves into a direction?"

"Probably best swap seats with me, James."

Meritus jumped into the co-driver's seat and began scanning the local area. "OK. One hundred metres over there." He pointed in a south-westerly direction. "Can you see that opening in the trees, Corp?"

"Got it." O'Brien restarted the engine and moved towards the gap in the forest. "If there are little tracks running through these woods, it might get a little tricky, sirs. As well as getting turned around, I'm sure it's escaped nobody's notice that this APC is pretty big."

"Aye, Ah wanted to bring young Billy Maxwell with us in case we got ourselves lost, but Ah think last night's..." he searched for the right word, eventually deciding on, "*events,* put the wind up our sixteenth century chums. What with the explosions and spaceships and – what the hell was that man in the fire, you mentioned? Some kind of ghost, or apparition? Well, Ah think they just needed a little readjustment time, safe inside the *familiarish* surroundings of Hermitage Castle. Ye'll just have to follow them as best ye can, Corp. Try not to break too many trees."

O'Brien grinned. "Yes, sir!"

After a few hundred metres, their equipment found the place where the horses had left the main path. By 16th century standards, the tracked personnel carrier was indeed heavily armoured and massive. It collected branches all along the main pathway, widening the brush considerably. "If we're to turn off here, we're gonna smash a completely new road. Not exactly low impact, Captain. What's your call?"

Douglas looked at his antique wristwatch. "With the chase, Ah'd forgotten about Gleeson. He was supposed to catch up with us hours ago. We could really do with his dirt bikes about now."

"We could call him, sir?"

"Ha, you're right!" Douglas snorted quietly. "We've all gotten so used to hiding comm traffic from Schultz and his merry band, Ah'd mentally removed radio from our toolbox. Patch me through to the commander, will ye, Corporal?"

On the third attempt, O'Brien received a response. "*Captain, is that you?*"

Douglas keyed to speak. "Commander, good to hear your voice. We need you. What's kept you so long?"

"We were real late leaving. Ya see, by the time our bikes arrived, the area around the castle was in the full throes of a peasants' revolt, mate! I had to dole out a load of the castle's food supplies just to quieten them down. Apparently, De Soulis had stolen most of the harvest for himself and these poor folks have had three hard years as it is – they needed every crumb. After that was dealt with, we got to spend all arvo riding round and round in bladdy circles, following your tracks! What have you guys been doing?"

A smile lifted the corner of Douglas' mouth. He went on to explain their circuitous chase after an extremely wily quarry. "Tell me more about what happened with the locals – did they come in arms to the castle?"

"Did they...? Bladdy 'ell, not many! They were pretty riled up and all, a hundred of them, at least. We eventually managed to get a spokesman to speak with us and, along with the food, were able to return those poor kids to their families – that went a long way to helping our *credibility. As for De Soulis, his name is mud, mate. There was no talkin' to 'em!"*

"What are ye saying?"

"I'm saying that if you don't get to him first, you'd better be packing a dustpan and brush!"

"Could ye no' have stopped them? Asked them to leave him to us? We cannae have the lass caught up in a mini war – especially if they think all the nobility are like De Soulis."

Gleeson's sigh travelled through the comm. *"Mate, you know I'm as diplomatic as the next bloke."* The APC crew shared a look. Douglas, rather decently, covered the mic so that the snorts and guffaws would not travel back to further highlight the Australian's failure. *"But a lot of these people have lost family to that monster. Without his walls or his soldiers, they're seeing the best chance they're ever gonna get to put things right, and damn the consequences. Are they wrong?"*

It was Douglas' turn to sigh. "Morally, no," he admitted. "Historically, Ah'd have to check with Mr Beckett. Anyway, Ah dinnae have time to worry about that now. How quickly can you reach us?"

"Well, if you'll keep bladdy still for a minute, we can be there in maybe... twenty?"

"Sorry, Commander, that's nae good to me. We're close now – and as you say – we need to find them first as a matter of urgency. Sorry, laddie, but ye'll have just have to catch up. Ah'm activating this vehicle's beacon – texting the frequency now. We should have done this hours ago, sorry." He motioned for O'Brien to send the code.

"*Got it. This is not easy terrain and some of my boys aren't too experienced on dirt bikes, but we'll be with you as soon as we can, Captain.*

"*Oh, and just before you go. The locals were all heading up to a hilltop, about three klicks north-east of Hermitage Castle. It's a place they call Ninestane Rig. They say it's a stone circle where De Soulis enjoys getting up to his tricks. They were convinced he would head for it.*"

Douglas frowned as a memory from his childhood surfaced, screaming for attention. *Ninestane Rig.* That name was important. Always more interested in exploration and flying, he suddenly wished he had paid more attention to his father's blah-blah about their local history. *Well, there's no time to worry about it now, is there?*

"*Hope that helps,*" continued Gleeson with an analogue crackle. "*Now, don't you fellas do anything I wouldn't do, will ya? Over and out!*"

"Well, that's a carte blanche," O'Brien remarked drily.

Douglas wagged a finger. "Dinnae forget, we're the good guys. Now smash those trees down – we need a road!"

Sir William de Soulis froze, as still as a tenth stone in the centre of the ring while his men arranged protectively around him and the Princess Elizabeth. He held tightly onto the rope lashed about her wrists and closed his eyes. Despite the fracas around, he fell into a trancelike state, repeating over and over the mantra that would summon Redcap.

Wherever the shade was, he did not appear to be answering.

De Soulis cursed him for leaving when he was needed most. Eventually, he was forced to accept that they were on their own. Perhaps it was no great surprise that demons could not be trusted, and judging by the crowd circling them, a full and frank apology was not going to get him out of this, either. Worse, the peasants were growing bolder.

A man carrying a scythe stepped into the circle, hesitantly. When he did not in fact disappear in a puff of smoke, his eyes hardened to iron, matching the vicious grin horseshoeing up his face. "*Get 'em!*"

The invisible ring of superstition holding the locals at bay collapsed out of nonexistence, freeing them to stream between the stones like a tide no longer dammed. De Soulis only wished he could say the same for himself.

The three soldiers, their greatest threat besides De Soulis himself, were mobbed instantly. With so many beating them, De Soulis knew he would never see them again in this life as he backed to the edge of the circle.

Seeing his chance, Wally ran for it, haring back into the forest.

"*Coward!*" screamed De Soulis.

"Aye!" the reply shot back from the trees.

"Son of a whore!"

"Och, aye. That *tae!*" came a second, very definitely and unapologetically Doppler shifting away from him.

A few men separated from the mob to give chase, but half-heartedly; quickly to return empty-handed. No one wanted to miss the finale to their orgy of violence and vengeance.

De Soulis held Bess to him like a shield, drawing his extra-long rapier with his free hand. He was a giant of a man, towering over the commoners surrounding him, but his black cape and frightening visage could not hold so many.

Even the terror of a man facing an enemy with powers beyond his understanding, may be reduced by numbers. The pack mentality of a hundred-person mob divides that fear between them – albeit with a penalty handicap bestowed upon the people at the front – only to recycle it into aggression.

Bess was snatched from his grasp and thrown unthinkingly to the snow-covered ground. Scrambling between the legs of the crowd, she was kicked unmercifully before she got far enough clear to regain her feet. Someone grabbed her by the hair and pulled her back, forcing the next queen of England to land the woman a beringed fist in the face.

With no time to tend her bruises, and before anyone else at the periphery of the engagement took an interest in her, she cast dignity to the wind and followed Wally's example, scarpering for her life into the treeline.

De Soulis was less fortunate. He briefly considered falling on his sword, but in less time than the thought took to process, he became pressed too closely to move. The sword was yanked from his hand as the mob grabbed whatever they could reach of him and lifted. Before he could even cry out, he found himself crowd-surfing his way back out of the stone circle.

While the men entrapped him, their wives and daughters had been far from idle. Lifted high above the heads of the mob, De Soulis could now see that a large pile of timber had already been amassed and the cauldron lifted down from the cart.

The stone circle vacated, they immediately suspended the heavy cauldron between the two largest stones and began filling it with snow. Meanwhile, others built a fire underneath, utilising kindling also from their cart. De Soulis kicked and wriggled with all his prodigious might, but despite their fear and poor diet, the villeins' forced labour in his fields had made them strong. They were also fuelled by an exultant bloodlust that left them wide-eyed and frenzied. No matter how he struggled, they had him.

Now mortally afraid, the fire was lit in what seemed like the blink of an eye for De Soulis. It soon began licking at the sides of the cauldron, melting the snow. While the flames' intensity grew, the villages fed ever more fuel into the conflagration until it roared – steaming wet timber cracking and hissing furiously.

"How did ye find me?" he bellowed. "Answer me, damn ye! How?"

"Drop him!" someone shouted, and the nobleman fell from head height onto his back, driving the wind from his lungs. "And *wrap* him!" the same self-appointed spokesman yelled, the light of anticipation burning bright in his eyes.

Coughing, De Soulis attempted to rise. "Tha Queen Regent will hear o' this – ye'll ne'er get away wi' it![20]"

"What did he say?"

"He said, we'll ne'er git awa' wi' it."

"*Really?*"

"Aye, Ah ken!"

---

20 Many great quotes have been handed down to us through history. Perhaps the least great of them all – but certainly not by volume – are variations on the idiom, "You'll never get away with it!" From royal villains to ordinary villains, from derring-do to Scooby Doo, this phrase must have been penned and spoken in extremis more than any other. Like a political manifesto, you know you have read it, but cannot quite believe it. In the interests of demarcation – and on the back of several complaints from the Pantomime Writers' Guild – the publisher apologises, and would have it known that a full retraction, along with some original cursing, has been earmarked for the second edition.

"Dae ye think he really believes it?"

"*That,* Ah dinnae ken. Let's wrap him up 'n' then we'll ask him."

De Soulis was furious. For a man so prideful that he once murdered another man of lesser station for having the audacity to save his life, being spoken about like he was not even there – by his own peasants – had him in spasms.

However, as good as their word, they began to wrap him up in the strips of lead from their cart. De Soulis, struggling for his life, nevertheless paused in shock and disbelief. There was a familiar detail in the material; he recognised it as belonging to a finial. Adding to his ignominy, he realised that this was *his* lead. "That's ma chapel roof, ye damned thieving serfs!"

His only reply was laughter. Moments later, mummified in lead but for the eyes, he was once again hefted onto powerful shoulders and carried towards the fire and its cauldron of now-boiling water.

They dropped him, rigid, onto his feet. "Have ye any last words, ye monster, ye?" the same man asked. Only muffled shouting came from De Soulis in his lead cocoon. Much to the merriment of all, their spokesman cupped his ear theatrically. "Ah'm sorry, ye'll have tae speak up, Wullie!"

"Ye'll pay fer this![21]"

The farmer turned back to De Soulis, all traces of gallows humour leaving him instantly. "Ye took ma Elspeth, ma wee girl. She was eight! Just eight year auld – she hadnae lived!" He spat at De Soulis and spun around to the crowd. "If he cannae be cut wi' steel nor bound wi' rope, let's see how he fares boiled in lead! Hid first!"

A roar of affirmation filled the clearing and above it all, the screams of De Soulis carried down into the valleys.

"We're close now, James," said Meritus, turning in his seat. "No more than fifty metres. We're starting to get infrared readings, too. At least a hundred people and what looks like a large fire. The trees are thinning – I think there's a clearing ahead."

---

21 Once again, the publisher apologises, but for such a theatrical execution, certain idioms and their use are pretty much, *ahem,* 'carved in stone'.

The APC crashed through the treeline, dragging at least a ton of arboreal detritus along with it. Six horses were tied to their left, all of them whinnying in panic. To their right, a crowd of villagers amassed, bunching up close to one another in terror as the monstrous vehicle burst from the forest.

"May I suggest we don't use the public address system to calm them," Meritus added.

"Seconded," said O'Brien. "That really didn't work out so well with those priests, last time."

"Really?" Douglas nodded. "Understood. Ah only hope De Soulis' jail can cope with all the bad guys we've collected!"

With the squeak of brakes, O'Brien brought them to an abrupt, rocking stop, just outside the stone circle. "Well, I think De Soulis himself has just made room for one more, Captain."

"How's that, Corp?" Douglas craned to see through the forward viewscreen. "Tell me Ah didnae just see a boot disappear into that pot."

O'Brien whistled. "Face down." She turned slowly. "There's a possibility we might be too late, gentlemen."

Bess was exhausted and starving, yet she ran. Lost in the woods and barely able to lift her legs any longer, she tripped over a clump of stubborn underbrush and collapsed, panting. In the near distance she heard the roar of the local people as they did whatever they were doing to De Soulis, but she could find no pity for the man. The things she had heard in his cells, especially the children, she would never forget.

Too tired to move, she thought, *What now?* The forest floor beneath her had caught very little of the day's sun, still less of its heat. The sweat on her brow cooled quickly, causing her to shiver. She dug deep for the strength to move again when the breath caught in her throat.

A *crack* from the trees, somewhere away to her left.

She remained perfectly still, listening hard. Hearing nothing but the blood rushing in her ears, she crawled on her belly to a gnarled tree stump. Looking gingerly around its sides, she scanned the forest. Even after the autumn fall, the trees were as tightly packed as a hedgerow. They tore clothes and skin mercilessly, resisting all her efforts to escape.

Snap.

That was closer. I am hunted, but by whom – or what? Holding on to the stump, she raised herself slightly, the better to see. Her skin crawled with trepidation. She needed to run, but was no longer sure if she could. Her body was battered and stiff from days of ill treatment and complained at every movement.

Holding her breath, she listened again. *Is that the growling of some sort of animal?* Not daring to hypothesise on its type, she noted that the growl coincided with a slight vibration through the earth beneath her freezing cold knees. Laying a palm on the ground, she could feel it becoming stronger, the noise closer.

"Got ye!" A hand reached across her mouth from behind, pulling her backwards. "Thought ye could flee us, lass, eh?"

Bess recognised the foul stench of her jailer as she fought to remove his hand from her face. "Release me, stinking cur!"

His chuckle was low, rasping and seedy. Bess heard the *siss* of his long knife drawing from its sheath. In a moment, it was at her throat. "Tha master may be gan, but ye'll fetch a fine price where Ah'm going."

The rumble and growl from the clearing seemed to have lessened, only to be replaced by screams of group panic. Both Bess and her captor looked back, instinctively. "Let's no' stay tae find oot what that's all aboot. *Shift it!*"

Wally dragged her roughly to her feet and shoved her forward. Stumbling, she tried to break free, but the small man was wiry strong, his grip like iron. All manner of shouts and cries followed them from the clearing, including a shrill, keening sound that stopped abruptly. Wally shuddered, in spite of himself. "He's gone then," was all he could say.

A little further, they broke out onto the path they used earlier. It was not as they had left it. Wide enough for two carts to pass and barely recognisable, the trees seemed to have been pulled out by their roots or pushed aside when their pursuit smashed its way through. The tunnel through the trees was roughly rectangular and much taller than a man.

Wally took a moment to look back and forth in amazement, along what was now a road. He had only seen the steel beast in the far distance, and knew it carried men inside its belly, but the strange tracks on the ground made it appear that the thing walked with some sort of grill on each foot, though he could not fathom how it moved. He grabbed Bess' arm with his left hand and, with the long knife in his right, marched back towards the main trail.

As they drew near the junction, they heard voices calling out to one another.

Wally instinctively pulled back into the trees, dragging Bess after him. They listened.

"Are we near?" A man's voice with a strange manner to it.

"Yeah, pretty sure, Commander."

"Right. Ah, yeah. Kinda hard to miss that, mate. Looks like a bladdy bulldozer's been through there. Come on, before we miss out on all the fun."

Bess thought she recognised that voice, and its bizarre mode of speech. Before she could move or make any kind of call for help, Wally brought his knife close to her throat once more. His breath, as he leaned in close to whisper, made her empty stomach churn in disgust. "No' one word from ye, lass, or Ah'll—"

"HELP!" she screamed.

"Ya silly boot!"

Of the six riders, Gleeson was in the lead. Hearing the scream, he slammed on the brakes. It was getting dark under the canopy. So, with his hand on the front brake, he throttled up the motor to spin the back wheel, using his leg to slew the bike, and its headlamp, in the direction of the cry. "Well bagger me, we've found her!" He kicked down his side stand and stepped off, swinging the rifle from around his shoulders in one easy motion. "No need to do this the hard way, mate. Just let the girl go."

"Come another step 'n' Ah'll cut her throat!"

"He will not! I am worth a queen's ransom."

"OK, mate. Enough's enough. Just put her down, gently."

"Ah'll kill her!"

"She says you won't."

"Ah'll dae it!"

Bess pulled at the elbow of his right hand, to gain a little clearance from the blade. "He would not dare, Commander."

"Dinnae push me!" Wally's voice was desperate now.

"Well, hey nonny no," chuckled Gleeson, switching on his rifle's laser sight. "You know, when somebody threatens three times in a row and still does bagger all about it, it means they're not going to follow through – so let her go." He sighed witheringly. "Listen mate, I don't want to shoot you, but—" The single shot *bang* from his assault rifle interrupted him. "OK. Maybe I did, a *bit*."

Wally shrieked, dropping his blade. He clutched his useless right arm with his left and vanished into the trees like a ferret.

"Ah, let him go. We've got the Sheila. Come out, sweetheart, you're safe now."

Despite her ordeal, Elizabeth patted down her dress, arranged her hair as best she could and walked straight-backed from the trees, showing all the bearing of a queen.

The Sarge kept a watchful eye on the entire clearing from atop the armoured personnel carrier. Rifle in hand, ready to stun any transgressors, he did not entirely trust the villagers. They had lived in the shadow of Hermitage Castle and its monstrous Lord de Soulis for years, finally winning their freedom through an extraordinary act of retribution. The Sarge knew such things left their mark. He did not blame them; he simply watched.

Off to his right, Douglas scratched his head. "Ah'm glad Ah dinnae have to put this one in a report." Before him, the villagers had already dug a grave pit in the centre of the stone circle at Ninestane Rig. "Historic Environment Scotland are going to have a cow when they schedule this place."

The diggers were just helping one another out of the hole when Meritus returned from a strenuous conversation with the villagers' spokesman. "What's that you were saying, James?"

"Oh, just muttering to myself. How did it go with the locals in the end?"

"Would have probably gone a little easier had you been there. I was struggling with the accent and dialect, some. However, long story short – they did see a girl dressed in expensive, if tattered, clothing. She ran away and no one paid too much attention to her after tha—"

A burst of static brought Douglas' comm to life. "*Captain? It's Gleeson.*"

Douglas pulled it from his pocket. "Commander, we *sort* of have things under control here now. Are ye very far away?"

"*Just a few hundred metres down the road you made through the trees, Cap, but I wondered if you would come to us. We have the girl. She's OK, but in no state to go pillion. She needs a ride – all the way back to Flannigan's ward, if you'll take my advice, sir.*"

"Excellent work, Commander! Send a couple of your people on to us. Captain Meritus will remain here to witness, er... what's happening, but he'll need a ride home afterwards."

"*Righto, Captain. They're on their way. Prentice is a little saddle-sore, I'm sure he won't mind a ride back in the tank. Tobo can have his bike. By the way, what* is *happening there?*"

"It's a very long story. Ah'll fill ye in later. Douglas out."

As he signed off, the melted and fused remains of one of the Borders' most infamous butchers, Sir William de Soulis, were *poured* into the ground.

Douglas turned to Meritus. "Boiled alive in a lead overcoat – he willnae be coming back from that."

"De Soulis... come to me..."

Strange. Ah thought Ah was going tae die in that boiling pot. Why can Ah hear a voice?

"De Soulis, *focus.* This is your one chance, or it will be oblivion for you. Come to me... Follow my voice..."

Redcap? Is that you? How am Ah still thinking – surely Ah'm—

"Oh, yes. You are. Quite. Being boiled in lead will do that to a body – now *focus.*"

But if Ah'm dead, how can Ah hear ye?

"Worry about that later."

So, ye're going tae help me – now?

"Yes."

Could ye no' have come a little sooner?

"Let's just say I have my own problems at the moment. I've been, for want of a better word, wounded – quite badly. This is all I can do for you – exorcism's a bitch! Now come."

Where?

"To the next level."

What does that mean?

"You'll see. *Come on,* William!"

Enchanted, Captain Jill Baines walked around the great hall within Hermitage Castle's Douglas Tower. She had seen it before, she knew, but it was like trying to reconstruct a dream from snatched, corner-of-the-eye recollections. A Baines from her youth leapt to the fore excitedly, marvelling at the architectural details of a *living* castle – not to mention the tapestries and wall hangings, even the floors. *What I wouldn't have given to see all this when I was a student. Incredible.*

Beck and Mother Sarah had clamoured to see her, ever since she regained consciousness, but she was not ready to have that conversation just yet, choosing instead to catch a flight back to the *locus in quo* – where she had almost died, *twice.*

What happened when she was last here left her with an impression of importance, but very little else. She had to cement it all together for fear of losing it beyond recall. Whatever Redcap was, it seemed he was gone, but gone forever?

Beck's words haunted her. '*All I'm sure of is this – if I can't make you believe now, by the time you do, it will be too late.*'

Was it too late? Or had she done enough to salvage things, barely? Hoping for the best was to court disaster. She could not simply assume it was all over; this was a reprieve, nothing more. Beck and Sarah would bombard her with questions upon her return and she knew that if the answers were anywhere, they were here.

Her musings were cut short by the approach of Lord Maxwell and Sir Nicholas Throckmorton. Neither man looked particularly happy. She had expected this. It was time to divvy up the spoils – trouble was, these two were probably spoilt enough.

Despite her concerns, she painted on a smile for them. "Please, won't you take a seat by the fire, my lords." Her attempts at conviviality fell on stony ground.

"Captain," Maxwell began immediately, "Hermitage Castle should be mine. Ah have the men tae garrison her and from here Ah can pacify all o' Liddesdale!"

"Unacceptable!" Sir Nicholas remonstrated, banging a fist on the arm of his chair. "For an enemy of the Crown to be ensconced so, and so close to our borders, is—"

"Gentlemen, *please.*" She took a deep breath as she studied them. "No one could accuse the two of you of prevaricating, I'll give you that." With a mischievous smirk, she added, "You haven't even asked me how I am."

Both men cleared their throats uncomfortably before making passable enquiries.

"I'm very well, thank you – all mended. Now I do understand your concerns regarding this castle. It's a powerful piece on the board with great strategic value along the Middle Marches." She looked directly at Sir Nicholas. "I also understand that several of her past lords were, shall we say 'amenable' to English... let's use the word 'influence'. I'm sure life in the Borders can be complicated, with some double dealing necessary for survival in such a fraught location – so let's not pass judgement on that. I can see why Lord Maxwell might not be your first choice, Sir Nicholas, but he *has* helped us – more than any other since we arrived here – and by doing so, has also assisted in the search for the Princess Elizabeth."

The noblemen looked away from one another, like schoolboys sitting in the headmaster's office after a fight in the playground.

"If we can find *her,* we may be able to get our history, and your lives, back on track. Perhaps all our efforts here might even usher in a new era of cooperation between your nations, hmm?

"With benefit of hindsight, we know, and most importantly, Lord Maxwell now knows, that Elizabeth will help her fellow Brits up in Scotland within the next two years – so it is surely in everyone's interests for him to hold Hermitage, at least for a while. We can hardly give it to an Englishman. Mary of Guise would have her French troops here by tomorrow afternoon!"

"Aye! The lass has some sense, eh?" cried Maxwell. Clapping his hands and rubbing them together, he gave Sir Nicholas a roistering thump on the arm.

Conversely, Sir Nicholas' expression more resembled that of a man answering the call, in darkest night, only to discover a gift from the family pet as it squelches between his toes. He did not actually swear, but the effort of internalising was clear on his face.

Baines did feel for the man. He only had his country's best interests at heart, but as the girl with a spaceship parked outside was calling the shots, there was little he could do to change the situation. She sought for a way to make things easier, when Corporal Jones strode across the hall and saluted before them.

"What is it, Dewi?" she asked, happy for the interruption.

Jones' face was not designed for smiling, but he did his best. "They've found her, Captain."

Sir Nicholas' face lit up immediately and he jumped from his chair. "Where? Doth she live? *Jones?*" He grabbed the lapels of Jones' tunic, attempting to shake the giant Welshman in his eagerness for news.

Jones gently peeled the nobleman off him. "She is well, sir. Captain Douglas has her safe in the AP— in the belly of our steel beast, isn' it."

"Is James taking her back to the *New World?*"

"Yes, ma'am. Apparently, she's picked up a few bruises, but nothing that won't be fixed by Dr Flannigan's care and a good meal."

"Excellent. You'll be wanting to go and see her, I expect, Sir Nicholas?" asked Baines, smiling. "I'll fly you back with me."

Throckmorton's ruddy enthusiasm paled. He turned to Maxwell. "Doth my lord have a mount for lending? Or hire? I have a purse of silver...?"

Baines laughed. "You'll be safe enough with me, Sir Nicholas. The quicker you're back with the princess the better, eh?"

She turned back to Maxwell, who remained seated by the fire. "And I assume you'll wish to stay here and begin reparations?"

The Scottish lord nodded, looking around greedily. "Will ye no' mend tha door yer man blew to smithereens, Captain?"

Baines' smile broadened, but without reaching her eyes. "Don't push it, Dave."

Chapter 8 | You Can't
Make an Omelette...

Lieutenant Devon watched the video intently. Sergeant Denholm Haig had been deliberately killed while they were mining uranium from the moon, that much was clear, and was reason for concern. The fact that it hardly seemed to matter to their captain or leaders also bothered him. He hoped their security footage would provide answers.

A keen military man, Devon knew he was guilty of a certain overzealousness when it came to weapons testing – even when that testing was carried out at an enemy's expense. After years of drill and training, any soldier would wish to put his hard-won skills to use, but there were limits. He was not a murderer.

Haig was originally rostered to the *Eisernes Kreuz*, the Old Man's flagship. After her destruction, he was rescued by Heidi and the then-Lieutenant Aito Nassaki before boarding the *Sabre*. Abandoned on an island off the west coast of Cretaceous Africa – when Captain Emilia Franke stole the *Sabre*, taking her for their last fateful journey – he had finally joined the crew of the *Heydrich*. Having been so widely posted, Devon knew the odds were against him in trying to solve the puzzle of Haig's death. He himself had known the sergeant only slightly. However, a seemingly diligent and upright soldier should not be so easily discarded and forgotten, and Devon intended to get to the bottom of it.

While the *Heydrich*'s science team buzzed about the wormhole drive, panicking about something to do with the wormhole itself, there was not a great deal for the rest of the crew to do. Devon had made sure the basics were covered; fresh water, fresh meat, that kind of thing, but for the first time since they had landed on Cretaceous Earth, he had time on his hands. Determined to put it to good use, he watched and rewatched the security footage until his eyes begged for a break.

Pinching the bridge of his nose, he rubbed tiredness from his right eye while keeping his left on the screen. When the picture seemed to jump slightly, he wondered if his own actions had created the effect.

Suddenly alert, he reversed the video and played the section again, this time at half speed. There was definitely a glitch. Making a note of the time signature, he allowed the footage to play on, and sure enough, four minutes and twenty-eight seconds later, there was another.

Four and a half minutes of nothing *have been cut into this film,* he thought excitedly. *I'm getting close.*

He had tried to view the footage from Haig's short conversation with Old Man Schultz, and then Schultz's second conversation with his granddaughter soon afterward, but simply did not have the skills necessary to retrieve such information. It was not as though he could recruit any help with this matter, either. So he decided to focus on the storeroom where their spacesuits and oxygen tanks were kept, and now he had a lead. Playing the second glitch back slowly, he felt sure something had changed. He split the screen and paused the footage one second before, and one second after, the glitch.

It felt like solving a spot-the-difference puzzle in a Sunday ezine. Staring closely, his brows knitted. Almost giving up on the enterprise, a thought struck him. He zoomed in on the air tank itself, the one that was to be Haig's, a few hours after the footage was captured.

Was the tank at a slightly changed angle in the racks? He played a four second slice of the film, resampling and zooming in on that specific area. Haig's tank did indeed jump. The movement was so slight as to be invisible without determined scrutiny, but it was there.

Right. I have proof. Someone did indeed slice in stock footage to cover their movements. Now, how will I find the real *footage?*

Ironically, he was fairly sure that Captain Nassaki would be able to help, but unfortunately, he was also Devon's chief suspect. Doubt had first surfaced when his crew tried desperately to locate Haig, just minutes before that section of the moon was scheduled for incineration. Nassaki had seemed strangely resistant to finding the man or bringing him back aboard, even though the time remained to do so, barely. His behaviour struck Devon as out of character.

Then there was the fact that Nassaki and Haig had both been captives aboard the *New World*, if only briefly, and he felt certain that while there, Haig had heard something he should not have. Whether it was something Nassaki had said – perhaps to his brother – or something that had been said about him, he could not guess.

Devon also suspected Haig of passing this information to the Old Man during their secret liaison, while Heinrich had been imprisoned aboard his own ship. Whatever their conversation entailed, the Old Man, for reasons known only to himself, had kept it *to* himself.

He sat back and sighed, rubbing his eyes again. *I need some technical help, but from whom?*

Devon's alarm went off at 3am. He sat up and stretched, rubbed his eyes, scratched his man-parts and pulled on his trousers.

Moments later, he was heading for the brig with a networked tablet under his arm. There was no one around. The guards were all posted elsewhere – *he* had posted them. Using the deceased Sergeant Haig's security code to open the hatch – a nice touch, he thought – he strode into the brig and froze.

"You're up late, Lieutenant," stated Heidi.

Factory Pod 4, USS *New World*, AD1558

"Donald, can you hear me? Donald, it's me, darling. Can you *see* me?"

Dr Donald Parrot had fallen asleep at his desk, again. Dr Patel had all his science team run ragged in what he called 'one last push to get us home'. Donald had his doubts. What Patel asked of them had never been attempted before – at least as far as they knew – and all they had to work with was cannibalised equipment from a broken ship. Not an ideal research environment.

It was not as though they could even pop out for a coffee or a stroll to clear their heads, either. The world outside was practically a war zone, and senior brass had warned most strenuously against wandering far from their front door. As if they did not have enough woes already, there were slavers about.

Donald was exhausted, mentally and physically. The one benefit he could draw from the insanity of their lives over the last few months, was that he was always too busy to dwell on the murder of his beloved.

"Donald?"

Still half asleep, he yawned. His mouth felt like a bear pit. Was someone calling him?

He looked around blearily – no one there.

"*Donald!*"

He rubbed his hands down his face, then massaged sleep from his eyes. "Great. Now I'm hearing voices. That's not good."

"Donald, it's me, Jamie."

"*Really* not good," he answered himself.

"You're not going crazy – it really is me! Can you hear me?"

"Jamie?"

"*Finally!*"

"Wha' – how – *what?*" Awake and alarmed now, Donald jumped from his seat and looked around his small office for any explanation for what he was hearing. His comm was switched off – dead battery.

"Sorry, that was me," said Jamie's voice. "I needed energy, so I drained its power."

His terminal had gone to sleep when he had, and remained in standby mode, and his door was closed against extraneous noise. "OK, now I'm freaked. Get a grip, Donald. It must have been a dream – that's all. Some type of hypnopompic hallucination. Yes, that's it. Nothing to worry about."

"No, it wasn't."

He jumped like a pond skater. "What the hell?"

"Donald, focus. Concentrate. I'm here, right here. Please try."

Before his tired eyes, an apparition shimmered into being – and what an apparition. It was the one person he most longed to see. However, on the downside, this was clear evidence that he was in fact losing his mind.

"*Jamie?*" He stared in total disbelief. "Jamie *Ferguson?*"

The apparition frowned back at him. "As opposed *to?*" Her forehead wrinkled in that familiar way it always had when she became annoyed or frustrated with him. Jamie's ghost glared impatiently, yet it was the most beautiful sight he had ever seen. It broke his heart. He reached out for her, to hold her close and never let go.

"Yes. Sorry about that, too." Her expression changed to regret as his arms closed about nothing at all.

"But... how is this possible?" was all he could manage.

"Perhaps you should sit down, darling," Jamie suggested kindly. "Actually, this is only possible because of my connection with you. Some links cannot be broken – even in death. I know that sounds a little pat, but actually, it's true."

Donald sat automatically, without even realising. He tried but could not find a single thing to say.

"Don't worry, dear. Let me explain," she soothed. "It seems there's vastly more psychic energy loose about the world in this time, than our own. Dr Patel would probably call it a *superfluity.*" She shrugged. "Have to admit, it's a fairly stark indictment of the twenty-second century, when you consider *our* population is more than a hundred times greater."

Bafflement joined shock on Donald's face.

Jamie elucidated, "You see, in the past – *these* times, if you will – people's minds lacked access to the sort of knowledge we take for granted. However, unfettered by the crutches we use to prop up *our* intellects, their psyches were actually far more powerful. Stripped of all aids and short-cuts, their minds had to *work,* you see?"

Donald was *at* sea. "How? And what does this have to do with your... your *condition?*"

"To answer your first question – our minds have been blunted by holos, TV, social media and the endless scrolling that erodes our minds like sandpaper. These people had none of those things. Everything had to be worked out – calculated from scratch from basic principles.

"They had no distractions at all, unless they made them themselves. They created their own entertainment – created their own world, in fact. What I'm saying is, rather than scour them clean with transient 'media', they *lived* in their own minds.

"Add all that to a binding and sincere belief in many things we would mock as mere hocus pocus – or at best, religion – and you breed an environment where we can harness enough psychic energy to penetrate the veil, as it were, and touch the ones we love."

"And the others...?" was all Donald could think to ask.

"Mario has found his brother, Georgio – no surprise there. The only one of us still struggling to regroup is Aabid Hussain—"

"*Him!* But he—"

"Oh, don't be so *corporeal,* Donald. Honestly. His part in what happened to us is all in the past now."

"Not for me it isn't." For the first time, Donald looked angry. "He was part of the group who took you from me."

"Perhaps. But we *will* be together again – we all will, in the end. I know it sounds obvious, but we're all made of the same star-stuff and, whatever we are, whatever we do, that's just inevitable. You'll see. And part of me will always be with you, Donald. You know that, right?"

His anger crumpled as he held a shaking hand to her face.

"This has all been a shock. I'm sorry, sweetie." Jamie continued, holding out her own hand to wipe his tear. He saw it, but felt nothing.

She smiled, kindly. "Thank you for being there for me – my anchor. You see, we've encountered a negative entity. One we brought with us from the Cretaceous, actually. A man Captain Baines had no choice but to kill, to save all our people from the Nazis. However, for the reasons I've described, he has extraordinary strength here."

Donald frowned with concern. "You're in *danger? Now?*"

She smiled again. "Some things don't change, darling. But don't worry. He dispersed us, but your love brought me back. As did the love of others on this crew, for my friends. We're all one – remember that. And I'm sure we'll help Aabid back, too, when we have our full strength again. Luckily, Captain Baines fought off the negative one, and with the help of a clumsy, long-distance exorcism – courtesy of Mother Sarah and Beck Mawar – he seems to have been sent away. At least for a while."

Donald looked afraid. She knew his fear was for her and so played the situation down. "I'm sure they'll be able to fully deal with him, now they've had a trial run. You know Captain Baines. God help anyone who threatens her people, right? So I don't want you to worry."

"Of course not!" he answered caustically. "The soul of the woman I love has apparently been saved by a demon exorcism. I wasn't concerned!"

"Now, now, Donald. Sarcasm doesn't become you. I just wanted you to know that we're grateful, and most importantly, that I still love you. You *will* get home, Donald. You're brilliant. And with the help of your brilliant friends, you'll put everything right again, you'll see.

"Now, it tires me to show myself like this – I haven't yet regained my full strength – so I'll say goodbye for now. Take proper care of yourself!" Her expression softened. "I love you."

She reached forward to gently touch his temple as she faded.

"I love you, too," Donald confessed to the empty room.

"I know that, silly," shot back a disembodied voice.

Donald placed a hand to his temple, where she had touched him, his smile, at once sad and yet hopeful. Taking the hand away, he sat quickly and brought his terminal to life with a zeal he had not felt in months.

He placed a call.

The screen came to life with the face of a very weary-looking Dr Patel.

Donald grinned. "Satnam, I've got an idea!"

"Dr *Schultz?*" Hardly a game-changing rejoinder, but it was past three in the morning and the best he could do.

"How observant of you, Devon." Heidi could be sharp at any hour – her bluntness cutting right to the point.

"But you...? Sorry, ma'am, I didn't realise you were... I mean, I—"

"Did not realise I was back? Then I am consequently forced to deduce that you did not drop in here to find me. That must surely mean your intention was, in fact, to speak with the prisoners – yes? Now, perhaps you will tell me, *why?*"

Devon swallowed. He was about to respond, when the word *prisoners* snagged at him. Plural. He had spent most of the last day and night in solitude, reviewing security footage, and expected to speak with Anne Hemmings alone. However, along with 'Two', as Heidi so derisively called her, the brig now seemed to have a second inmate, in the next cell.

Unfortunately for him, Heidi was most definitely *not* in a cell. However, Devon was struck by a certain resemblance between the new, rather drawn yet beautiful, blond prisoner, and his boss.

"You are no doubt thinking, she looks like myself," Heidi stated, incisive as ever. "You may also be gratified, possibly even a little confused, to learn that her name is also Dr Heidi Schultz. Dr Heidi Schultz, may I introduce Lieutenant Devon." Entertained by his bafflement, Heidi's eyebrow rose as she spoke. "What can I say, several generations of careful breeding pays."

Devon could hardly prevent the phrase '*in-breeding, more like*' from trotting across his mind. Fortunately, he had by now recovered enough of his senses to prevent it from falling out of his mouth on the way through. Heidi was, no question, one of the most perfect physical specimens he had ever seen, but there was also most definitely something *very* wrong with her.

Perplexed and off balance, the situation was getting away from him, as she had clearly intended. A jolt of adrenalin shot through his system, waking him to the danger of his confession. What could he possibly say that might convince Heidi that he had any agenda other than to speak with Hemmings?

"I see you have a tablet under your arm. Are you planning some sort of jailbreak? Perhaps a mutiny, hmm?"

Devon swallowed again and could see but one course of action – tell the truth. "I came for help breaking into our security files, ma'am. I believe I'm getting close to finding the murderer of Sergeant Denholm Haig."

"Who?" Heidi asked, uninterestedly.

"He died on the moon, ma'am."

"Ah, yes. The man in the moon. How quaint. Yet he proved useful in the end, did he not? Supplying us with the parts we needed to forward our isotope through time."

Devon's expression darkened. "*Yes,* ma'am."

"And if you discover his murderer, what do you intend to do, then? How will this change things?"

"I believe the reason for his *removal* might be important, ma'am. There may even be a... a *fifth columnist* working among us."

"How interesting. And who do you suspect?"

He most certainly was not going to offer that information without proof. Instead, he admitted, "That's why I needed Dr Hemmings' help – to crack the security footage, ma'am."

"Have you mentioned this to *mein Großvater?*"

Devon chewed his lip.

"Speak," she prompted, sternly.

"I think he may already know, ma'am. Haig visited him in this very cell, just before he was killed. I'm trying to put the pieces together, so that—"

"If *mein Großvater* already knows about it, perhaps *he* ordered Haig's death," she interrupted.

"I thought of that, ma'am, but he was powerless in this jail cell at the time."

Heidi gave him a wintry smile. "And?"

He had to concede that point, so he jumped tracks. "*And* I think that if he *was* killed, without authorisation, then there is something very wrong going on in our ranks – and we should know about it!"

Tired and on the back foot, his tone was harsh. However, rather than object, Heidi seemed to consider his words. "Very well. I will allow you to proceed with the help of Two, here. *But!* Whatever you do discover, you will bring it to *me*. Do I make myself clear, Lieutenant?"

Devon clicked his heels in salute. "Of course, ma'am." His mind reeled. He had expected serious trouble for being found collaborating with a prisoner – not to mention bringing her a networked tablet – but *if* he was clear of that, then what *would* his investigation turn up? The best thing about working for Heidi was that one could get away with literally anything, if she approved of the thinking behind an action and endorsed it.

The trouble was, if Nassaki did turn out to be the murderer, where would that leave the crew's coalition against the Schultzes? He massaged his temple. One problem at a time.

Heidi broke into his thoughts. "At the moment, we seem to have larger problems."

"Ma'am?"

"The wormhole we created continues to expand, and the rate is accelerating. Two, perhaps you would explain?"

Hemmings glared at Heidi. Still in her nightclothes, she pulled her dressing gown tight around her and retied its belt. "It appears that the wormhole is increasing at a logarithmic rate. We sometimes use logarithms to calculate atomic half-lives, so perhaps there is a causal link between the rate of growth of our isotope-tracking wormhole and the rate of our isotope's decay – or perhaps the connection is just a little universal irony."

Heidi crossed her arms angrily.

"Well, we don't know!" Hemmings spat. "And it is frankly no longer any of my concern. Now, goodnight!"

Heidi did not move. "I have made it your concern, Two. What can we expect?"

"A bigger wormhole – was I not clear?"

Devon scratched his ear with embarrassment; the loathing between these two was palpable. "If I may just ask, ladies, how *much* bigger?"

"That depends on when it runs out of power," answered Hemmings, casually.

Devon frowned. "But I thought it was drawing power from the planet's core?"

"So it won't run out of power for quite some time, will it? Look, what do you want from me?" Hemmings snapped reproachfully. "I told you not to open a wormhole through the planet until we were sure what the effects might be – but did anyone listen?"

"I'd like you to answer Devon's question," Heidi stated flatly. "How big will the wormhole become?"

It was Hemmings' turn to cross her arms, a weak smile tugging at her lips. "How much will the wormhole expand... hmm. With the power of our molten core, which has burned for billions of years and will burn for billions more, I would say, roughly... now, let me see, carry the three... hmm, yes. About as big as the planet itself."

"It will eat the *world?*" shouted Devon, his voice cracking.

Hemmings' smile broadened. "We Schultzes do think big, don't we?"

Heidi had barely swallowed the first instalment when this new horror launched itself upon her. "*We* Schultzes...?"

Jansen stretched, luxuriating in the freedom of an open collar. "It feels good to be back in fatigues again."

Heidi gave a half-smile. "I thought the tux rather suited you."

They geared up together in the *Heydrich*'s small hangar. Heidi stuffed two small cases into her flak jacket pockets, each containing four darts. She handed two similar packs to Jansen.

"Tranquilisers?" he asked.

"Concentrated carfentanil, yes. Each dart contains enough tranquiliser to knock out an elephant."

"Sounds a bit lightweight."

She shrugged. "If you recall, our original mission called for us to travel back just 100,000 years, to the Middle Palaeolithic. Early man had just about begun to place one block of stone on top of another by then. They would have made an exemplary slave labour force. Obviously, we expected a few wildlife issues – large elephants, possibly even mammoths, hippopotami, tigers, crocodiles and such. Had we realised how unsafe Geoff Lloyd would prove himself, or how spectacularly he would mess things up, we would have packed something with more kick – hence we are taking sixteen darts between us and an air rifle each."

"And if we have an accident?"

"If you are stupid enough to shoot yourself with elephant tranquiliser, things will not be so good for you, I think. However, if it makes you feel better, I will also take a pack of these." Heidi held up a small case with four syringes inside. "Naloxone. It's an opioid blocker. It might save you, if I'm quick enough."

"So *I'm* doing all the shooting?" Jansen asked, feeling sure of the answer.

Heidi surprised him. "On the contrary. I am simply reinforcing that *I* would never be stupid enough to shoot myself." She crammed the needles into a remaining pocket with a haughty expression.

Jansen frowned but changed the subject. "Have you decided what we're going after?"

"Indeed. I assume you remember the magnificent beast that cut us off from our ship, back when we were hunting spinosaurs?"

"The Carcharo-wossname?"

"Carcharodontosaurus, yes."

He looked at her askance. "You want to track *that* thing?"

"Not that one, specifically. Besides, we shall need a nesting pair."

Jansen's ears actually drooped at this revelation. "Can I await the outcome in Munich? I hear it's beautiful this time of year."

She smiled coolly. "But it's autumn there."

"And it'll be the autumn of our days, here, if we go with *your* plan."

"Really, Ben. You are becoming quite the old woman! Anyhow, as I was saying, we find a nesting pair of carcharodontosaurs. You see, using a little imagination, I placed myself in the minds of the world's greediest men—"

"Or women," he murmured.

Heidi glared at him. "The world's greediest *men*. Naturally, I had to compensate for their lack of imagination—"

"*Naturally.*"

"*Lack* of imagination," she repeated tersely, "and came to the following conclusion. They would want to own a Tyrannosaurus rex – which they would, of course, dumb down to *T* rex."

"But we don't have any T rexes," offered Jansen. "Not for millions of years, if I understand correctly."

"I *am* aware of it. What I am saying is, these unimaginative, greedy *men* will *want* a T rex, and that is what they will see. They will not be able to tell the difference. And there will be no point in trying to educate them as to the existence of a completely parallel line of theropod killers, who also reached gargantuan proportions tens of millions of years before the derived, iconic tyrannosaurs. They will simply see a T rex. So we shall simply *sell them* a T rex."

"Simply, eh?"

"Indeed. Come. We go."

"Wait, ma'am. May I ask a question?"

"Very well."

"When you were aboard the *New World,* after Lloyd set his bomb. You must have realised quite soon after, that your plan had gone seriously wrong. Almost a hundred million years wrong."

"Your point?"

"Weren't you supposed to destroy all evidence, in case NASA came poking around?"

She nodded. "I did attempt to destroy the *New World,* while it was still in space."

"You failed?" he asked in genuine astonishment.

"After a fashion."

He stared, waiting for more.

Heidi sighed. "I decided on a new strategy. Trust me, I had my reasons."

"May I ask what they were?"

"Of course."

"Will you answer?"

"Not today. Come. Let us move out."

"Captain Baines? It's Jonesy here, isn'it. I think we may have a problem. Two bodies of armed men moving towards us – that is, towards Hermitage Castle."

"Two armies to deal with before our morning coffee, eh? Well, I suppose it wasn't completely unexpected. We haven't exactly kept a low profile of late, have we? Do you know who they are?"

"Lord Maxwell's scouts tell us the nearest party are the Maxwell relief force, en route to take charge of the castle."

"If they're nearest, that's good news, Dewi, surely?"

"They're nearest, yes, but the *biggest* army are not friendlies, Captain."

"Who are they?"

"French troops, ma'am, and there are several hundred to Maxwell's few dozen."

"Great! I'm guessing the change of ownership up at Castle Grayskull hasn't gone unnoticed."

Jones chuckled. "You're remembering those old holotoon reruns, Captain? Never thought we'd actually meet Skeletor, though. Wasn't he meant to be in Snake Mountain?"

"If you look on your map, that's about seventy klicks north-east – a little place called Blackadder. Either way, we won't be hearing from him again, I hope."

"Skeletor or De Soulis?"

"Tomaytoes, tomartoes. What's Maxwell planning to do? Prepare for a siege?"

"What else *can* he do?"

A burst of static covered the worst of Baines' bad language. *"This is all we need! God knows what we've done to the timeline."*

"No point tamping and raging, Captain. Maybe we should just leave them to it, before we make things worse."

"*I hear you, Corporal, but leaving them to it might actually* make *things worse. Who can say? OK, help Maxwell fortify the place. Do you know how far out the two forces are?*"

"Maxwell's garrison are about four hours away – the French, maybe twice that."

"*Right. That gives us time to bolster their defences and get you and the others out of there before they show up.*"

"I like the sound of that, Captain, but if we *do* leave, we'll lose all control of events. Lord Maxwell's tamping, he is, about the French involvement, like. This could turn into the battle that should never have been."

"*That's brave, Dewi. Are you sure? The only way we'll be able to get you out of there will be to reveal all – I'm not sure Captain Douglas will wish to tip our hand to that degree.*"

"I understand, Captain. Outnumbered. Impossible odds. Just call me Dewi Glyndŵr."

"*Glyndŵr disappeared, Corporal.*"

"Don't worry, Captain *bach*. This is the rewrite, isn' it?"

"We've seen plenty of spinosaurs by the river, ma'am. Wouldn't one of those do?"

"No, Ben. We need *them* to carry our isotope throughout their natural lives or our Munich plan fails. They may even pass on the isotope via this generation's eggs. We cannot risk upsetting a plan we already know has worked."

Jansen blew out his cheeks as he looked out of the viewscreen from his co-pilot's seat. "This time travelling's hard to keep straight in your head. Just a thought. If we did *deliberately* scupper our own plans – so the isotope was never *present* in Stromer's Egyptian fossils – might that close this wormhole that's threatening to destroy the Earth?"

"No."

"No?"

"Time's arrow."

"Forget I mentioned it," Jansen murmured, refocusing on his instruments.

"There!" snapped Heidi, pointing ahead.

"Where?" he asked, simultaneously following her gaze and checking his instruments.

"There – *look!* Remind me again, what did I bring you for?"

"Oh, yes. I see them now, ma'am. On top of that low plateau."

"*So* glad. I'll put us down a klick to the west on that small hill. It should provide us with a panoramic view across those fern prairies."

"There are some *very* big animals down there, Doctor."

"They're only titanosaurs – Cretaceous cattle. Just keep out of their way, so they don't tread on you, and you will be fine."

"Hmm..."

Heidi sighed. "Alright, Ben, what is it?"

"Those huge long-necks are clustered near our target."

"And?"

"Well, it occurs to me that if they, too, are – can I use the word 'nesting' for something that weighs fifty tons and looks like two ostriches sewn together, back-to-back?"

"Nesting is accurate. What is your point?"

"There are bound to be egg snatchers, ma'am. Really fast ones."

"Ah..."

"Yer stayin' with us?" asked Lord Maxwell.

"Yes, sir," replied Jones. "Now Commander Gleeson has returned to help you hold the castle, there'll be ten of us. Also, Donald, De Soulis' captain, has offered the services of himself and his men."

Maxwell looked surprised at that. "Ah'm supposed tae trust him? A local man?"

"Perhaps *because* he's a local man, sir. His men have family in these valleys. And with the French coming and all... Of course, they'll want paying, boy."

"Oh, aye. Ah didnae see *that* coming! Tell him aye. Are ye sure you want to stand wi' us, Jonesy?"

"Captain Douglas still hopes we can keep the peace, sir."

Maxwell laughed. "And what would a Douglas ken aboot peace! Ah'll accept yer help, Corporal, but dinnae expect this tae go easy."

Jones took his comm from a pocket. "Time to try out the cameras Commander Gleeson placed in the path of the French."

The small screen came to life with movement. He opened it out to the size of a laptop screen and placed it on the trestle table before them. "Here they come. Do you recognise any of the officers, sir?"

Maxwell stared wide-eyed at the little screen, shaking his head ruefully. "I dinnae ken any o' them. And this is happening noo, three miles up the valley?"

"Yes, sir. Do you speak French?" Jones turned up the volume and they immediately heard the tramping of many feet and rumbling of male conversation.

Maxwell cocked his head to one side, listening hard. "Ma right ear's nae good from standing tae close tae one o' ma ain cannons, but it just sounds like soldiers' grumbling tae me. Nae help."

"Never mind, sir. We'll try again, when they reach the next camera, like."

"How d'ye make this happen, man?" Maxwell pointed at the screen in awe.

Jones took a small plastic box from his pocket. Opening it carefully, he showed Maxwell the pinhead camera and sensor array, wrapped in a gel pack and seated in the centre of the box. The Scottish lord bent to study it more closely. "Amazin'."

Jones waved his comm over the camera to activate it, adding it to his network. Maxwell's nose suddenly filled the centre of the comm screen.

"Is that me?" he exclaimed, jumping back. He raised his hands and lowered them, mesmerised.

Jones chuckled. "They'll be here in under an hour, sir."

"Aye," replied Maxwell, reaching up to clap Jones on a meaty shoulder. "But we'll be ready fo' 'em!"

"Perhaps you are right, Ben. It might be more dangerous on the ground than it appears. I'll take us in for a closer look." Heidi pulled the joystick back slightly and to the left, making their little ship climb and turn.

"Even from way up here our engine swell is panicking the animals," noted Jansen.

"You're right again. However, I think it will take more than that for a mother to abandon her nest." She threw the ship into a dive, levelling off at the approximate altitude of the nest in question, as it sat on the side of its plateau. Flicking a few switches, she armed weapons.

Jansen looked at her in astonishment. "You're going to try and—" His words were drowned by the launch of a missile. It was not a large missile, but the ship was going slowly enough for it to leave them behind instantly. "Scare it... *away?*" he finished lamely.

Heidi's plan turned out to be typically *Schultzian* in its directness. Most of the nesting mother's body evaporated in a flash of blinding heat, light and noise.

Jansen's jaw hung open. His last member of the majestic carcharodontosauridae had been glimpsed fleetingly, over a shoulder, while running for his life. He had never expected to feel sorry for one of them, but with Heidi, every day was a school day.

Before he could recover his wits, she was bringing their craft in to land, near the mess she had made.

They stepped out as the engines cycled down. Heidi ran straight for the nest. Over her shoulder, she called, "Bring the carry-cases— Oh... don't bother."

Jansen caught up and immediately understood why she had deflated. The dinosaur was now two legs, a head and a tail, at intervals around what looked to him like the biggest pavement pizza of all time – painted red. "I think you may have broken the eggs," he noted witheringly. "Was it always your intention to scramble them, only I thought we were poaching?"

From behind, there came a colossal *ROAR.*

Without even bothering to turn round, he shouted, "RUN!"

The thunder of massive feet shook the ground. Stumbling as he ran, Jansen cried, *"Daddy's home!"*

Their vessel was not far, but it was *too* far. Blind luck came to their rescue. He had been right, there *were* egg thieves about, and sure enough, tiny scavengers leapt from the ferns and cycads all around. Chirruping and calling, they snatched chunks of flesh in their jaws and ran, but the father's sudden return pushed and funnelled them back across the nest, turning Jansen's pizza parlour into a drive-through.

The distraction granted the humans a reprieve, a few precious seconds to cover the ground and throw themselves into the waiting ship's hatch.

They lay on their backs, chests heaving, finally daring to look behind. Even for the father-not-to-be, minced carcharodontosaur proved irresistible; certainly more so than a pair of tiny, two-legged running things, that did not smell of anything very much, and his presence on the scene put flight to the diminutive scavengers in a burst of faeces and feathers. Instantly nose deep in his mate's gore, he ignored the pygmies and their flight.

Jansen calmed his breathing and sat up. "He always said he loved her so much he could eat her all up."

"Theropod carnivores have long been attributed with cannibalism." She glanced at him. "Was that a joke, Ben? Only, I am never sure."

He shrugged. "So, do you have a plan B?"

"That *was* plan B."

The male dinosaur heard their voices and looked up from his feast to fix them with a furnace glare of unblinking malice.

Jansen gulped reflexively. "*Ooh,* he looks really annoyed."

Heidi scrambled over him in her urgency to reach the cockpit. Knocking the wind out of her bodyguard, she called, "Cut him some slack – he is from a broken home."

The engines were still hot and started immediately, which was fortunate, because angry theropods, even giant ones, were surprisingly quick off the mark when roused.

Carcharodontosaurus came on, roaring furiously as Heidi sealed the hatch and fired up the thrusters.

Dinosaurs over a certain weight were not jumpers, but this one had a spirited go. His jaws closed like a vice around their rear landing strut as the ship left the ground, pulling them down and sideways.

"Give it the beans!" screamed Jansen.

"I am!" she shouted back.

The animal attached was far from the largest of its species they had seen, but even as a young adult, he weighed many tons.

As the ship tipped, Jansen was on the side nearest the ground. "I thought this thing could lift ten tons?"

"For a properly centred load!" Heidi yelled as the ship pitched ever further. "Now tell me what is wrong with this picture!"

The dinosaur hung on with grim determination, flailing with arms, legs and tail. The small craft, already listing, wobbled terrifyingly with every movement it made as Heidi fought to keep them airborne.

The aerobatics could not continue; particularly with gravity on third fiddle, riffing an extremely mean 'baseline' below them.

"We are not going up," Heidi reported.

"I noticed!" Jansen panicked.

"So we must go down."

"*What?*"

Before he could remonstrate further, she allowed the ship to go *with* the weight of the dinosaur, rather than fight against it. It was a gamble, but she dared hope that their hanger-on was not enjoying himself any more than they were, so she dropped near the ground.

Heidi suspected the creature had grabbed them out of reflex. It seemed a safe assumption that nothing had *ever* picked *him* up before. As delicately as possible, she brought the ship down to five metres above the ground, where her gamble proved correct. The dinosaur simply unlocked his jaws and stepped off the ride.

With a bellow and tail-flick of indignance, he returned to his dinner – satisfied that he had scared away all comers.

Heidi expected the move. With perfect timing and the lightest touch, she arrested control from gravity's clutches and throttled the main engines up to a three-second, maximum burn.

Before Jansen could strap himself in, the little ship shot off like a missile, pressing him sideways across the co-pilot's seat. He vaguely remembered Heidi talking through the seconds running up to his blackout; something about returning to plan A.

"Open your gates, in the name of Mary of Guise, Queen Regent!" the mounted messenger demanded from the foot of their walls.

"Who's this French popinjay?" muttered Maxwell. "Ah can smell his perfume all tha way up here!"

Gleeson wrinkled his nose. "You're not wrong, mate."

"I like it," said Jones, inhaling deeply.

They stared at him.

"Reminds me of Christmas 2095, isn'it."

Gleeson and Maxwell looked at one another.

"How so?" the commander hazarded, cautiously.

"My mom gave my dad a Lynx Africa Centenary Boxset." He lapsed into reverie. "Only saw the old tosser at Christmas, after that."

Gleeson took a deep breath and blew it out slowly. "Look, perhaps we'd better just answer this bloke, I mean, if that's alright with you, Jonesy?"

"Carry on, boy. Don't let me stop you." Sarcasm was as impenetrable as any other chasm to Jones.

Maxwell leaned forward to bellow from the battlements. "Ah'm David, Lord Maxwell and Hermitage Castle is now *mine!*"

The man boomed from below, with all the practised cadence of a herald. "Your lands are well north of 'ere, my lord. We are instructed by the Crown to take charge of *le château*, this *'Ermitage*, and hold it from the English, who threaten the Queen Regent's borders."

"*We* can do that, mate!" shouted Gleeson.

The herald's horse skittered backwards. After fighting to bring it back under control, he looked up, scandalised. "You party with *l'Anglais,* my lord?"

"I'm Australian, ya wombat. And this isn't a bladdy party, either. Now bagger off!"

Maxwell burst out laughing. "This is Douglas' 'keeping tha peace', is it?"

Jones looked doubtful. "I don't know if you spoke with the captain, Commander, but he asked us to calm things down – didn't want us getting fractious, like."

Gleeson appeared genuinely astonished. "*Me? Fractious?* I thought we were meant to be holding the castle?"

Jones motioned him away, apologising to Maxwell. "Please excuse us for a moment, sir." Once alone behind a parapet, Jones showed Gleeson a message on his comm, originally from Thomas Beckett, forwarded by Douglas.

Gleeson read, developing a frown. "So, Captain Baines allowed Lord Maxwell to hold the castle because she knew that it was destined to end up back in royal hands?"

Jones nodded. "I don't know much about history, boy, but I trust Captain Baines – she knows what she's talking about. Sir Nicholas wanted to hold it for England, but if *he* gave it up *that* would be treason – he'd have to make a fight of it. Whereas Lord Maxwell will be just 'obeying orders', like. If we make things worse—"

"Look, Jonesy, no offence to Jill Baines – she's a damned good officer and leader – but do you really think Maxwell's the sort o' bloke who'll give up a castle? Especially to some drongo moonlighting from his day job at the *Eau de Paris* counter?"

"That's why we're here, Commander."

"I don't follow."

"How did Captain Baines explain it? Put it lovely, she did. 'To *smooth* the transition process' – I think that's what she said, boy. You know, with all your experience in advocacy, isn' it?"

"Oh, bladdy 'ell."

"You have been unconscious for a long time. I did not realise you were so unfit."

Jansen went from groggy to tetchy instantly. "Unfit, ma'am? I was lodged between the control console and the co-pilot's seat, with my face pressed against the forward viewscreen in a vertical climb! I would have been better off upside down. And what's that smell?"

He sniffed around the cockpit, eventually ending back where he started. "It's me!"

"Yes, you were quite ill, but rather than jettison you over North Africa, I have put up with it. I half expected to see a circling group of tiny stars, tintinnabulating about your head, after the cartoon fashion." Heidi glanced sideways. "But now you are awake, I would appreciate it if you would clean the vomit from your instrument panel and your fatigues."

Speechless, Jansen left his seat to fetch some cleaning wipes from a storage compartment in the ship's tiny hold. He returned a little cleaner, and only then did he notice they were no longer moving. "Where are we?"

"I managed to track down another nest – while you were sleeping. We are now about forty kilometres west-north-west of our previous location, out on the peninsula we can usually see from the *Heydrich*."

"That far?"

"Large predators range across vast territories. Moreover, they seem to nest privately. I would guess, to prevent their brethren from raiding their eggs or young. Earlier today, we witnessed their predilection for cannibalism first-hand. This time we must take a gentler, yet altogether riskier approach."

Jansen gazed out of the forward viewport. "The tranquilisers."

"Indeed. Take a look." Heidi handed him a pair of field glasses. "The nest is below us on that flattened ledge, two-thirds of the way up the next hillside – do you see it?"

"Hmm, yes. At least I see one of the parents. Do you think that's Mum?"

"Hard to know. They swapped a few minutes before you awoke – clearly taking incubation in turns. The nest is on the eastern slope. It is possible they might roam a little, once the sun is upon it during the earlier hours of the day."

"Are you suggesting we wait it out overnight, ma'am?"

"After the last debacle, why not? We can call it plan C. If they do not, in fact, leave the nest, we shall just have to revert to plan A, once the second adult leaves to hunt."

"Do you think the second adult will? I mean, if he or she returns with a kill, that might keep them going for days."

"That is a good point," Heidi agreed. "But they may leave for other purposes. Carnivores do not merely hunt an area – they also must defend it. They have to be *seen* – or at least scented – within the region, to warn off competitors. You know how you males pride yourselves on being able to urinate anywhere."

Jansen scowled but ignored the taunt. "So one of them always remains peripatetic to mark the area as theirs – is that your theory, Doctor?"

Heidi shrugged. "Perhaps, but if we're lucky, both will leave the nest with the morning sun. We shall see."

"You should really get some rest," said Baines, kindly and without bothering to 'hello'. "It's quite the day you've had, I hear."

Douglas looked up from his desk as she entered. Since the crash destroyed his captain's briefing room, he had been forced to take a small office within *Factory Pod 4*.

He smiled, exhaustedly. "Ye're telling *me* to rest, after what ye've been through? When Ah got back with the Princess Elizabeth, Ah went straight to see ye. Imagine my surprise to find that ye'd checked yourself out of Flannigan's care and flown off back to Hermitage Castle!"

Baines' smile subsided. "I had to, James. I had to remember something important. You see, I know what happened to you."

"Which bit?"

"The bit where you were rendered unconscious."

"Flannigan told you?"

"No, James. I was *there.*"

Frowning with confusion, Douglas stood and walked across the small room to pour them each a cup from the percolator. "Ah'm guessing this is going to be a conversation that will require copious amounts of black coffee."

He handed her a mug, which she immediately set down on his desk as she fell into his arms.

"J-*Jill?*" he spluttered, almost spilling his own drink.

"I don't want to hear regulations, James. Just shut up and hold me."

Never a man to disobey a direct order, Douglas reached around to place his own cup down with care as he held her. "Ah thought Ah'd lost ye, Jill – in that place." His voice cracked slightly. "Perhaps ye could tell me what happened?"

She could feel his awkwardness, which caused her to giggle. "Oh, James, what am I to do with you?" She looked up deeply into his eyes and kissed him. After all, NASA was very, *very* far away.

To rebuff her would have been the very height of bad manners; always a courteous man, what was Douglas to do?

"Get lost!" shouted Gleeson. "That bladdy lunatic, De Soulis, was well off the reservation! Lord Maxwell remedied the situation in the *name* of the Crown. He's already drafted an appeal to the Regent's offices, to hold this castle and these lands secure for the safety and well-being of the Liddesdale people, and under the very protection of the Queen Regent herself."

Twenty metres below them, the herald suddenly appeared less sure of himself. "I will seek advice from my masters, my lords." With that, he wheeled his horse and cantered away.

Maxwell, Gleeson and Jones watched him ride towards the French encampment, near the northern shore of Hermitage Water, roughly 200 metres south-east of them. From there, the Queen Regent's men had cut off any possibility of escape or resupply from the eastern and northern valleys.

While their attention was in the east, one of Maxwell's men brought news from the castle's north-facing battlement. A smaller force was making its way across the lower flanks of Hermitage Hill, almost certainly to cut off any retreat to the west.

Maxwell nodded with downcast approval for the French commander's good sense. He turned to Gleeson. "Do ye really expect a legal argument tae work? Ah cannae call ma entire force doon here wi'out leaving ma lands exposed."

Gleeson shrugged. "It's worth a shot then, mate, isn't it? It'll put 'em on sticky ground if they attack us, at the very least. And if we really do draft something, it might tie them up in legal wrangling for months, even years." He grinned. "By then, of course, you'll have been master of this place for quite a while – be a bagger to get you out, mate!"

The glint of avarice lit Maxwell's eye. "And how do we answer their claims of treason?"

"Taking lands from a rival lord is hardly treason, mate. Especially a bladdy nut job who butchered his own people. The burden of proof will be on them. Woolmington vs the Director of Public Prosecution 1935." He turned to Jones with a self-satisfied smirk. "Ya see, I've still got it!"

"*Nineteen*-thirty-five," repeated Maxwell, not sure he understood correctly.

"Yeah. In the year of our Lor—" Gleeson changed tack, clearing his throat. "Never mind, maybe we'd best leave that bit out of the application. But the principle is sound."

Maxwell shook his head, sadly. "Ah couldnae get one o' ma lawyers to ride all tha way oot here, even at the tip of a lang spear – and that's wi'out the *cordon sanitaire* thoughtfully provided by the Queen Dowager's French lackies! So who's to draft this *fiction of law*[22]?"

Gleeson's grin faded. He turned to Jones. "Did you confirm receipt of that message from Douglas? I mean, we could still just blow 'em all back to hell, right? If the message never got through?"

"Sorry, sir. The captain always insists on read-receipts, so that he knows his orders have been delivered."

Gleeson soured. "He's our very own Alfred the bladdy Great, making sure all his captains can read – another great legal precedent! Alright, alright, I'll do it."

Maxwell was astonished. "Ye're no' a damned lawyer?"

"No need to shout about it."

Noting the Australian's displeasure, Maxwell grinned. "Ye're a dangerous man, Commander."

By habit and training, Heidi Schultz slept lightly. The snuffling around their ship heightened her senses at once. Her last remaining orbital attack craft was a tough little ship, but it was far from indestructible.

She shook Jansen awake to remove his snoring from her awareness, instantly clamping a hand over his mouth before he could speak.

Once certain he understood the need for silence, she switched their electrical equipment over to stealth mode – the last thing they needed was to be revealed by their viewports lighting up, like so many television sets in the middle of a pitch-dark jungle, for the diversion of nocturnal hunters.

Infrared images came from several cameras built into the hull, all around the ship. Something had *been* there – it was there no longer. All that remained was the swaying and rustle of ferns where the something had made a sharp exit. If she had to guess, Heidi would have said that the *something* was quite sizeable.

---

22 Refers to an untruth taken as a truth, in order to help courts reach a decision or apply a legal rule. Although actually coined in the 1580s, more than twenty years later, after spending several days in the company of some of the world's most outrageous time travellers, Maxwell casts the ire of future legal historians to the wind on this point.

Jansen glanced at her. She shook her head. A heavy *bang* on the roof made them both jump, as a large creature leapt into the woods and vanished.

Jansen blew out a breath he had not realised he was holding. "Did you see what it was?" he whispered.

"No. Just a swish of a tail between the trees. Whatever it was," she turned fully to him, speaking normally now, "it was fast. We should get back to sleep now."

"After you," he murmured, uneasily.

Heidi's lip twitched into a smile. "Goodnight, Ben."

Douglas coughed to cover his embarrassment. "Right, now we've sorted that out, maybe you could explain what exactly was meant by 'you were there'?"

Baines took the seat across from his desk. "I thought he'd killed you – he did kill you! At least, that's what he showed me."

"He?"

"Lieutenant Robin Rotmütze. You see, while you were Heidi's captive aboard the *Last Word,* we put our satellite up into space to find you. It was captured in orbit by one of the enemy's attack ships. Luckily, Sam Burton had fitted it with a self-destruct. Unluckily – for the enemy – it was inside their ship when I gave the command to destroy it." She sagged a little. "You must understand, I had no choice. If I had not denied that asset to the enemy, they would have used it to hack our systems and discovered what we planned to do – and our plan to destroy Meritus' ship was desperate enough, James, without giving it away completely.

"When we tipped the ship down into that ravine, I..."

He reached out to take her hand across the desk. "Ah survived, Jill. Dinnae beat yerself up about it." He pushed back the memory of Lieutenant Elizabeth Hemmings' neck snapping, as he was thrown onto her by the turning of the ship. It was a tragedy beyond anyone's control; he would never put that on Baines. Instead, he asked, "What does this have to do with Rotmütze?"

"I killed him."

"Come again?"

Baines nodded sadly. "You don't know how long I've been working up to this conversation, James – admitting to what I did, my feelings about it, and you. Perhaps it's best all out in the open in one go, eh?" She smiled weakly.

Douglas gave her hand a squeeze. "Aye. It's OK, Jill, Ah understand. At least, with regards to the enemy soldier, you did what you had to. It seems to have been necessary, if regrettable, but if he was killed during military action a hundred million years ago, how could he be in a Scottish castle – no' to mention how could he make me..."

"*Faint?*"

"Ah was thinking more along the lines of 'manfully lose consciousness', but Ah'll no' argue semantics."

Her face lit up with its old mischievous grin. "You were lucky he only knocked you out."

"How could he—"

"James," she interrupted him before she lost her nerve. "When I ordered the satellite and his ship destroyed, he did not pass over, at least not as he should have, and not all the way. Beck Mawar believes he must have been such a piece of work in life that when his body died, he became a..."

As she tailed off, Douglas leaned forward across his desk. "Became a what? A saint? A legend? Elvis? *What?*"

"She thinks he's a demon, James. A demon."

He sat back. "Look, Ah know Ah've no' been around so much lately, but has everyone gone stark, raving mad?"

"I know what it sounds like, but I was there as he reached for you. He was about to stop your heart." Her voice wavered and a tear ran down her cheek. She wiped it away, crossly.

"So what stopped him – if this fellow is some kind of evil spirit, what stopped him?"

"I think I did. That is, with the help of Mario and the others."

Douglas straightened, concern etched into every tired line of his face. "Jill, perhaps you should take some rest. You've been through so much. Maybe all this, and what happened earlier, maybe it's just some sort of exhaustion-related breakdown."

"You think I'm *nuts?*" she bridled. "After I tell you how hard this has been for me to talk about – you think I'm nuts!"

"No." He raised his hands placatingly. "Of course not, no' entirely."

"Not entirely!" Baines shouted as she jumped to her feet. "You know what, James, you may be right – perhaps I *am* nuts. If we ever get home, the first question I'll be sure to ask my shrink is why I care so much about you!"

Douglas winced as the traditional internal door slammed shut in her wake, plunging a small cactus that had miraculously remained potted and shelved all through the crash, needles-first into the carpet.

He sat stunned for a moment. "That may just be the shortest relationship Ah've ever had," he pondered, rounding his desk to pick up the stricken plant. "Poor wee chap. Let me put you back— *Ouch!*"

Golden sunlight poured out across the Egyptian delta and north coast. Such early beauty nevertheless carried the promise of searing heat to follow. Unmoved by the vista, Heidi's attention was all on the nest and the billions of dollars it represented. She kicked Jansen awake. "Get up. They're moving."

"Wha'?" he answered groggily.

"Hurry, we must go. Before the whole jungle wakes up."

"Yes, ma'am," he answered blearily. "Just a couple of things I need to do first."

She sighed. "Hurry!"

A few minutes later, Jansen joined her, considerably lighter of step. "Right, I'm ready, ma'am."

She glowered at him. "Up with the lark! Come, and don't forget your weapons. We've wasted too much time as it is."

The hatch opened and they stepped out into a fresh morning. A lava flow of life crept down the hillside and across the delta below them. Verdant and vital, impossibly green, it shimmered in the low sun. Beyond the land, blue reigned supreme as the Tethys Ocean merged with the skies, a seemingly depthless horizon almost within reach.

"Wait," said Heidi.

Jansen stopped. "What have you seen?"

She raised her field glasses to scan the terrain before them. "Nothing, but I know they are out there."

"The carcharodontosaurs?"

She shook her head. "Them, of course, but it's the smaller, faster predators that should concern us. Did you notice how they exploded from out of nowhere, the last time we went for the eggs?"

Jansen nodded, swallowing his nervousness.

"And then there is whatever dropped on us in the night," she added.

"You think it might hunt in the day, too?"

"Quite possibly. Many of the dromaeosaurids, or raptors as they are commonly known, seem every bit as comfortable in the day as the night."

He looked down the slope to where the nest lay. No more than a kilometre, but through a jungle of ferns and cycads that were home to all manner of creatures from snakes to giant scorpions, and of course, dinosaurs. The hill was steep, too, he could not help noticing. An impossible landscape in which to make a quick evacuation on foot.

"What do you think that thing in the night was, Doctor?"

"I don't know, but if you take a look on the roof of our ship, you will notice that it marked us."

"Marked, as in...?"

"Urine. Yes. Not good, Ben. It thinks we belong to *it* now. And look at these footprints."

Jansen first glanced around them, instinctively, before stooping to study the marks and scratches in the soil. There were all manner of tracks, some left by birds or small dinosaurs, the multilegged trails left by millipedes and other large invertebrates, but the ones Heidi singled out left little to the imagination – at least, not for Jansen, not any more. Just three prints. Two, where the animal landed, having leapt from the roof of their ship, and one other, some three metres away. That third print clearly showed the first step of a sprint into the jungle and demonstrated the creature's stride on the run. It took no expertise at all to work out that whatever had left those tracks was fast. Even more worryingly, the prints were three-toed and *large*. Jansen swallowed again. "If it catches us down there, we *will* belong to it – so long as our quarry doesn't take us out first."

Heidi smiled and slapped him on the back, making him cough. "It is good to be alive, *ja?*"

He looked at her askance. "*Staying* alive's better."

Corporal Dewi Jones knocked on the solid oak door, leading to what used to be De Soulis' office and counting house. He took the muffled, disgruntled 'Mmph' through the heavy timber as permission to enter. Striding into the small room, he noted several heavy chests and boxes to his right. One of the boxes was open and showed a bundle of tallow candles. He sniffed and wrinkled his nose.

Before him, placed in front of the room's single, shuttered window, sat a heavy, carved desk, and on it burned two large candles in their silver holders. Between them, several parchments lay rolled out, held flat by small stacks of large coins in copper and silver. Behind the desk sat Commander Gleeson.

He lifted a quill pen from the parchment he was working on and looked up irritably.

Jones sniggered and turned away.

"What?" asked Gleeson, crossly.

The corporal fought to control his face as he turned back slowly.

"Well?" Gleeson leered in the half light, raising one eyebrow.

It was too much. "Er... Mr *Scrooge,* I presume?" Jones managed before bursting into laughter.

Gleeson glowered. "I preferred you when you didn't say much! Now, what do you want, Corporal Hyena?"

Still sniggering, Jones managed, "Lord Maxwell sent out a few lads to spy on the French, Commander – hiding in the darkness, like."

"And?"

"Two of them have returned, sir. One says they're up to something, isn'it. His French was limited, but he thought he heard the words *'briser le siège'.*"

Gleeson straightened. "I don't have much French either, but I'm guessing that means 'break the siege'?"

Jones nodded. "Apparently so, sir. He also heard something he believed was *'faiblesse'* and *'la porte'.*"

Gleeson jumped to his feet knocking over his chair. "*La porte?* That I *do* know. Grab that box!" he ordered, pointing. "No, the other one. That's it. I'll take this one. Follow me."

As they ran out into the corridor, they heard a thunderous *boom* and felt it roll through the stones beneath their feet. "Oh, crap!" shouted Gleeson. "Step to it, everyone – it's time to rumble!"

Heidi and Jansen cautiously made their way down the hillside as it dropped steeply into a gulley. The v-shaped cutting ran deep, the legacy of a hundred thousand monsoon years. Fortunately for them, it was currently dry.

Before they opened the wormhole, Heidi had glanced at a report submitted by One, where he speculated about a volcano far to the north, across the Tethys Ocean, causing the weather systems to move south. He believed it to have prevented the delta's usual monsoon for the last few years. He further speculated that the area might be undergoing a mini extinction event – if there was such a thing. The foliage was lush from the humidity and occasional rainy spells, but without the monsoon carrying fluvial minerals harvested from inland floodplains, the area would indeed begin to starve as the rivers dried up. His theory might also go some way towards explaining the large numbers of carnivores over such a comparatively modest area. They had seen small herds of large sauropods, even large herds of smaller iguanodonts, on the fern plains, but the herbivores were in nothing like the numbers they would have expected – not with so many savage, predatory mouths to feed.

Their flight in, the previous day, revealed a herd of Spinosaurus aegyptiacus – or so Heidi initially believed – several hundred of them, but a herd of apex predators made no sense at all. It took a low flyover to assuage her curiosity. From a distance, what looked like herding spinosaurs turned out to be Ouranosaurus nigeriensis – a hadrosauriform, related to both the famous Iguanodon and duck-billed dinosaurs. The row of neural spines along much of the ouranosaurs' backs and tails created a 'sail' that, from a distance, was similar in appearance to that of Spinosaurus. Upon closer inspection, Ouranosaurus were much smaller, and herbivorous, and that was the problem. According to the notes Tim Norris left behind for Heidi to devour, Ouranosaurus and similar herbivores should have strolled across the landscape in thousands, or even *tens* of thousands. It was just possible that One's hypothesis was correct – they were actually witnessing a localised climate change and extinction event.

Her reverie was broken by a loud *snap* and a call from behind. Jansen had lost his footing on their way up the other side of the cutting and slipped back down, causing much cracking of foliage and a mini rockslide.

Heidi rolled her eyes. So much for stealth. She made her way back and extended a hand to help him back up onto the narrow animal run they were following. Jansen seemed little the worse for wear, but she got to wondering just what *sort* of animals made this run. They were hardly in sheep country, after all.

She shook her head in annoyance, a finger to her lips warning him to be silent. They set off again, but Heidi was beset by a new sense of creeping horror. Despite having little imagination regarding fear of the unknown, she nevertheless could not shake the feeling that something, or some *things*, had been disturbed by Jansen's tumble. The jungle seemed unnaturally quiet as they approached the nest.

Cycads grew as large as trees in places, on this side of the ravine. Hiding behind a leaf the size of a small car, she pulled out a pocket set of field glasses. Their built-in electronic distance measurement system sent an infrared pulse before them. A moment of autofocusing brought the nest sharply to life fifty-seven metres ahead.

The small clearing where the nest lay bore all the signs of foliage smashed to make room. When in need of private habitat, it seemed the carcharodontosaurs were fairly adept at redecorating with prejudice. More importantly for Heidi's purposes, however, they were not there.

She turned to Jansen, and with a half-smile, spoke quietly, "Mummy and Daddy Bear have left the cottage." Her razor-sharp mind doggedly followed the metaphor to its natural conclusion, prompting her to add, "And if you call me Goldilocks, I *will* kill you."

Jansen held up his hands in submission.

She motioned for him to follow. *So far, so good,* she dared note in the privacy of her own thoughts. In no way superstitious, it still felt like wisdom not to comment on the fact that they had seen nothing bigger than a sparrow since leaving the ship. They crept closer to the nest.

"How good do these guys smell?" Jansen whispered.

"Is that just appalling grammar or is there a terrible joke coming?"

He frowned, bewildered.

"Never mind. I doubt they smell very *good,* but rest assured, they smell very proficiently – like most hunters and scavengers. And in answer to the question *behind* your question – they will smell *us* long before we smell or hear *them.* And talking of smells..."

At the edge of the trample zone, now visible to their left, were the remains of a hapless Ouranosaurus; a youngster and doubtless ex-member of the herd she had witnessed yesterday, but regardless of the stink in the fetid heat, Heidi could not help but marvel at the industry shown by such huge predators in the building of their nest. Much of the smashed material had been recycled into a large doughnut[23] structure in the centre of the clearing. Built up in layers to a thickness of almost two metres, the walls of the enclosure appeared woven into a curve, like a hurdle fence. It was a work of astonishing complexity by creatures with not a thumb between them.

The human housebreakers walked around, at once to avoid the rotting corpse, and to take in the intricacy of the nest; like a bird's, but sheer scale demanded greater neatness, in order for it to stand.

They looked at one another, shaking their heads in wonderment. Heidi could not help but speculate on whether the creatures had worked together to bring the construct home. Perhaps she would never know.

A shadow touched her heart. *If only Tim were here to see this.* The thought shocked her, but then they certainly had a bond – one neither of them wanted. Despite her grandfather's lies and machinations, she briefly toyed with the idea of leaving a camera to watch the nest – how Tim Norris was that?

She brushed the thought away and climbed onto the walls. They were no more than a metre high, but this proved deceptive, because the inside of the doughnut turned out to be bowl-shaped and more than two metres deep. "They must have dug it out before building the parapet around the top," murmured Jansen, "but with what?"

"Their hind legs, one would imagine. You know, the way chickens scratch the ground?"

Jansen's eyebrows rose as he smiled. "Times a thousand!"

Heidi scrambled over the wall into the nest's interior. The stench was overwhelming. Shards of bone and half eaten hunks of rotten meat were everywhere – and then there were the turds.

She held her nose as delicately as possible, considering her circumstances. "It seems we are lucky."

Jansen coughed, wincing as he tried to hold his breath. "*Lucky?*"

---

23   Ring, not jam.

She nodded, breathing through her mouth. "Indeed. From the state of this place, I doubt Mummy goes out all that often." Heidi motioned for Jansen to pass her the flat-packed holdall he had carried from the ship, as she unpacked her own. "We'll take two each, just in case—"

"Don't finish that sentence – please," he interrupted.

Removing the heavy and disgustingly stinky ferns from the bottom of the nest, she revealed the eggs. Had she not been holding her breath, it would have caught in her throat. Such perfect natural symmetry. She counted sixteen sandy-coloured eggs in all, laid in a near-perfect circle, and each pointing out from the centre of the nest like petals on a sunflower.

They grinned at one another, despite the danger of their situation. The 'other side' to these gigantic, murderous monsters was a revelation. They were builders, they were artisans, they were nurturing parents, they were... *close.*

A roar tore through the jungle from down in the valley.

Heidi redoubled her efforts as she packed four eggs into two bags, wrapping them as carefully as she dared within the time constraints they now faced.

A second roar terrorised the hillside. Heidi zipped up Jansen's bag and froze. They looked at one another. This time, the roar came from above them and was even closer.

"We need to go, *now!*" Jansen mouthed silently.

His argument was persuasive and with a single nod, Heidi handed him the bag, tied her own across her shoulders, picked up her air rifle and leapt out of the nest. She landed lightly on both feet and set off at a run with Jansen sprinting wordlessly after.

A third roar shattered the suddenly still air. This time it came from in front of them. They skidded to a halt, grasping one another in the nervous reflex of terror. In the path of impending death, Jansen looked deep into Heidi's eyes for the first, and what he suspected would be the last, time. Steeling himself, he took an equally deep breath and said, "Oh, shi—"

"Shine it over there!" screamed Gleeson. "Over *there!*" The spotlight moved, bringing its beam to bear as near as possible to the castle gates. A sea of bodies clustered in the forecourt between the Douglas Tower and Well Tower.

Unable to depress the mechanism any further, the soldier shouted back, "That's as far as she goes, Commander."

Gleeson looked up and right, towards the fighting platform that spanned the gap between the towers. "Why aren't those bladdy drongos pouring missiles down on them? *Oi,* you useless baggers! Don't just stand there like a bunch o' caged galahs! Get throwing or firing or do *something – bladdy 'ell!*" He drew his head back inside the small, high-level window. "Jonesy, you've got arms bigger than most blokes' legs – take that box and run up to the battlements, will ya?"

"What's in it?"

"Something I lifted off Merito's transport. Don't worry, you'll know what to do when you get there. Go!" Gleeson patted the giant Welshman on the shoulder as he ran past. "And wake those useless bludgers up when you get there!" he shouted after.

"OK, boy," Jones called over his shoulder.

"And I suppose *I'd* better take the other box and get down *there,*" he added with a sigh. "Oh, man. I wish I wasn't so courageous!"

Before he could think better of it, he ran back through the great hall to the main spiral stairway. Jones had already scrambled up them two and three at a time, but Gleeson knew he had to take more care going down. He could hear the raucous shouts of many men from below, and the unmistakable sounds of a violent tussle within an enclosed space.

As he reached the bottom, he could see Maxwell's men filling the entrance passage, five abreast and six or seven deep. They gave all, pushing back against vastly superior numbers of Frenchmen. Their one saving grace was that there simply was not enough room for the enemy to get in – as long as they held. The explosion Gleeson had heard from De Soulis' office was obviously the main gates going up in smoke for a second time in as many days. This time, there were no remains left to patch.

He had not noticed any cannon on the video captured by their spy cameras, laid high in the valleys and in the path of the oncoming French. *Maybe they have a couple of those little falconet things,* he wondered, although the bang sounded far bigger than they alone would be capable of. It was an interesting little conundrum, had he only the time to ponder it. "Come on, Jonesy," he muttered, anxiously.

From his position at the bottom of the stairs there was little he could do without harming his own side – and Maxwell's men were hard pushed as it was.

A succession of flashes and bangs lit the ruined gateway from the outside. Suddenly there was screaming and shouting, cutting easily through the grunt and snarl of the men in the passageway. Something had gone very wrong at the rear of the French line.

"Do we split up?" asked Jansen.

"You would rather die alone?" asked Heidi.

"I'd rather not die."

"Then *run!*"

She grabbed his hand and they made a final dash as a fourth roar came from behind them. It sounded more a bellow of rage than a call. "Mummy's found the nest!" panted Heidi.

The answering call came from ahead once more, but was further north, up the slope.

Heidi pulled Jansen down to hide behind a bush. She whispered in his ear, "Our double back trail is confusing them."

Another roar from behind.

She smiled wryly. "They're triangulating our position. Good job there are only two of them."

"Yeah, or we'd *really* be in trouble."

She frowned at his sarcasm. "You can be a real bore when you're afraid."

"I'm sorry, I just want to live!" he scathed.

Before she could retort, a scuttling and thrashing sound came from behind them. It sounded like a heavy wind tearing through the forest. "Oh, no," she said. "Climb!"

"*What?*"

Heidi was already two metres above him, scrambling up the bowed trunk of an enormous cycad. "*Climb!*" she hissed, but it was too late. Jansen had waited a second too long in his confusion and they were on him.

To Gleeson's mind, the foul language coming from the French rear could only mean one thing – Jonesy was in position. Maxwell's men filled the gateway. The French had no choice but to retreat or stay where they were, and that was no choice at all, for Corporal Jones was throwing hand grenades down upon them. They were not *all* explosives. However, the fact that they were a mixed bag, including tear gas and flash bombs, did not cheer the attacking force particularly. As one, they ran for their lives, trampling the officers at the back.

A mighty bellow of victorious jubilation tore from the throats of Maxwell's men as they ran out from their relatively safe bottleneck within the castle walls.

"NO!" shouted Gleeson, desperately. "Don't follow them! Have none of you guys ever heard of the Battle of Hastings? Come back – you'll lose the advantage! Jonesy, stop throwing!"

The triumphant rout he had hoped for turned to disaster over a matter of seconds. He pulled out his comm. "Jonesy! Is Maxwell up there with you?"

"*Yes, sir.*"

"Tell his nibs to order those bladdy drongos back here, fast, before we lose the whole shooting match. We no longer have a gate. Still, I reckon we can make a go of it. If we hold the entrance, it'll take away their advantage in numbers."

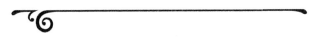

They came at him with terrifying speed through the dense foliage. Jansen could do nothing more than crouch, covering his face and head. The raptors were no taller than a metre at the hip, the youngest no larger than a chicken. When the pack attacked, they attacked as one, sickle-claws on the second toe of each foot shredding their victims, taking down all but the largest of prey.

Just a man in a world of monsters, Jansen had no chance at all. *Homo sapien* intelligence might well conquer the universe one day, but deprived of gadgets and planning time, man is a fragile beast. He requires the dinosaurs' absence to be.

Heidi watched in horror as her bodyguard vanished under lithe, feathered forms, shrieking, and calling up a storm. In seconds it was over, and they were gone.

The French rallied, especially when some enterprising crossbowman shot out the search light up on the battlements.

Gleeson stood at the mouth of the castle gate, screaming at Maxwell's men to return. By the time they woke to their danger, the French officers had picked themselves up and ordered flanking manoeuvres to cut them off. No more than half a dozen returned through the gateway before the trap closed around their comrades.

"You bladdy idiots!" Gleeson bellowed. Into his comm he screamed, "Jonesy! What have you got for me?"

"*I can't see who's who, isn't.*"

Gleeson cursed.

"Did our messenger get away with the first draft of the appeal for the Regent?"

"*Lord Maxwell says yes. Does that help us, Commander?*"

"Hang on – I'm doing the maths. What... five, *six* days? Before we get a response?"

"*If we're lucky, boy. If we're here a bit, maybe we could show them how to use email, like?*"

Gleeson barked a laugh. "Ha! Out of the mouths of babes and Welsh corporals!"

"*Sir?*"

"Hang on, mate. I'm sending an email!"

Heidi dropped silently to the ground. Jansen's fatigues looked like they had been through a cheese grater, but there was surprisingly little blood. His head was still cradled in his arms.

She tapped him on the shoulder. "You can come out now."

He looked out from the crook of an elbow, the whites of his eyes prominent in a petrified face. "I-I'm... *alive?*"

The roar of an immense creature shocked them. It was answered by another, just to their rear – the carcharodontosaurs were closing.

"Temporarily," she replied. "Get up!"

"I'm alive," he repeated, dully.

"It seems those dromaeosaurids had places to be – presumably far away from Mummy and Daddy Bear. I have to concur. Quickly – pull yourself together. Let's go!"

Stumbling to his feet, he looked around in confusion. Heidi sighed. He was clearly in shock. *She* had thought he was dead – who knew how *he* felt, after being swamped by raptors. Which raised another thought, *I suppose that little encounter answers the question about what made these animal runs.* She shook him with as much sympathy as she was capable. He almost fell.

Looking around for inspiration, she knew the giants were close, but lacked the technology on her person to pinpoint their position accurately. Heidi knew owls could locate a sound exactly within three dimensions, tyrannosaurs could scent for miles and had eyesight superior to eagles – the carnivores of this time were no slouches, either. The smell of blood from Jansen's cuts would be in the wind, free for anyone to use – the original wireless network.

By comparison, her human senses were woefully inadequate for the task, but did it matter?

That most human of traits, imagination, came to her rescue. *Those clever little terrors, and their advanced sensory toolbox, will know* exactly *where the giants are – so they can avoid them. If we follow them, we should* also *find ourselves where the giants are not.* She grabbed Jansen and ran, following the trail of broken twigs and stems left by the raptors. It was hardly a pathway, and certainly not wide or tall enough for humans to traverse easily, but as it twisted and jinked this way and that, Heidi got a sense of the dromaeosaurids stopping to make split-second decisions, en route. She doubted they had a specific destination in mind; they were simply vacating the immediate vicinity of the giants while they were roused and dangerous, but that was also good enough for her right now.

Another roar split the air. It seemed further away and that gave her hope, especially as they were travelling south-west and uphill – broadly the direction of their ship – when the terrain began to dip. Stopping to glance between the foliage, she realised they were back at the cutting where Jansen had slipped earlier. The crashing and clamour of the carcharodontosaurs was a little way behind them now. Following the trail of several dozen raptors must have confused their scent – great news. However, if the pack they followed worked out that they too were free and clear, would they stop running? More importantly, would they stop running right where Heidi and Jansen needed to be?

She chewed her lip as she mulled over their options. *This is no longer fun.* Jansen, still shaking, took the opportunity to sit and get his breath back.

They had retained their air rifles, but Heidi wished she had packed explosives. Despite the debacle at the last Carcharodontosaurus nest – where she overdid things with a missile – a lesser distraction would almost certainly be useful right now. If nothing else, it would probably send the smaller animals scurrying.

She sighed with exasperation. She knew they were there, could sense them, just a few hundred metres up the other side of the ravine. Mr and Mrs Carcharodontosaurus were the obvious power in the area. The raptors simply waited to see if the humans would escape the giants' net, before risking themselves. With a grudging respect, Heidi realised she would have done the same.

"How quickly do these tranquilisers take effect?" Jansen asked quietly, surprising her.

"Back with me? Good. It would depend upon the mass of the animal, and most likely kill the raptors who ran *you* down. Of course, by the time we had shot one each we would be shredded by the others."

"And the big ones – how long would they take to go down?"

She considered. "The tranquilisers we brought with us were designed to take down a mammoth, so it would need at least as much for each dinosaur, maybe even two shots each. And then of course, you must factor for attitude."

Jansen looked up questioningly.

"I may have mentioned this before." She sat next to him. "Elephants, although strong, tend to be relatively placid creatures most of the time. Which is why they made such reliable workhorses, right up to their extinction in 2062. Giant carnivorous theropod dinosaurs, on the other hand..."

"Have a temperament less like something that pulls a cart and more like an old supercharged V8?"

"Precisely. Although two shots would probably bring one of them down, I am not sure it would be in time to help us."

Jansen seemed to deflate further. "We need a new plan."

"I agree. Just a clear shot at a safe distance would even the odds, I think. As things stand, we cannot penetrate this jungle to see our adversaries – until they smash through the cycads to claim us."

"That's a nice thought. So do we go on?"

Heidi shook her head. "That steep-sided ravine you fell down earlier is like a ha-ha."

"It didn't seem funny to me."

"Dolt! A ha-ha is the type of ditch and wall arrangement often used in landscaped gardens to keep large farm animals out. I very much doubt whether an adult Carcharodontosaurus could cross at this point. Unfortunately, the cutting presents no barrier at all to the raptors."

"You think they're waiting for us?"

She nodded. Their ship was just a few hundred metres away and packed with enough ordnance to lay waste to the whole hillside, but it may as well have been on the moon for all the good it did them. "Perhaps an intelligence test?"

Jansen frowned quizzically. "Go on?"

"If we lured the apex predators here, would their presence be enough to send the raptors running again? Or do they know they are safe over there? This is their territory, after all. It is not much of a stretch to believe they have had to make themselves scarce before now."

"So we lure the giants here and then take our chances over there, ma'am?"

She shrugged. "I do not have anything better at the moment."

He blew out his cheeks despondently. "I suppose we had better—"

A nerve-shredding *crack* came from the foliage behind and just left of them, followed by another and another. By the time they were on their feet, the huge cycads were falling all around. The leaves were large and blocked their view, and when a massive leaf seemed to implode right in front of them, it took a split second to understand what was happening. They watched in stunned fascination as an enormous pair of jaws snapped closed around it, leaving Heidi and Jansen looking up directly into eyes of wrath.

The terrifying visage of Carcharodontosaurus saharicus burst through the brush. Shaking its head like a dog, it tossed the mangled greenery aside.

"I don't th-think he c-cares for his five a day," Jansen stuttered.

The dinosaur leaned down close and leered, abattoir drool dripping from its mandible to pool by their feet.

"What now?"

How did something so vast manage to get the jump on us? Heidi's desperate thoughts burst into a plan. "Jump!" she screamed, rolling down the bank into the ravine.

His wits rallying, Jansen dove after, the split-second delay and sudden acceleration making it appear they were tied by elastic.

A roar of frustrated fury from behind made their ears ring as they leapt and slid down the embankment, just as a second giant head crashed through the vegetation to snap for them, too.

Angered, the noise the carcharodontosaurs generated was appalling. Heart in her mouth, Heidi could only hope it would scare away any other creatures between them and their ship.

They hit the bottom of the ravine hard, but unable to spare themselves, climbed up the other side without missing a beat.

Gaining the top of the deep-sided cutting, they were suddenly out of the larger foliage as the ground levelled enough for them to run.

The ship was less than two hundred metres ahead as they pounded back along their animal track thoroughfare, but with just a quarter of the distance covered, the squawk and hiss of raptors awoke from the jungle to either side of them.

"You blokes stand to, OK?" Gleeson shouted at the handful of men who escaped the rout. He pulled out his comm. "Jonesy, send as many as you can spare down to the main ga— to the *hole*, where the gate used to be!"

Gleeson recognised a glimmer of good fortune as he peered out through the darkness. The French had made a mistake. He would have stormed the castle and held it *against* its garrison, rather than waste time corralling Maxwell's men outside her walls.

In the meantime, his few reinforcements, mainly from the *New World*, had been given time to run down several flights of spiral stairs to join him.

Within moments, he heard their running footsteps and turned to greet them. They all carried 22nd century weaponry. "Oh, you *beauties!*"

With them came De Soulis' erstwhile captain of the guard, Donald. "Where are ma men, Commander?"

Gleeson pointed. "Out there, mate. With most of Maxwell's crowd. I shouted myself hoarse to get 'em back in, but they wouldn't listen."

Donald released a heavy sigh and bent forward, hands on knees. "Tha damned fools! Ah trained them better than that! Ne'er leave tha walls if ye dinnae have tae!" he hissed waspishly.

The fifty Scots were surrounded by six times as many French. They backed up to one another bravely, forming a circle. "Hald steady, boys!" someone shouted from their midst.

The French tightened up, shouting demands for an immediate and unconditional surrender.

"You understand that wombat in the fancy rig?" Gleeson asked Donald.

"Aye. He's saying he'll slaughter them all and hang any as are left, if they dinnae doon arms. Tha pompous son o' a boot!"

Gleeson opened his mouth to respond when his comm crackled. He accepted the call. "Gleeson – go ahead."

"Commander, this is Lieutenant Singh. We got your message. I'm inbound in one of the lifeboats we fitted with a stun-cannon. Captain Meritus is on my wing in the other – how can we assist?"

A slow grin spread across Gleeson's face as he ordered everyone back inside.

"Ah'll no' desert ma men, Commander," Donald replied seriously.

"Don't you worry about that, me old mucka. You just get yourself inside before the fun starts.

"Sandy, you're more welcome than a pub in the bush! Can you see the castle on your instruments?"

"Yes, sir."

"Will the stun blast kill?"

"Depends on distance and how many people get in its way to disperse the bolt, Commander. What are you thinking?"

"Nothing flash. Just shoot everybody outside the walls. Do your best to keep casualties to a minimum, o' course. There will be friendlies in the way, but knock 'em all down, Lieutenant. We'll mop up afterwards."

"Got it. Lowering power to the weapon and running calculations now."

"Oh, and Sandy? It would give me a lot less to explain if no one saw you comin' – or goin' for that matter."

"*Hey, Commander – it's me!*"

Gleeson shook his head wryly. "Make sure you get well inside the gateway, boys." He opened another channel. "Jonesy?"

"*Yes, sir.*"

"Get everybody off the roof. God knows how this will go down!"

"*Alright, boy. It's good news, then?*"

"Well..." the Australian drawled. "It's hard to say for sure, mate. Gleeson out. *Bladdy 'ell!* Gleeson *in!*" he bawled, throwing himself inside just ahead of the blue light.

"Now what?" Jansen hissed.

"Do not move," Heidi whispered. She gripped her air rifle tight but knew its single tranquiliser dart would be useless against so many. Focusing on the big prize had distracted her from the considerable danger represented by some of the smaller creatures. Tim would have known better – that's not to say that he would have warned her. A distracting thought, offering no comfort whatsoever.

She took a deep breath and swallowed, waiting for them to strike.

Jansen turned to her, defeat in his gaze. "This will need a miracle."

Barely had the word left his lips when the small, birdlike raptors shrieked and streaked past them. In a blink, they were gone, leaving only a slight rustle in their wake as foliage fell back to its natural position.

Jansen's grimace turned to a smile of disbelief. "Looks like we're not the only ones having a bad day today."

Heidi did not return his smile, nor share his relief.

"Oh, come on," he continued. "What were the odds? Bad for them is good for us, surely?"

"You think so? I was just contemplating how much worse things may have just become."

Barely had the words left *her* lips, when a roar tore through the forest around them. Carried on the wind, it was difficult to tell from where it came, and it was surely that change in the wind that alerted the raptors to another presence – very much *their* side of the ravine.

"What was that?" asked Jansen, suddenly alarmed once more. The call was higher in pitch than that of the Carcharodontosaurus, more ear-splitting and somehow even more alien.

"Run!" Heidi put action to words, sprinting for their ship. The ferns were large, but in places she could see over them towards the clearing smashed flat by their landing the night before. The small vessel was less than fifty metres away and she gave all to the pell-mell, uphill dash. Heads down, neither she nor Jansen saw the creature as it leapt from behind to block their path. Having raced up the hill at easily four times the speed any human could manage in such circumstances, it now stood before them, claws grasping, jaws wide, eyes lit with a bloodlusting insanity. Pumped full of adrenaline and endorphins from the chase, it was out of control and *needed* to kill.

"That's why the raptors ran," Heidi breathed heavily as she pulled up short. The creature had timed its assault beautifully, to stand right between them and their ship.

"What *is* it?" Jansen's voice quavered with terror.

The clearly carnivorous theropod dinosaur before them stood half their height again at the hip, its giant scaly body and long hind legs at once massive, yet lithe. This animal was obviously built for speed. Red and yellow tiger stripes ran down its flanks all along the body and tail, while its head was mostly flame reds, fading to burgundy. Despite being eight or nine metres in length, Heidi suspected it to be the swiftest creature they had yet come across – possibly one of the fastest running predators of all time. Having recently pored over Tim Norris' notes, she fancied she might even put a name to it, too: Deltadromeus – the delta runner.

As remains of Deltadromeus were discovered without a head, some confusion persisted about whether this animal was merely a subadult Bahariasaurus – as discovered, also headless, by Ernst Stromer.

She could now lay that to rest. The three dinosaurs that almost claimed her grandfather so recently – deadly fast though they were – appeared heavyweights compared with this creature. Tim had explained that some theropods underwent significant changes in build as they grew to maturity, but the head of this creature bore purple crests above the eyes that the mature Bahariasaurus, caught on headcam, entirely lacked. Animals were more likely to gain a crest in maturity than lose one. Like early cinematic images of Velociraptor, this animal was agile, fast and deadly, but much larger.

Pupils dilated with excitement, the merciless eyes bored into them, its gaze locked and unblinking. As the sun exists at the edge of a thermonuclear explosion, brought to heel by its vast gravity, so this creature's glare hedged around a berserk rage, checked only by the reptilian chill innate to all birds of prey.

With painful slowness, Heidi raised her rifle.

Deltadromeus leapt.

She fired.

The roaring in the distance unsteadied the men every bit as much as it did the horses. With only flaming torches to see by, the French night-time raid had stalled, under the heavy bombardment of Jones' hand-grenade riposte.

Gleeson believed they may even have fled the field had not Maxwell's troops overplayed their hand by charging out to see them off.

The lightning from the eastern sky played further into their belief that a storm was upon them. Many deemed what they saw as the power of the Almighty Himself, though in fact, somewhere between rage of nature and wrath of God, science was happening – two kilometres out and cruising at eight hundred metres.

The 'lightning' leapt from sky to earth in sheets, carpeting the ground to the south of the castle. Men and horses were felled almost soundlessly in the velvet post-flash darkness.

Gleeson's comm beeped. "Go ahead, Sandy."

"*Sir, we've covered the area, but they're so tightly grouped that scanning their vitals will be impossible. If we hit them again, we'll kill them. Can you mop up?*"

"Indeed we can, Lieutenant. You've done enough and we owe you and Merito a couple o' cold ones in the Mud Hole. Cheers."

"*Do you believe you can hold now, Commander?*"

"Yeah, once we've separated our friendlies and got them back inside. Tell Douglas and Baines I've sent an appeal to the Queen Regent in Maxwell's name. Should keep them tied up in law for months to come – maybe longer. Long enough for the eggheads to get us out of here, I hope.

"People have very few rights in these times and simpler law is easier to enforce. However, the obstruse and conflicted 'spirit of the law' has barely moved on in half a millennium, so they probably won't tumble that I was spouting a load of old bull dust for a while yet!

"This attack came before we could get the word out, but if we can claim the attack was unlawful – say, during an unresolved dispute – we might just see our way clear to crowbar in a bit of mitigation, too. We'll see. Maybe I'll even sue the Crown!"

Engine swell from the lifeboats became more distant with each passing second. *"Never thought I'd hear you enjoying the law, Commander. What will you tell those Frenchmen when they wake up?"*

Gleeson chuckled. "That this is what happens when they tangle with the righteous! Even if they don't follow through, your 'light show from heaven' oughta make 'em open their lunches[24]!"

"Ah came to apologise." Douglas spoke into the video doorbell outside Baines' quarters aboard the *New World*.

"Did you?" came the curt response.

Douglas smiled disarmingly. "Aye. Also, Mother Sarah has been looking everywhere for ye."

"I know, that's why I'm in here."

He scratched his ear, still smiling. "Aye, that's what Ah thought, so Ah didnae mention Ah was on ma way over."

"In that case, I suppose you can come in."

The door slid open. Baines sat on a couch, gesturing for Douglas to take a seat opposite, across her small coffee table. Many of her things had been smashed in the crash, but she had clearly gone to some pains to tidy the place.

Douglas' smile turned to concern. "This is nae like you, Jill. To hide away when people are after ye. Care to tell me what's wrong – Ah'll rephrase that – what *especially* is wrong at this exact moment?"

---

24 'Opening your lunch' is a wonderfully colourful Australian metaphor for breaking wind.

Her frown subsided to a wan smile. "James, have you ever had your beliefs turned completely upside down and inside out? Or seen things you categorically *don't* believe in with your own eyes?"

He thought for a moment, his smile returning. "Ah remember stepping out of ma ship to check for damage and almost getting mown down by a pack of marauding Mapusaurus. That gave me pause. Oh, and then there was the time my old first officer pinned me to the wall with a kiss..."

Warmth crept into her smile. "You noticed that, did you?"

"Oh, aye. Ah also remember talk about angels and demons—"

"I never mentioned angels."

He winked. "That's where Ah come in. By the way, Ah didnae have the chance to tell ye when we last spoke – Ah saw ye, ye know."

She frowned. "Saw me?"

"In the castle. At least, Ah think Ah did. It was like a 'corner of the eye' thing. Heard you, too – telling me De Soulis had done a runner.

"You hear tell of such things, do ye no' – crisis apparitions and so forth, showing themselves in places they cannae be by way of a goodbye..." Leaning forward, he looked searchingly into her eyes and swallowed. When his voice returned, it cracked with emotion. "Ah really did think Ah'd lost ye, lass."

Before she could answer, he held up a hand, taking a deep, steadying breath. "Now, it's fair to say it's been a long day for us all – and tiredness can lead to mistakes, even, dare Ah say it, misunderstandings – so Ah'll be succinct. Ah'd love to hear all about what happened to ye, but it's getting late – so do Ah stay or do Ah go?"

Baines rose from her couch and slipped in next to Douglas. She leaned close, placing her arms about his neck. "You stay."

The dart struck, but as Heidi feared, it didn't even slow the creature. At one-fifth the body mass of a mammoth, it was nevertheless at least five times nastier. The drug would require time to bring it down.

She pushed Jansen right as she dove left. Not quick enough. The Deltadromeus snapped for Jansen, as the largest quarry, and grabbed his boot. Screaming, the powerful yet suddenly diminutive man was lifted bodily into the air, dropping his pack.

With no time to reload before the creature had her, she grabbed the bag and its eggs, and ran for the ship.

"*Heidi!*" Jansen screamed, a sound of physical agony interwoven with despair and betrayal.

Without looking back, she called for the ship to open and jumped through the hatch, sealing it behind her. Stowing the egg bags carefully, she threw herself into the pilot's seat and began a rapid pre-start cycle. Knowing there was nothing she could do for Jansen out there, her intention was to fire up the ship, scare the creature away, and hopefully rescue him. However, by the time the engines fired, she could see neither Jansen nor the dinosaur from her forward viewscreen.

Throwing switches crazily, she brought every sensor she could to bear, but the jungle was 'life unbound', with heat signatures everywhere. Scaling, she looked for the three largest in the locale. Two were obviously the nesting pair of Carcharodontosaurus. It would have been comforting to assume that the third was the Deltadromeus, but there were others too. At least another four of comparable size to the creature that had taken Jansen.

Hovering, the ship's engines created a fearful racket, and she watched as all the animals beneath her left trails through the underbrush in their panic to run away, but which one had Jansen? In all her years carrying out stealth operations for her grandfather, she had never had, nor needed, a partner. Although Jansen was a mere underling, and therefore expendable, she had to confess to a certain bond between them. He had been among the three who originally rescued her from Heinrich Schultz's captivity aboard the *Eisernes Kreuz*. If he was gone, that left only Commander Ally Coleman alive from those first loyal followers.

She and Jansen had been through so much together – and with so much of that muchness bordering on madness, his would be a presence not easily replaced.

She opened a channel to his comm. "Jansen? Jansen? *Ben?* Come in..."

Static. Was he dead or otherwise incapacitated? Was his comm damaged? For all she knew he might simply be unable to hear it with the swell of the ship's engines rolling across the hillside. Otherwise out of options, she typed a quick message and sent it.

Part of her screamed to remain, to search the area leaving no stone unturned. *Damn Tim Norris,* she thought furiously, and placing the ship on autopilot, left it hovering over the site of their altercation while she rummaged back in the small hold.

Opening the duffel bags, she carefully inspected their stolen eggs. Her own two had come through everything unscathed. She breathed a heavy sigh of relief for small mercies. Opening Jansen's bag revealed a different story. One of his eggs had been smashed and its yolk poured everywhere. Perhaps unsurprising, after all they had been through, but Heidi was furious. She had big plans and would need a *lot* of money to pull them off.

Replacing the eggs carefully, she returned to the cockpit. Her scheme would keep her here for the better part of the next ten years, but she had accepted that. It would purchase for her the entire world and was a price worth paying – it went without saying that, with such an endeavour, losses were inevitable. So it was with genuine regret that she turned the attack ship on a heading for home and the *Heydrich*. "Good luck, Ben."

Chapter 9 | Holiday

"From which faraway place do you hail?" asked Bess.

"You mean, where am I from?" Woodsey clarified. "New Zealand. And no, I'm not Australian."

"*New Zealand,*" she repeated in reverent tones. "Forsooth, an exotic-sounding place, young fellow. A place that doth boast all manner of strange vegetables, surely?"

Woodsey's mouth opened, but he was genuinely at a loss for an answer, so he closed it again.

"And tell me, what could it be, this 'Australian' of which you speak not? If it be an insult, I would know it. Forsooth, there are many within Mary's council who might benefit from a good insult."

"Back home, some might say so," he allowed with a cheeky shrug.

"And you yourself, from the farthest shores, hast surely shown much courage for a man of so few summers. The ship that bore you hence, what was her name? Was she a beautiful vessel?"

"It was a plane."

"A *plain?* And what was her name?"

"Erm, Boeing, I think. Then we boarded the USS *New World* for Mars – that didn't work—"

"Mars?" Bess interjected. "The Roman god of war – I know the tale about him."

"Nah, the red planet. Fourth stone from the sun."

Bess frowned. "You mean one of the brightest stars in our sky?"

"You've heard of it? Cool. Yeah, the red planet. Anyway, like I said, that didn't work, so we ended up in Patagonia – er, that's South America."

Bess soured a little. "Mostly the colonies of England's enemies. They build fleets with her gold, to bring against us."

"Well, not so much, not during the Cretaceous Period anyway. It was almost a hundred million years ago, ya see?" Woodsey stated, matter of fact. "Erm... do you understand 'million'? Let me see, a thousand thousand?"

"A *pusend pusend* – I know it." Bess smiled indulgently.

"Yeah, well, a hundred of those. Numbers get a lot bigger in the future. Anyway, we built a huge enclosure to live in – back in South America, that is, then we got moved to Britain, jumped forward through time and, well... here we are."

Bess' eyes began to glaze over as if Woodsey were speaking a foreign tongue – which of course, he very nearly was. She tried changing the subject. "A man so travelled around the world's great oceans as yourself—"

"Actually, I flew."

Bess frowned slightly before deciding she must have misunderstood. "A man so *travelled,* must surely be learned in song and verse from many far and strange lands, Mr Woodsey. I would dearly love to hear an ancient sea shanty, passed down through generations of your *New Zeelund* mariners." She looked up from her seat, expectantly.

"Erm... I, er, dunno really..."

"Oh, surely you must, Mr Woodsey." She clapped her hands, girlishly. "Please. I would love to hear one."

"Sea shanties, eh? Ancient... hmm," Woodsey repeated quietly as he searched his memory for anything that might fit the bill. A subject perhaps outside his usual remit, he was nevertheless buoyed by such intense interest from England's future and most famous historic queen.

"Hello, Your Majesty," Tim greeted respectfully, while Woodsey still wracked his brains to please. Tim approached them from the entrance to the now swept and cleaned embarkation lounge. "Woodsey," he acknowledged his friend with a casual nod.

"Mr Norris," Bess returned his greeting. "What a pleasure to welcome you once more into our audience. Mr Woodsey was about to provide us with a treat – a marvellous shanty from his many travels at sea!"

Tim raised an eyebrow. "He was? I didn't know he'd even been in a boat." When the stress of mental exertion suddenly cleared from his friend's expression, he knew it was going to be bad.

"Ah," Woodsey snapped his fingers. "Got it! I do remember one."

"An ancient sea shanty?" Tim stared in frank disbelief. "*This,* I'm looking forward to."

"Yep, no worries." Woodsey tapped his temple. "S'all in here, you know. Right, here we go, an ancient mariner's song and it's called—"

Tim marched his friend down the corridor in a foul temper. "*Friggin' in the Riggin'?*" he scathed. "Seriously?"

"What's the matter, dude? She wanted an ancient seafaring song and you've gotta admit, she loved it. She was still singing it when we left—"

Tim stopped dead, glaring at his friend. "I know! Honestly, is that all you have to say?"

"Well, she did, she loved it," Woodsey retorted. "Especially the bits about there being not all that much to do and the part about that bloke being unfit to use a shovel—"

"Enough. Stop. Please." Tim prevented his friend from breaking back into song. "*She* is the future Protestant queen of Tudor England – future head of the *Church* of England. Do you really think she's ready for the *Sex Pistols?*"

"She asked for something ancient. I saw it on HoloTube – what? You think I should have reached further back? Like something by Bang Crossly?"

"Bing Crosby – look, never mind all that, it's beside the point!" Tim blew out his cheeks to calm himself. "You know we're all under orders to take every care in preserving the timeline, right? You *do* understand that?"

"It was just a song, dude."

"You introduced Elizabeth R to punk rock!"

"I thought, you know, softly, softly," Woodsey mitigated.

"What do you mean?"

"Well, I thought we could work up to death metal, gently, you know, so as not to..."

Tim was lost in a private nightmare and no longer listening. "And I was stupid enough to be with you while it happened – roped in, guilty by association. Captain Douglas is going to kill us – he'll have a seizure!"

"Relax, dude. She's just curious about us, that's all. You know, the way we speak and what we like and stuff."

Tim seemed to visibly wilt. "Oh, my God. What else did you say to her?"

"Ah, nothin' really, mate. You know, just a bit of this and a bit of that."

Holding his head in his hands, Tim spoke through his fingers. "We're not supposed to influence her. 'Make her comfortable until we can get her home to Hatfield House and nothing more', that's what we were told – the captain was quite clear. She's to stay here until the seventeenth of November and then Sir Nicholas Throckmorton will lead a party south to make sure it's safe for her to go home."

"You need to lighten up, mate. She was loving it. She swears like a drill sergeant, too, I'll tell ya. I was quite shocked."

Tim glared at him. "We're going to get it for this. You may have corrupted history. I mean, it's bad enough teaching her lewd songs, without you clipping the coinage of conversation, too."

"Dude, what does that even *mean?*"

"We're in Tudor England – roll with it!" With that, Tim strode away, fuming.

"I disagree," Woodsey called after him, mutinously. "*I* reckon I did mankind a favour. In fact, I may have just saved future generations the misery of chamber pot music! They'll be able to shoot forward past all that, steal a bit from Beethoven and ragtime, then jump straight over Vera Lynn to get directly to THE GOOD STUFF!" He hollered the last, as Tim vanished around a corner.

Woodsey turned, stuffed his hands in his pockets and stormed off in the opposite direction. "There's always something with that bloke. If he's not being captured by Nazis, he's standing in for the fun police!" Turning a corner, he bumped into Rose.

"Oops. Hey, what's up with you?" she asked, noting his expression.

"Nothing!" he snapped, moodily.

Rose raised a delicately manicured eyebrow. "Really?"

"Oh, it's Tim," he admitted.

"What have you done?"

"Me? It's not me, mate. Why would you think it was me? He thinks he's on Her Majesty's Censorship Service, or something. There's no talking to him!" Stepping around her, he too strutted away.

The smell was fantastic. Too much, in fact. They could hardly stand it. Drool dripped from two very different sets of jaws, each designed for very different tasks, but with one shared ambition. Fruit pie.

Mayor had escaped when Woodsey forgot to drop the latch in place on the animals' container. Reiver had escaped on his own, after Woodsey told him to shut up when he howled along to the song he was singing to the new, strange-smelling woman.

Offended, he had left and run across Mayor, also skulking in one of the corridors. Now that most of the hatches were forced permanently open, the smell of cooking wafted all the way around the Pod. Reiver's nose twitched. He studied his new companion. Mayor was taller than he, with considerable advantage in reach.

Cunning connected collie synapses with culinary expectation. Concentrating, he slipped into his 'mind pantry' for a moment, perusing memories, all neatly arranged in order of smell. The kitchens were attached to the Mud Hole. Reiver had sneaked into them once before – only to be shooed out with a broom by the chef. He remembered well that the pie shelf was out of his reach.

He looked Mayor up and down once more, this time calculating. His nose twitched again as the little wheels turned.

Larceny, though often removed by training, is a built-in trait for dogs. They also have ideas. As one struck, Reiver's jaw dropped open and he panted happily, his tongue lolling in the canine equivalent of an ingratiating smile.

A small yip of encouragement was all it took for his larger, if less intelligent, lieutenant to follow innocently down the corridor towards the Mud Hole.

Douglas was a man who learned from his mistakes. This time, he made sure all the attendees were given '4i' as the venue for their meeting, after the recent unfortunate incident with room forty-one.

Baines arrived before he did – no surprise – but there was a secondary agenda behind her punctuality. When Douglas left her quarters early that morning, they had decided to keep the change in their relationship quiet for the time being. They held little hope for success in that regard, but nevertheless thought it prudent to try.

When Douglas arrived at room '4i', he was gratified to see Baines, Mother Sarah and Dr Satnam Patel already in attendance. "Good morning, everyone." He flashed a smile. "Glad we all came to the right room this time."

As he found a seat, the door slid open once more, revealing the historian, Thomas Beckett. "Good morning. Am I late?"

"Not at all, Thomas," Douglas greeted warmly, offering him a chair. "Mary will be along with coffee and biscuits soon, so don't worry – ye havenae missed anything." He winked.

As if summoned, Mary arrived behind her trolley of delights, just ahead of the Princess Elizabeth, ushered respectfully by The Sarge.

The men all stood to greet her, and Douglas pulled out a seat at the opposite end of the table from his own. "Thank you for joining us, Your Highness. Thank you, Sarge. I'd like you to stay, too, as this conversation may touch on security matters. You can report back to Major White."

"Sir," replied Jackson, finding himself a seat once Bess had taken hers.

Baines began to address the princess, "Your High—"

"Bess," interrupted Elizabeth. "Bess will do, Captain."

Baines smiled. "Bess. Are your quarters satisfactory? The ship has taken a lot of damage, as you've no doubt noticed. Our guest quarters have been tidier."

Bess returned her smile. "They are most admirable, Captain."

"Please, call me Jill."

"Actually, it gives me the greatest pleasure to address you as captain, Captain. Such an exalted title."

Baines' polite smile morphed into her more usual mischievous grin. "Not bad for a woman, is that it, Your Highness?"

"Oh, Captain, *really*," grumbled Beckett. "What century are *you* living in? Now, may we come to the matter at hand?"

Baines chuckled. She had forgotten just how much she enjoyed teasing Beckett. "Of course, Thomas. *When* you've finished your biscuits?"

Beckett checked his shirt for crumbs.

A titter of laughter squeaked unbidden from the future Queen of England.

Baines turned back to her. "Your clothes are being mended and cleaned, Bess. We should have them back to you later today. Sorry we only had military fatigues to offer you in the interim. Unfortunately, we don't have any spare clothing from this period."

"Actually, *Jill,* they're quite freeing. I have never before worn breeches. Forsooth, I feel I could run and jump, even climb a tree in them. I'm quite giddy!"

Beckett buried his head in his hands. "You see how much damage we've done already?"

Baines ignored him. She found the princess' relief and happiness to be free intoxicating. That and her freedom, for a little while at least, from the social expectations of her day. She knew Bess would have no understanding of the word 'bra' but fancied she could smell smoke – she was already wearing the trousers.

History hardly recorded Elizabeth I as a feminist, Baines was well aware. Once queen, her hierarchy would be simple. She would be on top – the end. Further down the food chain came the men, then the women – horses could be slotted in at any level below her own. Yet despite this, Baines got the sense of just a little wiggle room to work with. "Let me make some introductions."

Bess nodded politely all round, but was clearly as fascinated by Patel's dark complexion as she was mistrustful of 'Mother' Sarah. Although suspicion of her Catholicism quickly gave way to astonishment, when it was explained that Sarah was not a nun, but a priest. "It seems there is much I may learn from your people, Jill," she spoke in wonderment.

"Yes," agreed Baines, "and that's sort of the problem. You see, we crashed here, almost six centuries before we meant to."

"You are concerned that the future may be in some way changed by your time here?" asked Bess.

Baines knew the people of this time had less access to knowledge, but were by no means stupid, and here was the proof. She nodded with growing respect for this intelligent young woman, fallen into their care. "Exactly. You see straight to the heart of the matter. The thing is, if our history plays out differently, much of who we are may be lost or replaced by—"

"Something even worse?" Beckett quested.

Patel leaned forward. "We must preserve the timeline at all costs." He beat his fist gently on the tabletop three times to reinforce his last words.

A moment's silence fell upon them.

"I'm not sure I agree," Mother Sarah spoke into it.

"I'm glad you said that," Baines answered, relieved. "I'm not sure I do either."

Beckett was outraged. "You can't be serious!"

"The way I see it," continued Sarah, "our world's a complete mess and our *place* in it is probably comin' to an end. Maybe this is our second chance, *maybe* even from God, for us to put it right." She sat back, folding her arms, daring anyone to argue the point.

Patel was shaking his head. "This is a dangerous road, Sarah. We all want to save the human race, our history, our achievements, and allow everything to continue, but how much will be lost? What if it *all* is? Like Mr Beckett said, what if we make things even worse?"

Sarah raised an eyebrow. "Worse than the end?"

Realising that a dam had just burst, Douglas thought it wise to stem the flow before a free-for-all ensued. "Sarah, Satnam. No one is saying that either view is necessarily wrong. It's more a matter of whether we have the *right* to deliberately effect changes that will almost certainly lead to a new world being created? For all we know, millions of people from our history may never even be *born*. Ah mean, what if we wiped out our own ancestors?"

More silence.

"May *I* express an opinion?" asked Bess.

"Of course, Your Highness," Douglas invited.

"It appears that you all fear the times you live in, or *lived* in – perhaps *will* live in. You have vouched safe I shall be queen. Perhaps I, and my fellow princes, could, as you say, effect change to avoid this dread future you fear so?"

"If anyone could, it's you," agreed Baines.

"*Jill,*" warned Douglas.

"What if she's right, James? Alternatively, imagine we *do* get back home avoiding all changes. Then what? We wait a hundred years before lights out? We know we can't fix our civilisation – there are just billions too many of us to survive. Am I wrong, Satnam?"

Patel sighed. "No. But that does not give us the right to play God, Jill."

Baines smiled wryly. "You know, I may just start taking a little more interest in spirituality after what's happened to me over the last few days. I certainly remember an old saying – and perhaps Sarah will bear me out on this – an old saying, about God helping those who help *themselves.*

"We are the only people who have *ever* been given a chance like this, and I'm not saying it's without danger or potential losses – I'm simply saying that we have a chance here, just a chance, to save our race from *guaranteed* destruction. If we fail to act, we seal our own fate, and that of every man, woman and child to follow."

The free-for-all Douglas had hoped to avoid exploded around him. He tried to interrupt but was whispering into a gale.

"QUIET!" bellowed The Sarge. "That's better, people. We'll not achieve anything by shouting at one another, will we?"

Baines grinned at him. "Thanks, and you're quite right." She studied him for a moment. "What do *you* think we should do, Sarge. Please, speak freely."

His brows furrowed in thought. "I'm a soldier, so it's in me – *drilled* into me – to take action. But more than that, our world is ending. Mars won't save us. So, with the very greatest respect to Captain Douglas, I would have to ask, do we have the right *not* to act?"

Douglas knitted his fingers under his chin and leaned on the table, contemplating Sergeant Jackson's words.

"James?" Baines prompted after a pause.

Douglas took a deep breath and opened his hands, palms up. "Ah don't have the answer, Jill. Both standpoints have merit, and drawbacks." He snorted, gently. "Extinction being just one of them. But then maybe the answer is staring us in the face."

"Go on, Captain," Patel encouraged.

"Ah mean that just *maybe* we have less control of this situation than we think. The princess is already here with us. Our very *arrival* changed the timeline from the history we know. She's meant to be three hundred miles south of here awaiting a ring and a new throne – what's *that* about? The fact that she even *knows* this must surely demonstrate just how far off the map we are.

193

"Ah still don't believe we have the right to change the future – that is, our past – but neither does a judge have the moral right to take away another person's freedom. He simply must, to protect the many."

"So, is that how we're selling this?" asked Beckett, sharply. "The greater *good?* Where've I come across that before – oh, let me see, in almost every book I've ever read!"

"You're right, Thomas," Douglas agreed wearily. "When does that ever end well? Ah get it. Even when you start out with good intentions, but we're already *here*. So much damage has already been done—"

"So why stop now...?" Beckett goaded.

"Thomas!" snapped Baines.

"No, Jill. Thomas is right to upbraid us. But by the same token, what's happened has happened. We cannae take it back and must simply go from where we stand, but if we begin actively working to egg things along, we really are taking the power of God unto ourselves. Now, it may be that we must, but we should still be checked at every point."

"OK," agreed Baines, "but while we're trotting about on our moral high horses, perhaps we should also consider how much help we could bring to these people and how much suffering might be averted."

"Explain," prompted Beckett.

"I'm not suggesting we rain technology down on them like bombs, Thomas. It's just that our knowledge could further these people's endeavours and build a better world – for *everyone.* New medicines, new ways of thinking, new understanding about one another and the world around them, new means of cooperation and communication. What if man were to reach the moon by the eighteenth century? Where would that take us by the twenty-second?"

"Speed them on the road to enlightenment, is that what you're suggesting, Captain?" Beckett clarified.

Baines shrugged. "Maybe."

"And just what the hell would we know about *that,* with our spaceships and our broken world? We live in Death's citadel, Jill, built from the bones of every living thing *we* destroyed!"

"That's a good image, Thomas," Sarah interrupted his rant.

"Thought you'd like it. Sounds like something from *your* bible!" he agreed.

Sarah smiled disarmingly. "Perhaps. And isn't that exactly what we're talking about changing? *Our* mistakes. Or at least trying to. Well...?"

"Ah thought that meeting would never end," Douglas sighed heavily as he dropped into the shuttle's pilot seat, spinning it round to face the craft's small bridge. "Are you sure about this, Jill? Ah cannae help thinking this kind of thing is exactly the type of interfering Schultz and his Nazi chums are up to."

Baines seated herself in one of the bridge's other seats, Princess Elizabeth following her lead. "No. But I don't see we have much choice, James. We should show Bess as much as we can and – assuming we can find our way out of here – possibly even leave someone behind to assist and guide her."

Douglas' eyes widened in horror. "Ye cannae be serious! And just who are ye suggesting we leave behi— No! Dinnae even think about it. You're not staying and that's final!"

Baines held up her hands, placating. "OK. OK. It was only a suggestion."

"I have heard others tell of these *Nartsees,*" Bess butted in. "What are they?"

Baines turned to her. "They're a people who... well, it's a long story and hopefully, if we can change things for the better, we may never get to meet them. Now," she began, anxious to change the subject, "have you been able to work the shower in your quarters? Only, we take so much for granted..."

Bess frowned. "The young man, Woodsey, told me about these *showers*. He offered to show me how to use them, too."

Douglas coughed. Choking, he managed, "He did, did he?"

Baines grinned. "You're kinda meant to wash *yourself* in the shower, honey."

Bess frowned in consternation. "Wash myself? A royal princess, daughter of the Great Harry?"

Baines' jaw dropped. Her minor in Reformation and Counterreformation Europe never prepared her for this. "You... you wish someone to *wash* you?" She turned to Douglas for support.

"Dinnae look at me!" he snapped, getting speedily to his feet. "Besides, it's time Ah was leaving you ladies and wishing you God speed for your trip." With a small bow towards Bess and a fleeting grin towards Baines, he strode from the bridge. "And dinnae crash ma shuttle, either," he called over his shoulder.

"You say that like I'm always crashing!" she hollered after him. "Right, Bess. Let's get you into the co-pilot's seat and strapped in." She winked. "Safety first."

Reiver growled and stood on his hind legs, jaws closing gently around the soft feathers at the scruff of Mayor's neck. Unsure what to do, the dinosaur stopped walking – which was exactly what Reiver intended. Using innate herding technique, the border collie dropped to his haunches, lowering his profile, and shuffled past Mayor to the kitchen's entrance.

No one within the kitchen paid any attention to the open doorway, especially not at floor level. If they had, they would have spotted a black and white speckled snout with a twitching, shiny black nose, testing the air.

Reiver's sensitive scanning equipment spat out the results of his survey from the 'dog matrix' printer in his brain – where ones and zeros scrolled at the speed of thought to build complex chemical profiles for every scent in the room.

Were it possible for canine thoughts to be roughly adapted into English and then much simplified, for the benefit of any interested two-legs, they would translate thus: Three shaved apes, each working strange magic with food. Alert – one of them smells anxious, take extra care when rounding up.

The nose backed away.

Thoughts without words are difficult to conceptualise. It is easier to think in terms of action and reaction, or expectation born of experience.

The planning of a distraction – to disguise a pie heist, for example – may at face value, seem beyond the cognitive powers of a collie. However, animals are far more attuned to their surroundings than humans could ever remember how to be. They *use* the landscape around them, harmonising with it. Reiver understood his place in the world without need of words. His mistress, Natalie, knew thousands of words – but he could take them or leave them – and within the confines of a working kitchen, he instinctively *knew* that a distraction was already in the bag, when you were packing a dog and a dinosaur.

He glanced back at his companion. The only unknown was Mayor's capacity to understand *his* task in all this. The smell of the baked fruit in sugared pastry was making the small hypsilophodontid drool. Reiver licked his own lips triumphantly – it seemed that, when the time came, his friend *would indeed* know what to do. With a conspiratorial *yip* he ran into the kitchen barking like the place was on fire.

Mayor ran in after him as the men looked around in shock and alarm. One of them noticed Reiver had company, endangering the mission. Thinking on his paws, he jumped and knocked a large bin over to regain the limelight. He was glad he did so, too. A perfectly respectable chicken cadaver had been carelessly thrown away and it was barely rotten at all – these apes were so wasteful! He grabbed the treat in his mouth and ran around the men's legs, dodging their slow-witted attempts to grab him, all the while snarling past a mouthful of chicken.

Mayor easily reached the pie shelf that Reiver could not, and tucking into the future, was lost in a fourth-dimensional state of euphoria. The pies, made for serving in the Mud Hole, were about thirty centimetres in diameter; generous enough for Mayor to plunge his whole horned beak and half his face into.

It took a while for the men, now armed with mops and brooms, to notice the munching sound coming from the pie shelf. *"Oi!"* one of them bellowed furiously.

Mayor was by nature a nervous creature. After being overwhelmed by the heavenly smell, he suddenly woke to the threat and grabbed a second pie by the rim of its bowl. Dropping down into his natural posture, he lowered his head and ran.

His work done, Reiver ran after him.

The men gave chase in righteous anger, but the hare was all over the tortoise on this day.

Bess let out a small, involuntary scream as the ship lifted from the hangar deck. Determined not to call on the superior piloting skills of Sandip Singh, Baines gently eased Douglas' shuttle along the cutting that led out of the Pod's hangar. The airlock and outer doors had been completely destroyed in the crash and were now so much part of the Cheviot hillside.

"Don't be afraid, Bess. Captain Douglas and I thought it would be good to take you away from here to show you some of the world and its wonders. Safe and remote. We have time until Mary..."

"Until sister mine is dead," Bess completed, unemotionally.

"Well, until the seventeenth, anyway. I haven't really given much thought to *where* we should go, exactly. You have a couple of weeks before you ascend the throne of England, Bess. Think of this as a holiday – a last hoorah before starting the new job. So where would you like to go, if you could visit anywhere in the world?"

The shuttle crept out onto the plateau, created from earth removed when the entranceway was dug.

"The New World!" Bess exclaimed excitedly.

"From the *New World* to the New World, eh? That must be a bit like what happened when the early settlers left from Plymouth only to arrive in Plymouth."

"Can we, Jill?"

Baines winked. "Hang on." The small craft's powerful main engines engaged, causing them to climb steeply. In seconds they were leaving the Cheviot Hills far below and behind.

"Woohoo!" exclaimed Bess.

"Now you're getting it." Baines wore a wide grin as she set course west.

"Reiver!" It was unusual for Natalie to raise her voice with Reiver, or any animal for that matter, but word had got around.

Reiver was canny enough to know there would be consequence, even penance, should they be caught red-mouthed. So, after devouring their ill-gotten gains – leaving the evidential bowl outside a friend's quarters – he had rounded Mayor back into the animal pen within the main hangar.

He sensed his mistress' furious pheromones before she even entered the container.

"Look at you! You've still got pie all around your face! Ooh, it's everywhere, just look at your ruff. What on earth were you doing with it?"

As stated, dogs had little use for words. Unfortunately, they had little use for mirrors, either – he thought he had done so well, too.

Only one thing for it. He dropped to the floor, chin on his front paws and looked up dolefully. If that failed, he would have to fight dirty, and roll onto his back, belly-up, executing 'the full submission manoeuvre' – two-legs never knew how to deal with that level of penitence.

From Natalie's perspective, she saw only the huge eyes of innocence, backed up by a swaying rump as Reiver swept the deck with his tail. She pointed at him. "You *bad* dog!"

Genuinely surprised by the total failure of 'doleful', Reiver could also not help noticing that as a mere partner in their caper – albeit the draughtsman – he was nevertheless bearing the full brunt of his mistress' ire. His eyes told the story quite succinctly: *After everything you apes do, I'm a 'bad dog' for stealing a little piece of pie to keep me from starvation?*

It worked like a charm, and his beloved two-leg soon began to feel guilty for what *he* had done. Better yet, her thoughts soon turned towards who might *actually* be at fault for all this. "Woodsey!" she seethed. "I should have known I couldn't leave you with him – or him with you! Mayor, get back in your enclosure – come on, boy." She turned back to Reiver, pointing again. "And *you,* young man, with me."

Her loyal collie got up from the floor and wagged off after his mistress. It was nothing short of a gross injustice for him to take *all* the blame for what had happened. It was clearly time to turn king's evidence and spread it around.

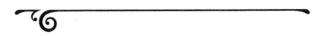

Smoke drifted through the workshop en route to the extractors. It bore the distinct stench of burnt-out electrics. Also wafting across the cavernous space were some astonishingly foul expletives. Fortunately, for Georgio Baccini, his grasp of Japanese was rudimentary at best.

To anyone entering from main manufacturing, Georgio seemed to be explaining plaintively that whatever had just happened, had not in fact been his fault.

Captain James Douglas sighed, straightened, tucked his shirt in, and continued towards what he now suspected would be a highly charged presentation. Here for a progress report on wormhole drive adaptations, the decisions made at his earlier meeting still weighed heavily on him.

Recently taken from the *New World,* the WHD now lived in one of the Pod's secondary manufacturing bays, where his engineers busied themselves running countless simulations before chancing a live wormhole. Douglas had been led to understand that uncoupling the drive from his ruined ship had gone by the numbers. However, he now inferred from the smoke and the swearing that, after much testing, two plus two may have just spat out a five. "Am Ah interrupting anything, gentlemen?"

Hiro's murderous expression turned to surprise. "Sir? You're early," he accused.

"Guilty. What have you?"

Hiro and Georgio shared a sheepish look. "Bit of a connection problem with the Pod's power core, Captain," Georgio confessed.

"Nothing you cannae fix, Ah hope?"

Hiro coughed and helped the smoke along by waving his hand. "Of course not, sir. No problem."

"Oh, my. What's happened here?" asked Jim Miller, joining them with Sam Burton, the Pod's chief of operations. Miller continued, "As head of manufacturing, I've been seeing all kinds of requisitions for new parts cross my desk. Thought I'd pop down and see how things were progressing – some of the units you've requested will have to be manufactured from scratch." He coughed as smoke from the burnt circuitry went up his nose. Bending to steal a furtive glance into an open hatch within the drive casing, he straightened up sympathetically. "Do I assume you'll need a few more requisition codes, Hiro? What went wrong?"

"Yes, I'd like to know that, too, Hiro," Burton stated coolly. "I've just received a bombardment of complaints about the lights going down in all the corridors on the second and third floors[25]."

---

25   As *Factory Pod 4* was essentially designed as a ready-made building, its inhabitants usually referred to the decks as floors.

"I—" Hiro began.

"I haven't finished yet," Burton interrupted. "And this affects you, too, Jim – I've also received three—" his comm binged, "*four* complaints from Mrs Miller about an arc from a wall conduit that seems to have fried her coffee machine."

Miller blanched. "Oh, no. Not Mr Skinny Latte..."

They all stared at him.

"That's what Lara calls hi— *it*..."

Hiro and Georgio glanced at one another.

"Expended resources, explosions, lights down across the Pod and now Mrs Miller's coffee machine," Douglas counted on his fingers. "What do we have to show for it all, laddies? In your own time."

"Erm..." they began in tandem.

When Jansen awoke, he almost cried out, so great was his pain. Only the huge, bloodied tongue gaping from the side of a giant, toothy mouth, right next to his face, gave him the fortitude to remain silent.

The Deltadromeus that carried him off by the ankle had eventually succumbed to Heidi's tranquiliser dart as expected. Upon hitting the ground, the creature had bitten deep into its tongue, which was still bleeding.

Jansen too had blacked out, but in his case from pain. Still dazed, it was hard to guess how long he had been unconscious. The sun was a little further in the west – maybe an hour? He also had no idea how long the drug would keep the dinosaur under. Fortunately for him, most of the other animals in this part of the forest were smaller than Deltadromeus and understood the idiom about sleeping giants instinctually, long before it was ever uttered by man.

He got to his feet and immediately fell back down, his face puce with agony. Realising the problem at once, he tried again, this time managing to get to his *foot*. His left ankle was badly sprained, possibly even broken. Fortunately, the Deltadromeus bit only to carry him, allowing his military boots and armoured snake gaiters to absorb the brunt of the reduced, though still significant, force.

Jansen closed his eyes in desperation. He knew he was lucky, not just to be alive, but to have kept his leg, too. *But how could she have left me?* It was certainly a shock, but perhaps no great surprise; he had seen so many used up and discarded by the Schultzes.

Not for the first time did he ponder whether the winning side was necessarily the *right* side.

A rumble from the beast's chest and a snort from its snout brought his reflections to an abrupt middle.

I need to get out of here! The trail back to their landing site was easy to follow. A large dinosaur travelling quickly through lightweight foliage cut a swathe of destruction impossible to miss. He leaned heavily as he hopped from trunk to stem to trunk, holding onto anything robust enough to support him. His confused stumble was pathetically slow, and potentially any minute now would see his captor regain consciousness again, too.

He remembered little but exquisite agony from his journey to this place. That and holding onto his air rifle like his life somehow depended on it. Despite the weapon being of no help to him whatsoever in the first instance, he had been right. He must have held on right up until the last moments, for he had travelled no more than twenty tortuous metres when he came upon it.

Reaching down to grasp his only remaining friend in a world of chaos and monsters, he kissed the barrel. That was when the weapon, up until then so useless, saved his life.

A roar sounded from behind him. Jansen turned to see Deltadromeus raise its head to look around. It appeared and sounded groggy, clearly not yet free of the drug in its system.

Jansen squinted vengefully. Leaning against a rotting stump, he took aim through the telescopic sights and fired. It was not a brilliant shot. A mostly paralysed, mid-sized dinosaur did not require one. The dart soared towards the prone creature with an angry hiss to strike it in the thigh.

Deltadromeus gave an indignant grumble and placed its head back on the ground, asleep again, before it was even down.

"Ha! Never go back for seconds, big guy!" Jansen was pleased with the result. However, his sneaky attack carried karmic repercussions as his leaning post chose that moment to completely disintegrate, dropping him with it. He cried out once more, in pain, yes, but also because he was instantly covered in scorpions, some as long as his forearm. He screamed and scrambled to his foot, patting himself down and smacking the creatures with the butt of his rifle.

"I *hate* this place!" he shouted, unwisely. Regathering his senses, he looked around nervously. What in the world was he to do? *Reload,* he thought, automatically. He searched his jacket and found he still had a pack of tranquiliser darts. He found his comm, too.

Opening it, he was astonished to find a text message from Heidi. While he was being savaged and carried away by a vicious, carnivorous dinosaur, had she helped him? Had she searched for him? No, she had sent a text. "Oh, how 'first-world' of you!" he sniped after he had finished swearing.

The text read: *Thought engines would scare animals away. Dino did not go down quickly enough for me to get you. If you are alive, drop me a line before I go back to Germany.*

It was a blisteringly hot and humid day, yet Jansen managed to turn the air in his immediate vicinity blue.

From his vantage point on the eastern hillside of the peninsula, he could see out across the sea to where the *Heydrich,* and presumably Heidi, now resided. It was easily twenty kilometres as the Ornithocheirus flew, double that by land. He sighed, his shoulders sagging once more with despair.

A possibly broken ankle, forty kilometres of rough terrain and thousands of dinosaurs between him and the relative safety offered by the lunatics he worked for. He was hurting badly, yet he hesitated to send an SOS to the person who had left him for dead – so that she could go and make a few bucks from stolen dinosaur eggs. The idea pained him almost as much as his ankle, but the angry haze eventually cleared to reveal the truth of his situation.

Choiceless.

"If I live through this, I'm taking a vacation – a nice holiday to a beach where nothing wants to eat me." Distress call transmitted, he switched the comm to send out a homing beacon and set about making a suitable splint for his leg.

Before he had finished, his comm buzzed with a return message: *Help on the way – Lieutenant Devon.*

The door slid open to reveal the gaping maw of Woodsey's yawn. Never a morning person, the way he saw it, he was doing his bit by staying out of everyone's way while they went about their important early business.

"What's this all about?" He leaned down to pick up a mostly clean bowl from the hallway carpet, just to the right of the Woods' apartment door.

Puzzled, he mussed his hair and smacked his lips, looking both ways down the corridor. No one. He was completely alone. A self-satisfied grin climbed the teenager's face to meet his eyelids on the way back down. "Ah, *that's* better."

For him, it was perhaps still too early to open his lunch... perhaps breakfast?

"*You!*"

Shocked alert, his eyes snapped wide with embarrassment.

"I knew I'd find you at the bottom of all this!" barked Dr Natalie Pearson.

"Wha'?" Woodsey removed a lock of tawny blond hair from his eyes.

"*You* know what I'm talking about."

"I beg to differ, Natalie."

"What do you call *that* then?" She pointed accusingly at the bowl in his hands.

"A bowl...?"

Reiver *woofed,* confirming for Her Honour that he did indeed recognise Exhibit A. Evidence given, he sat, to get on with a spot of tail wagging while he took in the show.

Natalie sniffed. "What's that smell?"

Woodsey blushed – a rare thing.

"Have you...?" Natalie continued. "Never mind! Just because I told you dogs are happier when given a task, you decided to put him to work stealing fruit pies, didn't you? And as for roping poor Mayor into your schemes..."

Reiver stopped wagging and gave a *yip* of indignation – what about *poor* him?

"I... *what,* now?" Woodsey's grin wrestled with a look of bafflement. "Look, lady. Your dog—"

"I should have left him in charge of you!" she cut him off furiously. "That way *he* would have been kept occupied while I was helping in the infirmary, and *I* could have relaxed, knowing I'd left the one with the brains in charge!"

"But I—"

"I see you've just got out of bed – did the rollocking I just received from the head chef wake you?"

"Look, I don't know—"

"Yesterday. While you were *minding* my dog, he robbed the kitchens!"

Woodsey burst out laughing and Reiver joined in, bouncing to his feet, barking and wagging his tail.

"*Be quiet!*"

He lay down and whined.

Natalie scolded him with a wagging finger, "*You* are becoming devious, young man." She turned to Woodsey. "And *you* are taking that bowl back to the kitchens to apologise."

"But he ran *away* yesterday. It wasn't my fault, Natalie."

"I left him in *your* keeping. One man and his dog – pah! I'd have done better to leave a budgerigar in charge of the pair of you!"

"Hey, I was busy. I was singing to the queen, dude."

Natalie gave a hard smile. "Yes, I heard about that. If you want my advice, you'll do well to return that bowl and then find somewhere quiet to lay low, staying off Captain Douglas' radar – apparently he wants a chat."

With that, she strode away. "Reiver!" she snapped over her shoulder.

Reiver nuzzled Woodsey's free hand with a wet nose, to express his condolences, before trotting after his mistress.

Woodsey looked down at the bowl in his hands, and then up to catch the fluffy rear and wagging tail as it disappeared around the corner. Shaking his head with chagrin, he said, "Well played, fur face."

Chief Hiro Nassaki's monologue came to a decidedly dissatisfying conclusion. "So, we're back to square one, gentlemen."

Douglas stood straight-backed, fighting the urge to cross his arms. "Hmm. Have we learned nothing from these tests?"

Hiro appeared deflated and demoralised, so Georgio took up the baton, earnest as ever. "We've learned that the WHD, when refocused to produce a small but sustained wormhole, requires more power than it does to make a much larger wormhole for only a split second."

"*I* know," agreed Burton sourly. His comm had barely stopped vibrating through the whole of Hiro's short presentation.

"But Ah thought we were only planning on sending a camera probe through?" asked Douglas. "Surely, the wormhole wouldnae need to be open for more than a few seconds—"

"That's the problem, Captain," Georgio cut him off. "When the *New World* jumps – or should I say, used to jump – she was firstly, travelling at speed. Secondly, she was drawn in by the immense tidal forces at the event horizon of the wormhole. In short, sir, her half a kilometre and more could enter a wormhole in less than a hundredth of a second. As no time passes within a wormhole, she would pop out the other side instantly. A wormhole remaining open for several seconds, as you say, would require vastly more power. Several orders of magnitude more, in fact. Were it not for the fact that we're only attempting to open a man-sized wormhole, the project would be impossible. Otherwise, we'd require a power source as powerful as... as..."

"The planet's core would do it," Hiro chipped in grumpily. "If we didn't care about destroying the world."

"Well, let's keep that plan on the back burner then, shall we?" Douglas suggested drily. "Do we have the power resources to achieve our goals or no'?"

"No."

"Yes."

Douglas looked between Burton and Georgio. "Which is it, gentlemen?"

Burton spoke first. "If we draw that much current from the Pod's reactor, we'll blow almost every conduit in the place and probably damage the power core itself. This is a civilian manufacturing plant. We have the power to run our machines, heat our quarters and charge our comms – it is *not* an interstellar battleship."

"True," agreed Georgio, "but we do have a much more powerful reactor aboard the *New World* that *is* built to carry a vast ship through space."

A grumble of disagreement began immediately, increasing in volume.

"Gentlemen, *please!*" barked Douglas. "One at a time. Hiro, why don't you think our ship's core will give you the power you need?"

"It will, Captain."

Douglas waited. Eventually, he remembered who he was speaking with and prompted, "But?"

Hiro looked surprised that more was required of him. "*But* we can't do it, sir. The core was damaged in the crash and attempting to bring it down here would require the entire ship to be remodelled to make room – that's not even accounting for the massive engineering effort required for disassembly and reassembly."

"So it's no' impossible, then?" pushed Douglas.

"Even if that *were* possible, sir," Hiro replied, tiredly, "that sort of structural alteration would likely bring the mountain down on us. As you know, Sekai's core spans several decks."

Another argument fired up.

Douglas sighed and placed his head in his hands until one voice caught his attention. "What was that, Georgio?"

"I said, sir, that I never intended for the core to be brought down here."

Douglas straightened. "Go on, laddie," he encouraged.

Georgio, as the most junior man there, swallowed as he re-entered the limelight. "The core is aft – now we're crashed, I suppose it might be more accurate to say *south* of us here. So, my suggestion is this..."

"That vast range below us is known as the Rocky Mountains. You know, now I come to think about it, that's not very imaginative, is it? Still, it's a heart-stoppingly beautiful place, don't you think, Bess?"

"I do indeed, though I find these translations fair difficult to follow. The left-hand parchment doth glow with more intelligent writings."

"The left? That's just the computer's recording of my speech. The right-hand side of the screen is *supposed* to be an Elizabethan translator," Baines elucidated.

"How gratifying. Art there other works named for us, also? And do *they* give such good service?"

Baines laughed. "Only an entire historical period. Look, forget the screen. I'll try to speak more slowly and clearly, so you can process my dialect. Please don't be offended. Perhaps the linguistics experts who threw this software together were a little too hung up on Shakespeare."

"Shake where?"

"Softspear— ware. Sorry, *software*. It's the progra... never mind, we'll get to that further down the line. Shakespeare, on the other hand, you'll get to know well enough in a few years – though, if you'll take my advice, you'll give your patronage sparingly or believe me, you will *never* hear the end of him."

"I see. Wait for the fullness of time?"

"Exactly."

"How far have we travelled, Jill?"

"Approximately four thousand three hundred miles. That's Yellowstone Lake down there."

"Such miracles," Bess sighed.

"This vast peninsula we're flying over is known as The Promontory. Again, perhaps not the most inventive nam— What is it?"

Bess' shoulders were rocking as she attempted to hide her face behind a delicate hand. "Perhaps your speech machine also writeth comedy, from time to time."

Baines leaned over to glance at Bess' screen and burst out laughing. "Perhaps it doesn't *hear* too well, either. Sorry, Bess. I said *vast pen-in-sula* is known as The Promontory. Nothing to do with man-prominences! Although you'll get used to Shakespeare going on about those a lot, too!"

"About what?"

The horrible feeling of digging a grave crept over Baines. "Well, not the 'P' word exactly. That comes later... I mean, that enters our tongue later... Oh, God." She closed her eyes – her mouth already had two feet in it. After a five count, she opened them to find Bess waiting patiently, wearing merely a look of polite confusion. Relieved, Baines continued, "More usually he used witty variances on the word for a male chicken."

Bess giggled. "He doth sound a saucy man."

"He certainly left us with many a catch phrase." Baines gave a brittle smile. "And endless willy gags," she added darkly. "Anyhow, more on him later." *And I hope we'll be long gone by then,* she thought, privately. "This whole area will one day be known as Yellowstone National Park. A national park is an area protected by the government, to preserve it for nature – that is, for wildlife. At least it was," Baines added, sobering. "Before the encroachment."

"Explain," Bess commanded. Seeing Baines' expression, she added, "*Please,* Jill."

"In the twenty-second century, very little of the natural world remains. Our population has become so enormous that any land unmarked by our sprawling towns is greedily used up by industrial farming.

"That's farming using gigantic machines and technology to produce food for billions of people. Our world's population is a hundred times greater than yours. Now, how bad do things get for *your* people if a harvest fails?"

"Forsooth, we have suffered three terrible years in succession under my sister's rule. Many believe it to be a sign from God."

"Well, *we've* survived so far by using science and ever more violent methods of extracting what we need from the Earth, but at great cost.

"Our world is several degrees warmer than in this time, too – which has sent our weather out of control. Let me show you something..."

Baines turned the shuttle and set a course both due north and upwards. After a hard climb, she spoke again. "We're now cruising at a hundred thousand feet – well into the stratosphere, we're near the limits of our planet's atmosphere. If you stepped outside now – apart from having a hell of a long way to fall – you wouldn't be able to breathe. Also, the air pressure is a tiny fraction of that experienced at sea level, which can lead to all sorts of problems for a human body."

Bess was spellbound. "I can see stars, yet I know it is day."

"Indeed, and coming up soon, far below us, is the North Pole. The world is so cold here that the sea is permanently frozen, all year round. It's very similar at the South Pole, at the bottom of our planet."

"I can see... the world *is* round..."

Baines smiled. "Oh, yeah. I never thought about that. It's a sphere, actually. Like a ball."

"I have read about such things, of course, from ancient Greek geodetics to the circumnavigation of Ferdinand Magellan and Juan Sebastián Elcano in my father's time, but to see it proved..."

Baines smiled, rejoicing in both the learned, questing intelligence of her charge, and being able to share these miracles with such a person. She gave Bess a moment to absorb the view beneath them, and its truth, before continuing, "Anyhow, in *my* time, all that ice has melted – the South Pole, too. We call it global warming.

"The world distributes its heat in many ways. One is through currents in the oceans. The largest of these conveyors, as we call them, is called the Gulf Stream. When the ice melted, it colossally increased the volume of near-freezing water, and as this water moved south, it began to disrupt the Gulf Stream. Parts of our planet began to cool, and quickly, while others began to overheat. We live at the absolute limits of our survival – although many of us don't realise it – and during that period our crops were dying at a rate to threaten our very existence.

"Again, we used our technology, pushing it to the very edge. Harnessing power from the sun and the wind to drive vast engines, we were able to reinforce the stream while warming the water – once more allowing it to convey heat around the planet.

"It saved us for a while, but of course, the process itself increased average temperatures across the whole planet.

"In the year 2112, we have over-farmed our land to the point where the topsoil is almost dead, and yet we keep using ever more invasive chemistry and mechanical technology to squeeze just a little more out of it. It's a road to total annihilation, but we see no way to break the cycle without allowing most of our population to starve."

They travelled in silence for a while.

"Your world doth sound a frightful place, Jill. But come, tell me how your people *live*. From whence do you hail?"

Baines brightened. "Would you really like to see?"

"Where do you think *you're* going, young lady?"

"Anywhere away from you and your stupid coffee machine!" Rose would have slammed the door to the Millers' quarters behind her, had it not been on rails and powered by heavy hydraulics. As it was, she made do with a flounce.

Ever since returning to the human world, her mother had become impossible. Her father had borne the brunt of her fury as ever, owing to the shortage of shops, restaurants, high-class boutiques and so forth.

"Well, *I'm* not married to her. I'm off!" Rose growled to herself.

Henry's life had also been far from easy, ever since his parents were mugged by a couple of women – one a politician, the other a Nazi. Rose could not choose which was the worse of that pair. Maybe she could cheer him up, *maybe* she could talk to one of the captains about getting her own quarters. They were in short supply, she knew, but if she were willing to share, perhaps? Henry would be behind that, she had no doubt; they got so little time alone. Captain Douglas was a kind man, but also a bit of a stick-in-the-mud. He would go straight to her parents and Lara would put a stop to it. Now, Captain Baines... *Yes,* Rose could imagine her helping them.

Deep in thought, she turned a corner and crashed into Woodsey for a second time. The bowl he had been carrying flew through the air to smash against the wall on its way to the deck.

"Oh, fabulous!" he barked. "What *would* I do without my friends, eh?"

"I'm really sorry," Rose pleaded. "What were you doing with that bowl, anyway?"

"Apologising. *Twice* now, it seems!"

"I, er... I'd better get on, then," she muttered awkwardly, picking up the largest of the pieces and placing them in his hands. *Perhaps,* she thought, *this is something best discussed at another ti—*

"Oh, no you don't," Woodsey barged into her thoughts. "*You* can come and explain this one!"

"I said I was sorry."

"Save it for the chef." He stopped and glared at her. "You know, I was having a real nice morning." His laugh straddled the ground between irony and hysteria. "I got up, just in time for lunch, and can you believe it? I was actually looking *forward* to spending a little time with me mates. But then I remembered Tim was still in a strop with me about the queen – or whatever she is at the moment – then Reiver sold me down the river, and now *you.* What's Henry got in store for me? A burnt effigy?"

"Christian! Is that you?"

Woodsey slumped against the corridor wall. "Oh, *man.*" There was only one person in the world who called him Christian – whatever period they happened to be living through. "Hello, Dad. Have you come to slap the cuffs on?"

"What? No," replied Dr Thomas Wood. "Hello, Rose."

"Hello, Dr Wood," Rose greeted meekly, while surreptitiously moving away.

"I'm *here,*" continued Thomas, furiously, "because you left the hatch open to our quarters. Careless, but not the end of the world, perhaps. *However...*"

Woodsey closed his eyes. "The place caught fire."

"No."

"Unsupported by the door, the walls fell down."

"No."

"The postman came and ate the sofa."

"*What?* No. You left our door open as second on the bill, after you'd headlined by leaving the animal enclosure open last night. I've been hearing all about it from Natalie – Dr Pearson, that is. Apparently, when she spoke with you, she wasn't aware that Henry's Cronopios had escaped, too – all nine of them!"

Thomas turned briefly to Rose. "Don't worry, I've already had a few choice words with your boyfriend about taking care of his animals." He rounded once more on his son. "Now, don't ask me why they came to us. Maybe they followed your scent. After all, you feed them – occasionally – when you remember to help Natalie out. Or perhaps they followed Reiver's scent? I know you've been spending time with him, too. None of this is the problem."

Woodsey opened one eye, just in time to grab Rose's sleeve and pull her back, mid-slope. "So what *is* the problem, Dad?"

"The *Cronopio* have eaten the sofa – they've chewed it to shreds!"

Woodsey put his head in his hands. "Oh, *man!*"

"Oh, I'm not finished," Thomas continued, quite uncharacteristically cross. "They then proceeded to break into my room and crap all over my bed!"

Woodsey fought it. He tried *so* hard, but his shoulders began to tremble and then rock. Completely unstoppable, a tsunami of laughter erupted out of him. Against her own will, Rose tittered, too, but had the grace to hide it behind her hand.

"*Oh,* I'm still not finished," Thomas hammered on, completely nonplussed by the teens' reaction. "Guess which room *you're* getting tonight! And you can forget about the sofa – we don't appear to have one any more! Still, never mind, eh? Maybe we could pick up another one online or nip down to the nearest showroom, hmm...? No, wait!" With that closing salvo of sarcasm, Dr Wood stormed away.

Laughter subsiding, Woodsey sighed deeply. "When will I ever catch a break?"

As the woe left his lips, another shout echoed down the corridor. "*Woodsey!*"

"Oh, for *real?* What now?"

"I'm gonna hurt you!" bellowed Henry. "I've just had a right chewin' out from your old man because *you* let the animals out!"

Rose burst into tears of laughter while Woodsey slipped down the wall, crumpling onto the floor. "Don't hurt me – just kill me, dude."

Chapter 10 | Video Nasty

Crack. Alone in the jungle, Jansen forced himself to look round, his flesh crawling. Suddenly, he was an island, poised to vanish under a tide of life and just waiting for the wave that would overtop him.

Moving away from the Deltadromeus had seemed like a good idea – an obvious choice to make. However, the further he travelled, the braver the woodland creatures became. Painfully aware that he was *not* 'Walking With Wind in the Willows', he checked the breech of his air rifle nervously. He knew it was loaded, but he was fighting panic now.

Snap! Crack! Louder this time. He spun to face the sounds. The foliage was thick here, blocking his view, but it was also weak, providing little protection. He guessed the plants around him were some type of gunnera. Many towered more than a metre over his head, with huge leaves drooping to the ground, but he knew their stems would not stand up to a large dinosaur in the way that a tree of similar girth might. They would snap.

SNAP!

And I will die, he thought. Adding to his woes, he now heard deep grunts and the rustle of heavy foliage being shaken, too. It sounded like a large animal straining at something. Now several hundred metres from the sleeping Deltadromeus, the activity of life was all around him. An eruption of squawking nearby, followed by a chirruping, made his blood freeze – raptors.

They were close, but not *too* close. Jansen's spirit drooped still further. *Great! A Faustian deal with God knows what.* It was the very last thing he wanted to do, yet if he wished to keep the raptors at bay, he must approach the larger creature – approach it, but not be seen by it.

Clearly a powerful animal, whatever was making all the grunting and violent crashing had opened an oasis of calm about itself – and like a planet orbiting a sun, Jansen found himself surrounded by moons. For now, all was in balance – so long as no one moved.

Oh, crap! he cursed silently to himself. *I can't stay here.*

His leg was murder as he dragged it, splinted, using his rifle as a walking staff. Movement took a lot of energy and he had little left to spend. Catching his breath against the thick stem of a giant plant, he used the rifle to carefully move aside the heavy foliage.

A clearing – but not a natural clearing. The large flora had been smashed down. Not the trampling of a herd, merely the path of a large animal. He stepped cautiously forward. The plant stems were broken, but there was other damage, too. Jansen smiled for the first time as he noted evidence of chewing.

Taking a huge gulp of air, he sighed heavily. *A plant eater,* he thought with relief. Smile still on his face, he turned straight into another face, but this one was huge. He had been wrong about the damage being caused by a large animal – there were *two* of them.

The furthest faced away from him, standing on hind legs to crash another giant gunnera to the ground.

The closest stared at him side-on, like a horse. It chewed. Jansen froze in shock, struggling for breath. He dared not move.

The animals were about five or six metres in length and had large sails along their backs. These sails were their most prominent feature, drawing the eye immediately and Jansen's terror spiked. Thinking he had bumped into a couple of spinosaurs – either young ones or a species smaller than the Spinosaurus aegyptiacus he despised so well – his observed chew-damage to the broken leaves was all in the wind.

Oh-my-God! Oh-my-God! Oh, my... oh.

Never in his life had he been so happy to be wrong. Despite the sails, these animals more exactly resembled the unfortunate, half-eaten creature he had discovered in the Carcharodontosaurus nest. *What did Heidi call them? Oorah something? Ouranosaurus, that was it.*

He remembered flying over a herd of similar animals the day before. Judging by some of the larger specimens, which were perhaps a third longer but much more massive, he guessed this pair were still relatively young. The closest continued to chew and stare.

Seized by a crazy notion, Jansen stooped to pick up a discarded piece of leaf from the ground. Leaning heavily on the rifle, he hopped forward.

The dinosaur jerked its head away, startled.

Jansen persevered, holding out the large remnant.

The giant head swung closer once more, slowly, sniffing at the proffered morsel. Still grinding away at its last mouthful, it nevertheless took the food from his hand, adding it to the mix. With leaves and plant stems sticking out from both sides of its chomping cheeks, there was something of Bugs Bunny in its manner.

Jansen grinned. "Hello, boy." Daring to reach forward, he gently patted the snout. "You like that, huh?"

The animal had no understanding of the affection he bestowed, but it chewed amiably enough, happy with his company. Its brother, or sister, Jansen had no idea which, also came to investigate. Once again, he stooped and offered up a large, green something or other to oblivion.

Chuckling at this extraordinary reversal, Jansen patted the second creature on the nose, too. It snorted, raising its head.

Within a heartbeat, the whole dynamic turned instantly perilous. Jansen had no idea what had changed; he simply leapt back as best his damaged leg would allow, giving the giants some respectful space.

The dull, bovine eyes flashed with the whites of fear. As Jansen awoke to the danger, he also began to realise there was something more going on than a beast spooked by his clumsiness.

Another crashing sound approached from the west. Something large was running downhill towards them. A huge, rending *crack* spat a Deltadromeus out of the dense foliage and into the area cleared by the foraging ouranosaurs.

"Whoa!" Jansen cried out involuntarily. His mind raced; this could not possibly be the animal he tranquilised. With two doses, that one must surely be down for hours to come, so this must be another of the dreaded creatures.

Behind him, the ouranosaurs were bucking and braying, filling the clearing with deafening honking sounds right next to his ear, or so it seemed. *This is going to hurt!* He dove into the brush, scrambling as fast as he could to hide out of sight. He would have kept going, too, but for the thought that tore at his heartstrings. Those young herbivores were the only creatures he had met in this hellhole that had not tried to eat, poison or dismember him – could he really just leave them to that *thing?*

He stood, using the rifle to keep his balance. The dinosaurs were roaring and braying furiously now. Jansen heard a loud *thump* followed by a scream. Pushing through the foliage he saw the Deltadromeus leap back after its first attack, blood on its claws and muzzle. One of the ouranosaurs was hurt.

He aimed the rifle at the predator, but it leapt so quickly at its prey that the dart missed. Jansen swore roundly, feverishly loading another.

Though huge, the Deltadromeus was unbelievably fast. A third longer than its prey, yet lighter, it made the ouranosaurs seem pitifully slow and plodding. The monster tore again at the hapless herbivore, but this time got more than it bargained for. By chance or design, the injured animal's sibling bucked, swiping its tail in a vicious arc that caught the predator, knocking him back several metres to crash into the giant flora at the edges of the engagement. Jansen fancied he heard a couple of ribs crack, too, but rather than cowing the theropod predator, the agony of broken ribs made it even angrier.

Weakness was death in this world, and it quickly rolled back to its feet and began a more respectful circling – claws grasping, head low, jaws wide. It wasted no further energy on threats or feints; it was looking for a kill.

Jansen fired a second dart, and this time he hit. Deltadromeus roared in furious anguish as the dart pierced its flesh near the broken ribs. The diminutive David realised his mistake at once, when Goliath skewered him with the molten stare of agonised accusation.

"Oh, crap!"

The huge jaws gaped wide as the dinosaur tensed to sprint at this new and conveniently bite-sized quarry. The roar tearing from its throat knocked Jansen to the floor. He could not *believe* how loud it was. So terrified was he, that it took several clenched seconds to realise that the deafening roar was actually engine noise.

The dinosaurs smashed their way through the foliage in opposite directions, desperate to escape what to them must have seemed apocalyptically loud.

Coming to his senses as he came to his feet, Jansen was as livid as he was grateful. He shook his fist. "What the hell took you so long?"

"And this is almost exactly where I used to li— *will* live. Five hundred years or so from now, I'll be born – just over there, as it happens." Baines turned to her silent passenger, who seemed temporarily robbed of speech. She smiled, kindly. "Bess? Are you alright? If this is all too much for you, we can go back?"

Lost for words, Bess merely shook her head in wonder. "Such..." Her voice croaked. She placed a hand gently to her throat and coughed to clear it. "Such grandeur, I..."

"Yes, it still does that to me, too, and I grew up here. However, this particular part of the moon looks very different from how I imagined. It's not merely that New Florida hasn't been built yet. Even the hills around the crater rim are nothing like I remember – they're further away, too."

"This doth alarm you, Jill? Could the land not be changed over such vast swathes of time?"

Baines frowned, searching her memory. "Look at this." She typed a brief query into the ship's computer and called up construction photographs from the New Florida project. "These pictures were recorded while our moon base was still being built. See the edge of the crater – how near it is? Even the shapes of the rocks are very different."

"Doth rock not wear down over time? We see them left carved by the ancient folk, all over our lands, and all worn smooth. I cannot imagine they always looked thus."

Baines was shaking her head. "No, there is little or no erosion on the moon. No weather, you see? No rainfall to rub away at stone. Little changes up here, notwithstanding violent intercessions from space debris. We have plenty of water, but it's all locked up in ice and doesn't tend to move around very much."

Bess frowned, thinking hard as she tried to unravel both Baines' words and the concepts expressed. "You believe some kind of nefarious event hath caused these changes?"

"If so, then it happened a long time ago – millions of years, most likely."

Bess studied her. She lacked understanding of deep time events but could read Baines' apprehension well enough. "*Jill?*"

"When we moved forward in time, Bess, we left others behind. Not our people. They were enemies, set on remoulding the world to their whim. Potentially, to the cost of everyone who has ever lived. You see, altering the timeline could cause some, many, or even all of us, to have never existed.

"We had no choice but to leave. They were about to destroy our ship, killing all our people, but now I wonder what happened afterwards...

"There has clearly been a devastating impact here at some point in the past – one that had not occurred in our original timeline. This is a worry, because now I can't help wondering what else may have changed, and did it happen naturally or was it caused by a deliberate act to suit someone's purposes? Purposes we don't yet understand."

"I see. And these others of whom you speak, who art they?"

Baines sighed. "There's so much you should know about the future, but before I show you, please understand that we intended none of this. We were thrown back in time by an explosion caused *by* this enemy. One of our own crew was corrupted to help them. His name is Geoff Lloyd."

"*Is* Geoff Lloyd – you mean he still lives?"

"Yes. Almost died several times, but he has more lives than a cat."

Bess thought for a moment. "And this Geoffrey Lloyd, he is with your enemies now?"

"No, he's in our infirmary. He's paid a heavy price for what he did. Never a pleasant guy, but I do believe he regrets his part in all this, and the deaths caused directly or indirectly through his actions."

"You have him, and he *lives?*"

Baines bit her lip. When she answered it came as little more than a sigh. "Yeah."

"You do not punish treason and murder?"

"We do, but we don't kill people for committing crimes, not any more."

"For heaven's sake, why not?"

220

Baines snorted softly. "Yes, it must seem hard to understand. We could have executed him. His life was in my hands, but I..."

"You spared his life. Why?"

"Trust me, I was tempted not to, but I genuinely believed he regretted his actions – still do. I gave him the opportunity to do something to make up for it."

"And has he?"

"He saved a young man's life. One of our engineers, Georgio Baccini."

"Baccini? A papist?"

"What? Oh, no. We don't have those sorts of problems now, Bess. At least, not often. No, Georgio is a kind and gentle young man, and brilliant too. Geoff was responsible for the death of his brother, Mario. If I had executed him, we would have lost Georgio too, when that dinosaur attacked. So I think I chose wisely. When Geoff saved him, he almost lost his own life. We thought he had, at the time. It remains to be seen if he can redeem himself further, but where there is a will..."

They sat in silence for a while, Bess clearly trying to understand the strange ways of these new folk who had appeared inside a mountain. "What is this *dinosaur?*"

Baines smiled. "Now *there's* a story that takes me back."

Devon helped Jansen hobble into the ship, closing the hatch behind them. "I'm sorry it took so long to find you."

"What happened?" asked Jansen, sitting heavily in the co-pilot's seat.

"In a word, apathy. I commandeered our attack vessel immediately upon receiving your distress call, but..."

"But?" Jansen prompted.

Devon let out a frustrated sigh. "The crew's efforts were directed elsewhere, kitting out Heidi for her trip to Munich."

"But she knew I was out here unprotected. *She* left me here. I got a text message explaining that she couldn't find me, but would come if I sent a message – what changed?"

Devon looked at the injured man directly; it was clear Jansen had been through the wringer. "You became a lower priority than whatever she intends to do in Nazi Germany. She told us that if you survived the dinosaur attack, then she had every confidence in your ability to continue to do so for a little longer."

Jansen huffed. "Was that meant to be flattery? And about her *trip* – did you know there *are* no Nazis in this new version of 1943 Germany?"

"No, but I surmised. From what the Old Man said after his return."

"Something has radically changed the timeline. Heidi thought it may have been Douglas' expedition."

Devon nodded. "Hmm. That's what he thought, too. Heidi said things were different and that might help our cause, but she didn't say exactly how different."

"Perhaps you're no longer a member of the charmed inner circle. It seems neither am I." Wearily, he added, "I can't believe she left me twice. Is she still on the *Heydrich?* Couldn't even be bothered to fetch me now?"

"No. She departed for Germany as I was leaving."

Jansen brought his fist down on a console. "Great! What a couple of fools we've been, eh? Siding with the Devil!"

Devon nodded agreement and understanding. He powered down the ship entirely, taking extra care to disable all sensing and spying equipment. "Yes, and to that end, I think we should discuss the future. Perhaps you would consider, *ahem,* siding with the 'Devon'?"

Jansen stared at him. Eventually he asked, "Do you have any water?"

"Of course." Devon disappeared into the craft's small hold and returned with a canteen, a power bar, and some painkillers. "These should help, they're strong ones. I don't want to return just yet. I've swept this ship for – shall we say 'after-market' bugs? She's clean. And we've things to discuss. Are you with me?"

Jansen threw back a couple of pills and swallowed greedily from the canteen. Wiping his mouth, he nodded. "I am. I'm a soldier, I understand that our mission is dangerous and there will always be losses. But I'm done risking my life for people who won't even help their own when it's easily within their power to do so. We don't matter *at all* to the Schultzes. Luckily, there are only two of them."

Devon smiled. "Just them and a hidden army of spies, but I share your sentiments. This world has everything we need to continue our race. I believe in that, but that's just never enough for the Old Man – or his granddaughter.

"I believe we could also have an ally in Commander Ally Coleman, although she has no transport to reach us here. However, principally, we must also speak about Captain Aito Nassaki and that business on the moon."

"The uranium harvest?"

"The murder."

Jansen looked surprised. "I have to admit, I'd forgotten about that."

"Everyone seems to have forgotten about it," Devon replied harshly. "Sergeant Denholm Haig was simply dismembered, stuffed into pieces of space suit – after being injected with our isotope – and left on the moon for the next hundred million years!

"I approached Heidi with fresh evidence about his killer."

Jansen gave him a sidelong look. "And?"

"She was interrogating the *other* Heidi Schultz from Munich and Dr Anne Hemmings at the time. She agreed to my continuing the pursuit of Haig's killer, and allowed me to employ Hemmings as a tech advisor – despite her imprisonment, but..." He tailed off, frowning thoughtfully.

"What is it?" asked Jansen.

"I don't know. She wasn't particularly interested in the death of one our people – not that I expected her to be – but there was something more. It was like she *feigned* disinterest, perhaps to allay suspicion. We all know what she's like, after all, so it's entirely likely her disinterest was genuine. Maybe I was imagining things, but there was just something..."

"*Or,*" Jansen took up the baton, "she wants the investigation to continue because she has her own suspicions but wishes to appear aloof, oblivious even." He lapsed into silent thought for a moment. "The only person she fears is the Old Man. Do you think *she* thinks he's involved?"

Devon massaged his temples, tiredly. "The webs they weave. Can you imagine what it must have been like growing up in that family?"

"You'd be very careful at mealtimes," Jansen quipped. "Do you suspect Nassaki's involvement, too?"

"I did. Maybe I still do, but the Schultzes are always up to something and I'm beginning to wonder if Nassaki's a blind – or a patsy. I couldn't find any link between him and the late Sergeant Haig, other than they were both captives, briefly, aboard the *New World.*

"This is where things could get risky. You see, my intention was to confront Nassaki with the evidence incriminating him – although now I'm not sure whether he left that evidence behind or it was *placed* to incriminate him." He sighed heavily, exasperated.

"And this risk you speak of," continued Jansen, "you're considering asking Nassaki straight out?"

Devon nodded. "But that would tip my— *our* hand."

"I've had enough of all this cloak and dagger stuff!" Jansen burst out angrily. "I say we do it."

"And if we don't like his answer?"

Jansen turned to face Devon directly. "Then we'll either secure a friendship or make another enemy – and we know how to deal with those, don't we?"

"A future king of England? One of *my* descendants? Gets the axe? At the traitorous hands of commoners!" Bess blazed mercurially.

"Not exactly," Baines placated. "He wasn't a *direct* descendant."

"Oh, then forsooth all is well and I'll allow it to vex me not!"

"The Crown was restored a few years later. In fact, it was a period *known* as the Restoration. Being completely honest, though, the Crown eventually came to serve a fairly titular role, becoming subservient to Parliament in reality, if not in ritual and protocol. It was the aristocracy's turn to rule. For a while."

"*I* would not trust most of *them* to rule what happens in their own codpieces!" bellowed the future queen.

Baines grinned. "Yes, well, after World War II, the common man not only agreed with you, but began to do something about it. Naturally, *they* then proceeded to make many of the same old mistakes, but in fairness, they did make some new ones, too. So in summary, *that* happened. World War II, or as the Brits call it, the Second World War, is next on our list. This is arguably the darkest period in world history. Though the battles tended to be less diabolical and drawn out than in the first conflict, there was an underlying evil in the governance of WWII that left an indelible stain. In terms of scale, it was far more atrocious than the religious burnings and injustices of this age. Millions were simply murdered – there's no other word for it, thanks to Reinhard Heydrich and his buddies.

"And this is where we get to the Nazis, our once and future enemy, it seems. It's the philosophical descendants of these guys who got us all into this mess. Can you believe they even named one of their ships to honour that monster, Heydrich?

"If we – *you* – can change the world and save our race, then maybe some good will come from their evil in the end. We can only hope – more to the point, we can only hope to avoid it, second time round.

"These films show a brief history of something we call the Holocaust. You will also see clips of the Nazi war machine in all its destructive brutality. A video *Nazi,* you might call it." Baines grinned. Noting Bess' expression, she cleared her throat self-consciously and simply asked the computer to 'play'.

They watched in silence for the next hour. Baines could feel the tension in the younger woman, building like a negative charge.

She focused on her breathing and swapped her attention to the view outside: Earth from the moon, her home. How she loved that spectacle, but it was more than that. For the very first time in her life, she realised that the Earth, in all its majesty, was merely the cream on the trifle – most people's favourite part, perhaps – but for her, the distance provided *by* that view was the foundation of the trifle, and she was a jelly and sponge gal, all the way.

To Baines, rather than mere kilometres, the space between Earth and the moon was also measurable in units of safety. Here she could admire the world from the comfort of her armchair, like a favourite movie – safe from its tribulations. In her time, moon base *New Florida* was a one-hundred-percent controllable environment, and her father one of its most senior men; her safety had never been in question. Earth was a very different story and quite literally always had been. Whether it was AD2112 or 99,200,000BC.

She glanced surreptitiously at Bess. The young princess' face was expressionless, but Baines could easily discern between genuine nonchalance and training. Elizabeth had lived with danger almost all her life. Had hardly known a time when she was out of it. Consequently, she had learned to keep her own counsel, learned to hide within herself.

Baines believed in their agreed course of action; believed they had indeed been tempted by a one-off deal offering the chance for a future – one where the looming extinction of the human race might be avoided, but she was not blind to the fact that there would be costs. Glancing at the young woman beside her, she wondered how much damage this imparted knowledge might do. Would it outweigh the good? Could Elizabeth change the world so radically that the end came even sooner? Was that even possible for one woman? Was it all simply too much to dump on her?

The answer, she suspected, was yes. After all, what could be more powerful than knowledge? She looked down on the Earth once more. *What have we done to you?*

"Enough."

Baines, startled out of her reverie, sat up sharply. "What?"

"That's enough. Please stop your moving paintings, Jill."

Bess' face showed no emotion, but there was a hardness to her eyes that had not been there before.

Baines stopped the video as instructed. "Are you alright, Bess? I know that's a lot to take in—"

"I'm fine. I have watched your pictures, have seen your world and it is a frightful place."

"There are good things you should see, too," Baines tried. "Extraordinary achievements of ingenuity and courage that—"

"No," Bess cut her off. "I believe I have seen enough. Already, I know more than any mortal should of the future and have reached a decision – forsooth, two decisions."

Unsure where this might be heading, Baines waited, saying nothing, asking nothing.

"Firstly, I see that it is my duty to do everything I can to protect England from the terrible certainty you hast shown to me. A world of smoke and fire, ruled by mechanical monsters, a world that must *not* come to pass.

"I am not too proud to admit that I shall require wise counsel to avoid this future, and I hereby accept the help you offer."

"We are sorry to put this on you, Bess. You will have enough to deal with without this, but it must be you, you see? We have this one chance in this one place. The industrial revolution began here and it must begin again here, but hopefully with a foresight our people simply didn't have the first time round."

"Indeed. I accept the task."

Baines waited, but as Bess was not forthcoming, she asked, "And the second decision?"

Bess turned her seat to face Baines directly. Her eyes were cold and weary, like she had aged years in mere hours. "I shall never deliver progeny into this world of yours. I wish no child of mine to live through such horrors. What will be will be, but I will end when my time runneth out, and leave to others what is required to complete your task."

Oh, crap! thought Baines. *Don't tell me I've just reinvented the Virgin Queen.* "The future is not set, Bess. God knows, we can vouch for that. Please do not let us—"

Bess cut her off with a hand. "I would return to England, please. I have seen wonders, but now it is time."

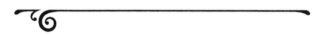

Later that evening Baines knocked on Douglas' door. It slid open momentarily. "Jill, come in. Ah was just... What's happened?"

"Oh, James," she replied tiredly, entering his quarters. "I've come to see if you might just possibly be able to save my soul."

"Ah take it 'the plan' hasnae quite gone to plan, eh? Well, Ah'll do what Ah can for yer soul. Maybe a wee dram will help thaw it a little, hmm?"

As the door slid closed, she fell into his arms.

He held her, frowning with concern. "Gratifying as this is, ye're beginning to worry me, lassie. What's happened?"

Douglas listened in silence until Baines ran out of words. She rubbed tiredness from her eyes. "So, what do you—"

"*Think?*" he completed. "Ah think, what's done is done. This was never going to be pretty, Jill."

"You were against it all along, weren't you?"

Douglas poured them both another measure of single malt, obtained with Lord Maxwell's generosity. "Ye know, this stuff's no' half bad. And Ah never said Ah was against it, by the way. Ah simply said Ah didnae know what to do for the best. The majority decision was against me and, well, Ah suppose Ah was glad to bow out, in a way."

Baines tilted her head quizzically. "How so?"

"Because then the decision wasnae mine to make. So, when it came to playing God, Ah was happy to take the coward's way out, for better or worse."

"Oh, *James.* You've never committed a cowardly act in your life. If ever there was anyone—"

He forestalled her with a hand. "Ah play by the rules, Jill. You're the one with the real courage, the maverick who'll do whatever your people need, with nary a single thought for yourself or what you'll have to live with." He gave her the smile, the one that melted her from her heart down to her socks, and always had. With a chuckle he added, "You're twice the man Ah am, Jill, and Ah love ye for it."

She took his glass, placing it on the coffee table so she could sit on his lap. "How do you always know what to say?"

"What, like 'you're no' *entirely* nuts'? Ah seem to remember *you* having something to say about that little nugget – Ah still have the holes in ma hand from the cactus!"

"OK, so you have your off days." She grinned and kissed him. "Hang on – cactus?"

He laughed. "Never mind. Ah think the wisest course now is simply to press on. We've made our decision – all we can do is walk from where we stand and carry out the plan to the best of our ability. Also, Ah think the quicker we get out of this time the better it'll be for everyone. We dinnae belong here. We have a job to do, but let's no' linger, eh?"

Baines nodded, pensively.

"Ah have to say, though, the changes you described to the moon's geology have me a little concerned. How do we account for it?"

Baines shrugged. "I checked and triple checked our co-ordinates. It was definitely... *home.*" Her voice cracked a little.

He held her close. "Aye, Ah understand... but we'll muddle through it, lassie."

She accepted the hug gratefully, then pulled away, to deal with a rogue tear. Smiling bravely, she continued, "You ask me how we account for it, but you know... I've seen the moon in the past, the future – I've lived on it, was even *born* on it, and after all that, about the only thing I can be absolutely sure of is that I have *never* seen Elvis there."

Douglas looked at her for a moment and they both snorted with laughter.

"On the up side," she continued, "Hitler never made it up there, either."

"Ah'll pass that devastating blow on to the fringe press," Douglas chuckled. He raised his glass. "To getting out of here."

They clinked. "I'm with you there, but I think there'll be tears before bedtime."

"Go on."

"We've lost people outside for a start."

Douglas sighed deeply. "Cocksedge and Schultz's aide. What was her name?"

"Erika Schmidt. Do we simply leave those two behind? To get up to who knows what? And then there's Hiro. Can you imagine what *he's* going to be like when we leave the *New World* entombed in this mountain?"

Douglas looked lovingly around his quarters and lowered his head sadly. "Ah'll miss her, too, but for Hiro Ah think it'll be far worse. The *New World's* ma ship, but for the chief, Ah dinnae joke when Ah say, Ah think she was his first love."

"Are you contemplating destroying her, James?"

"Ah was, until you and Sarah came up with our new direction. Now Ah think Elizabeth will need the knowledge contained in this old hull, if she's to have any chance of pulling this off. It's a heavy load we're placing on her – and she'll have load enough to carry. You know far more about this time than Ah do, so Ah dinnae have to tell you that. But she's a tough lass."

"I agree, but watching her absorb that information earlier was heartbreaking, nonetheless. No one should know about their future like that, James, but Elizabeth was just so... *stoic*."

"Ye didnae tell her about her own life and death, did ye?" Douglas looked shocked.

"Credit me with some restraint, honey. No, I carefully dodged anything that affected her directly. I hope it was the right thing to do, but we're so far off the reservation now..."

They sat in silence for a while, in one another's arms but in separate worlds.

"But concerning Hiro," Baines broke into the moment. "He certainly hasn't been the same."

"Aye, Ah think there's more to it than just his *Sekai,* though."

"Aito?"

Douglas nodded. "It nearly destroyed him to lose his brother the first time, but to get him back and lose him again..."

"But we don't know he's dead, James."

"*Jill,*" he drawled, shaking his head sadly. "Ah saw that creature take his hand and fling him at the cave wall like a ragdoll. Ah cannae see how anyone could survive that. The blood was everywhere, even from a distance as the hatch was closing behind me, Ah..." He tailed off, sickened. "Ah should never have let the laddie go."

Baines ran a gentle hand up and down his spine to relax tense muscles. "You had no choice, James. The hostage swap allowed us to kidnap Tim Norris away from Heidi, as you'd vowed to do. But saying that, I do understand your feelings. I wouldn't count Aito Nassaki out just yet, though. He came back from the dead once, after all."

"Ah, just the man I wanted to see! Lieutenant Devon, a word please."

Devon, recently returned from rescuing Jansen, was leaving the small infirmary his hapless co-conspirator now shared with Heinrich Schultz. At the sound of his name, he turned. "Captain Nassaki, how may I help you?"

"We have orders from Dr Schultz. She wishes us to find a location near to the wormhole where a large industrial facility may be constructed. We'll need good bedrock, and you know this area better than I, so I thought I'd enlist your help."

Devon had hoped for a little time alone to think, and plot his next move, but could see no way of refusing Nassaki his help without raising suspicion. Then a thought struck him. "Sir, there is one man who knows this area extremely well."

"You refer to Mr Jansen, I assume," replied Aito. "I thought he was injured."

"Not seriously. Once his leg's fixed up, he'll wish to leave the infirmary as soon as possible."

Aito gave Devon a secret smile. "I don't doubt it. How is the Old Man, by the way?"

Devon returned his smile. "He seemed in, er... *rude* health when I saw him just now, sir. Jansen should be out on crutches in a few hours, perhaps we could wait 'til then?" He shrugged. "Maybe take an armoured vehicle out to find our most likely location?"

Aito nodded. "Let me know when our colleague is ready."

Devon watched him walk away. *So reasonable. What* is *your story, Nassaki?* he wondered. *I must know.*

It was a fine morning. Douglas, Georgio, Hiro and Patel took a ride in one of their armoured personnel carriers, with The Sarge and O'Brien providing security and a driver.

"We're very lucky with the weather," remarked Douglas. "It wasn't uncommon for these hills to be under drifting snow by this time of year – during this period, Ah mean."

"It is a beautiful view," agreed Patel.

"Speaking of views," interrupted Georgio, "I think I can see our target. Shall we get out, Captain?"

O'Brien drew to a halt and popped the rear hatch for Douglas' engineering team.

"Using our soil-resistance and ground penetrating radar, and dialling it up to maximum, we should be able to get a picture of the *New World*'s aft section in the ground beneath us," Georgio explained for Douglas' sake. "Hiro, could you give me a hand with this, please?"

Between them, the engineers heaved the equipment from the vehicle. "It will take some time to build a complete picture, sir."

"Very well, Georgie. Sarge, go with them. There may be unfriendlies hiding in the heather."

"Sir."

The three men carried their equipment to Georgio's plotted start point and began dragging the machine across the face of Cheviot Mountain.

O'Brien armed herself to stand security for Douglas and Patel – two-thirds of the ruling triumvirate.

"To complete this work will expend much if not all of our material," Patel stated dispassionately. "Even to the point of disassembling our home."

"You don't think it's worth it?" asked Douglas.

Patel scratched a hand over several days' stubble. "It had better be, James. As you know, I have concerns about the plan to involve ourselves in these times, but I'm also most uncertain about creating a portal for our people to leave by. At least, in this way. Walking unprotected into a wormhole has never been attempted. Anything could go wrong."

"Aye, ye may be right, but we dinnae belong here, Satnam. We *have* to go."

"Yes – but go where? Have you fully considered that? There are plenty of empty spaces left on the map in this time. We do not necessarily need to resort to such desperate measures."

Douglas looked at Patel in surprise. "Starting a new colony with advanced technology in 1558? Ye cannae be serious, Satnam? Have we no' done enough damage already?"

"Why not? We would need to implement certain restrictions, but the world is a big place in these times."

Douglas was shaking his head. "Let's say you're right. We *control* ourselves, disallowing any kind of growth. Even if we placed ourselves out of the reach of these people, what about the generations who follow us? Sooner or later, someone would shout 'go' and it would be a free-for-all. Ye must see that."

Patel considered. He sighed with exasperation. "There is wisdom in what you say, James, but taking into account Jill Baines' concerns about the altered geology of the moon, what exactly do you think the *future* will reveal – assuming we survive our trip through the wormhole?"

Douglas grimaced. "Death or glory?"

Patel nodded silently, staring out over hills that seemed to roll on forever, peaking and troughing like an Einsteinian map of space–time itself. He let the point rest, returning to the work in hand. "Jim Miller will have to rip your ship apart, if he's to create enough power conduit to fuel our 'experiment', all the way out here. That must be hard for you, James."

"Aye. Georgio explained while Hiro tried not to listen. Most actions for the greater good tend to be like that. But hard or no', if it saves our people..." He tailed off. Drinking in the view, he continued wistfully, "They're a good bunch – mostly. If there's any chance at all we can get them home, we must try. And talking of good people, Mary packed me off with some breakfast wraps this morning – would you care to try one? It's veggie sausage. Ah cannae wait."

Douglas, Patel and O'Brien munched the morning away while the autumnal sun sailed low across a depthless blue sky.

Beneath it, Georgio, Hiro and The Sarge crisscrossed the hillside. By noon, they had toiled, tripped and sworn over every rabbit hole, heather bush and bog on Great Cheviot's south-west slope, but they were ready to view and share their results.

"Excellent!" the young Italian enthused as the holo came to life above the control console. He spun the three-dimensional display to take in all the angles. "It looks like we're in good shape. You see, Captain, most of the damage was inflicted to the bow section, as you'd expect. Apart from minor damage from the earth falling back in around the ship, we're really not bad at all.

"Now, I suggest we dig down to this point here." He pointed a finger into the holographic display. "It's about – what's the scale on that, Hiro? That's better, yes, it's about fifty metres below and in front of us – as we're oriented east. If we begin digging here, we can cut a shaft large enough for our machines and run the large power conduit back out from the *New World*'s core."

"And you think it will be OK to bring the WHD out here?" asked Douglas.

"For a short time, Captain," Hiro spoke for the first time. He seemed even more subdued than previously.

Douglas would check on him later, but in private. For now, they had work to do. "Are you planning on propping the shaft this time? Judging by how far down and in we need to go, we'd have to remove half the hill to create another cutting, surely?"

"Indeed, Captain," replied Georgio, the ghost of concern crossing his face. "Which will require even more of the resources we don't-a have. Unfortunately, there are very few large trees left this side of the border – at least, of the type we would need to build structural supports. Apparently, Henry VIII cut them all down a few years ago to build ships – a hundred thousand oaks, Beckett told me. So we'll have to carve the supports we need from *our* ship, too. Sorry."

"Very well," agreed Douglas. "Jen, open a channel to Bluey in the Pod's hangar, could you?"

O'Brien obliged.

"Bluey, this is Douglas. You can begin now, but stay close to your escort."

"*That's great news, Captain. We're on our way – Red's been chomping.*"

Douglas smiled and looked north, towards the plateau built upon their arrival. Bluey and Red, along with a team of other diggers and machine operatives, had worked the morning, widening the cutting that led down to the Pod's main hangar.

The fruits of their labour became apparent as the monstrous blade of a huge yellow bulldozer appeared from the cutting's mouth. Carving deep furrows, the mighty tracks turned the machine in Douglas' direction before working together to drive the behemoth forward. Behind the dozer, appearing slender and almost fragile by comparison, pushed one of their thirty-ton excavators. Douglas knew that one was driven by Red, Bluey's brother.

The 150-ton bulldozer – effectively mothballed after creating a thoroughfare across several miles of roughest Cretaceous Patagonia – now smashed its way across the undulating Cheviot, its eight-metre-wide blade turning landscape into roadway as it went. Bluey was in hog heaven as ton after ton of soil churned and rolled aside at his passing, only to be tidied and prevented from falling back by his brother's tender care.

Bringing up the rear, Captain Meritus drove a third tracked vehicle, another APC, carrying an armed detail.

Douglas watched the awesome display of power rolling towards them. Utterly lacking the merest scrap of humility, it somehow contrived to create a humbling spectacle. "The cat's well and truly out of the bag now, eh? Future landscape archaeologists will have to be blind to miss this one!

"Georgio, you planned this route – you did check there werenae any cairns or cists or any other archaeology in the path of that monster, right? This place is lousy with them."

"Erm..."

Douglas spared the young engineer a withering glance before closing his eyes with a sigh. "O'Brien! Open another channel to Bluey!"

Roughly two and a half thousand miles away, and the better part of a hundred million years earlier, an almost identical APC trundled across the top of a promontory in prehistoric Egypt.

Travelling away from the *Heydrich,* with the stunning North African Delta in the rear-view cameras, Devon set the vehicle's sensor suite to scan the ground beneath and around them.

"The top of the hill, from what I've seen," began Jansen, "is like a stone oval. The deeper soils in the centre are where all the trees grow. The largest and flattest bedrock is where the *Heydrich* sits."

Aito nodded agreement. The vehicle's scans seemed to bear out Jansen's observations. "I would imagine the depression at the centre of the oval has been filled in with earth and sand by the wind, over millennia. It might prove a quagmire in the monsoon season."

"Trouble is, the ground under the *Heydrich* isn't big enough to carry a large manufacturing plant. Besides, we need the ship to remain on station to provide protection for the wormhole – and any travellers. We can hardly park her where she'll sink! No, to meet Heidi's requirements, we'll have to clear the ground at the centre of the promontory and dig heavy pile foundations down to the bedrock, most likely."

"By hand, Captain?" Devon's tone expressed disbelief.

"Is that meant to be a joke?" Aito asked, acidly, waving his stump.

"Erm... I..."

Aito laughed. "Forgive my gallows humour, Lieutenant. And that's a *no,* by the way. Heidi's mission is to bring equipment and matériel through the wormhole. As it still seems to be expanding, we should soon be able to pass vehicular traffic – assuming the geography at the other end allows it. Perhaps she'll return with a few extra helpers, too. Once she's auctioned those eggs, naturally." Aito chuckled, wryly this time. "What a scam. I have to say this latest plan is one of the most audacious, if not craziest, schemes the Schultzes have come up with yet."

Devon and Jansen shared a secret look.

"Can you walk?" Devon asked him.

"He'll be alright," Aito answered for him, deadpan. "I'll give him a hand."

After an awkward silence Jansen burst out laughing and Devon groaned, all three men relaxing a little in one another's company.

Still chuckling, Jansen replied, "I can hobble about with my crutches. I was fortunate, my ankle's badly sprained, but not broken. Gonna take a while for the tendons to mend, though."

"Good man," Devon acknowledged. "Captain, I suggest we arm ourselves and go take a look over the ground we're recommending for a building site. Just in case there are any surprises."

Devon drove into the edges of the wooded copse at the centre of the plateau, pulling up when the foliage ahead became too dense for their vehicle to continue. "We should have a chance here, if any large predators arrive on the scene – plenty of trees to dive behind. I'll lock the hatch by voice command only – just in case we have to make a rapid withdrawal. *Valiantly,* of course."

Jansen held up a crutch, plaintively. "Let's hope not."

Devon's mouth twitched a smile. "Thank you."

"For?" asked Jansen.

"Making sure I'm not gonna be at the back. After you, Ben."

"No, *please,* officers first."

Grinning, Devon took the lead, stepping out of their air-conditioned environment into the baker's oven of a Cretaceous evening.

"You know I should be resting, right?" chuntered Jansen behind him.

They walked away from the APC. The trees within the small wood were not tightly packed, providing plenty of room for the men to move between. As they neared the centre of the copse, brighter daylight betrayed a clearing ahead, and within moments they were once more bathed in evening sunshine. Devon quickly scanned the clearing for threats before noting its size and composition. It was about a hundred metres in length, fifty wide, and kidney-shaped; slightly wider at the northern end facing the ocean.

Devon waited for Jansen to catch up before speaking. "I disabled the APC's external microphones, but you never know. We should be OK here."

Aito took an instant step away from his companions, making sure they were both within his field of vision. "OK here for *what?*"

"We need to talk," supplied Jansen.

Aito's eyes narrowed suspiciously. "I'm listening."

Devon and Jansen looked at one another. Devon spoke. "I need to ask you a few questions, Captain. I hope you will not be alarmed, but just in case, I've disabled your weapon."

Aito pursed his lips and pulled his sidearm from its holster. Checking the clip, he found it empty. "I suppose the spare clips you gave me are no good, either."

"Sorry, Captain, but we need to know where we stand."

"What the hell is this all about, Lieutenant?"

"Shall we call it an *addendum* to our conversation of the other day – the one where we discussed stranding the Schultzes in the future?"

Aito relaxed, but only slightly. "I thought that plan was well and truly blown."

"Perhaps, but the principle was sound. After all, here we are about to break ground on a permanent incursion from 1943 Munich to Cretaceous Africa. We have a wormhole that is steadily growing with no apparent way to stop it and Heidi is auctioning dinosaur eggs to pay for the beginnings of the next Nazi war machine. I mean, when are we going to say enough is enough?"

Aito's expression betrayed nothing as he asked, "What do you suggest we do about it?"

"If Heidi's already there," replied Jansen, "then there's not much we can do right at this moment. She will doubtless return with equipment and even more people for us to take care of. However, before we talk further of that, we need to know exactly where *you* stand, Captain."

"Where *I* stand?" Aito raised an eyebrow. "Without wishing to sound fatuous – in a clearing surrounded by carnivorous dinosaurs and without a weapon. Who needs a creek or a missing paddle with you two around!"

"I'm sympathetic to your plight, Captain," said Devon. "So I'll come directly to the point. There's something going on between the Schultzes. Something that will undoubtedly affect all of us, and almost certainly in a way none of us would want. It has something to do with the murder of Sergeant Denholm Haig."

"And this has *what* to do with me?"

"I believe you killed him."

Aito crossed his arms, staring both men down. "Your proof?"

"Security cam footage."

"You're lying."

"Nope. You did a good job erasing your entry to the locker where the air tanks were stored, but the film was just *ever so slightly* rough, where you cut it together. I can show you the slight judder in the video, Captain, if you'd like to see the proof of your mistake? I now have the missing footage."

"OK, Lieutenant. Why don't you tell me what *exactly* is on this film of yours?"

"A figure. Probably a man, tampering with the air tank Haig was about to take out."

"A figure? Probably a man? Is this a joke, Devon? You accuse your superior officer with *this?*"

"He did wear a mask, Captain. No one said the perp was a fool."

"So illuminate me, where exactly do *I* come into this?"

"The man wore a mask over his head, true, but the damning evidence was his hand."

"His hand?"

"Yes, sir. All *one* of them!"

"Ah."

What the quarter-kilometre road lacked in sophistication, it made up for in the brutality of its statement on the land. Douglas walked back along the new scar cut into the hillside, alone with his thoughts – and The Sarge, with a fully charged weapon.

Bluey had carefully tilted the dozer's blade to create a natural run-off for the rain and sleet when it inevitably returned. However, he cut the slope with a bias *towards* the hill, while his brother continued the process of cutting a metre-deep water channel all along the inside edge of the road, to carry the expected floodwater.

Every twenty metres, Red paused his trench *along* the road to dig a channel *across* the road. Also a metre deep at the hill end, these cross channels were dug with a fall of approximately one in thirty, towards the outer edge. Red took the extra time required to do this in order to slow the water's egress, so that it would carry away any silt or loose substrate left by the cutting of the road, down the side of the mountain. He knew from experience that if the water travelled too quickly, it would dump any suspended material, eventually blocking the new land drains. It was highly unlikely they would need the road long enough for that to happen, but the Australian twins were born of a breed who took pride in their work, and in doing that work properly – although, on this occasion, he refrained from checking the fall with his laser level.

Meanwhile, the teams further back towards the plateau were already using a lorry-mounted crane to offload large-bore polyvinyl chloride pipes, taken from their mining stores.

Cool, blue crystal skies provided Douglas with the crisp 'thousand-mile' outlook so indicative of a fine autumn day. He could clearly see the workers laying the pipes in the trenches across the road while one of the smaller diggers backfilled each trench and levelled the top surface.

It would have been much simpler and quicker to camber towards the outer edge when cutting the road, thus allowing surface water to naturally fall over the side and run down the hill. However, Bluey had argued that, should the weather take a serious turn for the worse, their heavily laden lorries might take a similar slippery route, and go over the side with the water – especially if that water happened to be ice or snow.

Douglas had learned to trust the Australian's instincts about such things. As he strode along the outer edge of the new road, making his way back to the Pod's entrance, he could hardly fail to notice that some of the drops to his left side were indeed alarming. Bluey's caution seemed well founded. Their weather had already gone from clear skies to blizzard and back to clear skies again, in their short time here; it might throw anything at them in the coming weeks.

He stopped a moment, just to take in the view across the valleys below. The sun was already dipping towards the west. With not a cloud in the sky to soften its brightness, hard shadows were lengthening across the landscape.

Douglas filled his lungs with air as crisp and sweet as he had ever tasted. He closed his eyes, enjoying the autumnal sun on his face. Every time the breeze dropped, a pleasant warmth penetrated his clothing and skin, undoing the knots of tension in his body.

He was practically home, but this was by no means the home of his youth – in so many ways it was better. With a rush, the realisation that he did not wish to leave this place swept through him, fomenting another desire – to protect all he saw for the future.

"Wishing we could take it all with us, sir?" The Sarge asked, gruffly.

Douglas had almost forgotten the other man was there. "Aye," he admitted ruefully. "If only we could bottle it, eh?"

The Sarge chuckled, making Douglas look at him quizzically.

"You got me thinking about a ship in a bottle, sir. We've certainly produced a trick, wouldn't you say? In the future people will go crazy wondering how the hell we did it, with no signs of the usual disturbances left by digging."

Douglas smiled. "Aye, they will at that—" His last word was clipped as something caught his attention.

"Sir?"

"Over there, Sarge. Ah dinnae wish to raise ma arm. West and just a little south, on the next hill over. Ah thought Ah saw movement."

The Sarge squinted for a moment before tearing open a pocket to retrieve a small pair of field glasses. "Here, sir. See if you can pinpoint it."

"Thanks." Douglas took the glasses and, focusing the electronics and optics, brought his quarry into view. What he saw was a young man, and it was a young man he recognised, staring back at him through a telescope. "What's he about?"

"Captain?"

"Here." Douglas handed back the binoculars, pointing out the location. "There's no pretending now, he's *seen* that we've seen him."

The Sarge refocused for his own vision. "Looks like that cheeky little sod we came across while searching for the princess. What was his name? Walter something?"

"Aye, one of the several Walter Scotts. We always knew our location could no' remain a secret, but what will he do with the information, Ah wonder?"

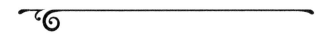

"May I ask, what do you intend to do with this information, Lieutenant?"

Devon inclined his head. "You don't deny it, then, Captain? I commend you. You see, despite cleverly pixelating even the film you removed from the logs, just in case, your... erm, *deficit,* may still be recognised, I'm afraid. I can, of course, show you the videos, should you doubt my evidence." He stared, daring Aito to refute his claim. "As for what I intend to do, that will depend on what you tell us. I have authority from Dr Schultz to find the murderer, Captain. So, how do you answer?"

"What a coincidence, gentlemen," Aito replied with a slow, confident half-smile. "I proceeded with that same authority."

Jansen glanced at Devon, who nodded, neither shocked, nor surprised. "Tell us, please, Captain."

Aito sat on the trunk of a fallen tree, taking his ease. "Just before Heidi left the moon, with Jansen here, to redirect that comet, she called me to her quarters. As I assume you've already found out, Lieutenant, she visited her grandfather while he was still a prisoner in our brig.

"I assume you also know, if you've been toing and froing through our surveillance logs, that Sergeant Denholm Haig also visited the Old Man, shortly prior to that meeting."

Devon nodded.

"But do you know *why* Haig attended on the Old Man?"

"There was no record of the conversation," Devon explained, for Jansen and Aito's benefit. "Only footage of him entering and leaving a few minutes later."

"As I thought," continued Aito. "According to Dr Schultz, and despite the Old Man's status as a prisoner at that time, Haig was called there to answer for a crime.

"Before I explain the details of that crime, let me just say that Haig was not a moral man. Although I took no pleasure in... in what I had to do, you should know he was a lascivious pervert and treacherous to his core – ideal security staff for Schultz's flagship, you might say."

Devon gave him a sidelong glance. "I found no evidence of this. His record seemed clean enough. A good soldier."

Aito swapped Devon's glance for one of long sufferance. "Tell me you're not that naïve, Devon. The public records of everyone on this mission aren't worth a damn. You didn't actually think we were the good guys, did you?"

"I believed we had this one chance to save our race," retorted Devon, irritated. "What's *your* agenda?"

Aito sighed. "Let's just say, it's not what it was and leave it at that, for now. Let's also put any pointless moralising aside for a minute, shall we? Haig was called before the Old Man to answer for, what Heinrich called, treason."

That surprised both of Aito's interrogators. "Go on," prompted Jansen.

Aito grinned, suddenly. "You see, he gave materials necessary for the building of a weapon to none other than Del Bond. You were there, Jansen. You surely remember Bond's pen – that little three-shot repeater he managed to put together as if from the air?

"Bond got the things he needed..." Aito was laughing now, "in exchange for some photos of that young girl – the one he dragged along with him when he escaped the *New World*. Remember her? The dishy young blonde?"

"Photos?" asked Devon, sceptically. "For *weapons?*"

"No, merely for a few innocuous bits and pieces that could, with a little imagination, *become* a weapon. And yes," Aito chortled, "in exchange for pictures Bond sneaked while the girl was undressing – that old dog! You know how strict the Old Man is about staff relationships: No breeding until *I* say we're ready," Aito intoned, giving his best impression of Heinrich's clipped, aristocratic accent. "That said, I would imagine those pics went round like prison currency!"

Remembering Rose Miller, Jansen, too, began to snigger. Only Devon remained aloof, frowning at them. "So he traded photos—"

"*Nude* photos," Aito cackled.

"Whatever. Bond traded them for the materials required to make a basic weapon. Are you saying that the Old Man *blamed* Haig, for Bond's attempt on his life when he destroyed the *Sabre?*"

Aito clicked his fingers and winked. "Exactly, Devon. No point arguing *mens rea* with a Schultz. Whether he was angrier about the attempt on his life or the breakdown of discipline, who can say?"

"OK." Devon massaged his temples. "The Old Man accused him. What did this have to do with Heidi *or* you?"

"Remember I told you Haig was treacherous? He bought his life by betraying me."

Devon looked pained. "*What?* Betrayed you how?"

"By telling Heinrich about an alleged conversation overheard aboard the *New World,* between my brother, Chief Hiro Nassaki and myself. While we were prisoners."

"So there *was* a connection between you from the *New World,*" Devon thought aloud. "I suspected there might be."

"Only an *alleged* conversation, mind you," Aito corrected him.

"And what was this *alleged* conversation about?" Jansen asked, gruffly.

"It never took place," Aito lied. "Haig was just desperate to offset his part in what had happened with Bond by dropping someone else in trouble. As we two were the only witnesses to this alleged event, no one could gainsay his story."

"Except you," noted Devon.

"Yeah, like the Old Man would believe *me*."

"OK. What did Haig tell Heinrich?" asked Jansen.

"Nothing, as far as I know. Heidi told me he *implicated* me in some scheme or other and then retired to gather the evidence. She was called to visit her grandfather so that he could inform her of a situation requiring resolution. In Schultz parlance, that usually means someone needs killing."

It was Jansen's turn to look strained. "So, why are you still at large, if the Old Man even suspects you *may* have been scheming against the Schultzes?"

"Am I?"

"Are you what?" asked Devon.

"Am I at large? You gentlemen seem to have me, wouldn't you say?"

Devon frowned, confused. "But Heinrich..." He trailed off as the pieces began to fit together.

Aito sighed. "As entertaining as it is to watch you struggle at this, Lieutenant, I don't wish to be out here on this game trail all day. So I'll help you along, shall I?

"Haig was a dead man. The moment Schultz found out about the business with Bond. How he found out, I've no idea – the man's damned near omniscient, so perhaps it's not that surprising. Haig bartered for his life. Heinrich accepted his proffered information. He then called for his granddaughter – and yes, it kind of makes you wonder who was in prison and who was actually in charge, I know. Heidi was told to deal with it, but she decided to do so obliquely and quickly – perhaps more quickly than her grandfather wished, I couldn't say for sure."

Devon's eyes narrowed. "You mean before he could report back on your tre— *alleged* treachery?"

Aito shrugged noncommittally. "Now, I'm offering conjecture here, but I believe something changed within Heidi after the incident with Tim Norris. It could be that some of her defences came crashing down, or maybe she has taken a few notes on how the enemy conduct themselves. Who can really say, but I believe she has become more attuned to the *possibility* of mutiny within the Schultz ranks. Such a concept was once unimaginable to her, so far did it fall outside the family dictum of 'rule by terror'. Before we destroyed most of our own fleet, she would have simply executed Haig, and as publicly as possible, to set an example to the rest of us. However, our numbers and resources continue to dwindle. So this is what I believe.

"She wished to avoid sending another disgusted shockwave through the crew by instructing *me* to deal with Haig. She kept the situation unofficial, naturally, but by telling me *and* selling me on the merits of covering my own back against Heinrich's suspicions – her words, not mine – she removed the problem. While it was *I* who committed the felony."

Devon nodded understanding. "And she was happy for me to bring you to justice, assuming you would be executed for murder, thus dealing with Haig and – should you actually be a traitor – any possible insurrection *you* might perpetrate in the future, all in one sweet little manoeuvre. And of course, the Schultzes are seen as the clean-handed seekers of justice. It's neat. It's very neat." He sat on an adjoining log. "Why do we always seem to be mere ants, in thrall to their controlling mind?"

"Oh, you had to say it!" Aito jumped to his feet.

"Aaarrgh!" Devon joined him. While they were talking, Aito's log had come to life as a whole colony of giant ants approached him from either end. "That explains why no one wants to live in this clearing – I thought it was quiet!" His voice shook as he spun, batting himself down.

"Let's get the hell out of here," snapped Jansen, already making his way at a high-speed hobble.

Aito brought up the rear, quickly catching them. "So, are we agreed?"

"About what?" shouted Devon, still shuddering and jumping in circles at the creeping horror he had just endured.

Aito batted a six-centimetre-long straggler off the other man's shoulder. "About this being an *ideal* location for Heidi's new factory!"

Chapter 11 | Local Troubles, Stranger Problems

"You and your men know the local terrain expertly. Once you have drawn them out, you attack them here." Erika Schmidt stabbed at the rough map she had drawn, with a finger. "You will not have the benefit of acting under cover of darkness, so, in order for your ruse to work, choose your frontman wisely." She glanced at the young Borderer to make sure he was still following her words, rather than her curves. "You understand, Sir John? Douglas' people will not be easily fooled. Our principal advantage lies in the likelihood that he will not wish to strike back with deadly force, and once you have your hostages, *we* have our leverage."

Sir John Johnstone nodded slyly. "And inside their fort, there are weapons?"

"More powerful than you can possibly imagine," Cocksedge chipped in. "You have a bit of a problem with David Lord Maxwell, I understand?"

"Aye, we have a feud."

"You *do* surprise me," she answered wryly. "Well, as your riders have very kindly brought us word that he's recently taken... what was the name of that place again?"

"Hermitage Castle," supplied Johnstone, darkly.

"Yes. Quite." She smiled, calculating. "*Hermitage.* Now, how would *you* like to take it from him?"

The young man looked astonished by the notion. "Hermitage is fair strong, ye ken?"

Cocksedge shared a secret look with Schmidt as she patted Sir John's hand. "Oh, I think we can accommodate. Besides, it sounds a much stronger and more appropriate venue from which to launch our campaign than this lumpen place, wouldn't you agree?"

"But tha castle? It will be mine?"

"Of *course,*" she assured smoothly. "We're only here to help."

Father Robert banged heavily on the rough oak door, making its planks shake on their hinges. The room he shared with two brothers from his order was small but reasonably comfortable. Yet it was a prison. When the castle changed hands, Maxwell's men, distrusting their religion, had locked the three monks away pending a decision on what was to be done with them.

He hammered again and presently a guard spoke through the door, "Aye?"

"I need the jakes[26], fellow!" Father Robert called desperately through the oak.

The guard laughed. "Use the pot, ye ken?"

"My needs are more... *solid.* Please!"

Robert heard a heavy sigh and the tinkling of keys. As the door opened, he greeted the guard with a warm smile. "Thank you, my son. Please, wilt thou accept a drink in gratitude? There's a pitcher and mug on the side. Help thyself to a sup of our wine while I... well, *you* know."

The guard grinned and moved to help himself. He was still grinning when he hit the floor, the back of his head full of splinters from the broken wooden candlestick holder Robert used to lay him out.

"Come, my brothers. For too long have we bided idle, whilst the works of our Saviour go untended. This is our chance!"

The monks under his command looked doubtfully at one another.

"We must go!" Robert hissed again. Seeing they were unwilling, he spat, "Cowards! You disgrace our order and the very cowl you wear!"

---

26   A common term for toilet from the early 15th century onwards.

With that, he snatched the keys from the guard and locked all three in together.

Hermitage Castle was in darkness. Only the occasional wall sconce lit its gloomy passages. Having dutifully obeyed the office of matins with his unenthusiastic charges, Robert had chosen the small hours to make his move, hoping the majority of Maxwell's force would be in their beds.

He and his brothers lived in a lower-status guest room on the top floor of the south-east Well Tower. The postern gate at the foot of the same tower, blocked up a couple of hundred years earlier, had been reopened and pressed back into service during the ascendency of Lord William De Soulis – ever a man who believed in keeping a functional back door. It was in fact the very postern Robert and his brothers had so recently been forced through, on that terrible, dark, snow-driven afternoon, to greet the newcomers and their demonic steel monster. His jaw clenched angrily at the memory – sent out with nought but a cross and two layabout lay brothers, to face the devil himself. He rapidly concluded that he was better off on his own.

The postern being on the ground floor of the Well Tower was convenient. What was less convenient, was the fact that it would almost certainly be guarded – unless Maxwell was a fool.

As hoped, no one had yet challenged him on the wooden stairs within the tower's upper floors. When he reached the head of the last flight, he stopped, listening.

Two male voices speaking quietly and, if he was not mistaken, the snores of a third.

He had factored for the help of his indolent brothers to bypass this last obstacle. As things stood, he would need a new plan. Thinking furiously, he knew De Soulis had kept poisons. Perhaps something in these men's drinks? It would not be murder, after all. He would not be damned. These men were reformers, heretics – God would understand. The problem was De Soulis' quarters happened to be at the other end of the castle and almost certainly occupied by the enemy's leadership.

Robert ground his teeth in frustration; he was so *close.* Although appalled by his old master's use of the black arts, he could not help thinking they might have come in handy at this point.

However, Father Robert was, above all, a survivor. Any port in a storm, he passed quickly from lamenting over a diabolical but occasionally useful master and moved fluidly onto prayer instead. Layer upon layer of doctrinal arrogance and zeal laminating his holier-than-thou armour, he played the chords of a carefully constructed conviction to place his desires once again in tune with the will of God. The Lord's will tracked his own with such surprising regularity that he saw no need to examine the circumstances of his miraculous escape in any great detail. Robert *knew* he was God's instrument. So, when Maxwell's guards cried out in fear or pain – from the top of the stairs, he could not discern which – he was not in the least surprised. He *had* prayed for them to be struck down, after all.

A loud *bang* made Robert's ears ring as the men ran screaming from the ground-floor well chamber below. Beneath the sudden onset of tinnitus, he heard the fumbling of a latch followed by the slam and rattle of a ledge and brace door.

Placing his hands together, he smiled, closed his eyes, and raised his face meritoriously towards heaven. It took only moments before he heard further shouting and the approach of running feet.

Moving swiftly now, he practically threw himself down the stairs to place the wooden peg that would act as a basic lock within the wrought iron latch. It would buy him mere seconds, so he wasted no time in running for the ironbound oak postern door.

Three heavy timber braces kept it fast against intruders. Feverishly, Robert had just thrown the last into its keep within the tower's thick stone walls, when he heard a groggy, "Whit's gaun on?" from the corner of the darkened chamber behind him.

The sleeping man had been left behind on his pallet, and from the lamentable rate at which he gathered his wits, Robert suspected the fellow was drunk, too.

God was indeed with him – or was he? The running and shouting drew nearer as he searched desperately in the gloom for inspiration. On the stone flags near the mouth of the well, he found it. A dagg – one of the single-shot wheel lock pistols favoured by the wealthier Borderers.

Robert now understood the source of the bang that left his ears whistling. The dagg, more than a mere firearm, once discharged had a secondary use, too. He snatched it up from the flagstones and pressed it into service. The guard was on his feet now, but before fully regaining his senses, he was relieved of them by a swing of the dagg.

Used club-like, it connected with a skull already thickened with ale, separating him from the conscious world.

Robert looked down at the prone man with satisfaction. Under the light of a single torch, he could see slick, black blood on the weapon's grip and fancied he heard laughter. Not from beyond the door, and certainly not from his victim, but from right behind him.

He dropped the weapon in sudden denial, and in a flight of panic, made for the postern. Using the frenetic energy his fear had provided, Robert lunged at the door, shoulder first, and disappeared out into the night.

The laughter continued within, rasping and sickly. As no living, or at least conscious, soul was there to hear it, it made no sound, and was forced instead to excite the room's air molecules in a bland, unphilosophical way.

The engineer squatted, squinting into the sun as he stared up at Heidi. "I was ordered here to pour concrete, not make biscuits, *Fräulein*." He dropped the handful of sand back to the ground with disdain as he stood.

"We have many tons of cement to carry through the wormhole," she replied levelly. "It will be most inconvenient to bring so much sand, too."

"More inconvenient than your new factory falling to the ground?" he retorted in clipped, concise tones. "The salt content is all wrong and as for the impurities..."

Heidi's jaw muscles bunched in annoyance. "So what do you suggest, *Herr* Todt? You are still the party's chief engineer, are you not?"

Todt straightened. "*Still?*"

Heidi treated him to a wintry smile. "Indeed. For now, and so long as you avoid any flights to or out of Russia."

Todt was clearly perplexed by her words and demeanour, but although this was entertaining, she required action. "I have given you a problem, engineer. Now, what is your solution?"

"Pump it."

"Excuse me?"

"The concrete," he continued. "I cannot work with this rubbish." He kicked his boot into the sand beneath their feet. "I suggest that your museum, if it is yours, should be remodelled to allow through-vehicular traffic. Once we can get our heavy mixers and pumping equipment to the wormhole, we can begin pouring. Of course, we shall need to bore for our piles first. This will not be so easy in this poor substrate."

"You have the capability to successfully pump concrete?"

"Of course, *Fräulein.*" He smiled superficially. "But forgive me, I had forgotten that your PhD was merely an insert-name-here-ology, *Doctor.*"

Heidi grabbed Todt around the throat, using his collar to restrict his breathing and constrict his jugular. "*This* Dr Schultz is a medical doctor, and among my other skills are methods of dragging out your death over many days, should you displease me. Perhaps you have me mistaken for someone else?"

In answer, he made yet another mistake by taking a swing at her. She ducked it, catching his arm as it passed overhead. Using his own momentum, she helped him to the ground, chin first. Flat on his chest with his right arm twisted upright at ninety degrees behind his back, Heidi's slightest pressure holding his hand flat and turning it clockwise with her knee on his shoulder blade, Todt nodded furiously. Apart from a small, ineffectual kick of his feet, it was the only movement of which he was capable.

She relaxed her grip on him. "Better. Now I suggest you begin moving equipment and personnel through the wormhole. I intend to break ground tomorrow and, Fritz, we have much work before us. Go." Heidi released him and turned once more to survey the mostly flat top of the prominence they now called home.

Soon it would be home to the Schultzes' first factory in the Cretaceous, the first step on Heidi's road to empire. Her lips turned up at the edges – it would be glorious.

Todt regained his feet, sulkily massaging his torn shoulder. When Heidi turned to find him still standing there, he clicked his heels and gave a brief nod in the military fashion. "Might I make a suggestion before I leave, Dr Schultz?"

She eyed him coolly. "If it will advance our efforts here, you may."

"Thank you. The woods at the centre of this escarpment are infested with giant ants. We must remove the trees, of course, but our work teams are suffering greatly from insect bites. Some have become quite ill."

"So I have been led to understand, and your suggestion?"

"Burn the trees to the ground – two birds, one stone."

Heidi's eyebrows rose in pleasant surprise. "Very well, Fritz. However, your people must first remove any trees near the *Heydrich* with chainsaws, to create a respectable fire break." She casually returned his nod. "Very well. Proceed."

With that, she turned her back on him, returning to dreams of empire.

16th November, 1558

"Are you sure about this? Last chance?" asked Baines.

Sir Nicholas Throckmorton nodded. "I must away to London, to secure the Princess Elizabeth's succession, both for her and for England, Captain."

"You may find yourself in bad odour at court, after snatching her away from the group of 'well-wishers' Queen Mary put on her tail a few weeks back."

"Yet I must do my duty. The fate of the realm hangs in the balance."

Without further ado, Baines led the nobleman from the shuttle's bridge, through her passenger compartment and into the small craft's hold. Within the hold, Dr Natalie Pearson was carefully unstrapping a couple of sturdy galloway ponies from their travel harnesses.

Sir Nicholas stared balefully at them.

"Something wrong?" Natalie asked over her shoulder as she brushed the first animal's back before saddling.

"Only that these poor creatures are hardly worthy of my status."

"They were the best Lord Maxwell's men could provide at short notice," Baines placated.

Sir Nicholas snorted derisively. "You think so?"

Baines hid her grin; Maxwell's magnanimous gift horses required no inspection of their mouths to see that they fell well short of true generosity. Despite this, they were no detriment to the mission or rider safety, either. The ponies were healthy and strong, more than capable of performing the two-horse relay required to speed Sir Nicholas on his flight to London. However, to the strutting Tudor courtier, they must have looked like hedgepigs compared with the fine grey that had borne him north some weeks ago – as Baines suspected they were meant to.

She could well imagine the Scottish lord grinning at the thought of Sir Nicholas bursting into the yard of St James' Palace, astride a shaggy-haired border pony.

Ever since the attack which culminated in Bess' kidnap and Sir Nicholas escaping pillion on Jones' bike, their horses had never been found – although Baines would not have been at all surprised if Maxwell's Kelso stables, far to the north, boasted a couple of fine new arrivals soon after De Soulis' fall. Furthermore, she felt sure Maxwell had a glint in his eye when he *gifted* Sir Nicholas these ponies. She would never voice that suspicion, for that was all it was. Instead, she attempted to soothe the Englishman's pride. "These sturdy mounts will serve you well, I'm sure." Baines cared little for which rich man owned which horses, so long as the animals were cared for.

She opened the side hatch. The estuary was heavily tidal at this location, and outside, the inky blackness was filled by the disconcerting roar of the sea. In the absence of all other sounds, or light to see by, their imaginations built high walls of water curling overhead, ready to smash them to pieces. Baines shuddered. "We shouldn't hang around here, especially with the tide coming in."

Natalie roped the halter of one Reiver pony to the saddle pommel of the other and led both animals out onto the sands, walking them in a circle to shake out any stiffness from their limbs after the journey.

"We're on the north bank of the Thames, just north of East Tilbury," Baines explained.

"East where?" asked Sir Nicholas.

"*Right*... too early. Erm, about thirty miles east of Central London," she tried again.

"5000-foot miles or 5280-foot miles?"

Baines opened her mouth and closed it again. She changed the subject. "I would have preferred to drop you closer, to make the journey easier, but the risk of being spotted was just too great. We've done enough damage without flying a spaceship over Tudor London."

He gave her a rare smile. "My lady hath done much exceeding valorous, too." Taking Baines completely by surprise, he bent to kiss her hand. "Until we meet again. For I shall not take rest until I slip the betrothal ring from Mary's finger and bring it as proof to my queen – Elizabeth."

Touched by his gesture, Baines stood to attention and gave the nobleman a smart salute. "Good luck, Sir Nicholas. And Sir Nicholas..."

He mounted the saddled beast, turning it back to face the women, standing in a shaft of white light thrown from the shuttle's hatch. "Yes, Captain?"

Baines grinned. "Just a small tit-bit that may cheer you on your way. Mary will pass tomorrow morning, but in the *afternoon* your dear friend Cardinal Reginald Pole will join her. That flu jab Doc Flannigan gave you should keep you safe."

They saw the glint of teeth in the darkness as Sir Nicholas Throckmorton turned his ponies and set off westward across the sands, at a gallop.

Father Robert collapsed in the snow. Exhausted and in shock after his escape, only the fear of being caught had kept him going through the night. Taking a high trail used only by shepherds and Reivers, he had suffered badly to get this far. Now, unable to move further, exposure would surely claim him.

With barely the strength to kneel, he prayed where he was and was rewarded by the rhythmic thud of hooves at the canter.

"Thank you, Lord," he mumbled before he passed out.

Commander Gleeson closed the door to De Soulis' study behind him, turning to the room's only other occupant. His shoulders rocked with barely suppressed laughter. "Maxwell's really blown a fuse, Jonesy. I thought he was gonna shoot that bloke for a minute there. Drunk on duty – guard duty, no less! Haha."

As a recently minted NCO, Jones took a dim view of this. "It was *sleeping* on guard that really sealed it, Commander."

"Yeah, well, in fairness to those three fellas, they were on rotation using the bunk. Not that Maxwell was in any mood for the mitigative details." He laughed raucously. "It's the other two I feel sorry for."

Jones raised an eyebrow. "The ones who ran away because they saw a ghost?"

"Exactly," Gleeson guffawed. "And then trying to convince the main man that *they* hadn't been drinking." He dissolved into laughter again, unable to continue.

Jones looked thoughtful.

"What is it?" asked Gleeson, calming.

"Just thinking about that lad we saw walk out of the fire, over at the chapel."

"What, you think they may *actually* have seen something?"

Jones shrugged.

"Look, stay with me, Jonesy. Don't leave me on me own with all these medievalists[27]!"

"You haven't spoken to Captain Baines, isn'it."

Gleeson looked at him askance. Legendarily unflappable, Jones seemed perturbed. "Alright, well, let's focus on the result of this little episode, shall we? That monk, or priest, or whatever he was, has done a runner. Where do we think he might have gone?"

"Lord Maxwell might have a few ideas, Commander."

"Maybe, but I reckon he needs a little cooling down time before we upset him again. If this bloke ran to one of the other northern lords, what damage could he do? That's what I'm getting at."

"The French might have him..." Jones postulated.

Gleeson tilted his head left and right doubtfully. "Hmm. I dunno. They may have captured him, I suppose. But it would have required near-psychic ability in the darkness and the foul weather last night. I doubt he'd have gone to them willingly. They may nominally represent the Crown, but I'm sure you've noticed that none of the people here really appreciate the French's involvement in Scottish affairs – and that's putting it mildly."

Jones thought for a moment. "Captain Douglas mentioned that he came upon a Sir Walter Scott while they were chasing down De Soulis – some kid, apparently. More importantly, he said that 'Sir Half-Pint' wanted this castle, isn'it. Seemed to think it was his, like."

---

27 'Renaissancists' would have been mere hair-splitting for Gleeson.

"Don't they all. Trouble is, all the nobs are related. You can bet two-thirds of 'em have a claim over this place."

They fell into silence, dwelling on broken gates and thoughts of isolation, within a turbulent sea of claimants and cannons.

Gleeson scratched his stubble. "Maybe we *shouldn't* wait to give Maxwell his ulcer."

30th November, 1558

Baines stood shoulder to shoulder with most of the *New World*'s senior staff as they examined the excavation down to their subterranean craft. Several of them had requested the inspection and Douglas had been pleased to agree. He wished to keep all the leaders and department heads in the loop, but also wished to hold a conversation away from any potentially prying ears.

"As you can see, ladies and gentlemen," he began, "our boys are about to break into the hull. As they are ahead of the teams working on the wormhole drive itself, the work will be halted at this point and left under guard."

"How far are the WHD mods from completion, Captain?" asked Mother Sarah.

Douglas looked to Patel. "Satnam? One for you, Ah think."

Patel cleared his throat uncomfortably. "We have enjoyed some limited successes, but the drive was never meant to be used in the way we now intend. I apologise for the delays, but have to insist on further rigorous testing, before we attempt a corridor to 2112."

Sarah gave him a nudge and wink. "So how long, fella?"

Patel looked pained. "I don't know."

Chief of Pod operations, Dr Sam Burton, sighed heavily, pulling his hand slowly down his face. "Our entire company stepping through a wormhole with all the protection afforded by a pair of trousers and a jumper, is about the stupidest idea *we've* ever had."

Baines threw an arm around his shoulders. "It's only eight a.m., Sam, give us time."

The Sarge frowned at the young man before him. He was short by modern standards, as was the way for most people of this period. Dressed in hand-me-down clothes of poor quality and boots almost worn through, he was a wretched creature.

With most of the senior brass a quarter klick south examining the works, The Sarge controlled the gates, and any flow of personnel.

It was hard to discern an exact age for this supplicant, requesting his help. Maybe late teens? Maybe thirty? He was too grimy to tell. As a southerner, The Sarge was amused to find out the young Scotsman's name was Jimmy.

Jimmy was asking for help with his 'hobbler', a Borderer term The Sarge understood to mean pony. Judging by the man's appearance, the beast known as 'Blossom' must be his only possession of value in the world – and possibly his only friend.

Never an unsympathetic man, Sergeant Jackson enquired further into the man's problems. That was when Natalie Pearson brought him a coffee and he lost control of the situation.

"I'll get my bag," she announced, running back down into the Pod.

"You'll what? Wait!" The Sarge called after her.

In less than a minute, Natalie sprinted back up the earthen ramp to where The Sarge and Jimmy still waited. "Where is she?" she puffed.

"Ah left her lying doon, o'er big yin hill," replied Jimmy, full of concern. "She widnae get up."

Jackson grabbed Natalie by the arm. "You're not going out there, young lady."

Natalie frowned at him, pulling her arm free, crossly. "I'm not standing by while an animal suffers. What could possibly happen to me here? There's no one around for miles, except Jimmy here, and he needs my help."

"What about the Reivers? Fancy being taken for a slave, do you?" The Sarge retorted while squinting at the Borderer. Not even as tall as Natalie herself, there was yet a wiry strength about him at odds with his bedraggled appearance. Sergeant Jackson was no fool; he knew that what these people lacked in knowledge, training and balanced diet, they more than made up for in toughness – a most hardy people. He had also witnessed a slyness in some, too, and refused to underestimate them.

Nodding for one of his men to take over, The Sarge spoke quietly to Natalie, "I'll come with you, Doctor." Making a point of swinging his rifle from around his shoulders and bringing it to bear on Jimmy, he motioned for the Scotsman to lead the way.

They turned north out onto the plateau, gradually bearing north-east and climbing towards the rounded summit of the Cheviot Mountain, under which their ship lay.

"She's nae farr," Jimmy encouraged, rolling his *r*s.

The three had walked about half a kilometre when Jimmy pointed to a depression in the moor. "She's doon in there. Ah cannae thank ye enough, lass. Ah couldnae get herr up."

"It's alright, Jimmy," Natalie reassured with a smile. "Let's see what we can do for her."

Presently, they arrived at the rim of the depression. No more than ten metres deep, it was bisected with a stream that cut into a gulley. The Sarge placed a hand in front of Natalie, forestalling her. There was indeed a pony at the bottom of the hollow, but she was on her feet and lapping noisily from the stream.

"She don't look ill to me, sunshine," he stated menacingly.

Jimmy bore an expression somewhere between hope and fear. "She widnae budge, Ah swear."

Jackson skewered him with a stare. "How did you find us, or even know about us?"

"Ah was with Laird Maxwell's main army – a few weeks ago."

"Right. So what are you doing here now?"

Jimmy looked shifty, but somehow *artfully* so. "The Laird likes tae..."

"Go on," Jackson prompted, leaning forward just enough to intimidate.

Abashed, Jimmy looked away. "He likes tae keep an eye on yer camp. Just in case..."

This made perfect sense, of course – Maxwell was no fool – but for reasons The Sarge could not quite put his finger on, he sensed Jimmy's reasonable explanation was masking a deception. Maybe it was that the explanation was one any soldier would have deemed sensible, beautifully crafted into a confession under duress to give it the ring of honesty.

Paranoia could keep a man alive, so The Sarge allowed himself his suspicions.

Before he could further interrogate Jimmy, Natalie snapped, "Come *on*, Sarge. Honestly! Just because the pony's back on her feet, doesn't mean there may not be any number of other underlying problems. We're here now. Let me take a look, won't you?"

Jackson sighed, nodding assent.

Natalie and Jimmy ran down into the depression to check on Blossom.

Watching them go, The Sarge was unable to shake the feeling that something more was going on. He took one last look around him: nothing but heather and black clouds in the north – harbingers of some unpleasant hours to come, perhaps, but nothing overly ominous.

Shaking his head, he radioed his position back to his men who guarded the Pod's entrance, and stepped down into the hollow.

"Nein, nein, nein!" shouted engineer Todt. "This will not do!"

Heidi's approach across the recently scorched earth had gone unnoticed in the man's agitation. She rolled her eyes. *This prima donna has missed his calling,* she mused. *If he refuses to shape up, he will be missing his head, too.* "What in the world is it now, Fritz?"

Todt jumped at the sound of her voice. He straightened his ruffled shirt irritably. "The bedrock is at too great a depth here. We cannot dig deeply enough with these small machines. To install the steel cages and fill them with concrete would be futile. As soon as the building's weight settles upon them—"

"Very well," Heidi cut him off brusquely. "I understand. What about using narrow-bore steel piles?"

Todt frowned. "I am unfamiliar with this system. Explain."

Heidi considered the engineer for a moment, wondering as to his competence. Remembering that, despite the huge alterations in the timeline, it was still 1943 in his world, she made an allowance and worked with what she had. "It is a system of galvanized pipes, supplied in various lengths, and led into the ground by a screw cap. A rotating head attached to the actor of your mini digger will spin the pipe and, along with the weight of the machine pressing down, bore it into the ground. Other pipes may be coupled on via a simple male-female connection. Several may be linked together for deep bore applications, to create piles many metres in length.

"The system was developed for use in sandy conditions. I believe they are used widely in Australia, among other places. Although the piles will have less compressive strength than your proposed design, they can be installed numerously, to achieve our goals. Especially as our building will be of lightweight portal frame design.

"Furthermore, as the sand you are drilling through is contained within a bowl of bedrock, our finished substrate and foundation system should be nicely contained, yes?"

Todt blinked in surprise as he backpedalled, "I... I had not heard of this method."

"It may not yet exist in your world. As you are here in the Cretaceous Period, I assume you understand that we travelled through time to find you?"

He nodded once, swallowing.

"Good. I have told you how it works. Now, I am sure you have the capability to put such a simple idea into practice?"

He nodded again when a loud roar from just beyond the treeline made everyone on site turn. Terror inflated, spreading among Todt's operatives. Heidi walked to the fore and turned, standing with hands on hips. "Get back to work!"

Despite being exactly what he had expected, The Sarge could not believe it was happening – the sudden roar of men leaping from the heather and streaming down into the hollow.

"Oh, Turkish delight!" At the speed of thought, he was already firing. Ten of the attackers collapsed, rolling down the slope before the main body of the force reached them. Jimmy was suddenly standing well back, grinning gap-toothed at his handiwork.

Had he the time, The Sarge would have removed what teeth the man had left. However, his main concern was for Natalie. He had to get her away before she was killed – or worse.

With only a second left to him, The Sarge dialled his 'Heath-Rifleson' up from ten percent to twelve and shot Jimmy in the face.

The gravity of Jimmy's situation hit him at 9.8 metres per second, per second – as did the ground – the fresh burn covering most of his face eliciting the squeak of a truncated scream as he went down.

Suddenly mobbed and barely able to move, The Sarge's final defiance was enacted upon another man's nose as the butt of his rifle left his hands.

Completely pinioned at every limb, he and Natalie shared a glance. Out of her wits, she was struggling to even breathe, but The Sarge's confident wink and half-smile air-transferred courage enough for her to stand.

Atop the bank, standing heroically against the blackened sky with legs apart and fists on hips, his cape flapping in the wind, Sir John Johnstone stared down at his prizes. He grinned and nodded to the archer at his side.

Bows were rare in this region, but the man clearly knew his business. He lit the awkward head of a flaming arrow from the flint of another man's pistol and fired high, to the north-west.

The Sarge followed the trajectory of the fiery signal, balefully. *Oh, Turkish delight...*

Private Pete Davies handed Baines a roll of parchment on her return. "A second message from Sir Nicholas Throckmorton, ma'am."

Baines took it and read. Both the hand and the syntax were difficult to her 22nd century eyes, but he had clearly tried to simplify where possible. She grunted satisfaction and handed it to Douglas. "Looks like things are settling down in London for the moment. Although Sir Nicholas is convinced that there will be another uprising if Elizabeth doesn't go back soon. Apparently, there is already some talk about her being dead and a few courtiers, like Nick, trying their luck vicariously."

"What's he proposing?" asked Douglas, still struggling with the first few lines.

"He and some of the other magnates are in the final stages of putting together an army to march north and bring her home."

"An army? Is that necessary?"

"He seems to think so. This is a very dangerous time for Elizabeth. Mary is gone but there are many powerful families, especially in the religiously more conservative north, who would give anything to see her *disappear.*"

Douglas scratched his chin thoughtfully. "But Ah wonder what the Scots will make of a major force moving north."

"Maybe we can help calm things," Baines suggested. "Perhaps recruit Maxwell? I think we can trust Nick. He really does care for Bess and certainly seems patriotic – at least, from a Reformer's perspective. Ultimately, I think we'll just have to let things play out now. We should, of course, encourage them to return south as soon as possible, but that's all we can do, realistically."

Douglas returned the parchment, giving up on it. "Ah think we should take her part way south to meet up with Sir Nicholas. Ye know, keep his army away from the border, and all that. This place is a tinder box on a good day, without thousands of English soldiers stomping along the borders, looking for a stolen princess."

"Queen," Baines corrected.

"Indeed," he acquiesced. "Making my point all the more urgent."

They stood in silence for a moment. During their conversation, Pete Davies had been joined by Corporal Thomas, bearing coffees. Baines realised there was something missing from the gateway furniture as she had left it, and approached them.

"Getting a nip in the air again, Captain," the corporal greeted her. "Sorry, if I'd known you were back, I'd have brought you a mug out. You can have this if you like – I'll get another."

"Thanks, Corp, but I'm good."

Thomas looked down at the letter in her hand. "The rider who brought that is still below. I thought the least we could do was feed and warm him, and his horse. The lad, Woodsey, is taking care of the mount. The rider asked if we'd like to send a return message with him, when he starts back."

Baines mulled it over. "Yes, perhaps we should. Thanks for taking care of it, Corp. Was Natalie unable to tend the horse? I'd have thought that was her thing. Also, gentlemen, I expected to find The Sarge on duty here. Is there something I should know?"

"He left with a Scotsman to look at an injured pony, ma'am," replied Davies.

"Is that your report or the beginning of a joke?"

Davies laughed. "Dr Pearson, as the closest thing we have to a vet, went with him."

Baines frowned. "Really? That doesn't sound like The Sarge."

Davies shrugged. "Perhaps it would be more accurate to say, Dr Pearson took The Sarge with *her,* ma'am."

"I see. So, who *was* this Scotsman?"

The men shared a wry look. "Some scruffy looking urchin named Jimmy, I think," continued Davies. "Dr Pearson's not someone to stand about while an animal suffers. She *insisted.*"

Baines was clearly nonplussed, secretly surprised The Sarge would have allowed this.

Davies grinned as if reading her mind. "I'd have never believed *anyone* could change The Sarge's mind like that."

"Oh, *really?*" Baines drawled, returning his grin now. "A little magic going on there, huh?"

Davies shrugged and Thomas gave him an admonishing backhand across the arm. "Not for us to say, ma'am."

"How long have they been gone, Pete?"

"Over an hour, Captain. He radioed their position about forty-five minutes ago – half a klick north-east of here."

Again, Baines frowned. "Get him on the radio."

Davies did as she ordered. No response.

Corporal Thomas began to look concerned. "Try again, lad."

Still no response.

"What was their last known position?" asked Baines, urgently.

Natalie and The Sarge were feeling bruised and ill-used. Hog-tied across the backs of a couple of ponies, they had been travelling for the better part of an hour. The steady trot over rough ground made ribs Natalie never even knew she had ache – not to mention the womanly discomfort in her chest as she bounced across moors, up dale and down.

Riding north into the storm clouds, the wind strafed them, exacerbated by driving sleet. Hands and feet hanging either side of her animal's flanks, Natalie was unable to draw in against the cold. She had never felt so miserable or hopeless, and regardless of what he showed the world, she knew The Sarge would be feeling the same.

Memories of shared dangers flashed through her mind. Despite The Sarge being once more at her side, their situation was grave. These were not dinosaurs eking out a meagre living, nor violent winds mindlessly smashing anything within reach. These were men and women; beings who set their will, their cunning and their intelligence quite deliberately against them. There was no doubt about it, powerless to even hold up a hand in defence of themselves, they were in trouble.

Just as she began to wonder how much more she could take, they topped a small rise to see a farmstead down in the wide valley below. With a jolt, Natalie recognised it as the place they found Mayor, after he escaped from the ship and followed a herd of cows home.

Though she shuddered to think what might happen to them next, the small smokestack rising from the house's chimney, and the huddle of barns without, looked surprisingly inviting. The combination of nervous stress, fear and bitter cold turned Natalie's metaphorical shudder into the real thing, and she began to shake uncontrollably as they drew closer. The smallholding took on more the appearance of an armed camp than a farm as they entered its yard.

Men greeted them, taking the ponies away to be unsaddled and tended while Natalie and The Sarge were dumped unceremoniously in the slush, against the wall of the bastle house.

Natalie's teeth chattered, but she found a grim satisfaction in seeing that at least a dozen of their attackers had returned in similar discomfort, having been stunned by The Sarge's rifle and swung across their mounts by comrades. Only Jimmy had been seriously injured. She hated to admit it, but she felt pretty good about that, too.

A ladder appeared to their side. A pair of legs. A familiar voice.

"Hello, my dear. Dr Natalie Pearson, isn't it?"

Natalie clenched her chattering teeth. "Allison C-Cockhouse, I p-presume? What have you d-done?"

"Cock*sedge*." The politician's false bonhomie wavered but recovered. "I am building a, *ahem*, 'new world' for us, and any with the vision to follow."

"Us?" growled The Sarge.

Cocksedge gave him a sickly smile, superficially to ingratiate while actually designed to infuriate. "Sergeant Jackson. I do declare." She bent close, so as not to be overheard. "I didn't expect these cretins to bag someone of your calibre – you must be crawling with shame."

Again, the smile.

"Perhaps you would explain why we're here," he replied unemotionally.

"Right down to business." Cocksedge clapped her hands together enthusiastically. "Of course, I can do that. You are here to provide me with leverage, so that I can get the things I need to make life here," she looked around contemptuously, "shall we say, a little more tolerable?"

The Sarge huffed. "Let's call a spade a shovel, shall we? We're hostages, right?"

Her sickly smile never wavered. "I prefer the term *guests*. However, having the *two* of you is quite the bonanza." She leaned forward again, conspiratorially this time. "*So* nice to have a spare. Which also means that, should there be any funny business, your buddy will pay for it." She smiled again. "I only need the one *hostage,* Sergeant – your word, not mine. Should you return to type, violent thug that you are, then your colleague here might go from hostage to *ghost*age. Do we understand one another?"

"You really are a piece of work, Cocksedge," Natalie spat.

"My dear, if you play your cards right, you'll be thanking me." Cocksedge turned to one of the men milling around the camp. "Put them in with the cattle. They're no good to me if they freeze to death!"

Chapter 12 | Tactics

"We have to produce enough power conduit to reach all the way down to the lower slopes," Hiro stated.

Jim Miller puffed out his cheeks. "I thought we'd be setting up the machine on our new road, just outside the ship. Does the operation really have to be so far away?"

Hiro nodded. "Sandy, explain."

Singh opened a topographical map on the wall monitor. "This is the geography outside our walls, taken by the Light Detection and Ranging equipment aboard our shuttle. The LiDAR scans clearly show the mound pushed up by the vast bulk of the *New World,* just under the hill – though I suppose it's technically a mountain after our... *insertion.* Now, *this* is a scan of the same area taken from our database. As you can see from the date stamp, this image was captured in AD2105 and it shows the Cheviot Nature Reserve, roughly contemporaneously with our departure. You can clearly see that the lines of the lower slopes are virtually unchanged."

"Does that matter, overly?" asked Miller. "We've changed the landscape for good now, surely?"

"Maybe, maybe not," Singh continued. "A lot can happen in five and a half centuries. Decomposition for one, an unforeseen explosion for another. What I'm getting at is that the *shape* of the *New World* might change over time. This is not a real mountain, after all."

"Exactly," Hiro joined in. "Were we to step through the wormhole at, let's say, eight hundred metres above sea level, in round figures, we might suddenly find ourselves a hundred metres in the air on the other side – should the ship collapse over time. On the last occasion, when we were forced to jump through time – against all sense, on the surface of our planet – we came severely unstuck. The changing geology causing us to reappear *inside* a mountain. I'm sure none of us need reminding about that.

"The *New World* saved all our lives, no doubt about it. So now imagine that our luck continues along a similar trajectory, but we reappear *without* her."

Miller scratched his head, grimacing at the thought. "You make a compelling case. But it's going to take time to build so much conduit. And without the benefit of stepdown transformers – because we need all the power we can get – the cross-sectional area of the cabling will be massive."

"Which is why we brought this to you as soon as we realised the problem," Singh explained. "And because we want you to—"

"We're taking a terrific gamble as it is," Hiro spoke over his colleague, hurriedly. "The least we can do is control the few variables we *can* counter for, wouldn't you agree, Jim?"

Miller was suddenly suspicious. "Have you told Sam Burton how much of his Pod he's about to lose?"

Hiro and Singh looked at one another awkwardly.

"We're heavily favouring the *New World* with our demolition work, in order to leave the Pod operational for posterity," Hiro ventured. "But, of course, there will be some, erm..."

Seeing his colleague falter, Singh stepped in to hover over the nettle without actually grasping it. "*You've* become quite good friends with Sam over the last few months, haven't you, Jim?"

Miller sat back in his chair, crossing his arms as realisation dawned. "Oh, *thank you!*"

Gleeson stood atop the battlements of Hermitage Castle, staring out towards the east. Below him, the Franco-Scot delegation withdrew to their camp. His letters to the Crown of some weeks back had received a response. Thus far, it had not proved all they could wish for, but dropping a spanner in the gears of government had garnered some success.

Mary of Guise, the Queen Regent, had indeed sent a couple of her closest advisors to open a dialogue with Lord Maxwell – Gleeson kept all *New World* personnel well out of sight for the duration of the talks.

The Crown ambassadors stayed for two days, while Gleeson reported their progress to Baines, second-hand, as he was able. Now they were gone, he would learn their final resolution – if they had one. He expected Maxwell to join him any moment.

"Commander," a hard masculine voice intruded on his thoughts.

Gleeson turned and nodded respectfully. "Lord Maxwell."

They stood together in silence for a while, watching the party ride away. Gleeson suspected that Maxwell was trying to find a beginning, which did not bode well. Eventually, he asked, "How did it go?"

"They left me with a choice," Maxwell growled. "Ah must be gone within tha week or forswear tha Protestant faith, and bend tha knee, offering ma allegiance tae tha Queen Regent."

Gleeson looked at him. "What will you do?"

"We'll quit oursel's as men, o'course," he grinned. "Ah cannae change ma faith."

"It means that much to you?" asked Gleeson, as only a moderner could.

Maxwell smiled slyly. "It's no' just religion. Ah love ma home. Scotland. Ye came here, yer people that is, tellin' us all sorts o' tales o' the future. And now Ah find masel' bound by them. Besides, bending tha knee tae Mary is tae bow tae tha French." Maxwell grimaced at that thought.

"I'm sorry, mate. We didn't mean to come."

Maxwell gave Gleeson's meaty shoulder a squeeze. "Ah know, lad. Although we're in danger now, ye've also brought us hope. Besides, when are we no' in danger, eh?" He soured, staring at the French camp.

"You want them out of your country." It was not a question.

"Aye. Ah hear rumblings from Edinburgh. Tha helping hand from tha regent's French royal connections is fast turning into occupation. They're stealin' and takin' whatever they want. If tha lass Bess is destined tae help us chuck them oot, then we must hold."

As a modern man, Gleeson may have found their demonstrative faith hard to understand, but he also saw the French force in a different light, too – simply no better or worse than anyone else at this point in the story of man, all living by the rules of *this* world.

Having lived for some time cheek by jowl with the people of this age, he had been forced to accept that the historian, Thomas Beckett, had been right – there was simply no point in judging history by modern standards. Perhaps their intervention would improve things, perhaps not. All he knew for sure was that he liked Maxwell, and some of the other people he had met here, but it was time to leave. They did not belong.

The Schultz camp had relied on a ring of explosives to keep the animals at bay in the early days, largely for the sake of expedience. However, the deep ditch and high wire fencing around the top of the escarpment were now nearing completion. Soon, it would be electrified, and powered by the *Heydrich*'s core, capable of delivering a charge distressing even to the large sauropods of the plains below. Some of the Paralititans approached thirty metres in length, from the tips of their long tails to the relatively small heads atop equally long necks, and weighed in excess of fifty tons. The fence would prove deadly to anything man-sized.

Heidi gave a satisfied nod as she surveyed the plateau. The foundations for their new factory were already laid, and out of them sporadic superstructure shot skywards, like steel weeds. The Nazi force had lived and worked aboard vehicles since the beginning of their campaign. Now, within a few short days, these jutting frames would be clad to form buildings, forever dividing the prehistoric world between *inside* and *outside*.

Things were proceeding well, helped along by German efficiency – a quality endemic to all timelines, it seemed, and something Heidi was only too happy to twist to her will.

She pondered the responsibilities of leadership. Like the factory they were building, there was an innocence to these people; a capability to build ploughs as easily as bombs, all at her whim.

Heidi had but two strong influences in her life. Looking through the eyes of her grandfather she saw weakness, but imagining the view from Tim Norris' perspective, she saw only potential.

She shuddered, despite the colossal heat. In her hands lay the power to build a new human civilisation, predating the one that was very nearly dead, or she could simply build another massive gun. Perhaps she would think on it.

Once brought to heel, Todt had proved deserving of his position as the party's chief engineer, too. After all, in what she thought of as *her* 1943, he had been a driving force behind the construction of the *autobahns*.

There was certainly an arrogance to the man. He was a fine engineer and an intellectual, but in this altered timeline, she could not see the Reich Minister for Armaments and Ammunition, who skilfully directed the whole wartime German economy – not to mention the building of the concentration camps.

In fact, by her 1943, he was already dead. Possibly murdered at Hitler's order for advising the *Führer* to sue for peace with Russia for the sake of that very economy.

She smiled, and her smile turned cruel; reinventing the world was invigorating. "Douglas has meddled. Now it's my turn."

"*A ransom note!*" bellowed Douglas, throwing the offensive scrap of parchment down. "What the hell is she playing at?"

"More to the point," asked Baines, "what the hell are we going to do about it? We haven't been able to find them. Perhaps we should reconsider aerial reconnaissance?"

Douglas subsided, suddenly realising their predicament. "Cocksedge knows Ah willnae send in the troops for fear of killing the locals – our ancestors, if you prefer. She's banking on it!"

"Quite literally *your* ancestors, James," Mother Sarah pointed out.

"Aye," he agreed. "And if we send out our ships to scour the land, we're going to attract *everybody's* attention. Ah'm just no' sure the world's ready for that."

Patel leaned forward onto the meeting table. "We are planning to leave soon. So, it seems that wretched politician has forced a choice upon us – one where neither option is particularly palatable. We either fetch our people back – which will require force, it seems – or we leave without them."

Douglas smashed his fist down on the table. "Unacceptable! There is no way Ah'm leaving Natalie or The Sarge in enemy hands. Aside from the personal feelings of friendship and respect Ah hold for each, they're *our* people! We've come too far, and Ah'll be damned if Ah'm leaving anyone behind now!"

Patel held up his hands, placating. "I agree, James. So do we attack?"

"No." Baines spoke quietly, thoughtfully.

The triumvirate turned to her in some surprise.

"You're usually our firebrand, Jill," Sarah stated. "You think we should do nothing?"

When Baines replied, it was with a glint in her eye. "No. I simply think there's a third alternative to fighting or abandonment."

"Go on, Jill," Douglas fished.

She spread her hands on the table, taking them all in, one by one. "We'll cheat."

Sir Nicholas Throckmorton set up camp a day's march south of Barnard Castle, when a messenger arrived from the north. Man and mount were fit to collapse, but almost eighty miles and two horses later, he dropped to a knee and handed Baines' letter to his lord.

Under pressure from the leading magnates in the south, Sir Nicholas had pressed his army to a forced march, in anticipation of retrieving their young queen. His men's gargantuan efforts had placed them just a few days behind the lone messenger sent on ahead.

Sir Nicholas took the missive, frowning. The dialect was taxing, though he knew Baines would have written as simply as possible. His society was yet to experience the full horror of autotranslators, or doubtless he would have accepted the paper and ink with better grace.

"Sir Nicholas Throckmorton – salutations.

We will deliver Elizabeth R on the fifth night of December, one hour past sunset, to the old Roman fort of Housesteads (also known as 'Vercovicium' – ten <u>long</u> miles east-north-east of Hexham). We bring E R south to you, in the hope of avoiding any confrontations caused by further increasing the English army presence so near to the border with Scotland.

Jill Baines, Captain.

Postscript: Bring only a small retinue of trusted men, lest our flying machine start a panic."

Sir Nicholas grunted. Folding the letter, he tucked it into his doublet. Although plenty of time remained before their agreed meeting, he would rest his men at the end of their journey. It made no sense to risk being caught out miles from their destination. Besides, he preferred to be within striking distance should the new people's plans go awry. He believed them to be largely folk of honour, but despite their wizardry and confidence, they did not always seem to know what they were doing.

"Sergeant!" he bellowed. "Bed the men down. We march on Hexham with the dawn."

From there, he would split his force into three smaller armies, basing himself at Hexham, nearest the Roman fort. The others he would send on to Otterburn and Chillingham. Sir Ralph of Chillingham would certainly know of Elizabeth's accession by now and would serve the Crown as he always had.

From these key positions, Nicholas would be able to move his forces in, to save his queen should the need arise. His entire purpose was to bring her safely to London, but with so many variables, not to mention the mercurial temperament of Elizabeth herself, he just knew it would not be that simple.

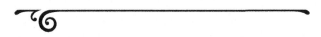

"Bring tha priest tae tha fire," Sir Walter commanded. "He looks frozen stiff."

"Thank you, my lord." Father Robert bowed and lifted his habit, bearing his backside to the hearth. As the cloth steamed, he began to regain some of the feeling in his extremities and nether regions.

"Bring us meat, cheese, bread and mulled wine tae warm tha bones," the young noble ordered.

"You are very kind, my lord." The priest offered the younger man another bow as he presented himself.

"Aye," Sir Walter acknowledged his introduction. "Now tell me, Father Robert, why were ye walking ma lands, and with nae provisions, to boot?"

The teenaged lord listened carefully to the priest's tale, ears pricking at the mention of Hermitage Castle's current weakened state.

"But whilst there, I heard tell of still greater treasure, my lord," continued Robert. "On Old Cheviot Hill. Where wonders defying description may be found."

"Aye, Ah've seen them. Damned dangerous wonders they are, tae. Monsters digging up tha hillside at the strangers' bidding. Ah understand they're led by a Douglas. Ye ken how this is possible?"

Robert's surprise showed in his face and Sir Walter grinned. "Oh, aye. Ah ken what's going on in the borders o' ma lands, Father."

"And you have seen the English Queen, my lord?" asked Robert.

"Ah saw her with Sir William de Soulis. He had her away, but as he's dead now, she must be in tha wind, eh?"

"I was led to understand she is also at Old Cheviot."

Sir Walter leaned forward, piqued. "*Is* she? Have ye news o' tha Johnstones hereabouts, tae? Ma spies tell me they've captured some of tha new people?"

"The Johnstones are a godless creed, my lord. If they have captives, they will use them to extract great wealth from these *new* people, these *devil worshippers!*"

Sir Walter grinned again. "Aye, but no' if Ah intercept them. Ma spies tell me Sir John Johnstone is working *for* tha new people. Or two o' them – a couple o' *women*." The young lord poured all his scorn into the word. "One's an old boot, but tha other's supposed tae be tha most dainty creature this side o' heaven, Ah've been told. Not that ye'd care aboot that, priest, eh?" He laughed. "They meet with tha other newcomers at noon tomorrow. Ma spy will be there. And when they make their exchange, *Ah'll* be there, tae."

North Africa, 99.2 million years BC

"I know I shouldn't be surprised," said Jansen. He, Devon and Aito sat astride three petrol-powered dirt bikes, requisitioned from their new contacts in Germany. Jansen's ankle was still tender, but the gear changes gently exercised the joint without too much discomfort.

"She still hasn't been to check on you?" Devon guessed the source of Jansen's mood.

"No," he admitted. "Nor will she, until she has need of me again – doubtless another suicide mission!"

Aito laughed, inappropriately, as he often did.

Jansen scowled. "What are we here for? It's damned dangerous down here by the river."

"Officially," explained Devon, "we're here to scout for the best place to lay pipework, so we can bring water from the river up to the factory. The main pumping and filtration station will be at the top, within our fortifications, for the safety of the staff and equipment.

"However, we'll need a 'first stage' filtration plant at source. The water's low, and thick with sediment – no point pumping all that muck uphill.

"There's talk that the rivers to the North African Delta might dry up altogether in a few years – all to do with a volcano pushing the weather systems south, or something. The eggheads are expecting a high proportion of the local wildlife to die off. But for now, we still have to keep all the animals out of the pipework."

"Won't the water running out be a big problem for manufacturing?" asked Jansen.

"Oh, *yeah*," agreed Devon. "But we can hardly move the wormhole, can we? So it's just a matter of making hay, I suppose."

"We could build drones with the Germans' help – if it becomes a problem," suggested Aito.

"What do you mean?" asked Jansen.

"If we send a number of remote vehicles up into the clouds we *do* have," explained Aito, "to pass an electrical charge into the water droplets there, they will attract one another. As they grow larger, they'll begin to fall – as rain. It was a technique developed for use in the United Arab Emirates, back in 2021, I believe. We can also use salts too – silver iodide, potassium iodide, and so on. One way or another, I'm sure Heidi will get her rain before it becomes a problem." He shrugged. "We may even avert a local extinction, and if we do save some of the animals here, that may be how our isotope through time was made possible – because we'll *one day* have to fix the weather."

Jansen groaned. "Don't give me any more 'time's arrow' – it hurts my head!"

Aito grinned. "I may not have my sainted brother's reputation, but I'm still an engineer, you know. Anyway, never mind Heidi's supply problems and the damned weather! Devon, you told us we're scouting for a pump site, officially – and *unofficially?*"

Devon nodded, holding in his thoughts a moment longer. "All comms off?" he asked. "OK. This is all coming together way faster than I expected. If we don't stop them, the Schultzes won't be in control of a prehistoric world where they can do little harm – they're going for *our* world."

"He's right," agreed Jansen. "The people of this 1943 are ill-equipped to deal with Heidi and her megalomania."

"You're saying they're weak?" asked Aito.

Jansen dragged a rasping hand across his five o'clock shadow. "I would say *innocent.* Look, Captain Nassaki, you were always the eco warrior in your youth, yeah?"

Aito shrugged acknowledgement.

"Well, from what I saw, and read in the news of that world when I was there, those people were well along the road to achieving balance – both in terms of population size and density, *and* technology. Strangely, they're still a little behind us in tech, but they've somehow managed to avoid many of *our* mistakes. I don't know how much can be attributed to the interference of Douglas and the *New World,* but they're certainly well ahead of where they should be for the middle of the twentieth century. Heidi thinks they're fifty, maybe sixty years behind us, at worst – whereas they should be more like a *hundred* and sixty."

Aito looked thoughtful for a long moment before he responded. "Are you saying they're worth saving?"

Ensconced within the captain's quarters and surrounded by such opulence as the *Heydrich* could offer, Heinrich Schultz called, "Come."

The hatch slid open, allowing his granddaughter to stride confidently inside. "You wished to see me, *Großvater?*"

"On the contrary, I *wished* to see you three hours ago. Now I am *ordering* your immediate report!"

Heidi smiled indolently. "Do not try and frighten me, Old Man. I have been busy, building what will one day be a new empire. I no longer have the time to pander to your whims. I am here now, so be content."

A slight twitch to the old man's right eye was the only outward sign of his annoyance. "You no longer believe you need me, *Enkelin?* Might I remind you that none of us would be here were it not for my genius and industry."

"I understand the meaning of 'the past' is more fluid than it once was, *Großvater,* but know that you are its icon. *I* am the architect of the future. There would be no permanent link with an industrial Germany were it not for *my* genius. *You* handed us failure – your continued existence, at my discretion."

"You challenge me?" Heinrich raised an eyebrow.

"*Nein.* I have vanquished you. Now do you wish to hear of my progress from your retirement chair, or should I simply dispatch you, to prevent any future misunderstandings on your part?"

He twitched a wintry smile. "Beware overconfidence, *Enkelin.* You may give your report."

Heidi snorted mildly. "We have converted the Old Academy to allow larger traffic, and the cabinet has sanctioned tunnelling work to begin from its basements to a large industrial unit, recently purchased on a nearby site. From there we shall be able to move all the material we need without raising suspicion. For a while."

"Until the wormhole outgrows your establishment?"

Heidi nodded. "You have seen the forecasts? It will be two years before the wormhole shows any outward signs of its presence."

"And in that time, you expect to have industrialised *this* location to the point where we will be well underway with the building of the next Nazi war machine, yes?"

"I do not expect. I *know.* We shall, of course, need more capital along the way, but we know how to get that, do we not?"

She straightened, looking down her nose at the old man in his comfortable chair. Recent musings had left her mind in some disturbance. It was time to put something long delayed finally to rest. "And now, I have a question for you, *mein Großvater.*"

Heinrich waited, offering nothing.

"Why did you lie to me about Tim Norris' heritage?"

A flutter of surprise crossed Heinrich's face. "What makes you believe that I did?"

Heidi felt it instinctively, knew she and Tim were kin, like the proverbial two-sided coin – and like a coin, once placed, one side saw all the light while the other hid in darkness.

During Tim's captivity, the coin fell on its edge, just for a little while – showing all its properties to the world. Of course, she would never admit to divining their true relationship from *feelings*. Her accusation would require more force, more *Schultz.* It would require a lie.

"I had another search – a much more *intensive* search – made of the quarters my cousin used while he was aboard *Heydrich.*"

"And?" Heinrich sounded bored.

"And this time I found *his* DNA, rather than the planted DNA you intended me to find." It was a complete shot in the dark, lacking any hard proof whatsoever, but Heinrich surprised her.

"He *is* my grandson – your cousin."

Her eyes narrowed. "Then what was the point in denying it?"

"Because you and I are very alike, my dear. Being betrayed by an inferior is unacceptable, but with possibly a hundred million years between us and the *New World,* the fires of revenge could, with reticence, be banked low.

"However, betrayal by one of our own... My dear *Enkelin*, to avenge that, I would expect you to break the world, even time itself in your rage. So I thought it best to let him go."

"Liar!" she spat. "You told me he was no relative, in line with your story about replacing me only to make me fight for my position – to make me stronger. The truth is, you *would* have ousted me – *killed* me – had my cousin served your purposes. Just because he was a male heir!

"You lied because you fear me – fear my retribution for your betrayal."

Heinrich smiled, snakelike before the strike. "Cannot both reasons be true, *Enkelin?* But now you have your truth, you must surely see that continuing down this road does not serve us. I made a mistake in bringing the Norris boy back into the fold. I accept that now, gracefully."

Heidi glowered, her eyebrows twitching up and down, lost somewhere between astonishment for his admission, and disgust for his treatment of his own.

"I thought blood would out," he continued, "but it seems that environment can indeed trump innateness. All that matters now is that we are here, he is gone. We must work with what we have – what we have *always* had – and, to paraphrase the English, not allow ourselves to be dazzled by the lawn next door."

Heidi's face seemed to contract with loathing. Until so recently, her grandfather's lies and intrigues were laid only to ensnare outsiders. Now, she hated him for casting her adrift in the world. What made matters worse was the fact that he was correct.

Before she could gather her thoughts, Heinrich changed the subject, as if they had been discussing the weather.

"Now tell me, *Enkelin,* what are your plans for the larger issue?"

"Speak plainly, *Großvater,*" she snarled.

"When the wormhole ceases to be useful and becomes destructive – you have a plan for that?"

Heidi viewed him coolly, changing down through her emotional gearbox until she was once more in control. *This conversation is over.* The thought rang through her mind like the slam of a door. When she spoke, her jaw and lips were taut. "I have work."

She turned on her heel to leave.

Heinrich managed a half-smile, then took a sharp breath, clutching his right hand to his heart. Recent stresses, barely survived, had left him weakened. He would never have admitted this to anyone, even his granddaughter, but now matters were worse. He knew her fury would have no mistress after this.

Having initially planned for everything, even his own mortality, fate had completely reshuffled the deck. So much had been lost, including his access to private medical supplies and 'spare parts', and were that not enough, queens were now wild.

Great Cheviot Mountain, AD1558

"I will do no such thing!" Bess retorted. "If all this cannot be taken south, then all preparation must be made for a permanent, heavy military presence here."

Baines leaned her elbows on the table, holding her head in her hands. This was not going at all the way she had planned. "Bess, I have to go and meet with our enemies. I can't get into this right now. Will you just promise me you'll think about it? Please?"

Bess stuck her chin out belligerently. "I pray good fortune doth reign over your mission, Jill, but forsooth, on the other matter, can promise nothing."

Baines stood and turned to leave.

"You turn'st your back on me?" Bess lashed out.

Baines rolled her eyes and turned back to lean on the table. "*We* are not your subjects, Bess. Furthermore, you need us, if you're to accomplish this – remember that!"

Bess stood, also to lean across the table until they were almost nose to nose. "And if *I* am to mend the world of the mess *you people* made, you need *me,* also!"

Baines smiled. "Yes, we do. Lucky for you, that, don't you think? You know it's only a matter of time before *Phil* comes for you, don't you – to defend his 'Holy Roman Empire'?"

"Philip of Spain always liked me!"

"Don't be so naïve. What are you going to do when he sends hundreds of galleys to England – rely on the weather? Think on what I've said. Take our help and advice."

Baines left, grinning.

Bess sat, drumming her beringed fingers on the table. Eventually, her petulant pout abated and she smiled. "Oh, Jill. What a chief minister you would have made."

"I believe their civilisation worth saving, yes," Jansen confessed. "And I've been thinking about a way to do it, too."

Devon grinned. "And I thought you were just feeling sorry for yourself. Come on, let's hear it, then."

Jansen gifted him a sardonic smile. "I've been *dwelling* on the way Douglas' people took us down the first time. They were in the position we are now – that being, without any serious weaponry. They had to use what they had and what was around them."

Aito yawned. "Is there a punchline coming? I'm aging here, and my lousy German prosthetic is hurting again. I asked for them to source Japanese, but did anyone care—"

"Alright, don't get tetchy!" Jansen snapped.

"That's easy for you to say," retorted Aito. "You're not the one with one white hand!"

"No, I've got two."

"Oh, har har. One of the nurses told the new Germans I'd had an industrial accident – an accident!"

"Well, at least the hand works." Devon tried to calm the argument.

"I heard them calling me 'Industrial White Finger'!" Aito snapped.

"You preferred 'Stumpy'?" asked Jansen.

Aito gave him a catlike squint, eyelids squashing his antagonist like a car crusher in the scrapyard of imagination. He opened his mouth to lash back, when they all heard a tumble of earth roll down the bank behind them.

Turning quickly, and with some alarm, they saw a dinosaur creeping along the side of the bank about five metres above them. Jansen recognised the animal. "It's a Rugops," he whispered to the others. "Scavengers or feeders on the weak. Last time I saw one of these, it was part of a pack, and chasing me!"

"A pack? What, like that one?" Aito pointed tremulously with his new hand, back the way they had come.

"Oh, crap! A bit like that, yeah. Except this one's bigger."

Flanked on either side by predators moving furtively to cut them off, their way back was blocked by at least a dozen more of the creatures, of various ages, all hanging around, indolent as a street gang.

The theropod carnivores ranged in size from two to six metres in length, the largest standing about man-height at the hip, vestigial forelimbs held uselessly alongside their rib cages; although Jansen did notice they occasionally swung them when changing direction, perhaps as a natural counterweight to their large skulls. Their colours were the typically predatorial reds and oranges that he could not help noting were also typically terrifying.

The pack's demeanour, however, was weird. They seemed in no hurry, casual even. Gone was the urgency Jansen had witnessed last time. Even so, the stealth with which they had flanked the distracted humans, promoted them to an exalted status on his things-he-hoped-never-to-see-again list.

"Oh, crap indeed," Devon seconded quietly. "The only way out is through the river."

"These are dirt bikes," Jansen hissed from the corner of his mouth. "I forgot my pedalo, did you bring yours?"

"*Now* who's getting tetchy?" Aito bit back.

All three turned in their saddles to gauge the threat posed by the Rugops pack, when an ominous scraping made their flesh crawl. It came from the shoreline, now behind them.

Slowly, Jansen turned forwards once more.

"Don't tell me." Devon closed his eyes, shaking his head. "I just don't need to know."

Jansen swallowed. Sunning itself on the baking sand at the river's edge was the biggest crocodile he had ever seen. Approaching fifteen metres in length, Sarcosuchus imperator made no move towards them, but merely opened its jaws to a height that would allow even the tallest of men to simply walk into its mouth. Whether it snagged an unlucky Rugops, or the Rugops' prey, it was just another day at the office for this emperor among crocodiles. He would simply wait for someone to make a mistake.

Despite Devon's request, Jansen could not help reporting his findings robotically, hoping for a reduction in share once the fear was distributed among his colleagues.

"D-don't worry," Devon quavered. "That's not threat behaviour, they break wind through their mouths."

"That's hippos, you idiot!" snapped Aito.

Devon tried again. "Well, we still have s-speed on our s-side. Maybe we can outpace the Rhubarbs."

"It's *Rugops!* And are you kidding?" Jansen looked at him as if he were mad. "You haven't seen these things run – it's not like we're on asphalt here!"

Aito turned to him, blood quickly draining from his face. "If you have a plan for dealing with the Schultz factory, Jansen, this might be the last chance to spill the beans – and quickly."

Jansen was transfixed by the gargantuan Sarcosuchus. "I do, but only survivors get to hear it!"

"I'm game," Devon recovered. "We should split up, then, yeah?"

"Good idea," agreed Aito. "You split up first, and *we'll* see if they follow you."

Devon turned to him. "Captain, sir."

"Yes?"

"You really are a dick, you know that?" Devon started his bike, revving the engine aggressively, and with that their whole world was suddenly in motion.

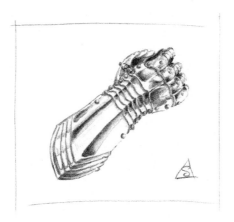

Chapter 13 | Armies

Baines noted the large Reiver entourage. An unsubtle statement of support for the envoy that made her wonder how many more were waiting back at their base – wherever that was. Casually, she greeted, "Mrs Cockshed. Been a while. How's living out here working for you?"

"Cock*sedge,* that's *Ms* Cocksedge." Her politician's mask fell to instantly cover any irritation caused by Baines' insults. "Why don't you simply call me Allison? And I could call you Jill. How would that be?"

Baines stared, allowing Cocksedge's smile some time to begin weighing her down, and then on a perfect eleven count, she answered, "Why don't you simply call me *Captain* and get to the damned point!"

Cocksedge's smile froze for a moment, then her expression began rearranging itself like a sliding block puzzle. Baines watched in fascination, waiting to see where the space would end up. The woman's mouth opened to speak. *Well, that answers that question.*

"My *dear,*" Cocksedge tried again. "There's no need for hostility. We're all part of the same crew, aren't we? Our very own clan, as it were?"

"Really? And these armed Reivers you've gathered to yourself – how do they fit into *our* crew? If you're going for *clan*-destine – surprise, surprise, I can see them."

"*Jill.*" Cocksedge patted Baines lightly on the hand in an attempt to ingratiate. "They're only here to make sure we get a fair deal. That's all this is about."

Baines looked down at the hand touching her. It would have been churlish to say 'touch me again and I'll kill you'. Nevertheless, her smouldering glare seemed to have the desired effect, and Cocksedge withdrew immediately.

"Release my people, Cocksend. *Then* we'll talk."

Cocksedge's mask almost slipped, but she rallied for one last stab at solidarity. "Jill, there's no need for us to be enemies. We simply have a list of basic requirements. Once fulfilled, you can have those two back." She steepled her hands prissily before her chest, smiling with all the disingenuousness of the career passive-aggressive. "*If* you still feel that you want them."

Baines soured further, her self-control twanging like taut elastic. *Spending time with this woman is like sitting a practical examination in anger management,* she thought. She *said,* "Give me the list."

Cocksedge handed her a scrap of parchment.

Baines could not help noting that the tear across the bottom of the list followed the same line as the one at the top of their ransom letter. *Written on the same piece of parchment,* she thought as she scanned the list. *They wrote the demands first,* then *the letter. Nice.* She looked up from the parchment. "I guess it's kinda hard to get your hands on paper out here, huh? As you tore this from the same piece as the note you sent us, I wonder what would happen if the wind just blew it away right now?"

A crack appeared in Cocksedge's demeanour, showing a glimpse of the real woman. "Your beloved Sarge might lose his head just as easily." Her expression, always fluid, slipped into one of regret. "My *people* have ideas about maintaining civilisation that differ somewhat from our own, I'm afraid. They like to make very clear, very bloody examples – hanging body parts on gates and such. I've been able to control them 'til now, but..."

Baines eyed the politician, poker-faced. "I can't help noticing how much of this 'essential equipment', to help you eke out a meagre living among the locals, is made up of weapons and ordnance."

Cocksedge's smile rebuilt itself immediately, like a video rewind; it was remarkable. She completed the effect with just a subtle frosting of reasonable. "These are hard times and hard lands, Captain. I'm sure you understand."

"I'm sure I do."

"And your response?"

"I wish to see Dr Pearson and Sergeant Jackson before we make any deals. After all, I've only your *word* they're even alive."

Cocksedge pulled a comm from her pocket, giving an involuntary shudder as icy wind blew into the garment. "Erika, dear. Please show our guests to the camera." She turned the device towards Baines.

The Sarge and Natalie were onscreen. "You guys alright?"

"*We don't need no rescuing, ma'am, we like it here!*" barked The Sarge, filthy-faced and clearly tied with hands behind back.

"*Don't give them anything, Captain!*" shouted Natalie as the camera was flipped to show the beautiful visage of Erika Schmidt.

"*They are in good health, for now,*" stated Schmidt. "*That could change with a night outside.*"

Cocksedge chuckled. "Really, my dear Erika, we don't need to threaten. Captain Baines has already vouched safe that she fully understands the situation, haven't you, Jill?"

Before Baines could answer, a man's voice bearing a cockney accent erupted once more from the comm, "*Tell the old bag to shut it*—" Cocksedge stabbed her thumb at the device, cutting off the rest of The Sarge's advice with a crackle.

Baines grinned.

Cocksedge's mouth screwed up indignantly, like she had been force-fed a lemon. "They may sing a different tune, were I to leave them entirely to the tender mercies of my colleague. I understand Erika's previous employment offered exemplary training in all manner of disciplines."

"I think we can agree that Heinrich Schultz is hardly the sort of man who bases hiring decisions on words-per-minute or the shortness of the applicant's skirt," Baines allowed.

"Oh, she excels there, too, she assures me."

There was absolutely no camaraderie between Baines and Cocksedge, but they were able to shove aside their animosity for a grudging moment of shared jealousy.

"Your answer, Captain," Cocksedge pressed again.

"Your list is long and impressive, but not exhaustive. What if I were to make you a better offer?"

Cocksedge gave her a sideways look. "Go on."

Baines allowed just the hint of a smile to twitch at her lips. "What if I were to offer you *everything?*"

"Don't you think we should tell the captain before we do this, Hiro?" asked Georgio seriously.

"Probably, but I really don't see the point in worrying him. This is what we're here for. If it goes wrong... well, it won't really matter where you are on this island, will it?"

Georgio's discomfort was replaced by a flush of fear. "By island, do you mean the whole of Britain? You think that's likely?"

Hiro glanced up from his instruments. "Very."

Georgio looked away with a shake of his head. "Thanks for breaking it gently. I should have asked Sandy!"

Hiro blinked, not understanding. "Shall we get on?"

"Why the hell not?"

"Very well." The chief engineer reached out for the large red button he had installed for this very purpose.

"*Hiro!*" Georgio almost screamed.

The chief's hand hovered over the button as he looked to his friend in bafflement. "What?"

Georgio blew out his cheeks, equal parts frustration and despair. "What about 'good luck'?"

"Oh, *that.*" He pressed the button.

The wormhole drive hummed to life and the focusing crystals, rescued from their armour-plated compartment in what remained of the ship's bow, began to glow.

Within their workshop, something resembling a liquid spiral came into being from nothing, not four metres from the machine itself. The wormhole opened to the size of a football and hovered about a metre above the deck. It appeared to neither produce nor absorb light. It made Georgio's vision blur as he tried to focus on something best viewed from the corner of the eye.

"Don't just stare!" shouted Hiro. "Send the camera!"

Shocked into life, Goergio cast the small device through the watery, disc-like event horizon, hanging on to the cable attached.

The device broadcast on every wireless frequency they could think of, including obsolete Bluetooth. Nevertheless, Hiro had insisted on a good old-fashioned cable to provide a backup, doubting they would get a second opportunity for testing.

Everything worked perfectly until all the lights went out. Despite this, the wormhole continued to swirl unnervingly, as backup emergency lighting woke up in fits and starts around them. Still giving off no light of its own, it became invisible for the split second they were in darkness, merely *existing* parallel to reality.

Hiro stared. "Why hasn't it shut down?"

"Hiro?" Georgio's voice had a tremor to it. "What have we done?"

"Ten, eleven, twelve, thirteen – whoa!" The chief stepped back involuntarily as the wormhole disintegrated. "What the hell was that?"

"I've never seen a wormhole do that," seconded Georgio. "Was that thirteen seconds after the power went out?"

Hiro nodded dumbly. Both of their comms noisily vibrated and binged for urgent attention in their pockets, but neither man could bring himself to move, let alone answer them.

"Hiro," Georgio asked again. "What have we done?"

Sir Walter Scott sent scouts ahead of his main force, as would any commanding officer. They reported a large build-up of Johnstone men to the west of Cheviot Mountain. Having recently scouted the newcomers' location personally, he decided to strike out east. Well to the north of Cheviot and the Johnstones, he would climb into the hills and turn south to come at them from the opposite side. However, he would not stray too far north as he crossed briefly into England. Thomas Percy, seventh Earl of Northumberland, and his brother, Sir Henry Percy, had a great number of soldiers guarding the south bank of the Tweed up past Norham and all the way to Berwick. A Scottish burning party led by French officers had already fallen foul of them earlier in the year, suffering heavy losses.

Also, and most crucially to his current endeavour, he wished to avoid giving any clue of his whereabouts or intentions away to the Johnstones. Hermitage Castle would have to wait. If the priest was right, there was a much larger prize to be had here. Having seen evidence of the newcomers' prowess with his own eyes, he believed it, too – such machines they built.

The young lord, still in his very early teens, put away his colossally expensive telescope and pulled on his gauntlet once more. As his fingers slid into the leather, he balled them into a fist. *Tha power of tha newcomers will be mine!*

Sir Nicholas expected to be in Hexham by nightfall. From there, he would let his men sleep the night and then choose two commanders to continue north. Each would take a third of his force and press on, with written orders bearing the royal seal for Northumberland's captain at Otterburn and Sir Ralph Grey of Chillingham. If he timed things correctly, and assuming he could still rely upon Maxwell's help, he could tie off almost the entire middle and eastern border with Scotland, then close in around the newcomers' craft like a tourniquet, sealing it away from the world.

He allowed himself a brief smile; the power soon to rest within his hands would be unprecedented. He would hand that power over to his queen, of course, but perhaps he might place just a few *requests* before letting go of the reins entirely. *Or should I say, letting go of the* reign? he mused. Although currently still secret on the world stage, the power of the *New World* could make a man like Throckmorton king of the old one. *Now, that is food for thought.* Temptation gnawed at him. He snorted ruefully. Shaking his head, he spurred his horse along the line of his men to catch up with the officers in the lead.

"Somebody, hold me back!" bellowed the usually affable Sam Burton. "Hiro! I'd just got this crate functioning again and you've blown it all – *again!* Just about every breaker in the place is down. Do you know how many software problems that's gonna cause when we reboot?"

Hiro and Georgio felt like a couple of rabbits on a motorway at night, as virtually every department head in the Pod stormed their little citadel – a workshop just off the main manufacturing bay.

Backing strategically towards the door, they bumped into Captain Douglas at his most unsympathetic.

The engineers quailed, but Hiro used the seconds Douglas took working up to an explosive rant, to develop his veto. "Sir, we must talk, urgently."

On the point of steaming from the ears, Douglas sniped, "Ye *think?*"

"Yes," Hiro answered simply.

Douglas took a breath. There was very little point in getting angry with the chief, it only confused him. "*Well?*" he asked, the timbre in his voice tight as drumskin.

"Firstly, we're sorry for the inconvenience," Georgio jumped in, nodding vigorously for his immediate superior to follow suit.

Hiro merely looked blank and then continued as if nothing had been said. "The wormhole did not behave as expected, Captain."

Douglas almost sissed as he secured the saucepan lid of his anger and tried to focus on the chief's words. "Did it no'?" was all he could manage.

Hiro began calmly, "When the power went down—"

"Good of you to notice!" Burton bawled at his back.

Hiro continued unabashed. "The wormhole should have disconnected immediately, but it didn't. It remained open for another thirteen seconds, sir."

"Ominous," replied Douglas, reeling his annoyance back in.

"Thirteen is only a number, sir."

"*Thank you,* Hiro. Ah was referring to the wormhole. And how is the drive, by the way – did that blow with all of our breakers?"

"We believe the drive is fine, sir," Georgio supplied. "The breakers saved it," he added with a forced chirpiness.

"Isn't *that* great to know!" sniped Burton. "You planning any more of these tests without telling anybody? I only ask, as I'm sure it said somewhere in my contract that *I* was in charge of this joint! Or should we just burn the place down and save everyone a load o' time?"

"I fail to see how that would help, Dr Burton," replied Hiro.

Douglas pinched the bridge of his nose, as he was so often disposed to do when dealing with Hiro or Sandy. "Look, can we get back to basics? Sam, could you please see about the lights? Hiro, explain – from the beginning – what happened."

Hiro did as instructed. Just as he got to the bit about the lights going out, some of them came back on again.

Douglas looked around, giving a single nod of approval.

Hiro completed his tale.

"OK." Douglas took a moment to digest the information. "So, we don't know how the wormhole stayed open?"

The engineers shook their heads.

Douglas looked to Patel. "Satnam? Thoughts? Theories?"

Patel almost jumped when spoken to, so engrossed had he been in the story. Rallying his thoughts, he offered, "There is only one way the wormhole could have stayed open – at least as I understand the technology. It must have drawn power from an alternative source."

"And what about the way it disintegrated?" asked Georgio. "Do you have an explanation for that?"

Patel shrugged. "Perhaps the power was in the form of radiation – moving in waves, they simply petered out? Might it be possible your brother left something behind in his work, that might explain this type of phenomenon? He *was* our chief expert in the field, after all."

Georgio thought for a moment. "I do have Mario's notes and all his papers, but he never described anything like this to me – and believe me, he loved to bore me with his work."

"So we think some kind of radiation might have bled energy into the wormhole after it was shut down our end?" clarified Douglas.

"It's probably the closest we have to a working hypothesis at the moment, James," Patel confessed. "But what could cause that energy...?" He trailed off, lost in thought.

Everyone waited while the astrophysicist's powerful mind slipped into overdrive. When he spoke, his words came slowly, thoughtfully. "We have opened a wormhole on the Earth's surface once before..."

When Patel trailed off for a second time Georgio spoke, "But we saw no evidence of this last time."

"Is that correct?" Patel asked immediately, thinking quickly now. "Or were we simply too busy crashing to notice?"

Douglas pulled out his comm. "Sandy?"

"*Go ahead, sir,*" Singh answered.

"When you went through all the crash data from our arrival here, did you notice anything odd about it?"

"*Odd, Captain?*"

"Odd, like the wormhole staying open after power was lost to it?"

"*No, sir. Nothing like that. However, we only moved a few thousand metres through space – certainly no more than two kilometres, and that includes our run up to the jump. We were under fire at the time, as I'm sure we all remember.*"

Hiro frowned, struggling to see where his colleague was going with this. "What does that have to do with anything?"

Before Singh could answer, Georgio snapped his fingers, after a small eureka moment. "Yes! There was something about opening wormholes through the planet in one of Mario's papers."

"But we didn't do that," Hiro objected.

"Yes, I know." Georgio's face fell, and his whole body sagged as a horror crept over him. "*We* haven't tried anything like that."

"Whoa, what's this now?" asked Douglas with concern. "Are ye suggesting someone else might be mucking about with these things?"

"Causing a cross-dimensional power surge," Patel completed in dead tones, paling at his own words.

Georgio stared at him. "But Mario theorised that such a wormhole might be impossible to close."

"More than that," Hiro joined in, catching on. "It might *eat* the world."

Everyone fell silent.

After several moments, Singh asked, "*Captain? Hiro? Are you guys still there?*"

"For now," replied Hiro.

"OK. This is all just a theory, right?" Douglas clarified, trying to get everyone back up from the metaphorical floor. "Is there any *good* news resulting from your experiment? Georgie?"

Georgio seemed to snap awake. "Sorry, Captain. Erm, let's see." Opening his tablet, he downloaded the camera information. "All data and telemetry, such as it is, was transmitted successfully, both via radio waves and the direct input." He held up the severed end of the cable where the wormhole had cut it cleanly as it frittered into nonexistence. "This happened when the wormhole shut down. Well, that answers one question at least, ladies and gentlemen," he spoke to the room at large. "We can pass radio waves back through an open wormhole, so that suggests two-way travel might be possible for matter, too."

"*I'd rather test that with a mouse,*" Singh interjected via the comm link.

"So what's on the captured footage?" asked Douglas, anxiously.

Georgio frowned. "I think that's grass." He looked up from his device, a pained expression crossing his face. "I never thought to switch it to night vision."

"*Those things have an automatic mode, you know!*" berated Singh, unhelpfully.

"It's OK, Georgie." Douglas placed a comradely hand on the younger man's shoulder. "It was a shock to everyone, Ah get it. And Ah'm sure it can be enhanced. Just tell us what ye see?"

Georgio took a deep breath and smiled in disbelief. "Yep. Looks like grass, sir."

Douglas returned his smile. "So, *home?*"

"Could be, Captain. What's also important to note is that the wormhole swallowed more than ten metres of cable before the camera gave any recognisable pictures—"

Hiro clapped his hands together in an uncharacteristic show of enthusiasm. "Yes! We theorised the wormhole might appear high in the air."

"*I wouldn't call ten metres* high," retorted Singh.

"Huh!" grumbled Hiro. "If you stepped through and fell ten metres, *you* would have something to say about it!"

"*Probably,*" Singh agreed. "*Something like, ouch, and your rubbish calculations have just broken my legs.*"

"You're the one who likes crashing things! I have simply—"

"Alright, alright, gentlemen," Douglas calmed. "Is there anything else, Georgie?"

The young Italian slowed the video right down and was able to discern movement, despite the lack of any light. No. That was not quite correct – despite the lack of any *local* light. He froze the frame. "I can see stars, Captain!"

"*Probably from falling ten metres,*" chuntered Singh.

Georgio ignored the comment. "Sandy, I'm sending you this. Break out-a your star maps!"

"You know the *New World* will never fly again," Baines elucidated.

"What of it?" Cocksedge asked doubtfully.

"Simply that when we go, we must leave *it* – and pretty much everything else – behind."

The politician's eyes widened. "When you *go?* Go where?"

"Not where," Baines allowed with a crafty smile. "*When.* Our scientists and engineers have found a way back to our own time. And now you have, what I am sure for *you* will be, a difficult choice to make."

"Go on."

"You can either come with us, which will of course mean your arrest, or you can stay here as sole heir to the *New World* and her technology. That would be wealth beyond compare for most people from our *own* time, but *here*... Madam Cocksick, it would practically make you a goddess!"

Cocksedge was so stunned by the revelation she barely noticed the slur on her name and salutation. "When do you propose to leave?" was all she could think to ask.

"Soon. Within days. If you would rather stay here and live your life wielding vast power over these people, there will of course be concessions."

Cocksedge suddenly looked distrustful. "Oh? Name them."

"Immediate forfeiture of The Sarge and Natalie."

Cocksedge laughed. "*Commander* Baines, you almost had me there."

Baines almost corrected her rank but realised it for the insult it was in time to stop herself. Rather, she scowled with a complete sense of humour failure. "Let me make myself absolutely clear, Cocksedge. You had better be taking good care of my people. If anything has happened to them or *does* happen to them, this world will not be big enough for you to escape me."

Cocksedge studied her strangely, trying to work out the truth of their situation. Eventually, she asked, "You're serious? About leaving, I mean."

"Deadly," was Baines' unequivocal response. "About my offer *and* my threat. It's all for you *if* you return my people to me."

"You'll understand, Jill, if I require a little more than your word."

"Like what?"

"Like some of the weapons from that list. Let's call it an advance, shall we? As it's all to be mine anyway, there's surely no harm, is there?"

Baines shook her head. "I'm not arming you while we're still here, and that's final. Do you want to try again?"

Cocksedge squinted with annoyance. "What about some of the other items on the list?"

Baines nodded. "I brought the remainder of yours and Schmidt's personal effects with me – as a *gesture*." She motioned behind her. "I can have the corporal here fetch them, if you wish to make a trade?"

Cocksedge calculated. "I want more."

Baines laughed. "You *do* surprise me. What else?"

"There are medical supplies, food items and blankets on there. I want those, too."

Baines' laughter died away to a smirk. "Feeling a little under the weather, are we? I'll tell you what, I'll agree to those terms, but only enough for your and Schmidt's personal use – that *and* your personal effects. It's a good deal, Cocksniff. I suggest you take it."

Cocksedge's countenance curdled. "Not enough!" she spat.

"OK," accepted Baines. "Is it enough for one of the hostages? I have all of the things I just agreed to right here in our baggage, ready to go."

"How prescient of you, Jill." Cocksedge chewed over the weaker offer with obvious distaste.

"*Allison*," Baines cajoled smoothly. "Just look to your greed, I'm sure you'll make the right decision."

Cocksedge hated it when people saw through her. It was a politician's greatest failure. She also hated being accused of being what she was, but with quite literally everything to play for, she swallowed her plastic pride. "Very well. I accept. I will have Sergeant Jackson brought here—"

"No," Baines cut her off. "I want Dr Pearson."

"Really?" Cocksedge seemed genuinely surprised. "I thought you and he were old comrades in arms. Won't he be hurt that you're willing to sacrifice him for that slip of a girl? Or do you have a pet goldfish requiring a course of Tapsafe?"

Baines remained impassive. "Those are my terms."

"Very well. I'll have the girl brought here as soon as I've looked over my items. I'm sure you understand, dear."

Gleeson roamed the castle's corridors and hallways searching for Lord Maxwell. He had grown rather fond of the old place during the last few weeks. Living in a real castle with conditions barely changed since medieval times was a life experience he would never forget. Despite the mental scars left by the use of its latrines, he would miss Hermitage.

"Commander Gleeson, Ah hear ye've been looking for me?"

Gleeson turned in surprise to find Maxwell bearing down upon him in a flurry of robes. "Lord Maxwell," he greeted. "All dressed up again, I see. Another meeting with the Queen Regent's stooges?"

"Aye, the old boot's pressing me for an answer. What did ye need tae see me aboot, Commander?"

Gleeson looked regretful. "I'm sorry, Dave, but we've got to go. Got orders from Captain Baines this morning. She's sending transport for us tonight."

Maxwell's expression darkened. "Ah'll be sorry tae lose ye."

"Yeah. I think some of us will be sorry to go, to tell ya the truth. There *is* good news, though. Apparently, Sir Nicholas is on his way north with the army he promised."

Maxwell snorted. "Ye have a singular idea aboot what constitutes good news, Commander!"

Gleeson grinned. "I'll have a word when I get back, I promise. Your holding of this castle and Liddesdale will be important. I'll make sure you're not overlooked by Queen Elizabeth when it comes time to be grateful, no fear. Also, don't forget she'll pass her crown to a Scotsman in the end, so the quicker you guys buddy up, the easier it'll be all round."

Maxwell shook his head in wonderment. "Of all the things ye've told we, that's the hardest tae believe."

"It's the truth, mate. I swear."

Maxwell could read the sincerity in the Australian's eyes. "Ah believe ye, but 'tis for the fate of ma home that Ah fear. Before ye go, will ye no' tell me a wee bit about yours?"

"Australia? She's a beautiful country, mate. She'll be discovered by a Dutchman around fifty years from now." He stopped to think. "Wow, that sounded weird."

Maxwell laughed. "Aye!"

"Then a little later the Poms will start using the place as a penal colony."

"Poms?"

"English."

Maxwell frowned in confusion. "A prison, ye say? Ah thought ye said it was a beautiful place? We dinnae send *our* footpads and outlaws tae anywhere ye'd wish tae see, Ah tell ye!"

"Yeah. That's the running joke – centuries on, the Poms still think it's funny." He laughed ruefully. "Maybe it is... a bit. Ya see, it's different in our time, Dave. I love my home, but the politics of the future is more about corporation than country. We have companies so big they can control governments. Even arm themselves and go to war against one another to defend their interests – or rob some bagger else's.

"Many governments are practically *owned* by them – they certainly kowtow to them. Can you imagine that? Whole continents ruled by the owners of a shop?

"Canada's whole space programme carked it after the computer games manufacturer controlling most of their cabinet fell out with their opposite number in the States, about a rights infringement." Through his dismay, Gleeson realised Maxwell was struggling to follow.

"The map's redrawn, ya see? Countries are just dotted lines under the shaded areas of conglomeration. Even our languages are watering down. Although a third of the world's population are technically Chinese, almost everyone speaks American, even the Poms. There's only us down under that speak the Queen's bladdy English properly, now."

Maxwell was indeed struggling to understand Gleeson's mode of speech and to take in all that was said. Thinking of the rows of small shops in Kelso, his home, he asked, "Merchants' *businesses* bigger than *countries?*"

"Yeah. Telling everyone how to think and what they can watch, read, listen to and eat. Removing anything they don't think's appropriate for us from the net – that's... erm, well, kinda like a trade route.

"No hard copies any more, ya see? Deletion's kinda like the burning of books, but more eco-friendly, so no one notices the shackles snapping closed.

"O' course, then there's the spying devices in every home – on every *person!* It's grim, mate. It's real grim. Everybody buys into it 'cause there's no choice. In this time, you'd call an entity that seditiously removes all freedoms and discourages imagination – even the use of your own memory – the devil!" Gleeson noticed Maxwell's confusion and changed the subject, brightening suddenly. "But you guys are gonna change all that, right?"

Maxwell had the grace to look doubtful. "Oh, aye. Nae problem."

Baines' transport returned to the *New World* bearing a tearful Natalie Pearson. "We've got to get him back, Captain. We can't just leave him there."

Baines held the younger woman. "Don't worry, Natalie. I swear to you, we won't leave The Sarge behind."

"Why did you choose me?"

"Because Sergeant John Jackson is the toughest man I've ever met – even Jonesy is wary of him. He's far more capable of dealing with the situation than..."

"A young zoologist?"

Baines smiled with understanding. "I was about to say *civilian*. You see, I understand how terrible you must feel, leaving him behind like that, but he'd prefer it that way. Trust me."

"Of course he would!" Natalie replied tersely. "Because he's so damned brave and noble."

Baines acknowledged with a shrug. "Perhaps. But mostly because *your* safety will have been his chief concern. With you gone, he can act, and act alone without fear of dragging you into further danger. The Sarge is deadly, on the battlefield or in an East End snug on a Saturday night, but that's just the veneer. His real job, his purpose, in fact, is to protect and save lives."

Natalie stared, tears streaming down her face. "What do you mean?"

"Look, Sergeant Jackson is probably the highest trained soldier we have. Now he's free to think only of himself, he'll probably give them the slip – and a few concussions – before we even get to free him. So don't you beat yourself up. It's better this way, see?"

Natalie smiled bravely, wiping her tears. "I think so." They drove down into the Pod's main hangar. As they disembarked, someone called her name. She turned to see Woodsey approach on the trot.

"Are you OK?" he asked, breathless. "I got word you were on your way back and ran down here. I looked after the animals for you. Even cleaned 'em out."

Natalie smiled sadly at the anxious teen before her. She really cared for Woodsey, but not for the first time saw him as very young. By contrast, The Sarge had merely winked at her when that creepy blond assassin and that awful politician had taken her away from him. She had kicked and screamed, but *he* merely told her to hide a couple of lagers for him, before the Aussies nicked them all. In that moment, she had chosen the man she wanted to spend her life with. Natalie had no idea if he felt the same. All she knew was that she was furious with the situation, but even more so with herself – why had she not realised all this earlier? Why had she waited until it was too late?

She allowed Woodsey to lead on towards her beloved animal enclosure. As they drew near, they heard a growling and a scratching from the inside of the door.

"What's that?" asked Natalie.

Woodsey suddenly became very sheepish. "I must have locked him in—"

Before he could fully confess, someone had heard his mistress' voice. The barking could be heard all across the hangar.

For the first time, Natalie smiled. Woodsey drew back the bar locking the large container. Reiver burst from the doorway like a bubbly-propelled cork, knocking him out of the way.

"Hey! Steady on, mate."

Natalie laughed as the collie leapt excitedly, almost taking her to the deck. "*Whoa.* Slow down, boy." She bent to kiss his head and was rewarded with a wet nose smear across her mouth and face.

Once Reiver had checked her thoroughly all over, using his full snout and tongue sensor array, he turned his attention to Woodsey, who was opening the door wide enough to allow them in. Reiver loved his friends, almost as much as he loved his mistress. He would never dream of biting them. However, his educational nip certainly made Woodsey jump on the spot, leaving a small bruise behind on his behind, as an aid to memory.

"Ouch! I'm sorry, boy. *You* shouldn't have followed me. I didn't know you were even in there."

Reiver glared, making him step back.

"Alright, alright. I said I was sorry, dude."

Natalie laughed and knelt to give the collie a full hug. Over her shoulder, Reiver watched Woodsey rub his posterior, his expression smug[28].

Singh opened his tablet with a solemnity that put Douglas, Mother Sarah, Patel, Hiro and Georgio on edge. He synchronised the small device with the main screen, built into the wall.

"This image – such as it is – was taken from the wormhole cam."

The image was blurred. It had been several years since she received the treatment, and for a moment, Mother Sarah wondered if she were becoming near-sighted again. She squinted. "Please tell us what we're looking at, Sandy."

"Well, as you can see, the pictures aren't great. The camera was spinning as it fell and set to a low ISO value, without benefit of night vision. Then, of course, it hit the ground. Unfortunately, the lack of preparedness—"

"Wormhole cam? Is that a thing?" asked Hiro. He turned to Georgio and whispered, "Are we making that a thing?"

Sarah shushed him. "Sandy, what are we seeing?"

Singh turned back to the main screen. Across the baseline was a row of smaller images. He swiped one of them up to the centre, double hitting it. The image expanded to fill most of the wall. "I've played with this one, enhancing it as best I can. As you can see, it's definitely grass. Not massively helpful, perhaps. But at least we know we're *sort of* in the right period and epoch. Now, moving on to the stars." He brought another image to the fore.

"This is the best we have, showing the constellations. As you will see, I've managed to pick out elements of the Ursa Major Family

---

28   For anyone yet to be blessed by a dog's love – yes, they can look smug. It's a bit like the cat who got the cream and can mean anything from 'now let that be a lesson to you' to 'look at this fabulous new toy I'm deigning to show you'.

here and here. They're streaked because of the camera motion, but the brighter 'streaks' do appear to match the stellar maps we have in our computer for the northern hemisphere."

Douglas leaned forward. "Match them for *when,* Lieutenant?"

Singh acknowledged him with a small nod. "That's the question, Captain. I can't be absolutely precise from what we have here, but I can tell you – that is, I *believe* – that these pictures represent the cosmos as we would have seen it from AD2112. Or at least, *very nearly.*"

Douglas sat back, blowing out his cheeks. "Ah understand your reticence to commit, Sandy, but is there no way to tie it down further? Even being out by a hundred years could be disastrous."

"Especially if we step," Patel interjected, "into a civilisation less advanced than ourselves, yet advanced enough to take our knowledge by force and adapt it to their own ends. If we materialised in, say 2012, we might prematurely bring on the very Armageddon we are desperately trying to prevent."

"That's a little 'glass is half empty', wouldn't you say, Satnam?" asked Sarah. "Surely we'd be better off among folks with a more comparable level of understanding to our own?"

"Or at least more comparably cynical?" Patel added ruefully. "Captain Douglas, what do you think would happen were we to be captured by the British government?"

Douglas shrugged. "That would depend on when. In 1900, they might take our knowledge by force, in order to build terrifying new weapons and the largest empire the world has ever seen.

"In the early 2000s, they would probably just look to social media to tell them what to do, so *anything* could happen." He sagged as he considered further. "We *really* need to get this right, people."

"A sobering thought, indeed," Patel acknowledged, puffing out his cheeks. "Lieutenant Singh, are there any other signs? *Anything* that might give us a timeframe? What about technology or landmarks?"

Singh shook his head. "This is all we have. It may be – and I must stress the *may* – that we can attribute some of the fuzziness and overall low quality of the image to light pollution."

"Well, that would put a rather different complexion on things," Douglas stated, perking up. "The Wooler City encroachment didnae reach all the way to Great Cheviot until the 2080s. That was when it was saved as a nature reserve."

Singh was shaking his head again. "Captain, this may *not* be light pollution. It could just as easily be an artifact of a low-resolution image. I urge you all to view it with due—"

"Cynicism?" Sarah cut in, giving Patel a wink as she squeezed his hand. "So what do we do, folks? Can we send another camera, one with the capability to test the air, soil and anything else you tech wizards can dream up?"

"No."

It was Hiro who spoke, and they all looked to him to elaborate.

"This test was purely to see if we could actually make a small wormhole and pass matter through it safely. The camera obviously survived the journey, so we can tick that. We also learned that it is possible to send transmissions both ways, so we can tick that, too. The suggestion is that matter may also be able to do likewise. But you see, although our experiment gathered *some* intel from the other side of the wormhole, it was never specifically *about* gathering information from the other side of the wormhole."

"Can we no' try again with that in mind?" asked Douglas.

"We don't have the power, Captain. It will take almost everything we have to open a wormhole with a lifespan capable of transporting us all to the future. It will almost certainly destroy all our equipment, too. Look at the damage we did with just a four-second test."

Douglas frowned. "Ah thought you said—"

"Thirteen seconds," Hiro interrupted, nodding agreement. "We've been over and over the figures – every piece of data we managed to harvest from the test, in fact. *Our* wormhole lasted 4.4356 seconds. The *extension* was 13.0129 seconds."

"Extension?" asked Sarah.

Hiro sighed. "*Something* kept the wormhole open. This was after we tripped the Pod's power grid again. No matter how many times I look over the data, I can't explain it. We've never come across *anything* that might explain it."

"Except Mario's theories," added Georgio.

"Look, we cannae allow ourselves to get sidetracked here," Douglas took control. "All we need to know about that anomaly is, did *we* cause it?"

"I don't think we can answer that, James," said Patel.

"Then we must proceed as best we can," continued Douglas. "Much of the evidence we *do* have – the fall of the camera due to subsidence in the mountain for example – all points towards home."

"So, what? We're ready to go?" asked Sarah.

"Not quite," Patel answered. "Sam Burton's and Jim Miller's people are working hard, along with practically every able-bodied person they can shanghai, to strip as much material as possible from the *New World* for the manufacture of cable. There is danger in this work, too. Some of the ship is becoming structurally unstable, thanks to our efforts. Jim is not happy with the quality, but believes the material will, however inefficiently, carry enough power from the *New World*'s reactor to the wormhole drive for our jump."

"So, in terms of a date?" Sarah tried again. "People will need time to prepare."

Patel looked to Hiro, who shrugged. "Maybe the sixth?"

"Of December?" Sarah clarified.

"I believe that might be possible," Patel hedged, looking to Hiro for his appraisal.

The *New World*'s chief engineer gave a curt nod. "*Hai.*"

"OK, great." Sarah leaned forward on the table, catching each eye in turn. "*But,* here's a question for ya – what if some folks don't wanna go?"

After a surprisingly emotional farewell, Gleeson, Jones and the other *New Worlders* returned from Hermitage Castle. The old fortress' main gate was repaired, her retinue well supplied. They had done all they could and all that might reasonably be expected of them – all except one thing...

"You know... that Dave Maxwell... 's a good bloke."

Forewarned, Bess' lips twitched with amusement at Commander Gleeson's awkwardness. "You refer, of course, to David Lord Maxwell of Kelso. You believe I should show favour...?"

When Gleeson left the room, he heaved a mighty sigh of relief. "Bladdy 'ell."

"What's that, Commander?" asked Baines, lightly.

"Oh, nothin'. It's just... well, she's a barrel o' laughs these days, isn't she?"

"Ah... the head that wears the crown. Hard work, was she? I heard you were putting in a good word for David Maxwell."

"Yeah, well, that Dave Maxwell... 's a good bloke."

Baines laughed and put her arm through Gleeson's, leading him away. "Don't worry, we've already made clear the situation with our friends over the border. Bess will look to build stronger ties, have no fear. Drink at the Mud Hole?"

"You already squared it and you let me go in there anyway?"

"Yes." She grinned broadly. "Still, you've done your duty to a friend, and that's laudable." Baines led Gleeson away for a beer that, for the first time in weeks, had bubbles in it and was chilled by means other than being left outside. "You missed a trick, you know. Should have tried singing to her. I've been told she likes that. Apparently, young Woodsey wooed her with a sea shanty."

"Really? Bladdy Kiwis."

A couple of days in the mucky hay on the bastle's lower floor had left The Sarge stinking and angry. *Do they ever change this Turkish delight?* He moved to find a cleaner patch, less soiled by cows. Arms still tied behind his back, he was about to make his grievance known, when he sat on something that made him curse. Not wishing to draw attention to himself, he internalised his shock and foul language.

Under all the hay and filth was hidden something sharp – or at least sharp enough to hurt. The object must have been there for some time, too, judging by the stench in the place, just waiting for his unsuspecting buttock to unerringly locate it.

Briefly calculating when he had had his last tetanus jab, he nevertheless passed a thank you on to whichever deity might have been laughing at him at that precise moment. It was a blade.

He began working on his ropes immediately. Once through, he kept hold of them, should he be interrupted. Arms still behind his back, he began massaging his wrists and hands to bring some life back into them. Despite being indoors and thus shielded from direct exposure to the elements, it was still freezing in the ground-floor room. The thick oak door was clearly part of the building's defences, with a heavy drawbar propped at its side, ready to be dropped into place in times of emergency. Yet, however defensive, it was certainly lacking in draught proofing.

The Sarge's only method of marking time since his captivity had been to periodically note the direction of the shafts of daylight penetrating the cracks around the door. Occasionally someone would check on him, or briefly untie him to eat or answer the call of nature, but during those times he was heavily guarded. Cocksedge must know he would make a break for it, if he could – and even if she failed to see it, Jackson knew Schmidt would not.

She was probably as beautiful and deadly as Heidi Schultz herself. Heinrich would have nothing less for his personal aide, he felt sure. He remembered his brief run-in with Heidi aboard the *New World,* months ago. It had not gone well for him. If he was to get out of here, despite the small army camped outside, Schmidt would be his biggest problem.

It was getting dark, and that was all to the good. He risked a glance at the rusty knife before putting his hands once more behind his back. It was about twenty centimetres long and poorly made. *Never mind,* he thought, *in these situations, you take your friends where you find them.*

He settled in to wait.

Geoff Lloyd watched black clouds gather in the north. The sun had dipped in the west. Within minutes the landscape would be blanketed in darkness.

He considered that for a moment. 'Blanketed' suggested a cosiness that could not be further from the truth. A frigid total absence of light would be more appropriate.

He took a deep breath of icy air. A guard stirred close by. In a way it was comforting. Although these people were little more than his jailers, they were at least *his* people. Pondering what he knew he had to do next left him as cold inside as he was without.

At least he could walk now, albeit with a stick. The guard would call him back inside soon, and he would go meekly. Despite the uncertainty of what was to come, he knew this was no life for him. They would keep him from doing any harm – it was understandable. Unfortunately, they would also prevent him from doing any good, any*thing*, in fact. It might be simpler to leave – but go where? If he hid, they would turn the place upside down looking for him. Besides, he lacked the fitness to run away right now.

Heaving a heavy sigh, he knew that realistically there was only one course open to him. He would have to speak with Douglas and somehow regain his trust.

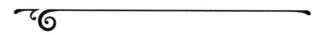

The cows were driven back into the bastle's ground-floor room at sunset. They would normally pass the winter nights in the barn, but it was full of Johnstone clan fighting men, just now.

The Sarge had mixed feelings about sleeping in a room full of cattle. He was tired of being stamped on and shoved into walls, but by the same token, he and Natalie would have caught nasty chills had it not been for their bovine buddies, warming the place. The draught cut knifelike through the tiny ventilation slots in the metre-thick stone walls, and the door fitted where it touched. Without even Natalie for comfort, he would catch his death without them – if he stayed. This evening, he was glad to see the old girls for quite a different reason, as he considered his next steps.

While most of Johnstone's force would be cosying down as best they could in the barn, he knew Sir John would be setting a formidable night watch. The young laird was no fool when it came to survival. Reiver stock through and through, he knew there were threats out there in the dark – and inside in the dark, with The Sarge. He trusted no one.

Each night, Jackson counted at least six men outside the door, standing around a brazier stamping their feet and telling bawdy stories. There would doubtless be several others set around the perimeter, too.

Above him, in the relatively civilised conditions provided by the bastle's living quarters, were just three women. They were the young Scottish girl, Aila, Cocksedge herself, and Heinrich Schultz's administrative assassin, Erika Schmidt.

Now it was a waiting game. The guard outside The Sarge's door would be changed at roughly 2200 hours and again at 0400. He would rest now. The change in guard always woke him.

Several hours passed in a fitful sleep, when sure enough, The Sarge woke abruptly. The men outside laughed and bantered, making no attempt whatsoever to keep the noise down. As expected, the changing of the guard.

Jackson was under no illusion that Schmidt might sleep through their racket. Her senses would be at least as honed to danger as his own. He sat up, huddling into his jacket. He would sleep no more this night.

Without his comm and equipment, The Sarge had no way of knowing the exact time. He guessed a couple of hours must have passed since the changing of the guard and made a note to buy an old-fashioned wristwatch, like the one Captain Douglas wore, if they ever got home.

He rose steadily to his feet. Quietly, he stretched, warming his muscles and joints. Even though the cows' heat radiated through the fetid air, the stone floor and walls were bitter cold. Once sure of his own body's cooperation, he moved around the room.

The door was the main entrance for both man and beast, and only lockable via a drawbar from the inside. It was kept closed, but he heard the guards prop something across the doorjambs outside each night, to stop the cattle from wandering should one of them open the door. It made a scratching sound when placed. He suspected it might be a short length of hurdle fence with a muck shovel leaned against it, to keep it in place. Enough to keep a mildly curious, somnolent cow indoors, but he doubted it would hold fast against any concerted effort.

The other way in, or out, was through the hatch in the ceiling. Everything he needed was in that room – not least, his weapons.

The hatch was for emergencies. When under attack, the bastle's occupants would drive their livestock inside the ground floor, bar the door and climb a ladder up through the hatch into the room above. As with the ladder used to access the front door at first-floor level[29], it too was pulled up and stored within the living quarters above. The hatch was well away from the walls, leaving no way for The Sarge to climb or jump high enough to reach it. For that reason, he hoped Schmidt would not consider the hatch a threat when the women slept.

The Sarge smiled. "Hello, Daisy," he whispered, almost silently into a cow's ear. "Cush, cush." He had heard Pte Adam Prentice say that northerners used the word 'cush' to call or calm their cows. As an East Londoner, he had no idea about cows or northerners, but had little to lose by trying. A Yorkshireman like Prentice was practically a southerner to anyone living in the borders, but to The Sarge, the north was the north – end of. Besides, the cow did not seem to mind.

Once sure the animal was calm, he leapt up onto her back. She moaned and stepped sideways, crushing his leg between her meaty flanks and one of her sisters.

The Sarge closed his eyes against the pain, trying with all his might to push the other beast gently aside – all without making a sound or crying out.

Eyes watering, he managed to make room for his throbbing leg while he waited for the beast to settle once more. "*Cush, bladdy cush!*" he breathed.

He patted 'Daisy' on the neck and tousled the long hair on top of her head between the ears – and more worryingly, between her huge and wicked-looking horns.

Once he was sure all was calm, within, without and upstairs, The Sarge began to manoeuvre himself to his feet atop Daisy's back. She moaned again but did not seem overly distressed by his comparatively meagre weight.

Again, he waited for her to calm and hold steady. It was quite the balancing act, but fortunately, the Highland cow was tall enough to allow him to comfortably reach the hatch, so at least he had something to hold on to in order to steady himself.

The Sarge grinned. Even the SAS never trained him to ride a cow. He lifted the hatch, gingerly. Warm air hit him in the face. The fire in the room above was burning low but still generated a

---

29   Second floor by American convention.

soporific heat. What he would not give to curl up on a fur in front of that fire, but that was not to be. He searched around for his weapons and equipment. They were piled next to Schmidt's sleeping pallet. Jackson almost swore.

With a sigh, he lifted the hatch enough to climb through and spotted a brace just to his side. He propped the trapdoor open and silently pulled himself up into the room.

Cocksedge groaned and pulled her silver emergency blanket closer about her. The cold draught from below must have followed him. He removed the brace and closed the hatch silently.

Moving as quietly as he could on the creaky boards, he made his way towards Schmidt, one step at a time. Despite years of training and surviving any number of crazy missions, The Sarge's heart was in his mouth – he was only human.

He reached out for his stun rifle and grasped it by the stock. That was when he felt the prick of the knife against his chest.

Erika Schmidt gave him the most erotic wink he had ever seen – of course, *she* probably thought it meant 'gotcha'.

The Sarge smiled uncertainly, then leapt backwards into a roll. Returning to his feet, he fired the Heath-Rifleson immediately.

The stun blast hit her bed, but Schmidt was no longer in it. Still in motion, she threw the knife at his throat before rolling back to her feet and straight kicking The Sarge in the chest.

He deflected the knife with his rifle butt, but her boot caught him right in the solar plexus, launching him through the air to land on Cocksedge – who screamed.

"Oh, Turkish delight!" he wheezed. Despite expelling the air from his lungs when he saw the kick coming, he was winded, but quickly staggered to his feet. By the time he fired again, the minx was already somewhere else. A crushing déjà vu re-ran the brief tussle with Heidi before his eyes. "Oh, Turkish delight!"

Night raids were nothing new to the Reivers and Sir Walter Scott's men made good time, moving from sheep track to drover's trail, every step of the way known intimately to each man.

There was no moon, and if Sir Walter was any judge, there would be an almighty storm soon, possibly bringing snow.

They were in the Cheviots now and looking for a sheltered spot to spend the night – sheltered being a highly subjective term. Sir Walter had four hundred men with him. They would be lucky to find so much as a cleft up here, to shield them from the worst of the wind and give them chance to light a few fires, unseen.

The wind seemed to increase as if sensing his thoughts. When one of his scouts returned with news of just such a shelter, Sir Walter shivered. He hoped it would be enough.

The Reivers were a hardy folk, but if they could not ride, even they preferred the hearth to the heather. Winter was not fully upon them yet, but it was close.

Walter gave orders to follow the scout to his dubious refuge. Their other scouts would soon find them; it was what they did.

Presently the ground dropped down steeply into a tight valley. He could hear the rush of a stream below as they dipped out of the wind. The location was by no means comfortable, but at least that wind was no longer cutting him in half. Had he a sympathetic nature, he would have realised that the situation was far worse for some of the older men. A north wind bit hard into mature joints. However, Sir Walter had no such sympathy; his mind's eye was firmly fixed on the work in hand. The Earl of Northumberland had men prowling the borders to the north and word had reached him, via a network of drovers, that another large English army was also heading up from the south, having split into three at Hexham.

Instinct told him they were all after the same prize. Then there were the Johnstones. He doubted he hated them any more than they hated him, but that hardly helped. If they got to the treasure first...

He cursed. On top of all that, there was the rumour that they had help from some rogue element among the new people.

The wind roared furiously overhead, making him glad for even this limited shelter, when the sound took on a strange property. Alien.

A deafening roar tore across the sky above them. Something huge was flying, *flying* through the air. Sir Walter covered his ears, but could not tear his gaze away. Just a couple of weeks ago, the sight would have had him running, screaming, filling his breeches most likely, but on this night his eyes burned with the light of avarice. He would have this magic for himself. After that, taking Hermitage Castle back to salve his family honour would be a mere formality – he would have the world.

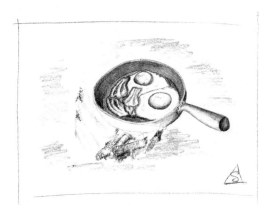

Chapter 14 | Dawn of a New Day

Dr Anne Hemmings passed her incarceration by cracking every security code she could access aboard the *Heydrich*. Her tablet was an allowance from Heidi, to help Devon solve his murder case. Access was limited and some of the codes were just too heavily encrypted. Nevertheless, her success rate was formidable; at least sixty-forty in favour.

Between them, she and Devon had already brought their investigation to a speedy conclusion; a conclusion known only to a select few, as no official report had yet been filed. Devon was anxious for her to retain access to the ship's computers for as long as possible. While his own orders took him away from the ship, riding the local terrain seeking development sites, he relied on Hemmings to undertake another essential task.

Commander Ally Coleman watched her workers from the viewport of one of the USS *Newfoundland*'s executive suites. Still convalescing after recent injury, she felt stronger for seeing their efforts – and the losses they had endured – come to something.

The new water pumping facilities had transformed their wilting crop. From her window, the fields were lush and vibrant with a dozen different yields.

Unfortunately, her eye was also drawn to a very different sort of crop – several new graves. She had not yet been mobile enough to visit them, but she would. In this time, the sort of flowers one might leave on a grave did not exist, so she would put together a wreath from the harvest, in remembrance of those people and what they had died for. She felt that more fitting.

Theirs was a weird landscape, the agricultural developments making it all the more so. On one side of their ship was the lake, much reduced by summer's heat, its beaches dotted with smoky fires to discourage the wildlife. On the other, verdant farmlands leading up into the forests that covered the foothills, nestling beneath the sharp and forbidding rocky crags that surrounded Crater Lake.

Coleman mulled over the name. Crater Lake. It was not a real crater, of course. Far more likely, it was the caldera of a giant – though thankfully now extinct – volcano, but the name had stuck. Now it was home.

She blinked. It really was. Made all the better by a total lack of interference from their masters – more specifically, their mistress.

Coleman had toyed with the idea of attempting communication. Yet something always held her back. For all she knew, the *Heydrich* could have gone down with all hands.

She mulled that possibility over for a moment, unsure how she felt about it.

Her orders were simple: develop the farm. That was all, and there was so much to do, she hardly needed to request new ones.

Perhaps the bed rest and light duties had given her too much time on her hands. Maybe that was why her mind turned ever more to what the others might be doing.

The others – another landmark in her philosophy. When did that happen? Yet, she could not deny it, that was how she thought of them. Indeed, her sense of autonomy grew proportionally to the time elapsed between communications with the Schultz camp – and she was not alone. Often, she heard her people talking about setting down roots here – even building homes. Could she blame them?

Her comm buzzed on the table to her side. She sighed. "Coleman."

"*Commander, we have a call for you from the* Heydrich."

Coleman groaned.

"*Ma'am?*"

"Nothing. Put it through to me here."

"*At once, Commander. But, Commander...*"

"Yes?"

"*The connection is encrypted.*"

Coleman frowned. "Encrypted? From whom?"

"*You got me, ma'am. Do you still want me to patch it through?*"

Coleman grunted, her ribs twinging as she sat up straighter. Her mind raced. *What the hell am I getting pulled into now?* "Very well. Put it though."

The voice on her comm was replaced by another. "*Commander Coleman?*"

"Speaking."

"*Good day, Commander. This is Dr Anne Hemmings. We need to talk.*"

99.2 million years later, The Sarge also had his hands full. He fired again but was only rewarded by Schmidt diving clear once more. Before he could take another shot, Cocksedge reached from her sleeping pallet to grab his legs; an uncharacteristically gutsy move that pulled The Sarge off balance. As he fell back, the butt of his rifle knocked Cocksedge senseless, releasing her grip. He shot her for good measure before diving himself.

The blade of a hunting knife took a chink out of the stone wall at head level where he had been standing. By binding his legs, Cocksedge had intended to make him a target. Saved by a combination of experience and luck, it was time to return the favour. Without even a thought, he instinctively launched his own sorry little knife for Schmidt.

She ducked immediately, but The Sarge had not aimed at her head. She cried out as the rusty blade buried itself in her leg as quick as sight.

Bringing his stun rifle round, he fired at the injured woman, but to his astonishment and consternation she was already on the move *again*. Worse, the rusty little knife was already wheeling its way back towards him.

"Aarrrgh!" he cried out, in spite of himself. The blade missed by millimetres, a mere distraction while she reached for something, but her speed and resilience were beginning to rattle – and were his eyes now deceiving him, too? Where the *hell* had she got that sword?

The Sarge scrambled to his feet, legs spinning like a cartoon escapee. The sword was not a good one, but like he cared, it would do the job. A chair flew at him, ruining his aim once more as shouting began outside. He was in trouble. The chair hit the shoulder he had injured in Cretaceous Patagonia, giving him a dead arm. He tried to bring the rifle to bear one-handed, but Schmidt was already on him, taking a swing that would likely separate him from his head.

Already falling, The Sarge went with it, dropping the rifle and reaching for the bleeding wound in Schmidt's thigh, instead. She screamed as he dug a thumb deep into the hole left by his rusty blade. Using her as an anchor to spin his legs around, he scissor-gripped Schmidt's own legs to bring her down – only to find that she was equally dangerous on the floor.

Her initial swing went wide, due to the speed of Jackson's reversal, and she buried the sword blade in the side of her sleeping pallet. Now it was a wrestling match to possess a weapon. For most men, struggling in close proximity to such a beguiling specimen would hardly have put them in mind of killing – but The Sarge was no ordinary man and the SAS never trained for sentiment. He dug deep into her leg and, regaining some feeling in his other arm, used his free hand to go for her eyes.

Schmidt screamed, her grip on his neck weakening. She turned her head away, elbowing Jackson in the face. He felt his nose crack, but this only got his motor running. Using his superior weight to pin for an instant, he reached for his discarded weapon.

Schmidt managed to get a hand between his legs, presenting The Sarge with a choice: forget the weapon or forget his family commitments.

He bellowed in rage and pain, letting the rifle go.

Bringing her other hand up under his nose, she struck him hard and they rolled apart, both limping back to their feet.

They faced one another. A smile gradually rose on Schmidt's lips – she had the Heath-Rifleson in her hands.

The Sarge knew it was over. He doubtless had a few seconds remaining to him, while she crowed, engaging some suitably cutting Nazi rhetoric, then that would be it. He was astonished when her perfect smile froze and she fell to the floor.

Standing behind her, wide-eyed and terrified, was the slight form of Aila. The young girl dropped a heavy iron poker to the boards guiltily.

The Sarge bent double for a moment to *centre* himself, before taking a step towards her with hands held high to show he meant no harm. "Thank you, miss." He smiled. Although, with the blood streaming from his broken nose, it was probably not his most charming first impression.

The shouting outside suddenly reached fever pitch. His personal crisis inside had distracted him from it. Opening his mouth to wonder aloud what might be happening, The Sarge caught something else. The roar of engines – heavy, military engines.

"You know, if this all goes wrong, we may never see one another again," said Henry. "I mean, like, what are the chances of this plan actually working?"

"Well, I'm glad *you* came," answered Woodsey.

"No – Henry's right," agreed Tim.

Woodsey gave him a sad shake of the head. "*You* always look on the dark side, dude."

"Tim's usually right, though," Clarrie jumped in, loyally.

"Well, *I* hope he's not," Rose stated flatly.

They sat in silence for a moment. Eventually, Rose asked, "How does everyone feel about this? Going home, I mean."

"If it *is* home," Woodsey mumbled.

"*Now* who's being negative?" Tim bit out.

Woodsey waved him down. "All I'm saying is, I'd rather stay here."

Tim could hardly believe his ears. After a moment's silence, he could not contain it any longer. "You, of all people, *like* it here? You know, I looked this up – it's called 'anemoia'."

"*Annannoying?*"

"*No,* Woodsey. Anemoia. It means longing for a time you've never actually lived through. A bit like nostalgia, but you were never there."

"But I was ther— *am* here," he shot back. "What's more interesting, I think, is why *you* looked that up – still longing for the dinosaurs?"

"No. Well, maybe a little. Look, that's not the point. I look stuff up – it's what I do!"

"Trying to diagnose your own sickness." Woodsey shook his head sadly. "Heartbreaking."

"I'm not sick, you numpty!"

"Yeah? Well, I'm not an amoeba."

"*Anemoia!*"

"Whatever. Look, let's think about it, shall we?" Woodsey began again. "What are the chances of us getting home?"

"That's what I said right off, dude, and you shot me down," Henry rebuked.

"No. *You* said what are the chances of this working. Not the same. I mean, seriously, what are the chances of us getting home? Ya see, the way I understand it, we've totally messed up the timeline. So even if this works, there's no guarantee that home will be... well... home."

"So what do you suggest we do about it?" asked Tim. "You know, I may be mistaken, but I don't remember our leaders asking our opinions on this move."

"Yes, you're right," agreed Rose. "And if they mess it up it will probably get us all killed."

"Maybe that's the plan," suggested Henry.

Woodsey laughed. "Wow! You're really in your dark place today."

"All I'm sayin' is that, maybe, they feel that *tryin'* to get home is safer than stayin' here." Henry looked uncharacteristically sombre.

"How's that safer?" asked Clarrie.

Henry's expression darkened still further. "I don't mean safer for us, Clarrie. Just safer for the world outside. Either we get home, or we just get out of the way."

"I think you're right," agreed Tim. "We're doing so much damage to the timeline here that we should just go – whatever the cost. Although, I find myself having to agree with Woodsey, too."

"No way!" Woodsey perked up. "This I've gotta hear. Spill, dude."

Tim rolled his eyes. "All *I'm* saying is, I also doubt home will be home, even if this does work."

"What do you think we'll find?" asked Rose, concern lining her pretty face.

Tim shrugged. "Anything is possible."

"Like T rexes running grocery stores, that kind of thing?" Woodsey grinned.

Tim shook his head. "No. I don't think we made that much mess in the Cretaceous—"

"Yeah," Woodsey cut him off. "*We* may not have done. What about those crazies we left behind? That creepy German chick that held you captive was a couple o' stormtroopers short of an interrogation party. She's capable of *anything*."

"Well, I'm glad *you* came," Henry returned the taunt.

Tim fell silent. He relived his captivity every day – and night – but worse than that was the possibility that Woodsey was correct.

"You think I'm right, don't you?" Woodsey read his mind.

Sullenly, Tim confessed that he did.

"So that begs one big question, then, doesn't it?" asked Woodsey.

"*What?*" they asked, severally.

"Do you think Mr T rex will serve booze if we find ourselves still underage there?"

They pelted him with paper cups. Some of them were empty.

The Sarge pulled open the first-floor door and threw the ladder into place. He beckoned to Aila. "Come with me."

Her eyes were large with fear, but after a second's thought, she nodded. He took her hand and helped her onto the ladder. Once down, she stood aside for Jackson to follow.

Just outside the enclosed farmyard stood Meritus' orbital attack ship, and to The Sarge it was glorious.

Johnstone's men had either run like hares or barricaded themselves up in the barn.

Captain Baines stepped out of the little craft's side hatch, with Meritus following immediately behind.

The Sarge grabbed Aila's hand and ran for them.

The only illumination across the yard came from a couple of braziers and the white electric light spilling from the ship's hatch. Baines blinked into the darkness. "Sarge?"

"Get back in," he shouted. "Let's get the hell out of here!"

"Wha—"

"Bladdy move!" he bellowed.

Baines quickly hustled Meritus back inside before he could say a word, as Sergeant Jackson and Aila flew in after them.

"Shut the hatch and get us out of here!" ordered The Sarge. He turned to see Schmidt standing at the upper storey doorway, backlit by the bastle's large fireplace. She seemed to stagger a little, but then brought the stun rifle to bear and fired.

The Sarge fell backwards into the ship, cracking his head hard off the deck. The hatch closed a moment later as the ship lifted from the ground in an explosion of light and noise.

Aila screamed.

Baines ran back from the cockpit. "Sarge? *Sarge!*"

Dr Flannigan stepped out of their ad hoc intensive care room, closing the door gently behind him. He turned to the group waiting outside, his expression grave.

"Captain Baines, how far were you away from the building when The Sarge got hit?"

"A hundred metres, hundred and change, maybe. Hard to be sure, it was dark. How is he, Dave?"

Flannigan considered. "A hundred metres... hmm. Well, that's probably the only reason he's still with us. Most hand stunners, even our souped-up rifles, don't do too well over distance. There's no doubt that when that weapon was fired, it was dialled up enough to kill a human being."

Natalie crumpled, sobbing. Douglas caught her and handed her to Baines. "Will he come through, Dave?" he asked.

Flannigan felt their eyes boring into him. "I... I don't know," he confessed, wretchedly. "He's strong—"

"No one stronger, boy," Jones interrupted.

Flannigan nodded.

Major Ford White held his head in his hands, finally free of the sling holding his arm. "I should have taken a force and just busted him outta there. *Damnit!*" He slammed his fist against the wall.

"Watch that arm," Flannigan warned. "This ain't a two-for-one sale."

"What can we do?" asked Baines, tremulously. "*I* left him there."

"No, Jill," Douglas countered. "This wasnae your fault."

"If we'd just been a few minutes earlier," Meritus muttered.

"Can I see him?" Natalie asked through her sobs.

Flannigan placed a gentle hand on her arm. "He's resting, honey."

"I only want to sit with him. Please?"

Flannigan looked to Baines, who nodded.

"OK, just for a little while, huh? He's in a coma and needs peace and quiet." Flannigan guided Natalie into The Sarge's room and to a chair.

"What happened to his face?" she asked quietly.

"I can fix that later. He's been in a fight. They weren't pullin' no punches, either. I'd hate to see the other guy. He's covered in contusions and has a knife wound in his..."

Natalie looked at him, sharply questioning.

Flannigan sighed. "In his, er... gluteus maximus."

"Up his *bum?*"

The doctor snorted softly. "Yeah. Well, *in* his butt rather than up it, thankfully. There are no internal injuries. I've given him a shot against tetanus, but that's the least of his worries right now. The high voltage shock is playing all hell with his central nervous system. The next twenty-four hours are gonna be critical."

Natalie took The Sarge's hand, looking up at Flannigan. "You can leave him with me now, Dave."

Flannigan smiled sadly. "Sure. If anything changes..."

Natalie nodded but did not answer.

As Flannigan closed the door behind him, she squeezed the hand, a tear running down her cheek. "You saved me again, you silly lump of a soldier. Now it's my turn, and when you come back to me, we're going talk about you getting a desk job." She leaned in close to him. "Sarge," she whispered, her breath warm and gentle upon his face. "*John.* I love you. Come back to me."

"The mission was a bust," Baines declared, disgustedly. She sat heavily on one of the couches that acted as a waiting area outside the infirmary.

Douglas sat opposite as they were joined by Dr Satnam Patel and Mother Sarah Fellows.

"Your talks with Cocksedge and Schmidt failed?" asked Patel.

Baines shook her head. "They never started. And there's worse."

Patel looked quizzically to Douglas.

"The Sarge has been injured. How badly, we're no' yet sure."

"I thought, with it being the middle of the night," Baines continued, almost to herself, "that most of them would be asleep." She looked up. "We only fly late at night to attract the least possible attention. I thought that if we could just..."

Sarah moved to sit next to her, placing an arm about her shoulders. "What happened, honey?"

Baines took a deep breath, settling her anger. "Captain Meritus and I took the orbital attack ship and went with the intention of speaking with Cocksedge one last time, as you know. My objective was to offer them whatever they wanted, within reason, to get them back into the fold before we leave. Naturally, the ship was a show of force designed to intimidate. I hoped to bring The Sarge home with us, *after* our negotiation. It was never my intention to start a fight."

"Cocksedge and Schmidt were unwilling to discuss terms?" suggested Patel.

"They never got to hear them. We landed, had barely stepped out of the ship, when all hell broke loose."

Patel was confused. "The ship landing caused this chaos?"

Baines gave him a sad smile. "Not the ship, The Sarge. Obviously tired of waiting for us, he decided to declare war on Cocksedge and the Johnstone clan – on his own." She thumped a fist on her knee. "*Damnit!* Why did I leave it so long? I put him in that position. I knew he'd try something as soon as I took Natalie away, but there was no way to tell him to wait."

"That's not your fault, Jill," placated Sarah.

"Try telling that to Natalie and The Sarge!"

"Sarah's right, Jill." Douglas spoke calmly. "Besides, we've no' lost him yet. The Sarge is as tough as old boots. Ma money's on him making it."

Baines smiled sadly. "If I'd known you had money, I'd have whisked you away from all this years ago."

Douglas snorted. "That's ma girl. The question now is, do we try again for Cocksedge and Schmidt or do we just leave them behind?"

"If we leave them, they could do untold damage to the timeline, James," Patel stated with concern. "With their knowledge, they might even create a counter faction to Elizabeth's reign. At the very least, they are bound to sow local discord. It's not like they were moral people to begin with."

Douglas sighed deeply. "You're right, but there are other factors to consider."

"Such as?"

"Such as this whole region is fast becoming an armed cam—*several* armed camps, in fact. And it's largely due to us and all our tempting goodies. We *must* go. And soon."

Woodsey was up early the following morning – for him. He pushed a broom around the animal container in order to put off doing any packing. It all just seemed so *final*.

Certain supplies would be essential if they were to take their animals with them. Concerned about how long it might be before they found suitable food on the other side, he stole a small handcart from the main hangar, so they could carry some with them. After that, he had run out of steam.

He initially hoped to find Natalie here, but quickly found out she was still with The Sarge – had refused to leave his side, all night. Woodsey knew this was the least he could do for her, but it felt wrong somehow. He was sure leaving was a bad idea.

"Hey," Henry called, pulling the container's door open wide. "I brought help."

Woodsey turned to see Tim, Clarrie and Rose bringing up the rear.

"Where do you want us?" asked Rose.

Woodsey smiled wanly. "Henry can pack up the raw meat for these fellas, for a start." He gestured to the small pack of nine Cronopio, snarling and nipping at one another around his ankles, each tussling for attention. "Natalie's been drying it out like jerky, so that it keeps."

Clarrie giggled. "I wish Dad had let us keep those little guys in our apartment."

Woodsey looked up sharply. "Trust me – you don't! It's a good job we're leaving here, otherwise I'd be paying for *their* damage for the rest of my life!"

They got down to it and between them, the teens made short work of the packing and tidying.

Woodsey leaned on his broom, something at which he was fast becoming expert. "You know, I'm gonna miss you guys."

"Eh? What brought that out?" Rose grinned mischievously.

"Won't have many more chances to say it, will I?" he continued. "We'll just step through that wormhole and either be whisked away to our old lives, or to completely new lives, or... or *no* lives."

Tim leaned companionably on his shoulder, nodding seriously. "You know, Woodsey, you really give my bottom a headache."

Across the main hangar, a mechanic returned to the vehicle he had been working on the day before. He opened the inspection hatch and nodded contentedly. Inspiration had chosen three in the morning as a good time to come calling. Then it proceeded to keep his mind active until finally allowing him to fall asleep twenty minutes before his alarm went off – but his inspiration *had* been correct.

He smiled, red-eyed. "I know what's wrong with you, old girl. Now, don't you worry none, Daddy'll soon put it right."

Still smiling, he turned to find all the tools and equipment required to undertake his task.

His smile froze. They were in total disarray and all over the deck, his expensive tool trolley stolen, without so much as a note.

Natalie stayed with The Sarge day and night. Flannigan ordered her to rest, but to little avail. On the third morning after his return, The Sarge stirred.

Natalie ran to the door. "*Dave!* Get in here!"

Flannigan came on the run with Matron Runde in tow.

"Sarge?" he spoke while taking the man's pulse. Flannigan grinned. "Strong. Stronger than in days. This is great, Natalie."

"You must go now," Matron ordered. "Allow Dr Flannigan to do his wor—"

"Like hell I will!" Natalie cut her off. "I'm staying."

Matron frowned, looking to Flannigan for support. He opened his mouth to speak, but upon seeing Natalie's expression, wilted. He shrugged. "I'm sure Natalie won't get in the way, Matron."

Matron glared at him, throwing her hands up in the air. "You people have *no* discipline!"

Flannigan felt like he was under siege in his own hospital. "Ladies, thank you both for your concern. I'll need you to remain quiet, but nearby. I'm gonna try and bring him round – get his vitals up."

He added a mild stimulant to The Sarge's saline drip. "Just give him a few minutes, now. Natalie, please, I need you to give him some room."

Matron pulled her away brusquely.

After a few minutes' anxiety, The Sarge opened his eyes blearily. Raising his arm, he felt the drip. "Wha'?" he croaked. Placing his free hand on his brow, he covered his eyes against the sudden brightness. "Oh, Turkish delight."

Natalie screamed and grabbed Matron, spinning her into a little dance.

Furious, Matron Runde brought the jig to a swift and unceremonious close. "*Most* improper. This is a hospital, girl!" she hissed waspishly, but Natalie could not have cared less if she had tried.

5th December, 1558

Wrapped in makeshift rain cloaks, Hiro, Georgio and Patel watched Bluey's team at work.

When they opened their four-second test wormhole, the drive had been bolted to the deck of their workshop. With the calamity that followed, they had not been able to ascertain what sort of stresses were present in the drive's housing.

Rather than take any chances on their one-shot plan, Hiro had insisted upon laying a heavy concrete pad *in situ*, where they intended to make their escape. Once in place, they would bolt their machinery securely to it.

This had caused a number of problems for the construction crew. Firstly, they had little in the way of hardcore, for a base. So Bluey and his brother had dredged the bottom of a nearby stream for small pebbles and silt.

On a nearby slope, Red spotted rock shale, which Captain Douglas assured them was known locally as 'glidders'. They collected some of this larger aggregate, too, using it to bulk out the material. The small, rounded pebbles and silt from the stream bed bound with the larger material, to provide a primitive 'crush and run' sub-base.

The peaty soil on the side of Cheviot where they worked, held together well, without need of shuttering. Although the vehicular descent was hair-raising, Bluey found a reasonably level plateau roughly halfway down the slope, where the heavy machines were able to simply cut and flatten a bed out of the soil.

Using their massive bulldozer as an anchor, the workers attached a heavy winch and used it to assist the lorries up and down as they delivered material to the new site earmarked for the WHD.

Bluey sat in his cab, cackling at his brother's discomfort. The excavator's single windscreen wiper worked hard to remove sleet from his field of vision. With every stroke, he watched Red's assent in one of their eight-wheel-drive lorries. The slope was slick with water and mud and every time the lorry slipped or jumped, he could just make out Red, swearing as he gripped the wheel. The lorry's ascent would not have been possible without the winch; even with it, he could fully understand how unnerving it must be for the driver, on the steeper slopes.

Still chuckling, he used his spreader bucket to level the last load of material and ran his tracked machine forwards and backwards to compact it, ready for the concrete.

Red's lorry reversed down to the new plateau again about an hour later, this time laden with twenty tons of cement, all palleted and wrapped individually in waterproof bags.

He jumped out of the cab and slipped immediately on his backside.

Bluey burst out laughing anew as his brother scrambled back to his feet, holding on to his vehicle. Had they been somewhere safer, he would have saluted with a string of horn blasts from his machine.

It may have made sense to keep the noise down, but as it turned out, signals were perfectly acceptable – as Red proved with a double-handed gesture that set Bluey rocking once more, within his cosy cab.

The weather was foul, possibly even getting worse. So, with help from a couple of other miserable souls, dragged from the dubious protection of their temporary shelter, Red made short work of unstrapping his load and crane-offloading it as quickly as possible.

He climbed back up into his lorry cab and removed his rain cloak, giving it a shake. Wiping his face, he sent a quick message to his brother – thanking him for all his help and concern – and another to the operator of the winch, high above.

The lorry began its climb once more, almost immediately becoming bogged down. With a kick and a buck, the winch took up the slack and together with what little traction the lorry's computer could find, began to wind the vehicle back up the slope.

The journey was even worse for Red now the lorry was empty. Despite vast amounts of low-range torque, his heavy wheels were prone to skip when powering uphill. When he did manage to find grip, the soil would soon shift under him as the grass or heather uprooted, leaving only the saturated mud beneath. This often caused the vehicle to slip backwards until the steel cables snapped taut once more, with a jarring *bang*.

His problems were not merely down to steepness, either. The ground also undulated left and right as he traversed its natural bumps and concavities. They had selected the best route down, but his several trips had churned the mountainside into muddy ruin. Several times, the lorry almost tipped, requiring some terrifying driving as Red was forced to power *into* the direction he wished to avoid.

A few hundred metres below, Bluey decided it was time for coffee and a sandwich. Just as he finished off with a piece of Mud Hole special fruit pie, his comm binged.

"*Bagger that!*" Red barked across the channel. "*That's the last time I'm going up and down on that winch. The wagon nearly turned over!*"

Bluey could certainly commiserate with his brother's fear. However, *could* did not necessarily mean *would*. "No worries, bro. I'll get one o' the Sheilas to finish it off for ya. Don't sweat it."

"*I'm serious, mate. It's dicing with death.*"

"Fair play, we don't wanna risk losing a rig."

The blast of foul language that followed Bluey's appraisal caused the Australian to grin broadly. "Steady on, bro. You're upsetting the ladies."

Despite his jocular response to his brother's terror, Bluey knew Red was not exaggerating, and that this would soon present them with another problem.

The Pod carried a large supply of cement, originally intended for Mars, and still unused. Together with a few night-time shuttle raids the previous evening – to a beach just north of Dunstanburgh Castle – for sand, they now had enough material to produce a rough concrete.

The construction may not have met the exacting standards of Fritz Todt's war machine, but Bluey knew he could rely on sheer bulk to get the job done. The concrete alone would be massed to more than a metre thick, with a steel reinforcing box-framework at its core, welded to heavy threads that would soon be used to bolt the WHD in place.

Bluey had meticulously set out the long steel threads so that once the concrete was poured, they would exactly line up with the fittings on the drive's base. He had wrapped the tops to keep the threads clean, and taped rods between each, to keep his distances. The whole framework sat on plastic cups to raise it off the ground, and was laid on a plastic membrane to prevent the substrate from leeching water and causing weakness in the base of the slab.

They had done all they could, and under fairly awful conditions, but now they needed to discuss phase two.

Bluey spoke over an open channel. "Well, that's it, boys. We're ready. So has anybody got any ideas about how we get one of our concrete mixers down here?" He knew the mixers carried aboard the Pod were not mobile. Designed for use on Mars, they were meant to be delivered to their place of work and permanently mounted.

"Don't all shout at once!" he taunted.

"*We can bring it along the road as far as the top of the winch by lorry,*" Red hazarded.

"You don't say," his brother replied. "And after *that?*"

"*We airlift it,*" supplied Hiro. "*Forget the lorry.*"

Bluey looked up to where Hiro, Georgio and Patel stood above him, peeking out from their temporary shelter. "In the daytime? I thought we were no-fly?"

"*You'd rather put this together in the dark?*" Hiro retorted.

Bluey shrugged. "We *could* use what we call 'site lights', mate. I understand the concept might be unfamiliar to you *indoor* blokes."

Georgio grinned. "*You're a funny guy.*"

"I think we need to report our position to Captain Douglas," stated Patel. *"There are armies to the north and south of us, I understand. So time might well be against us. It will be his call."*

Bluey shrugged again. "Well, don't let the grass grow, mate. It might only take a few hours to mix and pour, but I'm gonna need a couple o' days for this lot to go off before it's useful."

"In that case, am I to understand that we will miss our 6th of December departure window?" asked Patel.

"So, what...? You're gonna penalty clause me?"

Sir Nicholas Throckmorton struck out with a small but strong contingent for Housesteads Roman Fort – also known as *Vercovicium* from what records could be read in the stone.

Having never been there himself, he employed a local guide from Hexham; a man named Jack Forster, who was provided by Sir John Forster, a recent Sheriff of Northumberland and one of the larger landowners in the Middle Marches.

Sir Nicholas assumed Jack to be one of Sir John's minor relatives. However vital, being a guide was, after all, only a minor role – it was how patronage worked. Despite his low rank, Sir Nicholas had nevertheless provided Jack with a quality mount, so that his group could get in quickly, and more importantly, get *out* quickly, should the need arise. They were well south of the border with Scotland, but still within range for some of the more adventurous raiding parties.

Four further mounts came along to carry baggage and provide spares, should one of their beasts go lame. The best of the horses, discounting his own, was side-saddled, ready to bear the new queen to the safety of her waiting army.

They set off early, to understand the lie of the land. Should they need to run, it made sense to know where. By midday, they were scaling the gentle slope from what passed for the main track, up to the fort itself.

Practically all the nobility came from martial stock, and Sir Nicholas was ever impressed by Roman ingenuity. Well-educated in the classics, he knew the stories, had sometimes even studied them alongside the then-*Lady* Elizabeth.

The fort was built into the south side of the mighty Hadrian's Wall and was a later addition. Of the traditional 'playing card' shape, the walls were breached by four gates – one for each point of the compass.

How different warfare must have been. How glorious! Despite himself, he approached the south gate like a wide-eyed child, pondering the differences between Roman tactics and their own. The medieval castle, still so prevalent within the British landscape in 1558, was built with as few weak points as possible, to protect those within – who were also often few in number.

The Roman model was utterly at odds with this philosophy. They packed their troops in, using the walls only as temporary protection to avoid being surprised. When the enemy was sighted, all the gates would be flung wide to allow their legionaries and cavalry to rush out and amass in their fighting formations as quickly as possible.

Sir Nicholas took a deep breath, imagining the now-crumbling gateways alive with horse and men, all running, all armed to the teeth and screaming murder.

The fort's walls were still high and strong, Hadrian's Wall itself, at least twelve feet in places, and eight feet wide[30]. Inside the fort, Nature reigned supreme, her flora toppling walls and choking roads, yet Sir Nicholas was still awed by what he saw.

Just outside the gateway, to the south, were the remains of a vicus. Such small settlements often sprung up outside the permanent forts to exploit their trade. Some of the buildings were in stone, the remnant walls of one of them clearly having been used recently to corral animals. From the dung, almost certainly sheep.

"We'll hold the horses here," Sir Nicholas called. "Good job, Jack. Get us back as timely in the dark, and there'll be a gold angel in it for you."

---

30   The early stages of the wall were ten feet wide which was soon reduced to eight, presumably for logistical reasons. Although more than 1000 years of erosion had taken place by Sir Nicholas' time, Bede described the wall as twelve feet high in the early 8th century. Bede was extremely knowledgeable but not well travelled, so it is possible some sections of the wall may still have soared to their original theoretical height of fifteen feet – with a parapet on top. Much of the stone 'robbing' to build houses, walls, and especially roads in the 17th and 18th centuries, had yet to take place. Had Douglas been less focused on getting his people home safely, he might have thought to take photographs.

"I am glad your friend doth live."

"You heard about that? Thanks, Bess. The Sarge is very important to us," Baines replied with a nod. "Are you almost ready to leave us?"

Bess straightened and stepped before the older woman. "I am, Jill. And thank you for everything. Especially for saving my life."

Baines smiled. "Commander Gleeson was most directly responsible for that, as I heard it."

Bess returned her smile. "Yes, I have thanked him, and apologised for... what is the phrase? Winding him?"

Baines laughed. "Winding him *up,* yes." She gave Bess a hug, who responded stiffly, still unused to such familiar behaviour.

They made their way down to the main hangar, where the large vehicles had been cleared to the sides, leaving room for the entire crew to assemble.

Including Meritus' staff, almost two hundred people stood ready to give Elizabeth R a send-off worthy of a new queen.

As she stepped into the shuttle, she turned. "I thank you all and wish you well on your journey home."

A roar of applause and approval rang off the bulkheads as the last Tudor queen disappeared inside.

"Catch ya later, kids." Baines tossed them a casual salute, before she too disappeared, closing the hatch behind her.

Lieutenant Singh already waited aboard. As soon as his passengers were strapped in, he powered up the shuttle, lifting slowly from the deck as the crowd dispersed. He crept forward towards the main hatch.

"I found this bit a little nerve-wracking when I took her out," Baines confessed.

Singh merely flashed his perfect grin and steered the little ship as if she were on rails.

Once outside, they had a task to complete before setting off for Housesteads. Douglas was keen to keep all flight to the absolute minimum, so Singh had suggested dropping off the concrete mixer at the same time as they transported Bess south.

He hovered over the plateau while the people below attached cables to the three-ton mixer. Once the connections were made, a traffic controller waved a green light for Singh to proceed to the construction site.

"You know it's going to take a lot of shovelling to keep this mixer going," Singh commented as he flew. "I spoke to Bluey about it earlier today. They'll have to mix and lay fourteen cubic metres of concrete – that's about thirty-five tons – and preferably before the first lot goes off, tamping each level as they go. It's going to be tough work."

"Is that what Bluey told you?" asked Baines.

"Yes, well... *ish*. I had to fill in some of the blanks."

"What did he *actually* say?"

"He said, 'Yep. It's a ball-ache, mate'."

Singh set the mixer down gently in the designated area and waited for the cables to be released.

"This place is lit up like a stadium," Baines could not help noting. "I hope there's no one watching."

"Whit tha hell are they playing at?" Sir Walter spoke his thoughts aloud. Through the telescope he could see yet another vast flying machine, carrying a yellow silo under its belly. Every sinew in his body wanted to attack and take whatever they could steal, but he knew there was far more at stake here than a good night's reiving.

His informants had brought the news that none of the new people now remained at Hermitage Castle. He had also listened, with some merriment, to a tale about the debacle at the Johnstones' camp. The only conclusion he could draw was that the new people were leaving. Where or how they were going, he had no idea; all that mattered was getting his hands on their stuff – stuff they were bound to take with them.

He spat with frustration. Timing would be everything. He needed more information, and if that were not enough of a headache, his scouts had also seen the Johnstone clan packing up to move out. As he spied on his quarry, he realised that the only thing about which he had *no* doubts, was that the Johnstones would also be heading *exactly* here.

Sir Nicholas had warned his men about the flying machine. Some of them thought him mad, others thought him a liar, some both. None of them believed him. Nevertheless, he continued to split his small force.

The half left with the horses, he commanded to remain in a high state of readiness, hoping to keep the terrible noise of the machine as far from the animals as possible. He walked the rest around to the western gate, putting a lot of brush and stone between them as a shield.

Knowing Captain Baines, she would have some magic fox trick that would find them, even in the dark, but he wished to take no chances. His queen was coming home. So, Sir Nicholas bade them stand in a large circle about fifty paces across, each holding aloft a burning torch.

Now we wait.

They did not have to wait long. The roar of the shuttle's engines could be heard from miles away.

"A storm approacheth, my lord," said Jack.

"Forsooth, that is one description," he acknowledged.

As the ship drew closer, his men became more and more skittish.

"Calm yourselves!" commanded Sir Nicholas. "I told you all about this. There be no danger to any if you but stand."

The men looked from one to another, just waiting for the first to bolt so they could all follow.

"I said *stand!* Damn your eyes!"

The shuttle came into view, first as a flame in the sky; dark, silica ceramic re-entry tiles on its underbelly reflecting virtually no light.

Within seconds it was overhead – huge and deafening. The men in the circle screamed, crossing themselves against this demonic display.

"*Steady...*" Sir Nicholas countered their fear with orders and threats. "*Hold!* Or it'll be the worse for you, lubberworts!"

Singh landed the shuttle as gently as possible, but there was simply no way of disguising rocket noise.

Once the ship was down, Sir Nicholas could hear the terrified whinnying of their horses. He could only hope the walls and the men left in charge could keep them contained, or they would have a very long walk home ahead of them.

Once the ship was down, the silence that followed seemed unnatural by comparison. Sir Nicholas could hear some of his men praying, some were even sobbing.

"Shape yourselves and stand to attention, you dogs! Here cometh thine own queen!"

The shuttle's hatch hissed open, eliciting further whimpering from the waiting men.

"Call yourselves Englishmen?" Sir Nicholas hissed, furiously. "Stand to, I say!"

His men made a pathetic attempt to form a rank, but their torches were held at all angles, some visibly shaking.

Sir Nicholas rolled his eyes disgustedly, and then he saw her, took three long steps forward and dropped to one knee, head bowed. "Your Majesty, my queen."

"Not *just* yours, I hope, Nick. Please, rise."

He stood, and grinning like a schoolboy reached for her hands, kissing them. "Thank God you're safe, Highness." He turned to Baines, taking her hand too. "Thank you, Captain."

"Sir Nicholas," she greeted in return. "You have a lot of work to do, and Nick, you also have a great trust here... you understand me?"

He swallowed and nodded, formally. "By life or death, I am hers. Have no fear, lady."

"You see, I am well cared for." Bess smiled wanly. "Now I must away to begin anew. Do you have any last counsel for us, Jill?"

Baines appeared thoughtful. After a moment her expression cleared. "As a matter of fact, I do. Say *no* to tobacco!" She smiled. "Goodbye to you both and good luck."

The dawn of a new day, and it was dreadful. The skies opened before first light as though God simply left the tap running and went out to the shops. The entire top of Cheviot and the hills surrounding it were a mire – everywhere but the brilliantly drained roads, built by the Australian brothers and the rest of Samantha Portree's construction crew.

Douglas greeted Bluey as he entered the Pod's main hangar, returning from site. "Sorry it's so wet out there for yer people."

"Oh, it's not just wet, Captain."

"No?"

"Nah. It's bladdy freezing, too!" He sneezed hugely. "Sorry about that," he added, wiping Douglas' shoulder.

"Dinnae worry yourself, laddie. Ah didnae come here just to commiserate. Ah brought ye this and this, too." He handed the Australian a steaming mug and a towel.

Bluey took them, frowning. "*Tea?*"

"Aye," Douglas winked, "with a wee kick to it, to keep out the cold."

Bluey grinned broadly. "Good on ya, sport!"

"How goes the labour?"

Bluey blew on the hot beverage before taking a sip. "Mmm, some of the good stuff, eh? Nice. Yeah, it's progressing, Captain. It was the right call to carry on mixing through the night. This weather..." He wiped the water from his face. "We got it all in and it's already going off. But it's so bladdy cold out there... would have been nice to stand around it, to warm ourselves – that much concrete gives off a hell of a lotta heat. The exothermic reaction, see? It's called the 'heat of hydration'. It'll burn ya skin."

"So it's a bit more pleasant out on site, then?"

Bluey shook his head. "No such luck, mate. We had to cover it up, didn't we? Otherwise, the top would be ruined by laitance, with this storm. Don't want it to break up while we're making wormholes, do we, eh?"

"Good point. How's the other half of the operation going?"

"The cable?" Bluey began to laugh. "It's getting there."

Douglas smiled quizzically. "What's funny?"

Whatever it was, Bluey was laughing hard enough to spill some of his drink. "Jim Miller... Hahaha... What a day to pick to work outside for the first time!"

Douglas tried to cover his smirk, but the image of poor Jim Miller, away from his desk and plunged into the wilderness to drag cables through a freezing monsoon, proved too much and he burst out laughing, too. It had been a long time since he had laughed like that, and when the tears came they were not all of mirth.

To Sir Nicholas' horror and consternation, Queen Elizabeth I did not head for London to secure her throne, but instead set off north at first light. Riding at the head of her army with her stewing and furious childhood friend, she explained that the destiny of not only the realm, not only the world, but the very future of humanity itself rested upon her wresting control of the *New World*. Should one of the Reiver families take it, without benefit of the teachings bestowed by the *New World*'s crew, she shuddered to think what might happen.

Sir Nicholas had done his best. He had tried to dissuade her from this most dangerous course, but she had only replied, "We do not take this responsibility unto ourselves lightly, Nick. I made a solemn promise and now have a duty."

She would hear no more argument, so northwards they were bound, to meet up with Sir Nicholas' advance force at Otterburn.

Under the killing heat of an equatorial sun, Devon knew they were in trouble. A giant crocodile and an impassable river to their rear, with carnivorous dinosaurs forward and sideways.

Revving his small petrol engine violently, he confessed, "I thought this might spook the animals."

"I think it has," agreed Aito, "but what it hasn't done is frightened them away. Turning them from cold killers into angry killers might be one way to describe what you're doing."

"You got any better ideas?" Devon shouted, terrified.

"Well, I never go anywhere without these," replied Jansen, holding out a couple of grenades. "We could ride at the main pride and throw these ahead to clear the way. Trouble is..."

"Yeah?" asked Devon tremulously.

"The throttle is on the right-hand side, so we'll have to either *throw* left-handed – and I gotta say, I'm not thrilled about that – or we *stop* and throw them... with all those monsters chasing after us."

"They're getting a lot more agitated and a lot more *close*," shouted Aito.

"That's just bad grammar."

"Shut up!"

"OK," Jansen tried again. "Lieutenant, are you left-handed?"

Devon shook his head.

He turned to Aito – who scowled. "You're hilarious!"

"Right. Sorry. OK, left-handed it is then." Jansen passed one of the grenades to Devon. "I suggest we pull the pins now, unless you want to stop."

"Now's good." Devon pulled the pin, squeezing tightly on the lever. "Let's go!"

As the bikes roared away, rear wheels throwing sand and stones into the air, the pack of Rugops replied in kind.

Aito drew level with Devon, just as the lieutenant slowed and did his best with a left-handed bowl. "Is this how our story ends?" he cried as they waited for the explosion and hopefully a way through the pack.

"I dunno – keep reading!" Devon bellowed.

"OK. Today's the day, people," Douglas addressed his fellow triumvirates and department heads. "And Ah have to confess to a certain déjà vu as Ah see all of your faces here before me once more. Although, Ah'm honoured to welcome Captain Tobias Meritus into the fold this time – without whose efforts and the efforts of his people, we may not have survived. Ah can only imagine the courage it took to stand against a master like Heinrich Schultz. We're indebted to ye, Captain."

Meritus accepted compliments from around the table with no small embarrassment.

"Also," continued Douglas, "it's such a pleasure to have Dr Patricia Norris back among us – brave, brilliant and beautiful! Welcome back, Patricia."

"Thank you, Captain." Patricia acknowledged his words and the general good wishes of her colleagues with blushing smiles. "I asked Dr Klaus Fischer to accompany me, as he's really been running things for the last few months."

"Klaus," Douglas greeted. "We've sat around this very table so many times – all that remains of ma original meeting room – to discuss such things as the forming of governments, defence against Nazi

invasions, protecting ourselves against giant, flesh-eating dinosaurs..."
He tailed off with a smile and a shake of his head. "What a ride! And
now we're here to discuss our final journey, ma dear friends – our
trip home."

With a spontaneity that lifted Douglas' spirits, the room exploded
into applause and whoops of exuberance.

"Aye," he acknowledged, grinning in spite of himself. "We survived
it all, but now we face a new challenge, and it's nae small one, either."

The gathering sobered.

"Ah'm going to hand you over to Chief Hiro Nassaki in a moment,
to explain what comes next, as he and Georgio have been the main
movers behind our escape plan. Ah think that deserves a wee bit of
applause." He took a step back, allowing Hiro the limelight.

"Furthermore – and Ah hope ye'll pass this down the line to yer
people – Ah'd just like to congratulate each and every one of you for
your courage and hard work. We survived it all, ladies and gentlemen –
well done!" Douglas clapped again and everyone followed. "Now
Ah'll hand ye over to the chief. Hiro..."

Nassaki stood at the head of the table, sombre amid the adoration
and congratulation. He waited for everyone to quiet before he began.

"2000 hours, 31st July AD2112. That's when our collective story
really began. It may also seem the obvious time for us to return.
However, when the *New World* vanished, it set a whole chain of
events in motion. Returning before that date might draw us into a
paradox to confuse even Dr Patel's mathematical prowess, so we must
go forward.

"We suggest 0400 hours, 1st August 2113. We have several reasons
for suggesting this date. Firstly, it allows a whole year for the dust to
settle and allows Captain Meritus' people to escape the clutches of
the enemy – we simply have no idea what would happen if we met
ourselves on an alternative timeline, so we're avoiding the possibility –
we hope. Secondly, we expect to reappear in the Cheviot Nature
Reserve, an area of slightly less light pollution. Four a.m. should
give Sandy the chance to fix our date by viewing the last of the stars,
if the sky is clear enough, yet without leaving us in the dark for too
long before sunup. Thirdly, we've selected August as we'll have very
little equipment with us – aside from a few handcarts, pretty much
only what we can carry, in fact. Anyone who's been outside during

the last few days will see the sense in setting our destination for high summer.

"Now we move on to the journey itself. We'll be stepping through a wormhole, unprotected by any ship or vehicle. Theoretically, this seems viable, but we have never tried it before. Our test suggested no ill effects, but I have to warn you that we sent only inanimate objects."

"We should have tried the mouse," Singh muttered.

Hiro continued, unwilling to be distracted from the talk he had prepared. "We will have enough power to hold a man-sized wormhole open for three minutes."

Consternation and grumbling ensued.

"Alright, people, please," Douglas calmed the group. "Is that all we can manage, Hiro?"

Hiro shrugged helplessly. "If we're lucky, maybe three with a little on top, but no more, Captain. Thanks to Dr Donald Parrot's inspired equations – inspired, in fact, by a chat with his dead girlfriend – we've been able to program the Pod's power core to—"

"Come again?" prompted Baines.

Hiro gazed levelly at her. "Dr Jamie Ferguson. She was murdered by Heidi Schultz just before we landed on prehistoric Earth—"

"I know who she was, Hiro. What I'm lacking is context or explanation!"

Patel leaned forward uncomfortably. "If I may, Hiro. Dr Parrot had a visit from his beloved – or so he explained it to me. Something about there being much more psychic energy in this time. Anyhow, whatever the reason for his *inspiration,* his mathematics proved perfectly."

Baines shrugged, relenting. "Ah, what the hell. After what I've experienced here, I'm willing to go on a little faith. I'm sorry, Hiro, continue."

"Yes, well, I too had reservations, Captain. However, Georgio explained that this was only because I lack imagination." Singh snorted, but Hiro ignored him. "Besides, as Satnam has said, the numbers are good. Dr Parrot's equations will enable us to connect the Pod's power core to the circuit and use it to open the wormhole. This will save the *New World*'s reactor for the heavy lifting of *keeping* it open. You see, Donald's calculations have enabled us to program the Pod's power core to sense the wormhole's usage and disengage before damage occurs. This will leave the Pod's reactor intact to keep the Pod *alive,* as it were, after we're gone.

"In all likelihood, however, this operation will cause irreparable damage to Sekai's core. Once the power runs out, the *New World* will, in effect... die."

Sharing a glance with Douglas, Hiro's was one of abject misery and loss.

"You see," he continued after a sip of water, "the wormhole drive we have, was stolen from an enemy vessel. It's little short of a miracle we got it to work at all with our tech. It even has parts missing. Everything we've achieved has been by trial and error. Now, couple this with the fact that the *New World* is heavily damaged and already low on power..." He shrugged again.

"Look, if we had our ship intact, with our own wormhole drive, we might feasibly be able to hold a wormhole open for up to an hour – but, of course, were that the case we would simply fly home! As it is, we don't even have our principal wormhole expert any more." He glanced at Georgio. "Mario knew more about the phenomena than any of us, even Dr Patel.

"What I'm saying, Captain, *everyone,* is this is what we have, and nothing more. So, I ask you, ladies and gentlemen, do we stay, or do we leave?"

No uproar this time, just a heavy silence.

"Can we move nearly two hundred people in three minutes?" Douglas broke the reverie.

"One through every second," Major Ford White spoke his thoughts aloud. "It's possible, Captain, but we're gonna have to be really on it."

"We've done all we can to help the people of *this* time, Captain," Mother Sarah spoke smoothly. "We've no right to make it *our* time."

Douglas nodded, taking a last look around the faces gathered before him. "It's decided then."

It was raining again. A cruel, near-horizontal sleet that bit into any skin it touched. Almost the full complement of the *New World, Factory*

Pod 4 and the remnant crew of the *Last Word* stood miserable and shivering on the side of Mount Cheviot.

Captain Douglas stood four hundred metres above them, on their new road. With him, Geoff Lloyd leaned against one of Meritus' armoured personnel carriers.

"So this is it, Geoff. There's still time to change yer mind."

"No, Captain. The *New World* needs a sentinel to take care of her and protect her from prying eyes. I caused this mess. I have to believe some good can come of it."

Douglas took a deep breath. "If ye can help Elizabeth change the course of events to save our future, Ah think..." He tailed off, chuckling softly.

Lloyd viewed him quizzically.

"Aye, Ah think history will look kindly on ye."

Lloyd chuckled too. "I stole something from stores for this occasion." He took a small hip flask from his pocket. "Here's mud in your eye, James." He took a nip and handed it to Douglas.

Douglas smiled sadly and raised the flask. "To good times." He drank. "Hmm, some of Maxwell's finest, eh?"

"Well, if I'm to make friends here, James, I may as well pick someone who can also make a good malt." Lloyd held out his hand.

Douglas took it. "Good luck, Geoff."

Lloyd shook his hand firmly. "I think you'd better save the luck for yourselves. You're all crazy!"

Douglas smiled warmly. "You'll earn your forgiveness, Geoff. Goodbye."

"Goodbye, James."

Douglas handed back the flask, and without looking back, slithered his way down the slope to join his people.

Lloyd watched him go. He was about to leave when his comm began beeping insistently. Synced with the APC, the small display showed movement all around him. He jumped back inside the machine, locking the hatch. On the heads-up display, he could see four separate large bodies approaching his location. From the readings, the groups consisted of men and horses. *No surprise,* he thought. *So, they're here already, and the new queen sent away south. Fantastic. Good to see Douglas' plan is working as well as they always do – even in his absence. You'd better get out of here fast, James.*

He started the engine, spun the machine around and headed swiftly back to *Factory Pod 4*'s main hangar.

A sudden, almost debilitating sense of loneliness descended on Lloyd. He felt smothered by it. He also felt the need to speak, just to prove that he was still alive. "I'd better head back home and prepare a welcome for our guests!" With that, he began to laugh and continued laughing, almost maniacally. Tears streamed down his face as the tracked vehicle bounced and lumbered along the rough road. "Welcome to Geoff World!"

Douglas slipped down the last small slope to the plateau where the wormhole drive sat in the rain. Picking himself up, he grinned as Baines approached. "Let's hope that's the last time Ah end up on ma backside this trip, eh?"

She smiled warmly and threaded her arm through his. "Time to go, Captain. How was he?"

"Good, Ah think. He willnae let us down."

"You sure about that?"

"Aye, Jill. Ah have faith."

They walked into the group where, with a surreptitious hand squeeze, they separated to take their places in the queue – Baines at the front, Douglas near the back. The plateau was not big enough to allow a queue two hundred people long, so the whole group had been carefully choreographed into a spiral around the machine that would hopefully take them home.

"Who sorted all this out?" asked Douglas.

"This was all Ford's idea," Baines replied over her shoulder.

Douglas' eyebrows rose appreciatively. He singled the major out. "Hey, Ford. Ah'm loving yer work. Have ye no' considered domino toppling?"

White grinned. "You volunteering to fall over first, Captain?"

"He's already started!" Baines quipped and White laughed.

Despite the incredible danger and the insanity of what they were about to try, there was a real feeling of hope among the group. It nourished them all – they were going home.

"Good luck, Captain," called Tim Norris.

"And to you, Tim. God speed to us all, ladies and gentlemen!" He caught Hiro's eye.

"We're ready, Captain," he replied.

"Do you all remember how we got here?" Douglas called out for everyone to hear above the wind and the rain. "Let's go home the same way. TEN! NINE! EIGHT..."

The whole group joined in the countdown and at the call of one, the drive hummed into life and a small wormhole appeared in their midst.

Douglas had insisted that Baines be among the first to go. He had sold it to her on the basis that he needed someone to take charge immediately on the other side, to clear the wormhole. In truth, Corporal Jones would have been more than capable in the role, but Douglas wanted to make sure she made it through, should they run out of time. He also did not want her trying anything heroic should there be complications this end. He wanted her safe and home, but he also believed her to be the better leader. She would do whatever was necessary to make sure their people were looked after in 2113, whether that fell within the rules or not.

Unfortunately, his argument had backfired when Baines refused to be *among* the first.

He watched her disappear through the wormhole alone. Heart in his mouth, he prayed she was home and whole.

Her signal came back through the wormhole. She was alive. He raised his eyes in thanks.

Now they had not a second to lose, and Major White barked further encouragement, countering the growing fear that was inevitable now the time was upon them. "Move, move, *move!*" he shouted. All humour passed, he was suddenly the officer in charge of an evacuation. "Keep moving, everyone – you know what to do. Come on, let's *go!*"

For Douglas, his parade-ground bellowing seemed to fade as he watched the spiral queue continuously unspool around him. The grey light and jerky, fearful movements of his people as they took a leap of faith, gave the whole pandemonium the feel of a silent movie.

He saw Hank Burnstein jump through with his wife, Chelsea. Tim Norris and Clarrie Burnstein, followed by Patricia. It was like watching their whole nightmare unwinding back to start.

He looked around for young Henry Burnstein and saw him standing with Rose and Jim Miller, as Jim tended the WHD. He could not see Lara Miller. Perhaps she was already through? Just like Miller to put her first. He was most likely furious that Rose was standing so resolutely by his side, refusing to leave him, but there was nothing anyone could do about it now. They all had their positions and must keep moving.

Hiro and Georgio had taken their places in the queue, now it was clear their plan was working. Douglas had to hand it to White, the whole process was going like clockwork. He checked his watch – coming up on one minute thirty, but that was alright, because at least half of the people were already through. He watched Dave Flannigan limp into the event horizon. *This freezing sleet must be giving him hell with that duff knee,* he thought abstractly.

Douglas, by his own insistence, was among the last in the queue. Baines had railed at him, of course, but her arguments had no more effect on him than his had on her. They were who they were, and neither could change nor avoid it. Besides, he had led them into this mess; he must see them get out of it.

There were no more than thirty evacuees left now. They were going to make it. He could hear Miller shouting for his daughter and her boyfriend to go, but still to no avail.

Douglas stood next to the wormhole, opposite White, as they helped people through. There was not the time to help them find their courage, they just had to keep everyone moving, throwing them into the event horizon when all else failed. "Soon be our turn, James," White called over the driving wind.

It looked like a vast serpent, but while the adders of these hills were never more than a couple of feet in length, this was a giant beyond imagining – and it *buzzed.* Whatever witchcraft had summoned such a creature into being had also imbued it with heat and power. The sleet sizzled to steam upon touching its skin.

Sir John Johnstone was at a loss to describe it. Made from iron, or some metal he did not recognise, it led from a large cave all the way down the side of the mountain.

He called for his men to stop and dismounted, handing the reins to another rider while he unhitched his 'lang spear' from the horse's flank.

Nervously, he walked closer to the monstrous snake – at least a foot in girth. Tensing, he hefted the spear and stabbed hard into its side.

The tip of the weapon exploded, throwing him backwards to land in the soaking heather. Rather than the raucous laughter such an occurrence would normally draw from a large force of fighting men, there was instead only fearful murmuring and prayer. These men were no strangers to riding out to war or to burn, but this was sheer devilry.

Sir John picked himself up, throwing the useless staff away. "Bring torches!"

Stepping into the cave, half a dozen men at his back, Sir John waited for the torches to be lit out of the rain. Once the flames came to life, he took one and walked cautiously into the darkness.

The crew of the *New World* disappeared one by one into nothingness, but they did not go unnoticed. "Should we no' be preventin' them from leavin'?"

"No. With them gone, this world will be mine. There will be no one to stop me."

"Stop *you?*"

The shade of Robin Redcap smiled. "*Us.* But perhaps you're right, William. It would be of little consequence to our plans should a few of them get left behind, but it would be an agonising torment for Jill Baines." He chuckled nastily. "Why don't we go and take a look at their machine?"

Deep into the tunnel, Sir John stooped to inspect the markings on the floor. *Probably left by those monsters tha new people train tae dae their will,* he postulated privately.

The wind howled across the cave mouth behind and above them, but underground, all was still. So when a sudden blast blew his cape up over his head, it took Sir John by surprise. He stood quickly, indignant, as he looked around, trying to understand what had happened. *This is dark magic.* Shaking his head, he held his torch aloft once more and continued down.

Presently they came to a metal wall. Painted white, it was scratched, dented and scorched in places. In the centre of the wall was an open hatch. The metal snake – which he now knew was no living thing – continued onwards through the doorway.

He checked on his men, firstly to make sure they were still with him and secondly to bolster his confidence. He swallowed nervously and stepped through into the darkness.

His torchlight flickered, reflecting from metal surfaces and what he assumed were pipes. He had only ever seen lead pipes, and only then as a function of drainage on fine houses. These did not look anything like those. The floor beneath his feet rang as his boots struck them.

A little further on, he stepped out onto some type of gantry. The walkway was made of metal and led left and right. Of more immediate concern was the fact that he could see through the mesh floor. The iron serpent split at this point, dividing into dozens of smaller snakes, or threads as he was now beginning to think of them. Before him was nothing... void.

Sir John waved his torch as far out as he dared. Was there something out there? He could not quite tell.

From behind a *click* sounded, loud in the silent darkness – then there *was* no darkness.

His men cried out in panic and fear; perhaps he did too, he could not tell. Sir John no longer had full control of his actions, so terrified was he by what he saw.

The void was lit as if by lightning, but a constant lightning that neither wavered nor dissipated. It immediately became clear that the void was not a void, either. Some type of huge mechanism took up the space of several storeys.

Sir John held onto the rails of the gantry to relieve the feeling of falling. His head swam. He was terrified. With a powerful effort of will, he checked on his men. With dismay he saw one of them raise an axe.

The wormhole shimmered; something was wrong. White's suspicions were validated when he heard Jim Miller shouting and cursing, quite uncharacteristically coarsely.

"Oh, crap," White muttered under the howl of the wind.

Mother Sarah and Satnam Patel were next to embark. Sarah looked to White for guidance. Douglas had turned to see what was going on.

White grabbed him from behind. "Good luck, James, and God speed!" He launched Douglas through the now-fritzing wormhole to vanish with it.

The dull wash of otherworldliness was gone, possibly forever. Major Ford White, Mother Sarah Fellows, Dr Satnam Patel, Dr Jim Miller, Rose Miller, Henry Burnstein and twenty-three others were suddenly alone on the side of a hill in a raging storm.

He expected it to feel like being stretched, but in truth, there had been no sensation at all. He now felt a split-second tingling beneath his skin, followed by a collision; he was rolling downhill, surrounded by the smell and scratch of heather as he turned over and over.

When he came to a stop, the cold was gone. The icy wind was gone. On his back, he stared up into a cloudless night sky, seeing nothing but stars. The moment passed quickly, the stars replaced by flashing lights, dazzling him.

"James!"

He knew that voice. "James, where are the others?"

"Jill?"

"Help me get him up – somebody!"

Helping hands moved Douglas into a sitting position. "Ah made it?"

"Yes, thank God," Baines panted, holding him up. "But where are the others? There must be twenty or thirty people still on the other side. The wormhole just seemed to... to... What *did* it do?" she asked around for help.

"It looked like an interruption in the power, Captain," Georgio supplied. "Captain Douglas was very lucky to have made it through at all."

"No!" Douglas roared, throwing off the helping hands and getting to his feet. "We were *so close.* So close..."

Baines slumped to her knees. "We left them."

"No, Captains," Georgio insisted. "Whatever happened, it was nothing to do with us, nor do I believe they're in any danger. The collapse of the wormhole was almost instantaneous. Fortunately, it hung around just long enough to spit out Captain Douglas, but I doubt any of the others even got near it. There wasn't time."

"So they're stuck there," Baines intoned soullessly. "In 1558, just a handful of them, alone."

"They're not alone, Captain," said Hiro, joining them. "They have Sekai."

"They have Geoff, too," Douglas stated, automatically.

Burnstein shouldered his way to the front of the group. "Geoff? *Lloyd?*"

Douglas sighed, holding his head in his hands. "Aye. He asked me to allow him to stay behind to stand sentinel to the ship. He offered to teach Bess and her followers. It was his way of putting things right. He knew there was nothing he could do here. Ah agreed with his choice – respected it."

"Geoff *Lloyd!*" Burnstein bellowed this time. "Goddamnit, Douglas. My *son* is back there! And now you're telling me he's stuck with the guy who did this to us?"

Baines opened her mouth to flame at him but sagged as the enormity of all their loss struck her. "Oh, God..."

Douglas placed a hand on Burnstein's shoulder. "Let us get a fix on this, Hank, please. Ah understand, but we need to get our bearings."

He turned away and for the first time took a moment to look around. The starlight was *so* bright. Like it had been when they stepped out into that crisp October evening in 1558.

The moon was still large but waning, the Full Buck Moon having occurred three days earlier[31]. Behind him was the solid, reassuring bulk of Great Cheviot. They were essentially in the middle of nowhere, as intended. For the people who came through the wormhole, it seemed all had gone to plan, and yet... and yet.

Douglas groaned. "Sandy. Where's Sandy? Lieutenant Singh?"

---

31 The July full moon phase is known as a 'Buck Moon' – expected to wax fully at 1844 hours GMT, 28th July, AD2113.

"Here, sir."

Douglas grabbed his pilot's arms anxiously. "Sandy, tell me, *when* are we?"

Singh nodded and slipped the pack from around his shoulders. After a quick rummage he pulled out a tablet, activating it. He stepped away from the group, angling the device up at the stars to scan the local clusters.

"I wrote a program to calculate our location, and the date, from the positions of the stars..." He suddenly realised everyone was staring at him, desperate for answers. "Well, that was a while ago," he finished lamely.

It took the powerful little machine just moments to correlate the celestial magnificence overhead with what was expected for the 1st August, AD2113.

Singh cleared his throat. "OK. From the data, I can tell you all that it is four a.m., give or take a few minutes, on the morning of the first of August, Anno Domini two thousand, one hundred and thirteen."

The silence that followed his words was absolute. Even the mild breeze completely cessated on cue.

A cheer erupted almost simultaneously from many of the group, but by no means all.

"Wait! *Wait,* people," Douglas held up his hands in the moonlight for calm. "Where are the lights – the city lights? Where are the *cities?* The sirens, the noise, the smog? We should be surrounded on all sides by cityscape, but there's nothing!"

The fear rang through his words and the sudden silence like a death knell.

"Where are all the *people?*" he asked, more rationally. He spun round again, desperate to have missed something, *anything,* but a landscape of rolling hills under moon and starlight was all there was; black giving way to blue in the east as night gave birth to a new day.

"I can't answer that, Captain," replied Singh into the silence that followed. "We appear to be utterly alone."

"Oh, Sandy," Baines muttered, despairingly.

The historian, Thomas Beckett, approached Douglas. He spoke quietly, "What do we do, Captain?"

Singh pulled out his comm, searching for a digital link up.

Douglas noticed and waited.

Singh shook his head. "No signal, at least none that *this* device can find." He took a deep breath, expanding his chest fully. The air was sweet, far sweeter than at home. A thought struck him, and he brightened. "We may be alone in this world, but there is *something* I can tell you, Captain."

Douglas looked up hopefully – he would take *anything* right now. "Go on."

"This time I'm sure, it *is* a Tuesday."

Douglas gaped.

Beckett removed his rain hat and proceeded to batter Singh about the head with it.

Author's Notes:

To everyone working in the field of natural history, dinosaur research, historical research and archaeology, I once again send a massive thank you for your constant inspiration. As always, a few liberties have been taken...

Once again, I have included several dinosaurs within this book (shocker, I know), many of which I discussed briefly in previous notes. Like *Carcharodontosaurus saharicus* and the famous *Spinosaurus aegyptiacus,* some of them were also discovered by Ernst Stromer during his time in Egypt. I mentioned one of them in the notes at the back of the last book, another large theropod predator named *Bahariasaurus ingens*. The Allied bombing of the Old Academy, Munich, during spring 1944, destroyed Stromer's finds, along with the type specimen for *Bahariasaurus*. It is still unclear exactly which theropod family this animal belonged to. However, we can estimate that it grew to perhaps 12m in length and would have been a much lighter animal than *Carcharodontosaurus saharicus*, perhaps half the weight by similar length, and this fuels the imagination. How fast was it? How did it hunt? While we wait for the science to catch up on these questions, I'll look forward to writing more about *Bahariasaurus ingens* in the next book, CURSED.

The pack of *Rugops primus,* about to spring their trap on Devon, Aito and Jansen, were also mentioned in my notes for REROUTE, however, I'm not sure *Sarcosuchus imperator* got the paper and ink it deserved. Of the same family as the giant crocodile featured in some of the earlier books, *Sarcosuchus imperator* was one of the largest crocodiles known to science. With each jaw measuring at least 2m, it really did have a maw a grown man could walk into – if he'd really had enough!

Deltadromeus agilis was (possibly) yet another huge and terrifying theropod carnivore from North Africa. I add the 'possibly' only because some palaeontologists think the remains of this animal may actually have been a smaller *Bahariasaurus*. It seems entirely likely and believable that animals sharing a time and place might show similarities, even share ancestry, but as diggers are yet to find a head for either, the argument remains unresolved. For myself, *Deltadromeus agilis* was an irresistible force – an animal possibly the size of *Allosaurus*, but built more like a raptor – *come on!*

However, my personal exuberance aside, the hapless *Ouranosaurus nigeriensis* that crossed paths with *Deltadromeus* in the story, were understandably less enthusiastic. *Ouranosaurus nigeriensis* was a hadrosauriform, related to both the famous *Iguanodon bernissartensis* and the duck-billed dinosaurs. Despite being herbivorous, the row of neural spines along much of the ouranosaurs' backs and tails created 'sails' similar in appearance to those of several of the predatory spinosaur family.

Just a couple of editorial notes as I think of them: I stated previously about opting *not* to italicise the animal names in the main body of the story, hoping to avoid any confusing emphasis. Keeping all the capital letters in check is quite a job, too, as it happens – *Tyrannosaurus* vs. tyrannosaurs – see what I mean? (At this point, it would be remiss of me not to mention how hard my editor works to keep righting my wrong writing! Thank you.) While on the subject of wrongs... in chapter 10, Video Nasty, Aito says, "The public records of everyone on this mission aren't worth a damn." This is such a common expression that I spelt damn after the original four-letter word. However, it is believed that the derivation actually comes from a small Indian coin called a 'dam' – I assume they weren't worth very much. The phrase was possibly carried back to England by soldiers in the mid-18th century. 'I don't give a *damn*' was an Americanism first recorded in the 1890s. Correcting this typo in the story made it look like a typo, ironically – so it was just a case of, *ahem*, damned if you do, damned if you don't! (Sorry.) Mucking around with words leads us inevitably to Shakespeare. As with REROUTE, I have once again tried to include a *flavour* of the Elizabethan era dialects, hopefully without the confusion. In reality, it's fair to say that they would have been far more impenetrable to most of us moderners, as we would no doubt be to them. Can you imagine what they would make of emojis? Use of such glyphs would surely have been worthy of a burning at the very least! I remember one far-off day in English literature class, when the fourteen-year-old Stephen took his turn in reading Shakespeare to the class, including line numbers and all! I stopped reading when the rest of the class fell about laughing. I was completely baffled by this, until the teacher explained what I'd done. She was familiar with the condition where people walk in their sleep, but reading in one's sleep was apparently all new to her! Unfortunately, that is all I recall about my introduction to the Bard. I'm sorry to admit that is a true story. I may also have poked a little fun at one of literature's most important figures here, but most fourteen-year-olds probably feel the same. In any case, his reputation will far outlive my own, so he can get over himself! Here, have a smiley face, Shakey :o)

For anyone interested in the story of Sir William de Soulis, legend has it that he was bound by specially crafted chains and taken off to Ninestane Rig, where he was wrapped in lead and boiled alive by the people under his 'care'. The reason given for the chains was that his magic was so strong he could neither be bound by ropes nor cut by steel. The history tells it rather differently. As I mentioned in the last book, he was already long dead by Tudor times, but was such a beautifully crafted, semi-real villain, I just couldn't resist! Anyone who has ever visited Hermitage Castle in the Scottish Borders will understand; such a dark, menacing place simply had to have an evil, black-magic-wielding lord in its past. Fleetingly back to the history, Sir William actually died in the dungeons of Dumbarton Castle. It seems to have been common policy for the border lords of the time to consider whether their interests were best served by affiliation with the English or the Scots. In AD1320, it is believed that Sir William de Soulis (also spelt de Soules) was party to an English plot to kill Robert the Bruce, the Scots King. The scheme failed and he was rounded up with the other (presumably) guilty parties and taken to Dumbarton Castle where he died but, as far I can tell from the information available, was not executed. Dungeons were, after all, very unhealthy places to be, so this is probably not all that surprising. The legend that has stuck to him seems to come from a cross-pollination between Sir William's own black reputation (even by medieval standards, he was a seriously bad man) and the sticky end suffered by his ancestor, Sir Ranulf de Soulis (or possibly Randolph), who was murdered by his servants in AD1207. The legend of De Soulis and his familiar, Robin Redcap, fit so perfectly into the Hermitage Castle story that I intend to write about them further, once the New World Series is complete.

I probably should have mentioned this in my notes at the end of the last book: Lord David Maxwell is a fictional character I invented to bring together the *New World*'s crew and the indigenous Scots. The Maxwell clan was real enough, however, although I believe they were still followers of the Catholic faith at the time when this story was set. They really didn't get along with the Johnstones. Also around this time, the title of Lord Maxwell changed hands very quickly as several of the incumbents died in rapid succession. By 1558 it was the turn of John, the 8th Lord Maxwell who acceded at the age of two, following the death of his brother Robert at the age of four. Despite this, they were one of the most powerful families in southern Scotland during this time. David Lord Maxwell came to being because I needed a character who would be more radical and at odds with the Queen Regent – Mary of Guise – and of course, De Soulis.

To further foment confusion, there were also several Sir Walter Scotts, perhaps the most famous being the 18th century novelist so well known for Ivanhoe, Rob Roy, etc. The character in this story is loosely based on a young man who ended up being the first of the family elevated to the peerage – the 4th Baron of Buccleuch. The eldest son of Sir William Scott, he was the grandson of Sir Walter Scott, 1st of Branxholme, 3rd of Buccleuch. Our Sir Walter's father predeceased his grandfather, making him the 4th of Buccleuch at the age of just three. A fighter from his childhood onwards, he grew up among the Border feuds and despite his youth played a prominent role in 16th century Scotland's turbulent politics. In 1558 he was thirteen.

The Sir John Johnstone in this story was a largely fictional character, although there was a real John Johnstone alive at the time who would have been in his mid to late teens. However, that man was not knighted until 1584. Sadly, many of the Johnstone family records were destroyed in the burning of Lochwood Tower – courtesy of the Maxwells and the Armstrongs. When my fictional historian, Thomas Beckett, told the crew that the Scottish Borders of the 16th century were as dangerous as anywhere in the world at that time, he was probably correct.

Elizabeth I needs little introduction the world over, I'm sure. In reality, she awaited the news of her sister Mary's death at Hatfield House, roughly ten miles north of what is now known as Central London, on the 17th November 1558. Sir Nicholas Throckmorton did bring the news along with Mary's ring. History took a left turn with the arrival of the USS *New World,* leaving me with two stories I wish to tie up outside the New World heptalogy. My intention is to include both in the coming title, REBIRTH, but we'll see how the story develops – they may need a book each. Either way, I look forward to telling the story of how the infamous Geoff Lloyd inveigles his way into Elizabeth R's inner circle – accidentally taking on the name of a famous adviser and turning the forever intriguing Tudor court upside down in the process.

Martin Bormann was head of Adolf Hitler's Nazi Party Chancellery. He wielded immense power as private secretary to the *Führer,* not least by controlling the flow of information and access to Hitler himself. It is believed he flew the bunker after Hitler's suicide, himself committing suicide soon after – possibly a preferable fate to being captured by the Russians. He was condemned to hang posthumously after the Nuremberg trials.

Fritz Todt was a construction engineer and senior Nazi Party member who directed the construction of the German *autobahns* and later became the Reich Minister for Armaments and Ammunition. From that position, he directed the entire German wartime military economy. Earlier in the war he was a general in the *Luftwaffe,* having earned an Iron Cross in the *Luftstreitkräfte* during the First World War. He died in a plane crash in 1942, possibly on Hitler's orders, after trying to talk the *Führer* out of continuing the war with Russia.

The party members in this story are a softer bunch (possibly) because of Douglas' meddling with historical events during the 16th century. Without the terror and destruction of the First and Second World Wars, what might such men have become? Would they still have tended towards evil? I have tried to portray them as men who had the potential to go either way, though of course, for Heidi Schultz that would never do.

I hope you enjoyed this episode of the New World Series. It was always my intention for dinosaurs to provide the main set dressing and a continuous theme for this series, but with books 4 and 5 providing an interval, and taking the USS *New World* on a different course through time, in order to change the future. Now that stage is set, I look forward to taking you on the next leg of our heroes' travels in book 6, CURSED, where poor Tim Norris seems to be having another *roarfully* bad time, as he finds himself with it all to do over again...

Thank you so very much for reading. Take care, all,

Stephen.

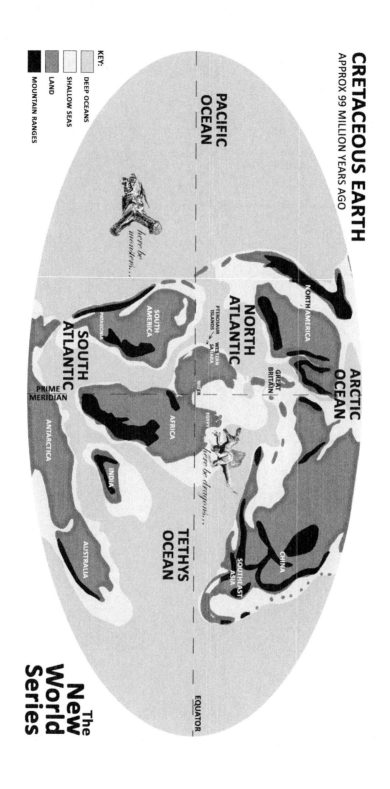

CRETACEOUS EARTH

APPROX 99 MILLION YEARS AGO

KEY:

- DEEP OCEANS
- SHALLOW SEAS
- LAND
- MOUNTAIN RANGES

PACIFIC OCEAN

here be monsters...

NORTH AMERICA

ARCTIC OCEAN

NORTH ATLANTIC

PTEROSAUR ISLANDS

WESTERN SALARA

GREAT BRITAIN

SOUTH AMERICA

PATAGONIA

SOUTH ATLANTIC

PRIME MERIDIAN

NIGER

EGYPT

AFRICA

here be dragons...

ANTARCTICA

INDIA

AUSTRALIA

TETHYS OCEAN

CHINA

SOUTHEAST ASIA

EQUATOR

The New World Series

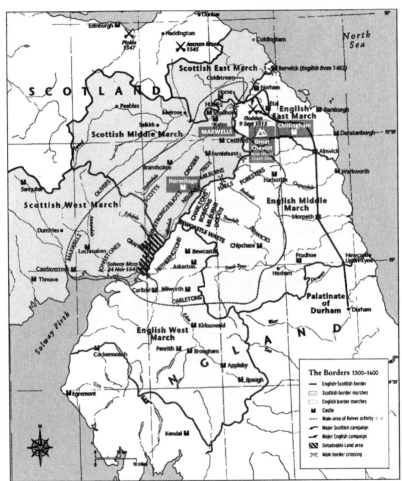

Coming soon:

CURSED

THE NEW WORLD SERIES | BOOK SIX

Stephen Llewelyn

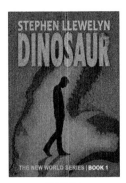

BOOK 1
DINOSAUR

BOOK 2
REVENGE

BOOK 3
ALLEGIANCE

BOOK 4
REROUTE

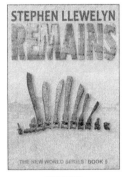

BOOK 5
REMAINS

BOOK 6
CURSED

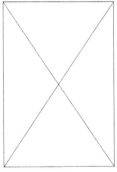

BOOK 7
COLLISION

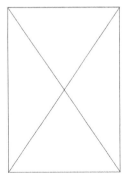

NEWFOUNDLAND

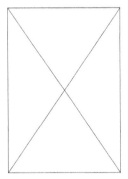

REBIRTH

The
**New
World
Series**

www.stephenllewelyn.com/books/

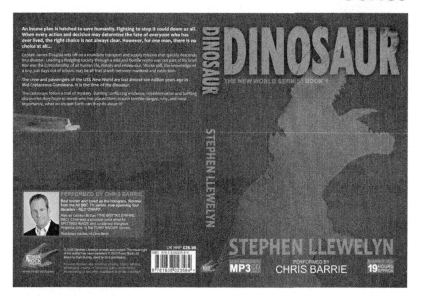

An insane plan is hatched to save humanity. Fighting to stop it could doom us all. When every action and decision may determine the fate of everyone who has ever lived, the right choice is not always clear. However, for one man, there is no choice at all...

Captain James Douglas sets off on a mundane transport and supply mission that quickly descends into disaster. Leading a fledgling society through a wild and hostile world was not part of his brief. Nor was the custodianship of all human life, history and endeavour. Worse still, the knowledge of a boy, just days out of school, may be all that stands between mankind and extinction.

The crew and passengers of the USS *New World* are lost almost too million years ago in Mid-Cretaceous Gondwana. It is the time of the dinosaur.

The castaways follow a trail of mystery. Battling conflicting evidence, misinformation and baffling discoveries they hope to reveal who has placed them in such terrible danger, why, and most importantly, what on ancient Earth can they do about it?

DINOSAUR

THE NEW WORLD SERIES | BOOK 1

STEPHEN LLEWELYN

PERFORMED BY CHRIS BARRIE

Best known and loved as the hologram, Rimmer, from the hit BBC TV series, now spanning four decades - RED DWARF.

Also as Gordon Brittas (THE BRITTAS EMPIRE BBC), Chris was a principal voice artist for SPITTING IMAGE and co-starred alongside Angelina Jolie in the TOMB RAIDER movies.

Photograph courtesy of Chris Barrie

© 2020 Stephen Llewelyn artwork and content. The moral right of the author has been asserted. © 2020 Fossil Rock Ltd. Music by Karl Mullen, used by kind permission.

UK RRP £26.99
ISBN 978-1-8380235-8-4

STEPHEN LLEWELYN

MP3 CD

PERFORMED BY CHRIS BARRIE

19 HOURS APPROX

DINOSAUR
audio performed by
CHRIS BARRIE
(Red Dwarf, Tomb Raider)

www.stephenllewelyn.com

Printed in Great Britain
by Amazon

74899908R00210